HAPPILY
EVER AFTER

By the same author:

Going Home
A Hopeless Romantic
The Love of Her Life
I Remember You
Love Always

HARRIET EVANS

Happily Ever After

HarperCollins*Publishers*

HarperCollins*Publishers*
77–85 Fulham Palace Road,
Hammersmith, London W6 8JB

www.harpercollins.co.uk

Published by HarperCollins*Publishers* 2012

1

Extract from *Forever Amber* by Kathleen Winsor reproduced
with permission of Penguin Books Ltd
Extract from *I Capture the Castle* by Dodie Smith reproduced
with permission of Random House Ltd
Extract from *The Best of Everything* by Rona Jaffe reproduced
with permission of Penguin Books Ltd
Extract from *Venetia* by Georgette Heyer reproduced
with permission of Random House Ltd

A catalogue record for this book
is available from the British Library

ISBN: 978-0-00-735026-1

Set in Meridien by Palimpsest Book Production Limited,
Falkirk, Stirlingshire

. Printed and bound in Great Britain by
Clays Ltd, St Ives plc

MIX
Paper from
responsible sources
FSC C007454

For Lynne
with thanks for everything and love x x

She read all such works as heroines must read to supply their memories with those quotations which are so serviceable and so soothing in the vicissitudes of their eventful lives.

Jane Austen, *Northanger Abbey*

PROLOGUE

August 1988

A Happy Ending for Me by Eleanor Bee
They laugh at me, the girls in the canteen,
But one day I will laugh at them.
Black boots jack boots they are everywhere
But I won't wear them just because they are trendy.
Oh, you treacherous night,
Why won't you take flight?
For I am like a little red spot that
That . . .

ELEANOR BEE PUT down her pen and sighed. She stretched her arms above her head, with the weary movement of one who is wrestling with her own *Ulysses*. Unfortunately, this action inadvertently caught her hand in the gleaming yellow headphones of her new Sony Walkman. The plastic case was yanked abruptly into the air, dangling in front of her face for a brief second before falling to the ground, with a loud crack.

'Oh, no,' Eleanor cried, talking to the floor in a tangle of long limbs, simultaneously pulling off her headphones and thus further entangling herself. 'No!'

The sound of Voice of the Beehive's 'Don't Call Me Baby' from *Now That's What I Call Music 12* in her ears was abruptly silenced. The Walkman lay on the floor, the lid of the cassette player snapped off and lying several feet from her amongst a nest of dust and hair in the corner of the room. Eleanor picked it up and stared at it in despair. The door of the bedroom was ajar, and through it she could hear the sound of glasses clinking, cutlery scraping on plates. And raised voices.

'You said you'd take her tomorrow, John. You did.'

'I did not. That's utter rubbish.'

'You did. *You just weren't bloody listening, as per usual. It's fine. I'll take her.'*

'Not if you're still in that state you won't. God, if you could see yourself, Mandana –'

'You sanctimonious shit. Listen –'

Eleanor jammed the headphones on again. Pressing her hands against her ears, she crawled across to the dusty corner and snatched the plastic tinted cover, brushing herself off as she stood up. She stared out of the window at the pale lemon evening sun, sliding into the clear blue sea. On the beach, the last few swimmers were coming out of the water. An intrepid band was building a fire, getting a barbecue ready, for this far north in August, the sun didn't set till well after ten.

But Eleanor did not see the view or the people. She stared blindly at the rickety wooden path down to the sea and wondered if she should burst into the kitchen, tell them she didn't want to go to Karen's in Glasgow any more. But she was also afraid of interrupting them; she didn't want to hear what they were saying to each other.

Mum's dad had died, two weeks before they'd come to Skye. At first it hadn't seemed like that big a deal. Eleanor

4

felt bad about it but it was true. He lived in Nottingham and they lived in Sussex, and they hardly ever saw him and Mum's mum. Mum didn't get on with him and Eleanor and Rhodes had been to the house in Nottingham only twice. The first time he'd smelt of whisky and roared at them when they played in the tiny back garden. The second time he'd had a go at Mum, shouted and told her she was a disgrace. He'd smelt of whisky that time, too. (Eleanor hadn't known what it was, but Rhodes had told her. He loved knowing everything she didn't.) Their granny visited them in Sussex instead or saw them for day trips to London, which Eleanor loved, even though nowadays it was annoying Granny didn't understand she was fourteen and didn't want to go to babyish things like Madame Tussauds; she wanted to hang out by herself at Hyper Hyper and Kensington Market.

But Mum had been much more upset about Grandpa dying than Eleanor would have expected. *Everyone's parents argue*, she reminded herself. Karen had said that last week, when Eleanor had cried all over her and said she didn't want to go on holiday with her parents and her brother. *Not like this, they don't*, Eleanor had wanted to say. She was so used to worrying about things – whether she would break her arm falling off the horse at gym, just like Moira at school, whether her mum or dad would die of a terrible disease, whether she herself was dying of a secret disease because she was sure her periods were heavier than everyone else's, and the letter in *Mizz* magazine had said if you were worried about it you should definitely go to the doctor – all these things kept her awake at night, till her heart pounded and then she worried that her heart rate was too fast and would explode and she had never noticed that all of a sudden her parents seemed to hate each other. Suddenly something was, she knew, wrong, terribly wrong, and it was only when she played her music really loud or curled up on her bed with a book that the tide of fear seemed to recede, for a little while.

They'd had an OK day today. A walk along towards Talisker Bay where the whisky was made; Dad had told Rhodes he could try some at the distillery, since he was nearly eighteen. The air was fresh and clear, the sky was a perfect powder blue, the last of the midges really had gone, and Eleanor was almost glad to be out of her room for once, outside with her parents and her brother. Just like a normal family on a normal holiday.

The trouble had started today when they got back and there was frozen pizza for lunch. Dad had had a go at Mum because it wasn't properly defrosted, soggy in the middle, and she'd shouted at him. Eleanor and Rhodes were used to this at home, but Dad was a GP who worked late and often didn't notice the burnt pasta, the half-cooked chicken Kievs.

'It's disgusting,' he'd said eventually, pushing the plate away. 'I can't eat it, Mandana. You should have defrosted it before we went for the walk.'

Mum was on her second glass of wine. 'Right. Of course, it's beyond the realm of possibility that you'd make lunch, John, isn't it? It's a holiday for me, too, I've had a bloody hard time and you don't even—'

Dad had stood up, pushing the table away, and stalked off into the sitting room; he'd stayed there with the door shut, watching the cricket till Mandana had gone in to remind him about driving Eleanor the next day.

A knocking sound made Eleanor jump. Her mother opened the door, slowly. 'Ellie, love?' she said. 'Are you all right?'

'I'm fine.' Eleanor took her headphones off. 'I just –'

Mandana came into the room. She wiped her face with one hand, tiredly. 'I'm sorry for the yelling. Just a misunderstanding, your dad didn't realise about driving you, you see. . . .'

Adolescent rage, made up of anger and fear, boiled inside Eleanor. 'I know, you didn't ask him. You drank too much and forgot. Again.'

'Ellie!' her mother said sharply. 'Don't be rude. Of course I didn't. It's not that. Your father and I just aren't getting on very well at the moment, that's all.'

'Are you going to get a divorce?' Eleanor heard herself asking the question, and held her breath.

'Love, of course not! What makes you think that?' Mandana patted her soft dark hair, rather helplessly, and said before Eleanor could answer, 'Anyway, I just wanted to apologise for all that noise. Daddy'll take you to the station tomorrow, it's no problem.'

Mandana's voice was trembling, and her cheeks were flushed. Eleanor rolled her eyes and crossed her arms. 'Why are you being like this?'

'Like what?' Mandana said.

'You're different since Grandpa died. I don't understand, you always said you hated him.'

'I didn't really hate him,' Mandana said. 'I just feel bad. I never saw him. He was a sad man, and it makes me sad, and it makes me think about things. It's just a hard time at the moment, that's all.'

'Why was he a sad man?'

'Look,' Mandana said, in the brisk way she sometimes suddenly had. 'Just be ready, get your things ready. It's . . .' She trailed off. Eleanor stared at her mother. 'Oh. I lost my train of thought, Ellie. Just be ready, won't you?'

'Don't call me Ellie.'

'OK,' Mandana said, one hand on the door. 'Supper's soon. On our knees, we thought we'd watch a video tonight. Won't that be fun? I'm making lasagne.'

It was pointless trying to talk to her. It was just pointless. 'Fine,' Eleanor said. 'Thanks, Mum. See you in a bit. I'll pack.'

'Good. And – please don't worry, love. Everything's going to be fine! You're just a worrier, that's your trouble. I think we should talk to Dr Hargreaves when we're back. Maybe some cranial massage would help you.'

The door shut softly behind her, and Eleanor was left looking out of the window once more.

It'd be better at Karen's – well, Karen's granny's – that was for sure. Only one more night and then she'd be there. She put the useless Walkman on the bed and hummed as she reached for her bag. She didn't hear the door open again.

'What the fuck are you doing?' Rhodes, her seventeen-year-old brother, stood in front of the bed. 'Why are you wearing your headphones with nothing plugged into them, you freak?'

Eleanor hugged herself. 'Shut up, you spazmo. I'm packing, to go to Karen's, not that it's any of your business.'

'You look like a freak.'

'Wow, Rhodes, you're so eloquent.' Eleanor made a face.

Rhodes laughed. Eleanor didn't say anything. She just shut her eyes and conjured up the image she liked best, that of her brother being slowly lowered into a pit of fire, screaming hoarsely, his eyes popping out, flesh starting to melt away, and her standing over him, nodding at the guard who asked, 'Lower, madame?'

She liked that image. She had called on it more and more over the last year. There was also the one where Rhodes, chained up and begging for mercy, got sliced into bits by a gang. But this one was the best. She was in control.

'What the fuck is this?'

'Get off, Rhodes, it's private.' Eleanor lunged, but too late. Rhodes snatched up her open notebook. His eyes lit up, he scratched the back of his fuzzy brown hair in excitement.

'Poetry!' He laughed. 'You're writing . . . ha ha!' He clutched his sides. 'Ha! You're writing poems! "They laugh at me, the girls in the canteen" – you bet they do, sis!'

'I HATE YOU!!' Eleanor shouted. 'I hate you, you . . . you bastard bitch!' She looked around for something to throw at him, and grabbed *Forever Amber*, which she was halfway through.

'What's it called?' Rhodes peered at the top of the page. '"A Happy Ending for Me." Ha! Ha ha ha!' He bent over, and slapped his knees.

'It's a good title. What would you know, you div? You can hardly spell your own name, let alone write poetry.' Eleanor was shaking with rage.

'God, you take yourself so seriously, don't you?' Rhodes said, his pleasure almost manifest in the room, like a dancing devil behind him. 'You think you're better than me, just because you read books all day and moon around writing stupid poems. You don't know anything about real life. You've never even snogged anyone, no boy'd go near you, unless they were gay, you look like a boy!'

'I'm not even listening, Rhodes. I feel sorry for you,' Eleanor said haughtily. She aimed the book at him. 'I just really do.'

'What does "A Happy Ending" mean then?' Rhodes said. His eyes were bright, his pupils dilated, his breath short. Like he'd just won a race. 'Come on.'

'It's called "A Happy Ending for Me", and actually it's—'

'No. I'm not asking that. Do you know what a Happy Ending is? Have you heard of it?' He laughed again.

'You're so weird, I don't even know what you're talking about.' Eleanor put the book down and stuck one finger up at her brother, which was about the rudest thing she knew how to do. 'You're such an idiot. You're only being like this 'cause you're upset about Mum and Dad.'

His face clouded over and his eyes narrowed. 'You don't know anything,' he said. 'No, I'm not, so fuck off.'

'No. Go away. I hate you.'

'What a weirdo.' Rhodes smiled. 'A Happy Ending is when you wank someone off. Give them a happy ending. Yeah? Wanking. Rubbing my dick till I spunk.' He grabbed his crotch. 'Like Lucy Haines did to me, last month. *That's* a happy ending. Oh, yeah.' He smiled, and rocked his hips back and forth. 'Oh, oh, oh, *yeah*.'

9

Eleanor didn't know what to say, or where to start. She was silent. 'You are disgusting,' she said after a pause. 'You are vile. Go away.'

Rhodes was still smiling. 'I'm going. Happy endings. Mmmmm.'

'Piss off.'

Eleanor slammed the door after him, then opened it and slammed it again, as hard as she could, and then she pushed the chair from the desk up against the handle and put her hand up to her mouth, clamping her lips together. She sorted her books into a pile: the Sylvia Plath poems, the Sylvia Plath biography, *Forever Amber* and a couple of spare books just in case so she didn't have to resort to those stupid magazines like *Just 17*, *19* and *Mizz*. They riveted her as well as terrifying her, full of silly girls going on about boys and rubbing almond oil into your cuticles – she didn't even know where cuticles *were*. It was so stupid, trying to pretend that silly stuff was part of real life, when real life was ugly and horrible, like Rhodes, like this house, like . . . everything.

She looked down at the poem. 'A Happy Ending for Me'. She ripped the page out of her notebook and tore it into tiny pieces, her bottom lip sticking out as the tears she had pushed down inside her came up; and as she sank to the floor, Eleanor Bee hugged her knees and told herself that one day, it'd be OK. She'd be a grown-up, and she *would* have a happy ending. The nice sort. Happily ever after, with a house full of books, a video recorder to tape *Neighbours* and all the clothes she wanted from Dash and Next.

But even as she sat there, rocking herself, tears dropping freely onto her scabby knees, her dark fringe falling into her eyes, she knew that sounded stupid.

'London eats up pretty girls, you know.'
'Not me!' she assured him triumphantly. 'I'm not afraid!'

Kathleen Winsor, *Forever Amber*

April 1997

'SO, ELLE, WHAT are you reading at the moment?'

Her palms were stuck to the leather chair and Elle knew if she moved them they would make a loud, squeaking sound.

'Me? Oh . . .' Elle paused, and tried to gently manoeuvre one hand out of the way, but found she couldn't. 'I don't know. Um . . .' She racked her brains for the 'buzz phrases' she and Karen had gone over that morning in Karen's tiny kitchen. Karen had written them on Post-it notes.

Buzz phrase. Buzz phrase. Oh, God.

'Well, I love reading,' she said eventually. 'I'm passionate about it.'

Jenna Taylor tapped her biro on the grey plastic desk. She cast her eyes over to the blue fabric wall dividers, then looked back, forcing a smile to her face. 'Yes, that's great, so you've said. What are you actually reading at the moment, though?'

Elle already knew this interview could not be going more badly. It was like when she'd begun her second driving test by pulling out and nearly crashing into a grey Mercedes which meant an automatic fail, and she'd still had to take the rest of the twenty-minute test. But her mind was a total blank. She could feel the angry red blush she always got when she was flustered starting to mottle the skin below her collarbone, creeping up her neck. Soon her face would be luminous red. She moved one hand. A high-pitched, farting shriek emanated from the chair. 'Um – what kind of thing do you mean?'

Jenna's voice was icy. 'I mean, can you demonstrate that you're up to speed with what's going on in the world of publishing at the moment? If you love books as much as you keep saying you do, it'd be great if you could give some examples of what you've read lately.' She smiled a cold smile.

Elle looked around the tiny open-plan office. It was almost totally silent. She could hear someone typing away at the next office space to Jenna's, and the whirr of the air conditioner, but apart from that, nothing. No one talking at all. They were all reading, probably. Being intellectual. Making decisions about novels and biographies and poetry and other things. How amazing. How amazing that she was even here, having an interview at Lion Books.

'Lately . . .' Elle knew what the truthful answer was, but she knew there was no way she could actually admit it. She was halfway through *Bridget Jones's Diary* and it was the funniest book she thought she'd ever read, plus at least once every other page it made her shout, 'Oh, my God, *me too*!'

But she couldn't say that. She was at an interview for one of the most respected publishers in London. She had to prove she was an intellectual person of merit. Intellectual person, yes. She coughed.

'Well, the classics, really. I love Henry James. And Emily Brontë. *Wuthering Heights* is like one of my favourite books ever. . . . I love reading. I'm passionate about . . .' *Oh, no.*

Jenna crossed her legs and wheeled the chair a little closer. 'Eleanor, look around my office. If you'd done your research you'd know I publish commercial women's fiction.' She slapped some spines on a shelf, dragged out a handful of thick paperbacks. 'Gold foil. Legs in lacy tights. I need a secretary who wants to work with commercial authors.' Her face was hard. 'If you like Henry James so much perhaps you should be applying for a job at Penguin Classics.'

Elle could feel hot tears burning at the backs of her eyes. The red blush was crawling across her cheeks, she knew it. *I don't understand Henry James. I only liked* The Buccaneers *on TV. I've applied for jobs everywhere and no one's interested. I've been sleeping on a friend's floor for three months and eating Coco Pops twice a day. I'm drinking in the last-chance saloon, Jenna. Please, please give me a break.*

'. . . If you'd told me you liked *Bridget Jones*, for example, or you were reading Nick Hornby, or Jilly or even bloody *Lace* I'd have some indication that, despite your total lack of office experience, you were interested in working in publishing. Hmm?' Jenna fingered a lock of long Titian hair with her slim fingers.

'I do like *Bridget Jones*,' Elle said softly. 'I love it.'

'Really.' Jenna obviously didn't believe her. She looked at her watch. 'OK, is there anything else you'd like to say?'

'Oh.' Elle looked down at her sweating thighs, clad in bobbling black tights and a grey and black kilt that, she realised now, was far too short when she was sitting down. 'Just that . . . Oh.'

I know I screwed this up, can you give me another chance?

I really need this job otherwise I have to go back to Sussex and I can't live with Mum any more, I just can't.

I have read Lace, *some bits several times, in fact, it's just I can't talk about it without blushing.*

My skirt is too short and I will address this issue should you employ me.

No, no, no. 'I – no. Thank you very much. It was lovely to meet you. I . . . fingers crossed!' And Elle finished by holding her hands up, making a thumbs-up sign with one, and crossing her fingers with the other.

'Right . . .' Jenna said. There was a pause as both of them

stared at Elle's hands, shaking in mid-air. 'Thanks for coming in, Ellen. Great to meet you.'

'Eleanor . . .' Elle whispered. 'Yes,' she said more loudly. 'Thanks – thank you! For this opportunity.' That was one of the phrases, she remembered now. 'I'm a keen enthusiastic self-starter and I'll work my guts out for you,' she added, randomly. But Jenna was ushering her out down the narrow maze of passageways, and Elle realised she wasn't listening, and furthermore she, Eleanor Bee, still had one hand cocked in a thumbs-up sign. 'Idiot,' she muttered, as they reached the lifts.

'I beg your pardon?' Jenna smoothed down her lilac crêpe dress and fanned her fingers through her glossy hair.

'Ah. Nothing,' Elle added. She got into the lift. 'Thanks again. Sorry. Thanks then – bye.'

The lift doors closed, shutting out Jenna's bemused face.

I MADE A thumbs-up sign.

Elle weaved her way down the Strand, swinging her handbag and trying to look jaunty. 'Let's all go down the Strand,' she sang under her breath. 'Have a banana. Oh, what . . .' Her voice cracked, and she trailed off. She glanced at her reflection in a shop window and shuddered. She looked *awful*, that stupid short skirt, why had she bought it? And that silly blue top, it was supposed to look like silky wool, but what that actually meant was that she had to hand wash it. Her light brown hair was too long and thick, tucked behind her ears and sticking out in tufts. She stared at the window again, and winced. She was looking into the window of a Dillons bookshop with a banner bearing the legend 'Our Spring Bestsellers'.

'*Captain Corelli's Mandolin* . . . I read that last summer, why on earth didn't I say that?' Elle smacked her forehead gently with her palm. '*The Celestine Prophecy* – oh, God, that's the crazy book Mum's reading, did she really want me to talk about that? That's not literature!' She stared at the array of books. '*The Beach . . . Men are from Mars, Women are from Venus* . . . what does *that* mean?'

Elle slumped her shoulders and stared at the Pret A Manger

next to the bookshop, where busy office workers were coming out clutching baguettes and soup. *She* wanted to eat in Pret A Manger. She'd never seen them before she came to London and to her it seemed the height of glamour, to go into a shop with other office workers and buy a proper coffee and a croissant.

But she didn't have the money for a coffee from Pret A Manger, nor a desk nor a job. Elle caught her bottom lip with her top teeth to stop herself from crying. *Come on*, she told herself, standing in the middle of the Strand as people pushed past her. *Buy an* Evening Standard, *go back to Karen's, have a cup of tea while you go through the Jobs section and you'll feel much better. There's something out there for you. There is.*

The truth is, Eleanor Bee was starting to get desperate. It was April. She'd left Edinburgh University the previous summer, and was still trying to find a job. It seemed all her other friends had something to do: Karen had a job as a runner at a TV production company, her old university flat-mate Hester was doing an MA in Bologna, and the other, Matty, was in teacher training college. Her ex-boyfriend Max was a trainee accountant, she'd bumped into him off Fleet Street the other day. It was just before an awful interview at an educational publisher where Elle had not really understood what they were talking about and when they'd said, *So do you think that sounds like something you could do?*, she'd replied, *Sure, can I let you know? No*, the grumpy, large, middle-aged man in cords had said. *I wasn't offering you the job. I was asking if you thought you'd be able to cope with the job. Thank you, we'll let you know.* She was sure bumping into Max was the reason she'd been so flustered. Not that she even cared about Max that much – he was using hair gel, for God's sake, and kept getting out his stupid new CD Walkman to show off to her. But it was the principle of the thing.

In February, Elle's best friend from school, Karen, had said she could come and sleep on her sofa. 'You're never going to find a job in publishing in a tiny village in Sussex, Elle,' she'd said briskly. 'Bite the bullet and come to London.' And Elle had accepted, nervous but also overwhelmed with excitement. *London*. She'd dreamed of moving to London, of living in the big city, since she was a little girl. She'd conquer it. She'd own grey wellington boots with heels. And have a matching grey briefcase, like the Athena poster of the city girl hanging off the back of a Routemaster bus blowing a kiss to her handsome boyfriend that Elle still had in her bedroom.

But London was very far from the welcoming and bustling literary salon Elle had expected it to be. Notting Hill was grimy, full of cracked pavements and crack addicts, and sleeping on the floor in Karen's was no fun. She'd been here two months now. She'd applied for every job going, written to every publisher she could find in the *Writers' and Artists' Yearbook* to ask them for work experience. But no one was interested. She was discovering she'd been totally naive to think they would be. She'd had four interviews, and this one today, at a major publishing house, was like the big one that had to work out, and she'd clearly totally one hundred per cent blown it. She'd thought she was so prepared: she had read everything, *everything*, in fact Karen said the trouble with her was she couldn't get her nose out of a book.

She hated the way she spent her days now. She'd sit in the silent flat, feeling crappy about herself and knowing she should buck up, watching Richard and Judy and dreading the moment when Karen would get back from work and say, in an increasingly unsympathetic tone, 'So, what did you get up to today then?' Her social life consisted of going to the pub or sitting around in the dark flat off Ladbroke Grove waiting for the electricity meter to run out. Plus Karen's other flatmates, Cara the chef and Alex the ad man, clearly found Elle a hindrance rather than a delightful addition to communal living.

On the Tube back to Notting Hill, Elle wondered for the

first time if she should have come to London at all. It wasn't how she'd expected it, and even though she was used to not fitting in, she'd never felt less welcome anywhere, in her whole life. It struck her that if she packed up her meagre possessions this evening and got a train first thing tomorrow, she'd be back at her mother's by lunchtime. But then – what? She and her mother, in the converted barn Mandana had bought after the divorce, doing what? Would it be worse than being here? Probably not.

Elle had a stroke of luck as she got off at Notting Hill Gate. Someone had left an *Evening Standard* behind on a seat and she scooped it up. It was a cold April day and she shivered in her thin coat, the paper clamped under one arm, as she walked through the empty streets, trying not to let her mood sink any lower.

It was just really hard, though, trying to find your place in the world. At university it had been so easy. You knew where you were going each day, what you were doing, and with whom. After university, the rules had suddenly changed, and Elle felt she'd been left behind. But the irony was, she knew exactly what she wanted! She'd always known! She just wanted to work with books, to read fine literature, to meet authors and to learn to edit, to have conversations like those she used to have with her Victorian Literature tutor Dr Wilson, about the Brontës and Austen and whether *Middlemarch* was the great Victorian novel or not and . . . that sort of thing. Of course, she knew she'd have to start at the bottom – she didn't mind that at all, in fact she rather thought she'd like it. But that didn't seem to make a difference.

What am I going to do? she thought to herself, walking briskly, head down. *Will I just be someone who falls through the cracks in society and never gets a job? And turns into one of those weirdos who keeps every newspaper from 1976 and carries a brown satchel and goes through the bins? Oh, my God, is that going to be me?*

The cold sharp breeze stung Elle's eyes. She wiped them with the back of her hand, and the *Evening Standard* dislodged and fell on the pavement, where a rolling gust of wind carried it off, into the middle of the road. She ran after it, and as she picked it up, noticed it was a week out of date. One whole week. She heaved her shoulders, and looked round for somewhere to dump the offending newspaper. There wasn't even a bin and she wasn't so far sunk into depression that she would just chuck it on the pavement. She stomped back towards the flat, muttering under her breath, not caring if she was taking one further step down the line towards being a newspaper-hoarding, bin-rifling weirdo, and thinking that the world was a cruel, cruel place.

ELLE SAT AT the kitchen table, reading the week-old newspaper and sipping a cup of tea, glad to be out of the cold, but still shaking at the injustice of the day she'd had. Absolutely no jobs yet again in the *Evening Standard*. She'd missed it last week; it had been sold out, and even if she'd had it a week ago it'd have been useless, unless she wanted to go into local government or work for a magazine called *Red Knave*, and she was sure she didn't.

Washing-up was piled high in the sink. They'd had people round the night before; Alex had made pasta and a bong, and Karen had made everyone sing 'Total Eclipse of the Heart' into wooden spoons. Elle had wanted to go to bed early to prepare for her interview, but she couldn't really get out her duvet and lie on the sofa while five other people were glugging Bulgarian white wine out of a screwtop bottle and yelling about the upcoming election.

Elle knew she should do the washing-up in a minute; perhaps then Alex would stop glaring at her when he came in and saying, 'Oh. Hi.' Which meant, 'Oh. You're still here, blighting my life.' She didn't like Alex much, all he seemed to do was show off his new mobile phone and take calls on it, then play *Tomb Raider* all weekend in the sitting room with his friend Fred. Elle had snogged Fred only the week before, more because she'd been trying to get to sleep and it seemed easier to snog him and then let them get on with playing *Tomb Raider* than tell them to leave. Plus Fred was actually an OK snog, even if she didn't have much to say to him. He'd been there yesterday too – but he'd been in a funny mood, and she wasn't sure he was interested any more, which wouldn't be a surprise, to be honest. He had a job and a flatshare, he wasn't sleeping in someone's sitting room and reading week-old newspapers.

Elle took another sip of tea, and turned from the out-of-date Jobs section to the news pages, cravenly aware this was a waste of time. There was a picture of Tony Blair, meeting some old ladies, and smiling. He looked young and tanned, and his hair was pretty good. Elle couldn't help thinking that was a plus point, not that it should matter but somehow it added to the overall romantic-lead sheen of him. Tony Blair always made her think of that line in *Pride and Prejudice* when Jane asks Lizzy how long she has loved Mr Darcy for, and Lizzy replies, 'It has been coming on so gradually, that I hardly know when it began. But I believe I must date it from my first seeing his beautiful grounds at Pemberley.'

Thinking of this now made her smile weakly. She closed her eyes and thought about Lizzy Bennet and Mr Darcy, wondering how they'd talk to each other after they were married and living at Pemberley. Because that always bothered her, what happened after the couple got over their misunderstandings to live happily ever after. She couldn't help thinking Mr Darcy wouldn't be sympathetic if Elizabeth ordered the wrong dinner service when a duke came to stay. She had seen what had happened with her parents, how vicious it had been, and Elle couldn't ever imagine that they'd once been in love.

John and Mandana had been divorced for seven years. Sometimes it seemed ages ago, sometimes she could still remember, as if it were yesterday, their old, cosy, normal life at Willow Cottage. The final papers had come through as Elle was preparing for her GCSEs. There was a lot of lip service paid to not letting it affect her exams, and people treated her very carefully, as if someone had died: the head-mistress even called her into her office for 'a little chat', to see if she was all right. Elle hadn't known how to answer when Mrs Barber had asked her how she was coping. How did you explain that you were a horrible person, because you were glad they were splitting up, glad they wouldn't be together any more, glad her dad was going away because these days he just seemed to upset her mum so much? Even when they had to sell the house and move to a barn outside Shawcross, and even when John remarried with what Elle overheard a friend say to Mandana was 'insensitive haste' she knew she didn't care in the way she should. She'd wondered whether she was a homicidal maniac – she'd read a book about them and one of the first signs was a lack of empathy. But Elle was just glad it was over, because it was horrible living like that.

To her secret relief, however, Rhodes obviously felt the same way. He'd gone to college in the States and was now an analyst, working for Bloomberg in New York. The last time she'd seen him was at Christmas at Mum's, and it had been awful – Mum had been drunk, Rhodes had told her she drank too much and was pathetic and anyone could see why Dad had left her, and then stormed out. Elle hadn't spoken to him since. Mum always drank too much, but it had got worse, that summer in Skye, as their marriage got worse. Elle never knew what came first, like the chicken and the egg. She only knew their old life, where her parents had seemed OK, was over.

So Elle didn't wonder what might have happened if her

parents had stayed together. She knew the real ending after the ending. She wondered about people like Lizzy and Darcy, or Beatrice and Benedick instead. Often she felt she was the only person who didn't believe they'd stay together, after the book or the play ended. She couldn't help it; she just didn't believe it.

She was pondering this, her knees under her chin, legs wedged against the table, when the door slammed and Alex came in.

'Oh, hi, Elle,' he said, not looking at her, and slamming his man-bag down on the table. 'How's it going? Any luck today then?'

'OK, thanks,' Elle said. 'Yeah, I—'

'I'm not staying,' Alex said. 'Meeting some guys from work at the pub. Just stopped off to change my shirt.'

'Oh, right,' said Elle, who found Alex's obsession with sharp Ben Sherman shirts half tragic, half touching.

'Hey.' He stopped and grabbed the paper from her. 'Can I just check something? Were you looking at it?'

'At the jobs, but it's fine, there's nothing in it,' Elle said, desperate to talk, even if Alex obviously wasn't interested. 'It's a week old, anyway –'

Alex ignored her and started turning the pages. 'Our new print campaign for Cape Town should be in here somewhere, we rolled it out last week and the fucking muppets haven't sent us any copies yet.'

'But this is last week's –'

He ignored her, and struggled to turn the pages. 'That's fine. Where is it? Hey! There! How cool is that? Yeah, looks good.'

Elle followed his jabbing finger. '"Visit Cape Town, for a World of Possibilities",' she read. 'That's great.'

She nodded politely as Alex talked, and looked down again, her eye caught by something, she didn't know why. And there, right in the middle of the Travel section, amongst ads for holiday lets in Cornwall and cheap flights to Thailand, she suddenly saw the following:

Editorial Secretary Required for Established
Independent Publishing House

Enthusiastic Self-Starter / Graduate. Must
have office experience

Competitive Salary: £11,000

Please send *curricula vitae* by post to:

Miss Elspeth MacReady

c/o Bluebird Books Ltd, Bedford Square

'What's that doing there?' Elle asked. She snatched the paper out of Alex's hand. 'It's – what's it doing there?'

'Don't know.' Alex stared at her, annoyed. 'Actually, Elle, I was looking at that.'

'Sorry, Alex,' Elle said, clutching the paper to her bosom and looking at him imploringly, almost in a panic: what if he took the paper away, flung it out of the window, how would she get it back? 'It's a job, it sounds perfect. . . . I don't know why it's there, it's in the wrong place. . . . Please, let me . . .' She stared again at the text. '"Send *curricula vitae* . . . care of Bluebird Books".' She bit her lip. 'Bluebird Books – I've heard of them! They're proper, they – they're old!' She ran into Karen's bedroom and scanned the precariously built IKEA Billy bookcase, crammed full of well-worn blockbusters, their cracked spines stamped with gold. 'Yes, I knew it! They publish Victoria Bishop! And . . . Old Tom! They publish Old Tom. Well, Granny Bee would have been pleased.' She glanced at her watch. It was nearly five thirty p.m. Too late to catch the post. There was no telephone number, either. *No*, a voice inside her head said. *You're going to go for this. You're going to do something about this, instead of sitting there feeling sorry for yourself.*

Elle bit her lip and marched back to the hall, pulled out a telephone directory, and thumbed through it, kneeling on the ground. Alex came into the hall and watched her.

'Can I have the paper back now, please?' he said, reaching forward.

'No! Just give me ONE SECOND, Alex, PLEASE!' Elle heard herself bellowing. Alex stepped back, annoyed.

'You're really starting to outstay your fucking welcome, you know,' he murmured.

Elle jabbed her finger on the page, and started dialling. It was a week old, that ad – even if it was in the wrong place, what were the chances? 'I'm sorry, Alex,' she said. 'It's probably hopeless, but I've got to give it a go— Hello?'

'Good evening,' said a low voice, a girl's. 'Bluebird Books, how may I help you?'

'Hello – yes. I – er – I just saw an advert in last week's *Evening Standard* for the job of editorial secretary – I wanted to ask if I could still apply? There wasn't a closing date.'

There was a silence, and then the voice spoke again, this time even lower, much closer to the speaker. 'The job ad? You saw it? You want to *apply*? Oh, thank fuck.' She coughed. 'I'm so sorry. I mean, thank goodness.'

'Thank goodness?' Elle was astonished. This wasn't the reception she was used to. The last job she'd rung up about, an editorial assistant's job at an independent publisher in Bristol, the man on the line had said, 'Sorry, position's been filled,' and put the phone down, like a scene from a film about the Great Depression.

'You don't understand.' The girl on the other end sighed, and Elle realised she was around her age, despite the huskiness of her Lancashire-tinged voice. 'No one's applied,' she

27

said quietly. 'Not a soul. I don't understand it. And Miss Sassoon keeps checking, and we have to have someone in soon, otherwise she'll go totally mad – it's been a week, a *week*, and nothing! Nothing!'

'Look,' Elle said. 'I think I know why.'

'Why? Why what?' The voice rose sharply again.

'Well. The ad's in the holiday homes section,' she said quickly. 'It's a total fluke I saw it.'

'The *what*?'

'Holiday homes. Between an ad for a nice cottage in Norfolk and a bungalow in the Lizard.'

There was a terrible silence, pregnant with meaning.

'Oh . . . FUCK,' the voice whispered. 'FUCK. She is going to kill me. K.I.L.L.L.L. me. How did I—'

'I don't think it's your fault, is it?' Elle said. 'It's the people who do the ads, they put it in wrongly.'

'She won't see it like that. Oh, God, oh, Jesus,' the voice said. 'What am I going to do? That's why. Oh, Jesus. She's going to ask me tomorrow. Oh, Christ.'

'Listen here –' Elle said, authoritatively. She nodded to herself. *Go for it!* 'Why don't you get me in for an interview. Eh?'

There was another silence. 'Yes,' the girl said eventually, breathing out with a long whistle. 'OK, can you come in tomorrow, first thing? She's not got anything on then, neither's he. And if you're rubbish, I'll just confess and we can do it again so we've got someone by the time Posy comes back from holiday. 'Cause she said she'd leave if she came back and they hadn't replaced Hannah . . . Man alive.' There was a loud thudding sound.

'What was that?' Elle asked, alarmed.

'I was banging my head on the desk. Look, if you come in, *please* don't tell Miss Sassoon. Please.'

'Of course I won't,' said Elle. 'Who is she, anyway?'

'You've never heard of Felicity Sassoon?'

'No, never.'

'And you want to work in publishing?'

'Yes,' Elle said. 'Oh, I really do.'

'Well, you've got to get this job. So I'm going to help you. Hold on.' There was some rustling on the line. 'Just checking everyone's gone, it's Rory's birthday, they've gone to the pub. Well, Miss Sassoon's father set up Bluebird, ages ago. It's er, something like the last of the old publishers in Bedford Square and she's really into that, so go on about that, I did and it worked a treat. You'll be working for her son, Rory. And Posy, who's another editor. Rory does crime and young trendy fiction, Posy does women's fiction, sagas, some of Felicity's authors.' She stopped. 'I mean, I presume you actually want to work with books like that, don't you? You want to get into publishing? They'll ask you what you've read lately, all that stuff, if you know any Bluebird authors. Have you got something to say?'

Elle took a deep breath. 'Well, I loved *Captain Corelli* and I'm halfway through *Bridget Jones*, plus I'm a huge fan of Victoria Bishop and my granny had all of Old Tom's Devon stories, but I also studied English at university and my favourite author is probably Charlotte Brontë.'

'Oh, they'll beat that out of you soon enough, but it's a start. OK, so next—'

'Hold on,' said Elle. 'What's your name?'

'It's Libby,' said the voice. 'Libby Yates. What's yours?'

'Eleanor Bee,' said Elle. 'But call me Elle, everyone does.'

'Do they now.' The laconic tone was back, and you'd never have known she'd been so flustered. 'Hello, Eleanor Bee. On with the tutorial. So . . .'

JUST UNDER TWO weeks later, on Tuesday 6 May, Eleanor Bee stood at the bottom of the steps of a big house and stared at the blue enamel sign hanging above her.

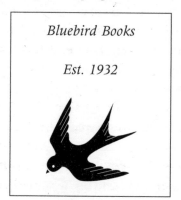

Bluebird Books

Est. 1932

'I have confidence,' she muttered to herself. She looked down at her smart charcoal grey trousers – new from Warehouse, on Saturday – and the raspberry pink short-sleeved jumper, at her beautiful soft black Mary Janes with the small heel from Pied a Terre which were only twenty pounds in the Christmas sale and which she was still unable to quite believe were hers. It was a beautiful spring day, and the newly green trees in Bedford Square swayed behind her. In the distance she could hear the clanging of a Routemaster bus bell, but otherwise it was completely quiet. Eleanor climbed the stairs and rang on the front door.

She was so nervous, she felt her knees might give way underneath her. She'd been here before, for her interview the week before last, but it seemed ages ago. Perhaps the whole thing was a huge mistake. Elle couldn't shake the feeling that she was an imposter – she was only standing here because no one else had applied, and because the terrifying Miss Sassoon, who'd briefly interviewed her, had been impressed that she'd heard of *Forever Amber*, because the only other person she'd seen had been some daughter of a friend of a friend, and she'd never heard of it. Well, Elle had thought, why were you interviewing the daughter of a friend of a friend? That's no way to find the best people, surely?

'So you've read it?' Miss Sassoon had asked.

'Oh, yes.' Elle was very fond of *Forever Amber*. She'd been reading it during the awful holiday in Skye all those years ago. 'I couldn't put it down. I – I enjoyed it even more than *Gone with the Wind*.'

'That,' Miss Sassoon had said firmly, 'is a subject for another day.' Elle thought she'd annoyed her, but Miss Sassoon had smiled and called for Libby to show her out, and then she'd been interviewed by Rory, who was very nice, in his early thirties, friendly and far less scary than his mother, so she'd relaxed and just chatted, and he'd teased her about liking the Spice Girls and then she'd left, and Libby had rung her at home that evening to say thanks. 'I think they liked you. I know Rory's bored of temps and the old lady just wants it sorted out, ASAP. You're definitely in with a chance.'

And for once that chance was hers. They'd given her the job, and she was here and now – she had no idea what came next. Elle rang the doorbell again, more firmly.

'Helloooo?' an elderly voice said into the intercom.

'Hello? It's Eleanor . . . Eleanor Bee. It's my first day, I'm

31

Rory and Posy's new secretary, they told me to get here for ten . . . ?'

'First floor. Please commmee innnn. . . .' the intercom said in querulous tones.

Elle climbed the wide stairs to the first floor and at the top she pushed open a swinging door to be greeted by Elspeth MacReady, office manager, wiping her hands on her skirt, and bending double, her rheumy eyes darting unhappily about her.

'Good morning, Eleanor,' she said formally. 'Good to see you again. Welcome to Bluebird Books. Mr Rory is in a meeting. He asked me to get you settled in. Here we are.'

Elle looked around her, taking it all in once more. A real-life publishing house. Where people made books, all day. And she was here, she was one of them! What a magical place! Strung out across the oatmeal carpet on the huge first floor were a collection of yellowing wooden desks surrounded by wall dividers, greying filing cabinets, and books. There were books everywhere, on shelves, in piles on floors, spilling out of cardboard boxes. It was strangely at odds with the beautiful old wood panelling on the walls, the four or five old portraits in gilt frames. She could see Bedford Square in the sunshine from the huge windows.

'Do you know where you will be sitting?' Elspeth asked. 'Has anyone explained to you the rules for the kitty, or about the keys?'

'No,' said Elle. 'I only really – I met Rory briefly and then—'

'Oh, dear. Oh, dear.' Elspeth shook her head. 'Someone should have told you –' She sighed, and her long thin frame shuddered.

'I'm sorry,' Elle said.

'It's fine. Now. Where to start. Firstly, each employee is issued with a key. This key is extremely important. The last person to leave the building at night turns the lights off and locks the front door with the key.'

'Yes . . . ?' Elle said weakly. 'Then what?'

'Well, that's it,' Elspeth said. 'But it's *very important.*'

'Of course.'

'And we ask that people, if they wish to join, contribute two pounds a month to the kitty for tea and coffee, and Miss Sassoon *very kindly* provides biscuits.'

'Right,' said Elle. 'And . . . ?'

'Well, that's also it,' said Elspeth. 'For the moment,' she added, firmly. 'Ah. Here is your desk. And this is Libby. Have you met already?'

'Yes,' said Elle, smiling gratefully at Libby, who was typing furiously, a Dictaphone machine next to her keyboard. Libby stopped and took her headphones off, raising a hand in greeting and pushing her dark blonde bob out of her eyes. She was wearing Anaïs Anaïs; Elle remembered it from their first meeting.

'Hi, Elle. Nice to have you here.'

Elle looked away from her, blushing as if they had been caught red-handed, like secret lovers. She stared at the desk in front of her. 'Oh, my goodness,' she said.

'Is there a problem?' Elspeth asked, panic in her voice.

'I have a phone,' Elle said, unable to believe it. 'And a computer.'

'Of course you do,' Elspeth said. She looked at her suspiciously.

A voice from the office behind them boomed, 'Elspeth. Come here, please.'

Like a cartoon character, Elspeth shot across the floor. Elle watched her open the old wooden door, saw a flash of a flared dark pink corduroy skirt, a woman whose hair was swept into a big bun, fat fingers with two massive rings cutting into them, and the big carved wooden desk she'd sat at the previous week for her interview. *Felicity.* 'Rory says the manuscript—' she heard, and then the door shut.

'Take a seat then,' Libby said, watching her. 'Don't stand around looking like a lemon.'

'No,' Elle said hastily. She sank down into the scruffy black chair in front of her and put her hands tentatively to the keyboard. There was an empty blue plastic in tray, a shiny black phone with a tangled cord, and a wire pen holder, with four biros and a pencil in it. She stroked the keyboard of her computer, opened the top drawer of the desk. 'There are Post-its,' she said, almost to herself. 'I have my own Post-its.'

Libby smiled. 'You are daft.'

She put her headphones back on and carried on typing. Elle opened the drawers a couple of times and pressed the button on the front of her grey computer monitor. She stared at the shelves by their desks. Trying to look like she had something to do, she reached over and picked some books out. There were old hardbacks, each stamped at the bottom of the spine with a gold bluebird, and lots of paperbacks, most of them pretty old, some green and orange Penguins. Lots of Victoria Bishops in hardback, all called things like *To Carry the Night* and *Lanterns Over Mandalay*, lots of Thomas Hodgsons: *Old Tom On Dartmoor, Old Tom's Springtime, Christmas with Old Tom* . . . She rolled her eyes. How boring!

There were lots of thrillers. She stood up and picked a few off the shelves. *Funeral in the Bunker,* which had a big swastika across it. Old historical novels, called things like *Katharine's Promise* and *To Catch a King*. One shelf had a row of copies of the same book, *Quantox's Dilemma*, the only vaguely new thing she could see anywhere, by someone called Paris Donaldson, with a hilarious photo of the author, in black-and-white, posing looking moodily into the distance. Elle wanted to laugh. He looked a bit like her flatmate Alex.

But it was the bottom shelf that was most alarming. It stretched out on either side of the desks, row upon row of books all with a heart on the spine entwined with the words 'MyHeart'. Elle's eyes nearly popped out as she read the titles. *He was a Sheikh . . . She was a Nurse. My Lord, My Captor. The Dastardly Duke's Revenge. Devil in a White Coat.*

34

'Oh, my goodness . . .' Elle whispered, trying not to laugh. 'Libby . . . what's MyHeart?'

Libby looked up at her, and then took off her headphones again with a sigh. 'What?'

'What's MyHeart?' Elle pointed.

'Our romance list. We publish two a month. Posy's in charge of it.'

'So . . . I'll have to work on those books then?'

'Er – yes.' Libby raised an eyebrow. 'Why, is that a problem?'

Elle blushed. 'No, of course not! It's just . . . they've got such funny names, don't you think?'

'MyHeart is the most successful part of the company, apart from the four big authors,' Libby said. 'I wouldn't make fun of it anywhere near Felicity, if I were you.'

Elle flushed with shame, feeling perspiration flowering on her forehead, under her armpits. 'Yes, of course. I'm sorry, I didn't mean to . . .' How stupid she sounded! Her eyes were dry; she rubbed them. She thought she might still be a bit hungover. The bank holiday weekend, despite her best intentions, had been a big one, from which she was still recovering. The beautiful weather and the Labour landslide meant everyone was in a euphoric mood. They'd stayed in Holland Park all day, drinking, chatting, flirting. She'd even snogged Fred again, and this time she'd really enjoyed it. It was nice, kissing someone in a park as evening came, feeling the moist grass between your toes, his lips on yours, your fingers twining with his . . .

Libby carried on typing. Elle sat up straight and blinked hard, wondering what the hell she should do next, when the door to Felicity's office opened and Rory emerged with a woman in her mid-thirties. The carved wooden door closed again as though someone was standing behind it, showing people in and out, in the manner of an audience with the Queen.

Rory was frowning. 'We should have gone for it, Pose. It's lunacy to be turning it down. Don't listen to her.'

The woman ignored him and walked towards Elle. 'Eleanor? Welcome! I'm Posy. Nice to meet you. Sorry not to have before. So glad you're here!' She was pretty, rather flustered looking, with pink cheeks and thin hair which curled tentatively at her neck and behind her ears; she looked the way a Posy should. 'Now –' She pulled up a chair and sat down next to Elle at her desk. 'Let's go through some things, shall we?' She smiled, and ran her hands over her forehead. 'You've met—'

'Hey, Posy, give the kid a chance.' Rory stood behind her and put his hand on Posy's shoulder. 'Hi, Eleanor. Great to see you again. Welcome. Has Libby been showing you the ropes? You should cultivate her, even if she is a bit stroppy and supports a rubbish football team.'

Libby, who had carried on typing throughout this exchange, could obviously hear enough of it through her headphones, as she raised one palm. 'Talk to the hand,' she said.

'Rory,' Posy said. 'Why don't I run Eleanor through some stuff, take her round and introduce her to people.'

'Good idea, very good idea,' Rory said. 'We can take her to lunch afterwards.'

There was a slight pause. 'Well . . .' said Posy. 'Abigail Barrow's just delivered and I have to – I can't really.' She turned to Elle. 'Sorry, Elle. We'll take you out another time.'

'Oh, no, please, I'll be fine,' Elle said hurriedly. She couldn't imagine anything worse, sitting with her bosses making small talk. And anyway, she wanted to fulfil her cherished lunch plan: find a Pret A Manger, have a sandwich, and sit in a park with the *Evening Standard* like a proper office worker.

Rory leaned forward. 'I'll clear out. Why don't we have a chat after Posy's finished with you. We're really glad you're here,' he said. 'It's a nightmare, getting used to things. I hated it, when I first started.'

'Were you a secretary?' Elle asked.

Posy gave a snort of laughter. 'Rory! That's a good one. He's never sent a fax in his life. Now, come on, Elle, let's—'

'Only ever worked at Foyles and here, for my sins,' Rory said, ignoring her. He grimaced. 'I'm nepotism in human form, you know. My mother wanted me to be involved in the business, and – well, I love books, of course, though we need to change. It's an interesting time to be in the game.'

'"The game",' Posy scoffed, sitting back down again. 'Rory's very flash, Eleanor. I'm staid and boring and like actually editing my books and building authors. Rory has a horror of the mid-list and he only likes authors who look attractive in photos.'

'Like Paris Donaldson,' Elle said seriously, but was surprised when Posy roared with laughter and Rory, after a second of looking annoyed, slapped his hands on the desk and joined in.

'She's sharp, that one,' Rory said. 'Yes, like Paris Donaldson, exactly. All the guys wanna be like him, all the girls love him. Gold dust.'

'I think he's a prick,' said Posy. 'But we don't agree about anything, do we, Rory?'

'No, my love,' Rory answered easily. 'We don't. I'll leave you two to it. Good luck again, Elle.'

He wandered off, whistling. Elle saw the look Posy gave as her eyes followed him. 'Er . . .' she said, after a moment. 'Right, let's get on with it.'

By lunchtime, Elle was ready for food, and she could have done with a large drink, too. Her head was buzzing. She had been walked through everything by Posy, who would say, 'It's *very* important you don't forget to do this,' and, 'Please make sure you *always* check this *extremely carefully*,' but if Elle was honest she hadn't understood about seventy-five per cent of what she'd been told. Posy kept explaining things and Elle kept writing them down in her ring-bound notebook, sentences that didn't seem to make any sense.

You need to keep an eye on Jews to make sure you don't run out of stock didn't look right, in fact it looked downright disturbing.

When proof covs come in from prod send 1 to agent 2 to the author, with note from Posy pp me file the other two, one in the author file, one in the covs circ file. What did this mean?

If Ed Victor or Abner Stein phones get Posy immediately. No matter where she is. If someone called Lorcan phones put him on hold and find P or Tony, don't let him ring off, <u>impossible to track down</u>.

But if woman called Georgina King phones saying she's a MyHeart author and she has the support of the RNA, get rid of her. Do <u>not</u> put her through to P. She is a lunatic. Elle had nodded and stuck a Post-it on the bottom of her monitor with 'Georgina King Lunatic' in large letters, trying to look as though she was On It. Finally Posy said, 'Is that all starting to make some sense? Is there anything you're not clear on? I know it must seem a bit overwhelming, but just ask if there's anything. Really important you ask.'

Just ask. Elle was so used to hearing that, in every job she'd had, temping, summer jobs, Saturday jobs. *Just ask.* It was a load of rubbish. They never meant it. If you did pluck up the courage to ask they looked at you as if you'd just been sick all over them. And where should she start, anyway? RNA? Grid? Jews? But this time she had to try. She took a deep breath. Which should she pick?

'Who's Lorcan?' she asked.

'Lorcan?' Posy nodded. 'He's the model we use on nearly every MyHeart cover. Big muscly guy, long hair, white teeth, you know the kind. He's almost as popular as the actual books. We're always trying to pin him down for shoots and he's never around. So when we can get hold of him, we have to cling on for dear life. He's the bane of Tony's life.' Elle looked blank. 'Tony the art director. Look, why don't I take you round to meet everyone now?'

She walked Elle around the floor, briskly introducing her to a sea of faces Elle knew she'd never remember. People were friendly but uninterested. When Posy said things like, 'Sam's the marketing assistant, she works with Jeremy, our marketing director,' Elle would smile and nod, though she actually wanted to shout, 'I've no idea what's going on! I can't shake your hand because I've sweated through my stupid new jumper and you'll see my armpits are wet!'

'Fetch your jacket and I'll walk out to lunch with you. I need to get a sandwich too.'

Elle swivelled around and realised she had no idea where she actually sat, she had lost her bearings completely. Posy looked at her as if she were a complete moron.

'I'm sorry,' Elle whispered. 'Just a bit confused, can't remember where I'm going.'

Something in Posy's expression changed. 'You poor thing. I remember what it was like, my first day in my job. I cried in the loos.'

Now I want to remember where the loos are and go and cry in them, Elle thought.

'SO THEY'RE ALL nice, then?'

Elle took another sip of her wine. 'I think so. They seemed nice. Rory's really funny. Posy's a bit strait-laced, but I think she's OK.' She rubbed her eyes. 'I'm exhausted. It's mental, first day at a job, you have no idea what you're doing or where anything is.'

'You'll get used to it.' Karen patted her arm. 'You'll be brilliant.'

'Oh, thanks.' Elle smiled affectionately at her old friend. 'And Karen, thank you so much for having me to stay.' She glanced at Alex and Cara, who were next to them, whispering to each other – Alex and Cara had one of those tedious 'flirty relationships' where everyone around them wanted to tell them to just get on with it and shag. 'I know I've outstayed my welcome. I'm really grateful to you, to all of you.'

Karen shook her head. 'My pleasure. You'd do the same for me.' She drained her pint. 'Another drink?'

'My round,' Elle said, standing up. 'I'll get these.'

She was tired, but she practically skipped to the bar. It was so nice to be able to get the drinks in, for once. It was so nice to be able to go to the Lav Tav, the Lavenham Tavern, their local, which was a proper gastropub, with nice food and floorboards, a log fire, and lovely rickety old tables and chairs. It didn't do cashback – the Elephant and Castle, round the corner, was much dodgier but it always gave you cashback, no matter how perilous your finances. She'd been drinking a lot at the Elephant and Castle the last couple of months but that period was over, she hoped. No more men with scary dogs on bits of old chain or women with no teeth wearing their coats inside and sitting in silence. It was the Lav Tav for her from now on – lilies on the counter and David Gray on the stereo.

Standing at the bar, Elle inhaled with a sense of weary satisfaction. She was in the pub after a hard day's work. It was a good feeling. She—

'Eleanor? Wow!' someone said in her ear. 'I didn't realise you lived round here!'

Elle turned. 'Oh!' she said. 'Hi there!'

It was a girl she'd met at some point in the day. Elle stared at her blankly, and then she remembered her: buck teeth, short blonde hair, unfortunate sparkly grips in her hair and too keen. She was assistant to Handsome Jeremy, the saturnine marketing director; Elle remembered *him*, he'd smiled and said, flirtatiously, 'How very lovely to have you here.' This girl had been bobbing around next to him, and she'd kept saying, 'Another girlie! Brill!' Shit. What was her name?

'I'm Elle,' she said, hoping to buy time and prompt a response.

'I know that!' the girl said. 'Durr! Can I get you a drink? Are you with some friends? I'm with my boyfriend Dave, shall we join you?'

'Sure!' said Elle. 'Um – I'll just get these.'

By the time she'd taken the drinks over, the girl and her boyfriend Dave had sat down at the table, and had introduced themselves to Karen and Cara and Alex, who were ignoring them and whispering in each other's ear again.

'So how long have you been at the company?' Karen was asking.

'I've been there a year,' the girl said. 'It's a marvellous place! Miss Sassoon is amazing, last year she gave us all a five-pound Marks voucher for Christmas. When I phoned Mum to tell her, she was like, that's what the *Queen* gives everyone at Buckingham Palace! Amazing.'

What the hell is your name? Elle smiled. 'It seems like a nice place to work,' she said.

'Oh, yeah,' said the girl. 'It's great. Dave says I go on about it all the time, don't you, Dave!' She nudged Dave, who said nothing and went back to staring into his pint. 'So where do you live, Eleanor?'

'Just round the corner, for now,' said Elle. 'But it's only temporary, I need to find a place.'

'Seriously? That's so weird.' The girl sucked on her straw. 'My flatmate's just moved to South Africa, it was all really sudden. *Really* sudden – like she went last week, only told me the week before that.' She stuck her tongue out. 'Dave said she was sick of me, but it wasn't like that! Anyway, you should come and see it. The flat, I mean.'

'Wow, that's – where is it?' said Elle. She didn't want to commit, but then she caught Alex's eye, and he gave her a cold look.

'It's at the top of Ladbroke Grove, above a cab company, right by the Sainsbury's. You know that big sign appealing for witnesses for that assault? Right there. It's actually really safe round there, that's not a problem, honestly.' She smiled her toothy smile. 'Anyway, I'm looking for someone, and the rent's like eighty quid a week each which is amazing, so—'

A shadow fell over the table. 'All right, mate?' Alex said, leaping up.

'Hi, mate. Hi, everyone. Hi, Elle.'

'Hi, Fred,' Elle said, her heart thumping in her chest. 'How're you?' she said nonchalantly, flicking her hair and sounding uninterested – this was something she'd picked up from observing Cara, who had men flocking round her like bees round honey.

Fred nodded. 'Good, good. It's nice to see you, Elle, how's the first day been?'

'Good,' she said, pleased. The girl from work was grinning expectantly up at her. 'Yeah, this is one of my new work colleagues,' she said. 'Um –'

Fred waited, as Karen stared at her.

'I'm sorry,' Elle blurted out eventually. 'I can't remember your name. I'm really sorry. I – I met loads of people today.'

'That's OK. It's Sam!' Sam stood up. 'Hiya! This is my boyfriend Dave. I'm Sam! What's your name?'

Fred smiled at Elle. 'Go on,' he said. 'What's my name?'

'Er –' Elle couldn't believe it, but she had to think for a moment. 'God. It's Fred. I'm going mad.'

Fred sat down, next to Alex, who slapped him on the back, while Cara smoothed her short Afro back from her forehead, and took another sip from her drink. Karen smiled at Fred ingratiatingly, while Elle, thoroughly flustered now, stared at the ground, thinking she'd better go to bed early, and then remembering with a sinking heart that the bed that awaited her was orange and green seventies acrylic, and had fag butts stuck down its back. She was so tired all of a sudden, all she wanted to do was sleep, get into work and attack this job properly. *Tomorrow is another day*, as Scarlett O'Hara would say.

'So –' Sam leaned forward, speaking loudly into her ear. 'Do you want to come and see the flat? I mean, I don't want to pressure you or anything, but it's pretty nice and cheap, and I'm going to be spending lots of time with Dave, obviously, so I won't be around much, and it's Ladbroke Grove, and you could move in right away, and we could go to work together and be like amigos, you know, look out for each other.' She lowered her voice. 'I think it's actually amazing,

43

in fact, don't you? The universe is telling us it's supposed to happen, otherwise why would me and Dave come in here the same night you're in here?'

There were several things Elle could have said to this speech, and if she'd been older and more jaded she might have done, but she was sick of sleeping on a manky sofa, and she wanted to put her books out and her CD player up.

'I'd love to come and see it,' she said, turning to Sam. 'When's good for you? Tomorrow?'

'Yeah!' said Sam, clapping her hands together. 'Amazing!' She clinked her glass against Elle's. 'You'll love it. What a day! Just think, this morning we hadn't even met!'

This morning seemed to be a thousand years ago. All the things that had happened. It felt as if, finally, she was on her way somewhere. Elle pulled discreetly at the armpits of her raspberry sweater. Amidst the maelstrom of new faces and facts she'd learned something concrete today, at least. Don't wear tight-fitting, pale-coloured, wool-mix knits when you're nervous.

September 1997

ON THE FIRST day of the month Elle woke early, with a pounding headache. Her throat was dry, her eyes puffy and sore from the crying she'd done the previous day. The room was too stuffy. She opened the window and lay on her back, looking up at the ceiling, blinking. Cool air blew in from the street, though Ladbroke Grove was quiet, and Elle knew suddenly that, even though it was only the first day of September, autumn was here. She sat up in bed, rubbing her tender eyes, as the memory of the previous thirty-six hours slowly returned.

She wished she didn't have to go to work. Could she just call in sick? She'd drunk an awful lot over the weekend, which was partly why she felt so dreadful, but it was the crying too; she'd cried all day. She had forgotten how crying always made her feel rubbish the next day, as if she'd been beaten up and left for dead.

Elle and Libby had been at Kenwood House on Saturday night, listening to the open-air concert (on the other side of the boundary, so they didn't have to pay). They'd taken a blanket, some crisps and wine, and though they didn't have a corkscrew and Elle had had to jab the cork into the bottle with her hair clip, it had been loads of fun. It always was fun with Libby, whether they were eating pasta at La Rosa, the tiny Italian place in Soho that only bouncers and strippers frequented, or arguing drunkenly over books (Elle, at Posy's recommendation, had just read the *Cazalet Chronicles* by Elizabeth Jane Howard, and thought they were the best books she'd ever read; Libby refused to touch them on account of their pastelly covers), or films (Elle wept through *The English Patient*, Libby snorted with laughter every time burnt-out Ralph Fiennes appeared on screen), or boys in the office (to Elle's fury, Libby tormented her about her alleged crush on Rory, and Elle couldn't come up with anyone in return for as Libby said, 'Publishing boys are total losers, Elle, get a grip').

They'd ended up at the Dome in Hampstead, and drunk even more. It had been a brilliant evening. When Elle had fantasised about the life in London she'd wanted it had been something like this, sitting in cafes discussing life and books long into the night, feeling the city under her feet, the still-terrifying but exhilarating sense of possibility out there. Daily life at Bluebird was alternately monotonous and scary: after four months she was starting to see just how far away was her dream of being a glamorous editor. You didn't get to be a glamorous editor by sending faxes to important literary agents called Shirley that began, 'Dear Shitley'. Glamorous editors didn't leave prawn sandwiches in filing cabinets, stinking out the office for a week with a smell so awful Elspeth became convinced they were being haunted by the ghost of a disgruntled author. They didn't photocopy four hundred pages of manuscript upside down, resulting in an entirely blank pile of paper, and they certainly didn't pass out in a corner of the pub after too many house whites, to the amusement of their colleagues. Yes. Elle knew she had a lot to learn.

The two of them had stayed out so late that they were shivering in the night air as they said their goodbyes. As ever,

Elle had felt guilty, creeping back to Ladbroke Grove at two in the morning, but Sam had been fast asleep. However, the next morning she woke Elle up by knocking on her door in floods of tears, her eyes huge, her fingers in her mouth.

'Princess Di's dead,' she said, and Elle made her repeat it, because it just didn't sound true.

They had spent all day crying, watching TV and listening to Capital play sad songs, going out in their pyjamas to the shop next door to get chocolate and Bombay mix and cheap wine and now it was Monday, and life was supposed to go on as normal, and of course it would, because it was stupid, Elle hadn't actually *known* Princess Diana. But, like so many girls, she felt as if she had, as if she – not that she *belonged* to her, that was stupid. But as if she sort of knew her, that if they'd ever met they'd have been friends.

Tears pricked Elle's eyes as she remembered the coffin coming off the plane, the Prince of Wales standing ready to greet it, his face lined with grief. 'The breaking of so great a thing should make a greater crack': that was Shakespeare, wasn't it? Oh, how pretentious it was, quoting Shakespeare. If Libby could hear her, she'd laugh her head off. Elle pulled the duvet over her; the Monday morning feeling of dread stronger than ever.

Suddenly, footsteps came padding loudly towards the bathroom, and the door was slammed with a bang. Elle winced, preparing herself. The radio came on, Chris Evans's voice slow and clear.

'It's Monday and, well, look, it's a hard day for us all, and we want to remember a wonderful woman, so here's Mariah Carey and "Without You". In memory of our Queen of Hearts.'

'YOOOOOU . . .' came Sam's voice, shrieking tonelessly through the paper-thin walls. '. . . WITHOUT YOOOOOOOU . . .'

Sam was 'a morning person', as she frequently told Elle when Elle asked her to please not tunelessly wail 'Mr

47

Loverman' at 6.45 a.m. Being a morning person, it seemed, meant not being bothered by the fact that you were totally tone deaf. Elle turned onto her stomach and screamed into her pillow, as she did every single morning. If she was ever called for jury service and there was someone on trial who'd killed their flatmate or neighbour for something similar Elle knew she'd have no hesitation in finding them not guilty. Every evening, she told herself Sam wasn't so bad, that actually they had a laugh over a glass of wine and some trashy TV. And every morning she woke up to what sounded like a drunk tramp gargling with petrol and razor blades, and she felt murder in her heart.

She even blamed Sam for the break-up of her semi-relationship with Fred. They'd seen each other, admittedly rather half-heartedly – he'd gone away for two weeks and not told her – during the summer. The second or third time he'd stayed over, Sam had woken them both up by singing the Cardigans' 'Lovefool' in such a painful way that Fred had left without having a shower, claiming he had an early meeting and needed to get home and pick up a suit. Since Fred was, as far as Elle knew, working in a cafe off Portobello while writing his screenplay that was going to win him an Oscar, this was clearly a lie, but she couldn't blame him. He hadn't called her since. Elle had tried to mind, but she didn't, to be honest. Fred belonged to the era of sleeping on sofas, watching daytime TV and feeling totally hopeless, and that all seemed years, not months, ago.

Forty minutes or so later, Elle was showered and dressed. It was still early, just after eight, and as she stood in the kitchen, her hands wrapped around a mug of tea, she sifted through her feelings, trying to work out why she still felt she'd missed something. Was it Princess Di, throwing her off? Or was it work? The trouble was, she could never remember anything specifically she hadn't done. It was the horror that there was another bomb, an uncollected urgent manuscript waiting in the post room, or another Dear Shitley fiasco, just waiting to explode, that she feared the most. In her darker days – and this was one of them – she wasn't sure what the future held. How on earth was she supposed to show them she'd be a good editor when no one had the faintest idea who she was, except maybe vaguely as the idiot who'd ordered Rory a cab that took him to Harlow instead of Heathrow? She was still staring into space as Sam came in.

'Hiya,' she said. 'What a strange morning. I feel very emotional still. Do you feel emotional?'

'Yes,' said Elle coolly, the post-shower-singing fury having not quite worn off. 'It's weird.'

Sam looked pleased. Her nose twitched. 'We're so similar. Ready for another Monday?'

'Not really,' said Elle. 'I feel like crap.' She sighed.

'I don't,' said Sam. She tucked her hair behind her ears and slung her flowery Accessorize bag over her shoulder. 'But then I'm not the one who stayed out with Libby all night Saturday! Am I!'

She laughed, just a little too heartily but Elle, still cross, bit her tongue. Sam always wanted to come along with Elle. Elle hadn't minded at first, but after Sam had fallen over onto Karen's birthday cake at her party in July and then got so drunk she'd passed out at Elle's friend Matty's housewarming in Clapham under a pile of coats in the hallway, Elle had started reining in the invitations. They were flatmates, they weren't joined at the hip. She'd spent her university years being the one who took the drunken mess home and she was damned if she was going to do it any more.

'I'm off,' Sam said. She was always in by nine, and usually left before Elle. 'You in this evening?'

Then Elle remembered. She said, 'I knew there was something I had to remember. Rhodes is coming over tonight.'

'Your brother?'

Elle nodded. 'I totally forgot. That's why . . .' She trailed off, and added, 'I haven't seen him for –' She tried to remember. 'Well, since Christmas, and then he left early.'

'How come?'

'Had a big row with Mum.' Elle didn't say any more.

Sam picked up her rucksack and changed the subject. 'Wow, this manuscript's heavy. I'll see you in a bit?'

Putting her mug in the sink, Elle grabbed her bag. 'I'll come with you,' she said. She double-locked the flimsy wood-chip door, and followed Sam down the stairs, out into the September sunshine.

'Did you finish it?' Sam said. Elle looked blank. *'Polly Pearson*? Isn't it brill?'

Her handbag was suddenly heavy on her shoulder. Elle peeked at it, saw a thick manuscript, untouched since Friday. 'Oh, my God.' Elle's face paled. No wonder her hungover brain was trying to tell her she'd forgotten something. It was two things. Rhodes tonight and now . . . and now this. She clutched the heavy bag. Of course. 'I promised Rory . . . I said I'd finish it over the weekend.'

'But you've read most of it,' Sam said perkily, holding the straps of her rucksack and whistling as she strode along, like one of those stupid creatures in the Girl Guide handbook. Elle looked at her with loathing.

'That's not the point –' Elle squeezed her eyes tightly shut. 'I wanted to gather my thoughts, have a proper response. Be . . . you know, like Libby. Have something to say.' Rory and Posy *never* asked her opinion on anything. She was virtually invisible, to them, to Felicity, to *everyone*. This was the first manuscript about which they'd said, 'Elle, we'd like to know what you think.' As though they were interested in her opinion. Libby was the one who could chat fearlessly to Rory and Jeremy in the pub, whom the authors knew when they rang up: 'Yes, Paris, it is Libby,' she'd say, if she picked up Elle's phone for her. 'How are you? What can I do for you today?' She was able to go up to agents at launch parties and introduce herself, and she always knew the right thing to say: 'Hi, I'm Libby, Felicity's assistant? Yes, we spoke last week! I just wanted to say how much I loved *Broken SWAT Team / Mother of All Ills / Lanterns Over Mandalay*.'

Sam cut in on her thoughts. 'Hey, do you want to go to Kensington Palace after work and lay some flowers?'

'No,' said Elle crossly, though she did want to, very much. She pulled the dog-eared manuscript out of her bag and started reading it as she walked along the street. 'I need to finish this before we get in.'

'Fine,' said Sam. 'I'll hold you.' She took her elbow and grinned at Elle, as Elle walked off the kerb. A bus swerved to avoid her, then hooted loudly, the passengers shaking their fists at the pair of them.

SAM RABBITED ALL the way in on the Tube, about how much she loved Dave (though Elle had met him but once since she'd moved in), and about how her sister had told her yesterday if the baby was a girl she'd call it Diana Frances, in tribute. But Elle had become adept at blocking out Sam's voice. She smoothed the manuscript on her lap and began to skim the last seventy pages, eyes darting in panic over the double-spaced lines. It was eight thirty. She had an hour.

The novel was called *Polly Pearson Finds a Man*, and unusually it had been sent to Rory, not Posy. It was by an Irish fashion journalist called Eithne Reilly, and already there was an offer on the table of £150,000 for two books, a sum so huge Elle found it hilarious.

'Jeremy says everyone's going to go mad for it,' said Sam. 'Oh. We're at Oxford Circus already, isn't it amazing how quickly the journey goes when there's someone to chat to!'

Elle looked up, wild-eyed. 'Help me. Does Colette get her comeuppance?'

'Yes, she gets fired. And it turns out Roland is a real bastard, and Max is lovely, and she's got it all wrong, because Colette lied to her about the Gucci account.'

Elle turned to the last page.

'Damn you, Polly!' Max Reardon said, striding towards her. 'I want you to come back to Dublin with me. As my wife, not as my features editor!'

'Max . . .' Polly stared at him with huge blue eyes, filling up with water and running down her cheeks. 'Oh, Max . . . Yes, please! Only one thing?'

'What, darling?' said Max, enfolding her in his arms and kissing her.

'I want the job too. And I know what my first commission will be. "How To Find A Man".'

The End

'That'll have to do,' she said, stuffing the manuscript into her bag. 'At least I know what happens in the end. Big surprise, it ends happily ever after.' Elle followed Sam as the Tube doors slammed open.

'Isn't it amazing? Did you like it?' Sam said, as they climbed onto the escalator, surrounded by silent fellow commuters.

'Sort of,' said Elle. 'It's so cheesy but it's romantic. I loved Max even though he's got the same name as my awful ex, which shows it must be good.' Libby had thought it was rubbish, but Libby would. Elle couldn't help it, she'd enjoyed it, but was that wrong?

'I couldn't put it down,' said Sam. 'So funny! The bit in the All Bar One!' She hugged herself, and then whipped out her TravelCard. 'Here we are, back on Tottenham Court Road,' she sang. 'What a lovely—'

'Look, Sam,' Elle said, suddenly desperate for a moment of peace and quiet, 'I'm going to treat myself to a coffee and a croissant. I'll see you in the office. Don't wait for me,' she added, amazed at how firm her voice was.

Elle stood in the queue, hugging her bag to her chest, smelling the coffee and feeling calmer already. Yes, this was a good idea. Sure, it was £3 she didn't have, but she needed a pick-me-up, because all that crying and wine-drinking had left her feeling very feeble. She'd think of something intelligent to say about *Polly Pearson* as she walked to Bedford Square, and all would be well.

As Elle turned off Tottenham Court Road, clutching her paper cup of coffee, with her croissant in a waxy paper bag, she inhaled again, and smiled. It was a beautiful day now, the trees in the square at their darkest green, about to turn. She was early, too, for once. *'Polly Pearson is a serviceable piece of chick lit, which I found to be—'* No, too pompous.

'Polly Pearson? Oh, thanks for letting me read it, Rory. Yes, it's very much of the genre but there's a refreshing lightness of touch which reminded me of a – of a . . . a sherbet fountain. A feather. A feathery syllabub. Syllabub? Or do I mean sybil?

She turned the corner and checked her watch. It—

'AAAAAAAAAAAAAAAHH! OH, MY GOD!'

Elle had bumped into something, and the shock made her fingers squeeze together, popping the plastic lid off her cup and pouring scalding coffee into the air.

'My – God!'

'Shit!' Elle cried, seeing her coffee everywhere, all over this large bulky shape, which she realised was a person, a woman. It stared at her, blazing anger in its green eyes, and she felt her bowels turn to liquid. Oh no. *Noooo.*

'What on earth,' Felicity Sassoon bellowed, brown liquid pouring down her face, 'are you doing, you *stupid little girl?'*

Passers-by on the wide pavement ignored them as Elle dropped her bag and croissant to the ground, and started dabbing at Miss Sassoon, who stood still, dripping with coffee, her huge bouffant grey hair flattened, her pale blue tweed jacket stained with brown. She resembled an outraged plump exotic bird stuck in London Zoo during a downpour. Elle ineffectually patted her, blotting the coffee with her thin brown Pret napkins. She reached her chest, and was about to start there, but Miss Sassoon pushed her away, furiously.

'Clumsy creature,' she said. 'Get off me.' She looked at Elle properly for the first time. 'Oh, for God's sake,' she said. 'It's you.'

'Yes . . .' said Elle. 'I'm so . . . I'm so sorry . . . Miss Sassoon . . .'

Felicity Sassoon stared at her, and her eyes narrowed. Elle stood still, the feeling in her stomach confirming what she'd known since she'd woken up.

This was going to be an awful day.

SHE'D ESCORTED FELICITY to the office, into the care of Elspeth, who nearly fainted with alarm when her great leader had appeared stained and bedraggled, the damp residue of coffee-stained napkin clinging to her jacket and skirt, and Libby, who had rolled her eyes at Elle, as if to say, *What the hell have you done now?* After everyone else had gone back to work, Elle turned on her computer and then, telling Libby she was off to get something from the stationery cupboard, she escaped to the Ladies, where she cried for what seemed like hours but was in fact only a few minutes. She would be fired. Felicity would ring up everyone in publishing and warn them against hiring her. Probably she was doing it now.

When she'd finished, Elle went to the sinks, wiping her nose and staring at herself in the mildewy old mirror. She looked awful: red eyes, red nose, still puffy and ravaged from a weekend of crying and drinking. She rinsed her face with cold water and patted it dry, because that was what heroines always did in novels when they'd had a shock, but it just made her face even redder than normal and took off the Boots concealer she'd so carefully applied to the spot on her cheek. She looked down at the newly laundered towel on the handrail: it was streaked with light brown.

She was just giving another shuddering sigh, when there came a knock at the door.

'Elle?'

It was a man's voice. 'Hello?' she said suspiciously.

'Elle, it's me, Rory. Open the door.'

'No,' Elle said, not knowing why.

'Come on. I wee in the men's loos, don't worry. Open the door.'

Elle unlocked the bathroom door and Rory's head appeared. 'Dear me,' he said, looking at her shiny red visage with alarm. 'What on earth's wrong?'

Elle burst into tears again. 'Coffee . . . Miss Sassoon furious . . . Poor thing . . . a punk outside Buckingham Palace, he brought flowers . . .'

'What? Who brought flowers?'

'The punk, he came straight from a night out clubbing and left a wreath.' She wiped her nose with the back of her hand. 'I cried all day, those poor boys . . . oh. Then this morning . . . wasn't looking where I was going . . . I probably scarred her, I'm so stupid.' Elle sobbed, her hands over her face.

Rory patted her arm comfortingly. 'It was an accident, Elle. Felicity's fine. The jacket's at the dry-cleaner's already and Elspeth's bought her some more Elnett, so everything's OK. Don't take on so.'

Elle cried even louder. 'Oh, God,' Rory said, squeezing further into the tiny bathroom and putting his arm round her. 'What on earth have I said now?'

'Granny Bee always said, "Don't take on so,"' Elle told him, staring up at him. 'It just reminds me of her, and she's dead now too . . . oh . . .'

Rory squeezed Elle's shoulders and smiled. 'Well, she was right. Elle, please don't cry. I hate seeing you like this,' he said solemnly. 'Now, dry your eyes, and come back out. Felicity wants to see you.'

Elle felt as if ice had been poured down her back. 'Oh. No,' she said.

'It'll be about *Polly Pearson*, don't worry. She's not going to yell at you.'

Elle didn't believe him.

'It'll be fine,' Rory said. 'Trust me?'

'Yes.'

'There you go. Don't look so dramatic, sweetheart.' He bent down and kissed her, only on the top of the head, but Elle stiffened.

'I'm OK now,' she said, and stepped away, trying not to blush.

'Sorry,' Rory said easily, after a tiny pause. He patted her arm. 'I was channelling your granny again. That's the kind of thing grannies do, isn't it? I have no idea. Mine ran off with a bearded lady from the circus when I was a young boy. Ready?'

'Er, sure,' said Elle. She wished she had some powder – her face was gleamingly shiny – but if she was about to get fired perhaps it didn't matter. She held her head up high and marched out of the loo, followed by Rory, past an astonished Sam.

'Don't let her boss you around,' Rory whispered in her ear. 'Good luck, kid.'

Elle knocked on the door. *It's fine,* she told herself. *I hate it here anyway. I'll leave and work in a bookshop, and I'll never have to read another stupid romance novel again.*

She knew as she thought it that this was a total lie. That she didn't mind the monotony of photocopying, the fear of failure, if she could just stay a while longer. She liked it here. She liked the feel and smell of a brand new book, fresh from the printer's, Jeff Floyd the sales director's shout of joy when Victoria Bishop went Top Ten, the notion that, unlike school, you went somewhere every day and you wanted to be there so you worked hard, you even enjoyed being bottom of the class, because one day, just one day, you might get better.

'Come,' the voice from inside the office boomed, and as she opened the door, Elle was surprised bats and grovelling henchmen didn't fly out to greet her.

She peered inside. 'Ah, Eleanor,' Felicity Sassoon said, behind her vast mahogany desk. 'Come and sit down.'

'Miss Sassoon – I'm so so sorry,' Elle began, shutting the door behind her. She sat down and took a deep breath. 'Are you – all right?'

'Yes, of course I'm all right,' Felicity said impatiently. She fiddled with the ring that was always on the second finger of her left hand, a huge antique amethyst in a claw setting. She was wearing a different jacket. Elle's eye strayed to the locked cupboard behind her, containing, she knew, the fully designed layouts of the *Illustrated Queen Mother Biography*, ready to go to press the moment the Queen Mum died. No one had seen inside it for years. What else did Felicity have in there, aside from several Harris Tweed ladies' jackets? A policeman's uniform, a sexy maid's outfit?

Elle blinked. Felicity wasn't the kind of person who you imagined having a romantic life. Though she had been married to Rory's father Derek, no one knew his surname, and she was always referred to as 'Miss Sassoon'. Office legend had it that Felicity had given Derek a heart attack, and that, according to Jeremy, 'He was glad to get away from her. Died with a smile on his face.'

'Elle,' Felicity said firmly, looking down at her jotter. Elle suspected she had her name written down there. *Eleanor Bee. Mousy. Moronic. Shy. Skirts too short. Scalded me Monday 1st September 1997.* 'I wanted to ask you something. I noticed earlier, as you were attempting to mop the contents of a paper cup of boiling coffee from my person, that you had the manuscript for *Polly Pearson* in your bag. Have you read it?'

59

'Er . . .' Elle was blindsided. She swallowed. 'Yes, almost all of it.'

'Did you like it?'

'Um –' She hadn't had time to come up with the apposite, one-line summing-up. Elle cleared her throat and sat on her hands, breathing deeply. She had to tell the truth, otherwise it'd be obvious.

'Well . . . I actually quite enjoyed it.'

Felicity frowned. 'Why?'

Elle fidgeted. 'It's romantic, it's funny, it's really readable,' she said, trying to explain.

'I don't understand how that's different from a MyHeart book,' Felicity said.

'It's very different,' Elle replied. 'I like MyHeart,' she added nervously. 'But they're . . . sometimes . . . maybe they're a tiny – a bit old-fashioned. Um –'

She slumped down in her chair again, afraid she'd gone too far, but Felicity leaned forward. 'Go on.'

'Well, one of the last MyHearts I had to check over, the nurse who had the affair with a doctor had a baby by him and she ran away and never told him because of the shame and now he's all wounded and thinks she hates him,' Elle said. 'That wouldn't happen nowadays. If I got knocked up by someone at work, you know –' she waved her arms around, getting into her stride, 'say Jeremy, I wouldn't go into hiding, I'd say, "Er – hey, Jeremy, what are we going to do about this then?"' She paused, as Felicity's eyebrows shot together. 'Or – or anyone! You know.' She could feel her old enemy, the blush, spreading over her collarbone. 'It's just a bit unrealistic. Like a Ladybird fairy story where everything's fine in the end. Women aren't idiots. I mean, those books are really good, but . . .' She trailed off again. 'That happy ending business – it's all a bit contrived. I don't ever believe it.'

'You don't believe it?' Felicity smiled, and her eyes searched

Elle's face. 'How unromantic of you, Elle, what terrible talk for a young girl.'

It wasn't true either. The truth was, Elle wanted to believe in happily ever after, more than anything. But to admit it would be to discount what she knew to be the real facts of life. So she didn't know how to reply to this, didn't know how to admit that she longed, secretly, to have her perspective changed, by something or someone, she didn't know which.

'Look at Princess Diana,' she said eventually.

'Diana, Princess of Wales,' Felicity said, correcting her sharply. 'She was never a princess in her own right, merely by marriage. A fact she would have done well to remember. She is not the example I'd choose, Eleanor.'

'But she – ' Elle began, then saw they had veered way off territory. 'I just don't like stories where it's obvious who they're going to end up with. Real life's just not like that.'

Felicity shook her head, as if she didn't know what to do with Elle. 'Well, I'll believe you, though I do think that's sad, dear. Everyone needs some escapism, now and again. What about Georgette Heyer? Do you like her?'

A childhood of Saturday mornings spent at the Shawcross library, reading while her librarian mother stamped books and made recommendations, meant Elle knew Georgette Heyer's name. She said, 'I've heard of her. I've never read her.'

Felicity looked absolutely astonished. 'What? You've never read Georgette Heyer?'

'No, sorry.'

'I am amazed. Never read Georgette Heyer. My God.' Felicity bowed her head as if she were a medium, acknowledging Georgette Heyer's spirit in the room. 'She is, quite simply, the best. *Jane Austen* would have liked her.' She breathed in slowly through her nostrils. 'And I do not say that lightly.' She reached behind her and handed Elle a copy of *Venetia*. It was a seventies paperback with a view of a girl in a cornfield. 'Take this. I am dumbfounded you haven't read her. You, of all people.'

'Why me?' Elle said, biting her finger nervously.

'Well, Eleanor, you won't remember, but I was impressed with you at our interview. You had opinions about books. And you were enthusiastic. *That* –' Felicity stabbed a pencil into her jotter, 'is a very good thing. Don't lose it.'

You won't remember. Elle wanted to laugh. 'Thank you!' she said, her face lighting up with pleasure.

'Go away and read that. What a treat you have in store. Now, I've gone off-piste again. One of the pleasures of discussing books, I'm sure you'll agree.' She glanced at her watch. 'Back to business. *Polly Pearson*. Why's it so marvellously different?'

Confident now, Elle spoke in a rush, the words tumbling out of her. 'Well. It's about someone near my age, living in London, having fun, trying to sort her life out, and she likes watching *Friends* and ordering takeaways and even though it's not the best book I've ever read, I know about five people who'd like it, and we've not had anything like that at Bluebird before.' Elle wanted Felicity to like it, she didn't know why, other than that she wanted Rory to be able to buy it and she wanted him to be pleased with her. She delivered the killer line. 'After all, you always say if when you're reading it you can think of three people you know who would like the book then you should definitely publish it.'

The dark green eyes – so like her son's, Elle had never noticed it before – were scrunched up tight. 'Hm,' she said, and Elle detected a note of uncertainty in her tone. 'Very interesting. I'll be honest with you, Eleanor. Rory wants us to bid for it. He wants us to go to £200,000, blow the other offers out of the water. He says it'll show everyone Bluebird can compete at the top. But it's a hell of a lot of money . . .'

She trailed off and stared thoughtfully at Elle. 'This *Bridget*

Jones vogue, it's lasting much longer than I suspected. *Bridget Jones in New York. Bridget Jones Moves to the Countryside.* And I'm afraid I simply don't get it.' She sighed; a shadow passed over her face. 'Rory thinks I'm past it, that I can't spot a good book when it's right under my nose,' she said unexpectedly.

Elle wanted to reassure her. 'Look, like I say, it's not completely fantastic. Perhaps it's a bit cynically done.' She stopped, and realised this was true. 'And the characters are cardboard thin, like she read some other books like it and thought, "I can knock one of these off myself." But I still enjoyed it.'

Felicity's eyes gleamed. 'Right,' she said. 'That is what I wanted to hear. Thank you.'

Elle smiled with relief. 'Oh – good. Um – is that all, Miss Sassoon?' she asked politely.

'Yes, dear,' Felicity replied. She got out her Dictaphone. 'Libby. Email to Rory Sassoon, Posy Carmichael . . .' She pressed the Pause button. 'Read Georgette Heyer. Let me know how you get on.' She made a shooing gesture, and Elle shot out of the cool dark office, shutting the door gently behind her.

'How did it go? Are you clearing out your things?' Libby asked, sotto voce, as Elle sank into her chair.

'No, it was OK.' Elle's shoulders felt as though they'd sunk four inches lower with relief. 'She just wanted to ask about that *Polly Pearson* book.'

'Hope you told her it was total rubbish,' said Libby.

'No,' said Elle. 'I said it was OK.' She paused, and looked down at the battered old Pan paperback in her hand. 'At least, I think that's what I said.'

It wasn't till after lunch that Elle came back, much restored by a tuna baguette and a walk to the British Museum in the sunshine, to find Rory standing by her desk.

'What did you say to my mother?' he demanded. He ran his hands through his light brown hair, scrunching it till it stood on end. Elle looked blank. 'To Felicity, Elle,' Rory said. 'About that damned book. Come on, what did you say to her?'

Elle sat down and put her bag on the floor. 'I don't know,' she began. 'Why?'

Rory had his shirtsleeves rolled up and his hands on his hips. He glared at her, his face grim, his eyes dark. She'd never seen him look so angry.

'I went out for the rest of the morning and I get back to this. She's sent the most fucking absurd email, saying she won't authorise a bigger offer.' He scratched his scalp furiously. 'She says we can match the first offer but no more. We won't get the bloody thing now, the agent's after money. This was our chance to show we're not some piddling old-fashioned grannies' club, that we're in the game! She was going for it this morning. *What did you say to her?*'

'I didn't say anything!' Elle said, trying not to squeak. 'I just told her I really liked it, that it was a lot more realistic than most MyHeart books, and I said I enjoyed it, Sam enjoyed it—'

Behind her, Libby coughed loudly.

Rory brandished a piece of paper. '*Asking the younger members of the office for their views,*' he read, in a low, angry voice, '*and trusting to my own instinct as well, I came to the conclusion that, in the words of a junior employee, "It is cynically done, with cardboard-thin characters, as if the author had read other books and merely thought she could knock something similar off herself." And therefore not something Bluebird should be spending its money on, no matter how forceful the desire to surrender to a seductive albeit – I believe fleeting – zeitgeist.*'

He bent down, so his lean face was near hers. 'Did you say that?'

Perhaps if Elle had been older or more experienced, she'd

have told Rory not to drag her into his feud with his mother. But she wasn't. 'I – I did,' she said quietly. She couldn't believe this was the same Rory who laughed and joked all day long, who'd been so sweet a few hours earlier, kissed her on the head. 'But I also told her I enjoyed it a lot, despite all that, I promise, Rory—'

'Elle –' he began, and then stopped. He closed his eyes briefly. 'For God's sake, you don't get it, do you? This is a commercial business.' He clenched his hands into fists. 'It's not your fault,' he said, after a moment. 'I'm sorry. It's just – now someone else will make it a huge best-seller and we'll be left trying to persuade Smith's to take the umpteenth Jessie Dukes about sisters in the Blitz.' He leaned forward again. 'You're a snob, Elle, you know that?'

'No, I'm not,' Elle said indignantly.

'Yes, you are. I saw you last week, devouring that book at your desk. You told me you liked it.'

He looked genuinely upset. He'd never been cross with her; it was awful. Posy was stern, sometimes a killjoy: Rory was funny, kind, a bit lazy, sure, but she'd always thought he was on her side. 'I was, I enjoyed it, but I'm just saying it's not—'

'Not what? Proper art? Oh, for God's sake.' He waved his hand at her, as if she'd disappointed him, played the wrong move in a game she didn't know she was in. 'Forget it. It's OK. It's her, not you. She's going to learn one day, and then it'll be too late.' He wandered off, and left her staring after him, bewildered.

RECOUNTING ALL THIS back at home to her brother that evening, Elle was still in shock.

'So I spilled coffee over her, and she didn't even seem to *mind* too much! She didn't shout or anything. I thought I was going to get fired, and then she asked me what I thought of a manuscript!' She poured Rhodes another glass of wine and drained her own. 'Honestly, Rhodes – well, you have to meet her to see what I mean, but she's an amazing woman, really remarkable. Her husband died when she was thirty, left her alone with a small son, and this company to run, and she's done it – she knows everyone, she's always going to the most glamorous parties. Last week, she went to the Women of the Year lunch, and Joan Collins was there, can you believe it?'

'Right,' said Rhodes, stuffing his face with Twiglets. 'So then what happened?'

His tone suggested polite boredom but Elle, wanting to make her older brother see how wonderful her new world was, couldn't stint on any of the details. 'Well,' she said. 'So . . . We have this really great conversation, you know, about literature. About all these really interesting things.'

From the battered old sofa in the corner of the kitchen

Libby chimed in. 'Elle, that's rubbish. You talked about romance novels and then she stitched you up. If you ask me she played you like a Stradivarius.' She threw some peanuts in her mouth and crossed her legs, as Rhodes watched her admiringly.

'. . . Anyway,' Elle ploughed on, 'Rory was really cross with me, he said I was the one who'd stuffed everything up.' She remembered Rory's grim face as he stood over her. *You're a snob, Elle.* She hated him thinking badly of her.

'He's playing you too,' Libby said. 'The pair of them. Sometimes I think I can't wait to leave that place. It seems all cosy-cosy, but the politics will ruin them in the end.'

'Mm.' Elle didn't like it when Libby talked like that. 'Supper's nearly ready.' She drained the pasta and stared at it, desperately, not sure what to do next.

'I'm starving,' Rhodes said, as though he could read her mind.

'Just applying the finishing touches!' Elle trilled, slightly too loudly.

If Sam was here she'd have bought some four cheese pasta sauce from Sainsbury's just in case. Sam planned her meals in advance. But Elle liked to wing it, with mixed results. She grabbed a glass of red wine that she happened to know had been there since the previous day, and chucked it into the pan, then some basil leaves from the withered plant on a saucer by the sink. It didn't look like much so, rather desperately, she shook some soy sauce and vegetable oil in after them.

'Who's hungry?' she said, clapping her hands and trying to sound like an Italian mamma. 'Hey? Come and get it!'

Rhodes sat down at the tiny table and stared at the pan, and Elle felt a flash of weary despair. They had a whole evening to get through. Her own brother, and he was a stranger to her.

'Mm,' Libby said. 'Smells delicious. Is Sam coming back?'

'No, she's out tonight.' Sam had gone to Kensington Palace after all, taking Dave with her. Elle was glad she wasn't here. There was a guilelessness about her that made Elle fear for her at Rhodes's hands. She knew he'd be vile about Princess Di, for starters. She handed Libby and Rhodes each a bowl. The winey-soy-oil had gathered at the bottom, leaving a faint red sediment on the pasta. 'So,' she said. 'Sorry for going on about work, it's just been a crazy day. It's brilliant, but it is weird. You know.'

'Not really,' said Rhodes. Elle opened her mouth, but he carried on. 'Ellie, you didn't do anything wrong. They're the ones using you, not the other way round.' He took another mouthful and stopped, then waved his fork in the air. 'Hm. What's in this pasta?'

'Yes, it's delicious, Elle,' Libby said, cutting across him. 'Rhodes is right, don't let them mess you around, Elle. Just be careful next time. Rory's out for himself, you know, so's Felicity.'

'Rory's not out for himself.'

'Ya-hah,' said Libby, sardonically. 'Right.' She turned to Rhodes. 'So, what do you do? Something with money, then?'

'I work at Bloomberg. Analyst,' Rhodes said. 'In New York – went to college there, stayed on to do an MBA, got the job at Bloomberg after that. They love the Brits.'

'Hm. Isn't New York dangerous?' Libby said. 'My dad wants to go, and my mum's always terrified. "No way, Eric! I'm not setting foot in that place! Who wants to be mugged and shot, eh?"' she said, exaggerating her Northern accent. Elle knew she was deliberately provoking him; Libby was always going on about how they should go to New York for a few days. She was obsessed with the place.

'What? No way is it dangerous,' said Rhodes. He seemed incensed by this. 'Typical small-minded Brits, that's what it is. You know, it's bollocks, this is 1997, those were problems in the eighties, they're long gone. It's a fucking great place.'

He pushed his plate away.

'Sorry, Ellie. I can't eat this. I think it's the jet lag. Have you got a pizza menu?'

Elle stared at him, a red flush of fury mixed with embarrassment creeping up her chest to her neck. 'No, I bloody haven't!' she said.

'What's that on the fridge?' Rhodes pointed to a takeaway menu.

She hated the way he wound her up, she wished she didn't care what he thought, didn't want to try and make him like her, be impressed by her. It was pathetic. Something inside Elle snapped. 'You're not having a fucking pizza,' she shouted.

'Why?'

Elle was practically gibbering. 'You can't just rock up here and be all, "Oh you're being stupid and I work in New York and I'm soooooooooooo amayyyyyyyyyyyzing." You always have to be the coolest person in the room, don't you?'

'I am cooler than you,' Rhodes said, blankly. 'I mean, Jeez, Ellie—'

'Don't call me Ellie! It's babyish!'

Rhodes watched her impassively. 'Look, don't go mad,' he said. 'I only wanted to see how you were and find out about your job. *Ellie.*'

Elle wiped her nose with her arm. 'No, you don't! You come because you have to, you never ask about Mum and how she is—'

Rhodes interrupted. 'Hey! You haven't asked me a single question about how I am. You rabbit on about your job and these people I have no idea about, you serve some kind of soy sauce pasta mulch, and then you start throwing stuff around and shouting at me.'

Elle stared at him. It was horrible how much she let him wind her up, always had done, how they wouldn't ever talk about the stuff that lurked just beneath the surface. 'Don't you understand –?'

'Yes,' said Rhodes, nodding, as though he was trying to be

reasonable. 'I do. Promise. It's just the facts are quite simple. You chucked coffee over the head of your company. Because of this she is aware of you for the first time since you joined, so you actually effectively networked, though I wouldn't use that method again. She asks your opinion because she needs back-up for her own strategy, and your boss is angry because she used you against him. That shows they both value your opinion, to an extent. It's a good thing. And it shows it's not your fight, it's theirs.'

'That's what I said,' said Libby.

'So the question becomes,' pursued Rhodes, putting his fingertips together, 'what do you do next to maximise this situation for yourself?'

'Er – does it?' said Elle. 'Isn't that a bit – creepy?'

Rhodes laughed, and flung his leg out, pulling his trouser leg up. He put one hand on his thigh, and cupped his chin with the other.

'It's business. The business may be selling books to grannies who like knitting patterns, but it's still a business. And if they're at loggerheads you can use it to your own ends. But first, you've got to work out who's got the biggest dick. Pick that person and stick with them. The old lady, or the son? Sounds like the old lady to me, he sounds like a prick.'

'Rory's *not* a prick,' Elle said. 'He's great. Isn't he, Libs?'

Libby cleared her throat and said, 'But Rhodes, if he's a prick, doesn't that mean the same thing as the biggest dick?'

'No,' Rhodes said, still serious. 'It's totally different.'

Libby got up, shaking her shoulders. 'Right,' she said. 'I have to go. I said I'd meet Jeremy and some of the others at Filthy MacNasty's.'

'What the hell is that?' Rhodes said, looking cross and yet intrigued.

'It's a bar, Shane MacGowan goes there all the time. They do book events, readings, it's kind of rough and ready. It's cool, you know.'

Elle had been to Filthy's over the summer and didn't like it. It was full of young editors and agents in thick black glasses all trying to outdo each other, and when one of the authors had talked about books being the new drug of choice she'd wanted to laugh out loud. She had tried reading one of his novels and it had been in blank verse with no punctuation and no one had names, they were all called Red-Haired Man, Brown-Eyed Man, and Blonde Woman, and of course Blonde Woman had taken her clothes off several times in an allegedly necessary-for-the-plot but basically super-sleazy way and everyone said it was art, unlike the MyHeart books which were of course beneath anyone's notice there, even though Elle thought the sex scenes were considerably better written. Of course, if she'd said any of this to anyone at Filthy's they'd have looked at her as if she'd just said she thought Hitler was a tad misunderstood.

Rhodes looked impressed; he was impressed by Libby overall, Elle could tell. She said, 'Are you sure, Libs? It's in Clerkenwell, and it's nine thirty.'

'It's fine.' Libby picked up her coat. 'I really want to go, and I know you hate that kind of thing. It's not that far for me to get back from once I'm there. I'll see you tomorrow, thanks for the lovely pasta soup. Rhodes, great to meet you.'

'Great to—' Rhodes began, standing up, but Libby had gone, waving a slim hand in farewell.

'She's cool,' he said, staring down the corridor at the front door.

Elle put her palms down on the table and wearily pushed herself up. 'The pizza place is just next door. I'll order you something, shall I?'

Rhodes turned back. 'Thanks, Ellie. I mean – Elle. That'd be great.' He cleared his throat, brought his thick black eyebrows together. 'Sorry. This was nice too – you know.'

She took a breath and smiled at him. 'Like a . . . starter, maybe.'

71

'That's it.' Rhodes smiled back at his sister. Pulling the pizza menu off the fridge, Elle said, 'So, Rhodes – are you seeing anyone? Sorry to be nosy. I kind of thought maybe you might be, from something you said.'

Rhodes's head flipped up. 'I am. That's weird, how did you know?'

'I read about two romance novels a week at the moment,' Elle said. 'Call it intuition based on experience.'

'We both have our own skill set, then,' Rhodes said, and Elle wasn't sure if he was joking or not. 'Well, yeah. She's called Melissa, and I've been asking her out on dates for a while, but her boyfriend was this mega-rich WASP and I thought I stood no chance, but she dumped him over the summer, so yeah – I moved in there. Took her for cocktails at the Plaza, played up my British accent, told her all about my idyllic upbringing in the English countryside and – goal.'

'That's great – I'm happy for you,' Elle said, after a pause. 'How do you know her?'

'She's an analyst at Bloomberg too, assessing global risk,' Rhodes said. Elle nodded as if she knew what that was. 'She went to Brown, so she's super well-connected, but she's fun too. I want her to visit England with me but . . .'

He trailed off, and they stared at each other, as though he knew Elle could see the collapse of the shiny artificial world he'd created, of a charming English cottage with a mum who bakes biscuits and has apple cheeks, and a super-involved dad amicably divorced from her and with two great new kids and a lovely new wife. '*Yes,*' people would say, in this fantasy world. '*The Bees managed it so well. They're just one big happy family.*'

Elle couldn't say anything back to that. She just nodded.

They went next door to wait for the pizza in the cramped takeaway place with the minicab drivers and the hoodie boys on their pushbikes, and the glassy-eyed skinny blondes, then they came back upstairs and ate the pizza and Rhodes said it wasn't too bad, not as good as New York pizza but good for London. They watched the news together on the sofa, the hordes at the palace, the Spice Girls in black at some awards ceremony, the funeral set for Saturday, five more days of revelling in this unaccustomed, unBritish grief. 'It won't always feel this sad,' Rhodes said, when Elle gave a small sniff, and she was touched. 'Promise, Ellie.'

He helped her make up the sofa bed, and then they carried on talking, and Elle asked him about Manhattan, and he told her about the steam rising from the subway, the place he'd been for breakfast only last weekend which was where the orgasm scene in *When Harry Met Sally* had been filmed. About how when he'd taken Melissa for their first date, they'd walked up 5th Avenue afterwards and a tramp outside Central Park had shouted, 'Marry her, you should marry her!'

'That's what it's like all the time, there,' he said. He asked some more about her job, how Karen was, whether autumn was a busy time in publishing, how long she saw herself staying at Bluebird. But he didn't ask about Mum, or Dad, once, and Elle didn't mention them.

March 1998

'WELL, I THINK it looks *really* nice,' Sam said doubtfully, as Elle stared in the tiny mirror of the Ladies' bathroom.

'I hate it,' Elle said dramatically. 'I don't know why I had it done. I look like a brassy whore,' she said, running a strand of hair through her fingers. 'My hair was fine before. Now it's insane. Look at it.'

'It's great, I promise,' said Libby, applying some lip gloss. 'It's the crappy Bluebird sales conference, not the Oscars.'

There was a sharp rap at the door. 'Hurry up, please,' came Posy's voice. Elle, Libby and Sam hurried sideways out of the cramped room. Posy was waiting for them, resplendent in a floral bias-cut Jigsaw dress. She was wearing blue eyeshadow and mascara and her hair was up. Elle stared; she'd never seen Posy dressed up before. Posy tapped her foot. 'The authors will be arriving soon,' she said, in the tones of one announcing the Apocalypse. 'Let's go.'

Elle had never heard of a sales conference before she'd gone to work at Bluebird. It was basically the chance for an almighty piss-up, as far as she could tell. There was a presentation, some flashy music on in the background, and then dinner with authors and the reps from all round the country, at a Georgian townhouse in Soho.

The marketing department was in charge for the weeks before the sales conference, and exciting-looking things started arriving for the event: Post-it notes in the shape of hearts and 1998/99 diaries with Victoria Bishop's new title printed on them – *Diary of a Well-Worn Heart* – and torches with 'Be Afraid of the Dark' for Oona King's new thriller. Elle thought it was amazing, what they could produce; there was still so much about the whole business that, even after nearly a year, filled her with a kind of wonder that she was here at all. She knew it was tragic to look forward to a work event this much, but she couldn't help it. Besides, after ten months of working there, she loved nights out with her Bluebird colleagues. Everyone got the same jokes, there was always someone to talk to and something to gossip about: whether Jeremy and Lucy the publicity director were having an affair, what Rory had allegedly said to Felicity during their latest row, how much of a bitch Victoria Bishop really was, and so on.

For this anticipated event Elle had even bought a new dress – dove grey chiffon with beading from Oasis – and the previous night, flushed with excitement and an all-consuming urge to be bold and embrace life, she had walked into a hairdresser's at the top of Tottenham Court Road and apparently blacked out in an episode of lunacy, because when she came to she saw she'd asked them to cut all her hair off into a crop, which wouldn't have been so bad if it hadn't been teamed with a dye job the colour of a field of rapeseed. And it was then that she remembered too late that the urge to be bold and embrace life usually had catastrophic results. 'Oh, dear,' she said sadly, grabbing her coat and turning off her computer, catching sight of the yellow hair in the black screen.

Someone lightly touched her shoulder. 'What's up?'

Elle turned quickly. 'Hello, Rory.' She put her bag over her shoulder, trying to look professional. 'Right, I'm ready.'

'Why are you sighing like an old steam engine?'

Elle rolled her eyes back into her head. 'Er – nothing. It's silly.'

'What? Tell me. I'm your boss. We have no secrets.'

'It's my . . . hair. I changed it.'

'Yes, I noticed that,' Rory said.

'Of course you did, it's horrible,' Elle said. 'It's just horrible.'

'You look great, Elle, stop complaining. That crop suits you.'

'Oh.' Elle smiled at him, but then her face fell. 'But the colour's so—'

'It looks lovely,' said Rory, slightly impatiently. He looked at his watch. 'Want to come with me?'

'Oh. Thanks a lot.' Elle stared at him. 'You look lovely too. Black tie's so flattering, isn't it.'

'What a barbed compliment,' he said, laughing as she flushed with embarrassment. 'Bet you wouldn't say that to Jeremy.'

'Jeremy's different –' Elle began in confusion, but Rory steered her towards the stairs.

'Enough. We're off to the ball, Cinderelle. Or rather, Soho's glamorous backstreets. It's going to be a great night, so stop complaining and enjoy it, your first sales conference. And don't,' he said, as they walked towards the front door, 'drink too much. The wine flows like water at these things. Be careful. I'm responsible for you, after all. No misbehaving.' He waved his finger at her.

'Of course not,' said Elle, feeling much more cheerful.

She annoyed Rory the moment they reached Auriol House by giggling at Jeremy, who was welcoming guests in the doorway. They arrived just after the Irish rep Terry, whom Jeremy was clapping heartily on the back. 'Go on through, Terry, good to see you, mate. Oh. Hello, Rory. Elle – wow. You look great! Love the hair, babe.'

Elle blushed, stood on one leg and then the other. 'Oh. Thanks, Jeremy!' She ran her hand over the back of her head.

'Come on,' Rory said testily, pushing her forward with a thumb on her shoulder blade. 'I have to find Tobias Scott, and you should see if there's anything you can do.' He fiddled with his bow tie and Elle thought again how serious he looked. 'Don't just stand around looking like a spare part. Felicity hates it. Mingle.'

She nodded vigorously. 'Tobias Scott the agent? He's coming?'

'Yes.' Rory said, as they walked down a corridor decorated with fairy lights and a huge sign saying, *Welcome to the World of Bluebird*. 'He's being a right slippery old bastard at the moment. I need to corner him.'

'Why, what's he done?' Elle liked hearing about things like this.

'They've asked for much more money for the new John Rainham contract. Felicity wants to go on with him, of course. I want to tell them to – oh, there's Emma. I need to talk to her too. Get working.' He patted her shoulder and wandered off.

Typical Rory. Elle rolled her eyes and turned into the first room, where a pink banner hung outside reading, *MyHeart. Enter the Land of Happy Endings*. Inside, a few guests stood around with glasses of champagne and in the centre of it all, a beautiful man with no top on, surrounded by women. 'They are releasing the calendar early this year,' he was saying. 'To fulfil *your needs*, that's what I haff said.'

Elle stared at him. This must be Lorcan, the famous male model they used on MyHeart's covers. Lorcan got about fifty letters a week; Elle knew because she had to forward them on to his manager. He had long, thinning, crunchy blond hair and an aquiline nose. His chest was totally hairless – she looked at it suspiciously.

'Well, I'm *very* grateful to you, I must say,' one of the ladies, short and plump and wearing a silver sequinned jacket, was saying. She licked her lips. 'I always tell people, without you on the cover, no one would buy any of my books!'

Next to her, a rather harried-looking Posy said automatically, 'Oh, come, Abigail, that's just not true! Elle, there you are! Come over here, meet some people,' she cried with a mixture, Elle thought, of relief and annoyance. Posy was often annoyed with you, even if you'd just arrived in the room – you should have been there earlier, or not at all, or something. 'This is my wonderful secretary, Eleanor,' Posy said. 'This is Abigail Barrow, Elle.'

Elle blushed. Abigail Barrow was one of MyHeart's biggest authors, and a notorious cow. But she wrote the most hilarious sex scenes, and Elle and Libby often took it in turns to read them out on slow afternoons when everyone was still out at lunch. She was very keen on two things: animals and sex noises. Her heroes always grunted, her heroines always moaned in ecstasy. She and Libby had a favourite sentence, culled from a particularly ripe episode in *An Engagement with Heartache*, when Lady Anthea is receiving attentions from Lord Rockfort: '*With a strangled grunt he knew her then, like a neighing stallion knows his sweet lady mare.*' 'How well do I know you?' they'd ask each other. 'Oh, about as well as a neighing stallion knows his sweet lady mare, thanks,' and then fall over with hilarity.

'And here's Nicoletta Lindsay, and this is Regina Jordan.'

Three authors all in one place; Elle shook hands with them each in turn, politely, trying not to stare, but she couldn't help secretly feeling slightly disappointed. She'd expected them to be shinier, glowing with some secret creative juice that made them more beautiful, more glamorous, somehow. Regina Jordan wasn't even a woman; he was a short balding man wearing a blouson leather jacket. He turned away from Elle, addressing Abigail Barrow.

'I didn't know you'd been nominated for—'

'It's lovely to meet you,' Elle said to Nicoletta Lindsay, who gave her a thin smile. 'So, how did you—'

But the sound of a gong, growing louder, came down the corridor, and Floyd appeared in the doorway. 'Dinner is served,' he announced.

Lorcan took the lead. 'Let us leave, ladies,' he said and held out his arms.

Upstairs, Elle was looking at the seating plan. She flinched in shock as someone pinched her arm.

'Come here,' said Rory quietly. She turned round. 'I've moved you,' he said in her ear.

She could feel his breath on her cheek, and she shivered. 'Why?' she whispered. She caught sight of the two of them in the window nearby: her in her floaty grey dress, he in black, whispering in her ear, illuminated by the candles on the tables, like a scene from a story.

'I was next to Tobias Scott, and the old bastard hasn't come. He's sent his son along instead. And I'm not wasting my seat on Tom Scott, he's absolutely useless. Plus the table's miles away. So I've shifted it around. You can go next to him.'

'But you'll be on the—'

Rory shook his head impatiently. 'It doesn't matter. Just go and sit down, will you? Table Three, I've moved your name card.'

Elle shrugged her shoulders. Fine. If Rory would rather end up on the MyHeart table listening to Lorcan talk about his 1999 calendar than sit next to Tobias Scott's replacement for the evening, well, his loss. She weaved her way back to table three, as Felicity, resplendent in gold satin, her hair even more magnificently bouffant than usual, sailed through the crowd towards the top table, escorted by the famous Old Tom, here in person, thin, bearded and bent nearly double.

'Good evening!' Felicity was saying to everyone, as though she were Queen Victoria at the Great Exhibition. 'How lovely to have you here. Thank you for coming. Hello!'

Elle found her place and sat down. 'Hello,' she said to the

man next to her. She looked at his place name. *Tony Rooney.* 'Lovely to meet you.'

Tony Rooney nodded and stared into space.

'So, then . . .' said Elle. 'What do you do?' She realised she was unconsciously channelling Felicity.

'I'm the London rep,' Tony replied, putting down his pint and staring at her. 'And who are you?'

Elle was discomfited. 'Oh. Sorry. I'm Elle, I'm Rory and Posy's secretary,' she said.

'Oh, right,' said Tony. He gripped his tankard and took another gulp, staring morosely into space.

A couple of other people sat down opposite them; Elle looked at Rory, laughing with the MyHeart authors she should have been sitting with, his hand on Posy's shoulder. Posy was glowing like a Christmas tree. Elle shrugged, trying not to seem disappointed. She had been looking forward to this evening for weeks, but so far the reality was quite different. It was like the evening version of job hunting, where no one is interested in you and the party seems to be happening at another table.

'So you're Rory's substitute, then,' someone said, on her other side. 'I wondered who he'd get to swap with him.'

Elle turned round. There was a man next to her, about Rory's age, maybe younger. He had dark hair, cropped short, and he was tall and angular; his evening dress hung off him, as if made for a larger man. 'Oh – no, I think the table plan was wrong,' she lied. 'I'm Elle, Rory's secretary.'

'Hello, Elle,' he said, shaking her hand. 'I'm Tom Scott.'

'Hi, Tom,' Elle said. There was a silence again, and she said desperately, 'And what do you do?'

'I'm an agent,' he said, looking at her slightly irritably. 'I work with my father, Tobias Scott.'

'Oh,' said Elle, enlightenment flooding over her face. 'Of course.'

From their table, which really was situated in the most distant corner of the vast room, Tom Scott stared out over the massed crowds. 'I'm not nearly important enough for Rory to waste his time on,' he said. He took another sip of his wine.

He was kind of rude, Elle thought; there was something she didn't like about the awkward way his jaw clenched, how his grey eyes narrowed as he scanned the room. Like he simply didn't want to be there. Libby was next to Paris Donaldson, who was alternately tossing his hair and whispering in her ear. She caught Elle's eye and winked at her and Elle winked back, trying to look as though she was having the best time of her life, that her corner of the room was a veritable Annabel's, champagne flowing, gay laughter, wacky fun.

But by the time the first course was served, Elle and her companions had descended into a silence that confirmed what all of them knew: they were on the duff table. This silence was broken only by Elspeth saying in her fluting voice, 'What lovely leeks!'

Elle, desperate, turned to Tony Rooney.

'So, Tony,' she said. 'What books are you most excited about for summer and autumn?'

'I've been doing this twenty-five years,' Tony said, lighting up a cigarette. He drummed his fingers on the table. 'Hard to get excited after a while.'

'That's good to hear, good to hear,' Elle said, nodding furiously.

'Are you taking the mickey?' Tony asked.

'No, no!' Elle said. What was *wrong* with him?

'Are you a rep?' Tom Scott, next to her, leaned forward and asked Tony.

'Aye. London,' Tony answered. He balanced his cigarette on the edge of the ashtray, and shook Tom's hand. 'Tony Rooney.'

'Tom Scott,' Tom answered. Tony leaned forward, across Elle, as if she wasn't there.

'Who are you here for then, Tom?'

'I look after – well, my father does – John Rainham,' Tom said.

'Your father?' Tony asked.

There was the minutest pause and Tom looked uncomfortable. 'He runs the agency, I work there. He couldn't come tonight, so I stepped in. I'm an agent too . . .' He trailed off.

Only got a job because his dad gave him one, Elle found herself thinking, meanly.

Tony nodded. 'Well, John Rainham's been good for us,' he said. 'Good books, great sense of place, good fan base in the shops. They love him in Greenwich, I suppose they would, eh!'

He smiled, and Tom smiled.

'Wish you'd have a word with Rory then,' Tom said. 'He doesn't seem to see it your way. He's being pretty difficult about a new deal.'

Elle interrupted, she knew she had to. 'Oh, Rory loves John Rainham, he—'

Tony cut straight across her. 'I'll see what I can do,' he said, as if she hadn't spoken. 'That'd be a shame. He's a big author for me, Tom. Good man.'

Elle sat between them, and drained her wine glass. She tried to tuck a lock of her newly blonde, stubby hair behind her ear and frowned: usually she didn't need any help to feel stupid. It was more than that though – she felt irrelevant, like a silly girl whose voice was higher, a waste of space. For the first conscious time in her adult life, Elle wondered how she'd have been treated if she'd been a boy.

'Tom, my dear, how are you?' Felicity was standing behind him, her hands on his shoulders. He stood up and she kissed his cheek.

'I'm good, thanks, Felicity, how are you?' he said. 'You look wonderful.'

Creep, Elle thought.

'I'm extremely well, thank you. Now, how's your dear papa? *Such* a shame he can't be here tonight, but you know, we must speak to him and sort out that new contract for John.'

'Talk to your son about it,' Tom said, smiling though his eyes were cold.

Felicity seemed to ignore this; she actually batted her lashes at him. 'That piece on Dora in the *Guardian* Review was wonderful,' she said. 'Were you pleased? I loved it. I can't wait to read the rest of the biography. It sounds marvellous.'

'It's good,' Tom said, and then stopped. 'Lovely to see you, Felicity.'

He sat down again. If Felicity was surprised at this abrupt termination of the conversation, she didn't show it. She patted Elle's shoulder. 'Good work, Elle, my dear, good work,' and moved on.

Flushed with kind words from her idol and full of sudden confidence, Elle turned to Tom. 'Who's Dora?' she asked.

'My mother,' Tom said. He ate some bread, chewing it with his mouth open, and pretending to listen to the conversation on his other side, between Nathan the art director and Lorcan's agent, about Lorcan's next shoot, recreating a Bavarian castle in Teddington.

In one of those strange moments where a greater force takes over and the imagination leaps further than the facts, Elle pressed her hands together. 'Dora – *Zoffany*?' she asked. 'She's your mother?'

Tom nodded. 'Yup.' He didn't seem particularly amazed she'd worked it out.

'That's incredible!' Elle shook her head. 'Oh – oh, my goodness. She's one of my favourite novelists, we did her at university.'

'You "did" her,' Tom Scott said. 'What does that mean?'

God, what a prick. 'Studied her, sorry.' Elle was still red with excitement. More than Barbara Pym or even Rosamond Lehmann, Dora Zoffany had been her favourite of the authors she'd studied as part of the Twentieth-Century Female Novelists course. She had read everything she'd written

– eight novels, letters, short stories – umpteen times. In nearly a year at Bluebird, she had met lots of authors and spoken to even more, but to be seated next to Dora Zoffany's son was something else. Dora was a proper novelist. People wrote biographies of her! Bookprint Publishers had only recently been taken severely to task in the *Bookseller* for letting her go out of print, Elle had read that very article only last week. And here she was next to Dora Zoffany's son, even if he was an arrogant loser! She smiled happily at him. 'I'm so – so . . .' she started, and then trailed off.

Tom said, 'What? So impressed? Think I'm more interesting now?' He ate some more bread.

Elle was stung. 'No –' she said. 'I didn't mean it like that, it's just I really do love your mother's books.'

'So do a lot of people,' said Tom, folding his napkin up into a tight square.

'Well – all I mean is, you must be very proud of her.'

'Of course I am,' he said. He turned to her, a frown puckering his forehead. 'It's just I don't generally sit there thinking of her as a world-class novelist, you know. She was just my mum.'

'OK. I'm sorry.' Elle gave up. Fair enough. He obviously didn't want to talk about her, and she could hear her voice, sounding high and stupid again. She wished she could simply say how much his mother's books meant to her, and how sad she'd been when she'd died, three years ago.

But Tom Scott didn't seem to need her sympathy or attention. He turned away and began a conversation with Lorcan's agent, so that his back was almost facing Elle. Thankfully, just then the tables were swapped so that each rep was moved around, and Tony Rooney left after the chicken, to be replaced by Jeanette, who covered Kent, Surrey and Sussex, and who was lovely, if a little obsessed with the sales ordering systems and their implementation. At least she looked Elle in the eye, though, and they had a long conversation about stock levels and ordering up books from the warehouse which Elle, after the evening so far, found extremely comforting.

By pudding, Elle was a bit drunk. She was two glasses of champagne and several glasses of wine down. Not that it seemed to matter – everyone else was, too. The noise was louder and as pudding was served, the dinner began to break up. Tom Scott stood up and nodded at her.

'Nice to meet you, Elle,' he said. 'Good luck with the job.'

'She doesn't need any luck,' a voice behind her said, and Elle looked up to see Rory behind her. He patted her head. 'She's the best, aren't you, Elle?'

'Sure she is,' Tom shrugged, and the shoulder pads in his too-big dinner jacket rose up and down again. 'Sorry to have missed you this evening, Rory.'

'Yes,' Rory said easily. 'We need to talk soon. Are you around tomorrow?'

Elle saw the flash of panic in Tom Scott's eyes. *He's totally out of his depth*, she thought. 'Er, sure. Give me a – no, I'll call you.'

'I'll try you as well. Thanks for coming, Ambrose.'

'Ambrose?' Elle said, more to herself, picking a grape off its stalk.

Tom ignored this. 'Bye, then,' he said, and walked away.

'Why'd you call him Ambrose?' Elle stood up, feeling a bit dizzy.

Rory laughed. 'That's his real name. Hilarious, eh? Changed it when he went to university. His mother knew mine, I used to have to play with him when we went for lunch there, he was a total square, really holier than thou.'

'I felt a bit sorry for him,' Elle heard herself say, to her surprise. She watched Tom walk towards the exit, unnoticed by anyone except her, his thin shoulders hunched, his expression dark.

'Don't,' said Rory. 'I can say this 'cause I know what it's

like. Loathes the job, loathes himself. I just want to shout "Get a Life" whenever I see him. Anyway, forget about Tom Scott. What's going on?'

Elle shrugged. 'I don't know. Is there anything that needs doing? Anyone I need to look after?'

'Me,' said Rory, and he put his arm round her. 'Let's get another drink. Jeremy's settling in at the bar over there. Come on.'

It was about one thirty when Elle looked around the room and realised she was, now, way too drunk to be out any more. Four years in Edinburgh had taught her many things, possibly the most useful of which was that she knew she could drink up to a certain point, but after that never did anything interesting like dancing on the bar with her top off or snogging random strangers. She would merely fall over and then probably be sick. The disco had started at eleven and was still going strong; Jeremy was singing along to the Proclaimers and dancing with Oona King. Floyd and a few of the reps were standing around in a circle, pints in hand, tapping their feet to the music and eyeing up various people. Posy and Loo Seat, aka Lucy, were having an intense conversation in a corner about something that involved them stopping to drink more wine and hug each other every few minutes, both with tears in their eyes.

Elle was standing at the bar with Rory, Joseph Mile – the reference books editor – and Sam. They were talking about their favourite books. 'Your favourite book is *Live and Let Die*?' Joseph Mile was astonished. 'I must say I'm surprised, even for you, Rory.'

'Well, it's just a bit of fun, isn't it?' Rory said. 'It's a bloody great book. What's yours?'

'I struggle between *Felix Holt, The Radical*, or *Jude the Obscure*,' said Joseph Mile, pushing his fingertips together. 'Probably the latter.'

How can he be this sober? Elle thought. She shrank against the counter, hoping he'd ignore her.

'And you, Sam?' Joseph Mile said.

'*Autumn of Terror*,' Sam said promptly. 'It's the best book there is on Jack the Ripper. It is amazing.'

'Oh.' Joseph Mile looked as though someone had just presented him with a bucket of vomit. 'Hm. Elle? You have a favourite book?'

Elle put her hand on the sticky bar surface to steady herself. She couldn't think of what her favourite book was, all of a sudden. She racked her brains. '*Jane Eyre*,' she said, which was partly true and also because, the previous Saturday evening, she and Libby had rented the video of the newest version starring Ciarán Hinds. 'Ah,' said Joseph Mile, drawing a deep breath to expound further. 'How interesting.' Next to him, Rory watched Elle, a strange expression on his face.

'She's the best heroine –' Elle began, feeling she ought to expound on exactly why *Jane Eyre* was a good book. Then she heard herself and stopped. It was suddenly too hot in the room; Elle put her hand to her forehead. 'The red-room,' she muttered, turning away from Joseph and Rory towards Sam. 'The red-room.'

'What?' said Sam.

'Sam, I have to . . . I'm going . . . go home.'

Sam nodded enthusiastically. 'Cool, cool.'

'I'm getting to go a cab, Sam?' Sam nodded again, and Elle shook her by the shoulders, intently. 'Sam! I'm getting to go a – getting to go a cab! Listen. You come with me?'

'I'm going to stay a bit,' Sam said happily.

'You sure? You can come with me.'

'Sure.' Sam looked at Jeremy, who was now dancing to Stevie Wonder. She waved at him, and he waved back at her, then at Elle: Elle blushed. Rory caught her eye and smiled. 'Think I'm going to stay,' Sam said. 'See you later.'

'OK, well, OK then.' Elle raised her hand. 'I'm off.'

'Bye,' said Sam. Joseph Mile raised his eyebrows very delicately. Rory kissed her cheek.

'You be all right?' he said.

Another flush of heat and wine flooded through her. She needed to get out. 'Yes, yes,' she said, almost impatiently, and she went downstairs gingerly, her feet now aching in her shoes.

It was a wet, cold night as Elle emerged into a rubbish-strewn side street in Soho. The rain was slick on the ground, and it was eerily empty. She shivered, and looked back up at the lights of the house, still blazing in the dark. She wasn't quite sure where she was, she still found Soho extremely confusing, so she set off to walk towards what she hoped was the direction of Regent Street.

Her heels clicked on the splashy streets. She pulled her coat tightly around her. There was a noise behind her, and she heard someone running.

'Hello?'

Elle kept on walking, slightly faster, and didn't turn round. 'Hey – Ello?'

Were they saying Elle or Hello? She couldn't tell. Elle started to trot.

'Come back!' The footsteps were almost behind her.

'Elle! Eleanor Bee!'

She stopped and turned around, as the person caught up with her.

'Rory?' she said.

'I came down to make sure you were OK,' he said. 'Suddenly occurred to me I shouldn't be letting my employees stride off on their own. Especially when—'

'I'm not drunk!' Elle said indignantly.

Rory changed the subject. 'I saw you leave and I know this is a dead end –' He gestured ahead of him, and Elle saw that the space she'd hoped was a passageway was in fact an entrance to an office block.

'Oh –'

He steered her back down the road, and turned left again.

'Don't worry,' said Elle, embarrassed, as they walked through the quiet street. 'I'll be OK from here. You can go back.'

'I was leaving anyway,' said Rory. 'It's fine, honestly.'

There was an awkward silence, as Elle tried to think of something to say, not fall over on the cobbles, and not be hopelessly drunk in front of her boss. Eventually, they turned into another street.

'We're on Wardour Street,' Rory said. 'Here we go.' He stuck his hand out. 'I'll see you part of the way, is that OK?'

'Sure, sure –' said Elle, as Rory opened the door to the cab and she climbed in. 'Aren't you – don't you live the other way, though?'

'I'm staying in Notting Hill with some friends,' he said, climbing in after her. 'I'm having my kitchen done.'

She turned to look at him as the cab moved slowly off. 'Well, thanks,' she said. 'Thanks a lot. You're good boss.'

'Am I?' Rory smiled down at her, his face dark in the cab. She knew his face so well, knew *him* so well, how he drummed his fingers on any spare surface, how he looked vague when trying to get out of things, how his mouth curled to the side when he was making a joke. But she'd never sat this close to him before, because he was her boss. It didn't feel like that tonight. It was as if they were different people. It was nice. Rory *was* nice, but then, she'd always known that.

'Yes, you are,' she told him. 'Sorry, I'm a bit drunk. But I can say it 'cause I'm drunk. You're really nice man. And I like you.'

'Well,' Rory said softly. 'I like you.'

He leaned over, and put his hand gently on her cheek, and kissed her. Elle didn't move for a second, but then she relaxed, and kissed him back. Rory slid his other arm round her and pulled her towards him. She could taste wine and cigarettes on him; she knew he was drunk too. The funny thing was, it should have felt odd. But it didn't. He carried on kissing her, and she slid her tongue into his mouth, loving the taste of him, suddenly desperate to feel more. His hand moved over her body, gently tracing the outline of her breast, and it felt wonderful, his fingers on her dress, the fabric moving against her hot skin.

After a minute, Elle broke away, her lips throbbing, her cheeks burning. She looked into the rear-view mirror, but the cab driver was gazing straight ahead. She glanced at Rory, and gave a weak laugh.

'What?' he said, stroking her cheek.

'I'm going to wake up tomorrow and think, "Oh, my God, I kissed Rory last night,"' Elle mumbled, into his shoulder.

Rory closed his eyes and smiled. 'What will you think after that?'

'How lovely it was.'

He kissed her again. 'Really?'

'Really,' Elle said. 'This is weird,' she added.

'I don't think so,' Rory said, smiling, and she looked at him and knew he was much drunker than she'd realised, but it was Rory, it'd be OK, wouldn't it?

Vaguely Elle wondered if she'd wake up in a minute, or what would happen tomorrow, at work: would she lose her job, would people find out, was this the right thing to do? But as she looked down at his hand, moving up her leg, she knew that at this exact moment, she didn't care. He was a man, she was a woman. Worry about it tomorrow, Elle, she told herself. Just for once, worry about it tomorrow.

'I thought you liked Jeremy,' Rory whispered in her ear. She could feel his warm breath against her skin, her neck.

'I like you more,' said Elle simply, without time to think this through, and she realised it was true as she said it. She kissed him again.

'Oh, really,' Rory said. 'Well, I'm glad to hear it. Very glad.'

He pulled her towards him, as the cab rolled west through the rainy, deserted streets.

I have noticed that when things happen in one's imaginings, they never happen in one's life, so I am curbing myself.

Dodie Smith, *I Capture the Castle*

November 2000

IT HAD RAINED for almost two weeks now, non-stop. Huge swathes of the countryside lay under water, and Elle was becoming used to opening her curtains every morning to grey skies, slicing rain on metallic streets. Her umbrella was never dry; it sat, soggy, in the bottom of her damp handbag.

Elle hurried up the stairs of the Savoy and paused at the entrance to the American Bar, gathering herself. She ran her hands through her hair, then rummaged for some lip gloss. She had dressed with care this morning; but she wished she wasn't so nervous. Coming somewhere like here didn't bother her these days. Agents didn't bother her, authors, bosses – she wasn't a little girl any more, she was twenty-six now. No, it was the meeting itself she was dreading, and why? It was only *them*, after all. She smiled at the urbane waiter at the door and scanned the room, trying to look calm, confident.

'Elle, love? Over here!' someone called from the furthest corner of the bar. 'We're here!'

Her mother was standing up, waving enthusiastically. Her voice was too loud; Elle walked over, feeling herself flushing with embarrassment. Mandana was smiling, her face red with pleasure. Elle returned her tight hug, thinking how thin she was, birdlike in fact.

'Hi, Dad,' she said, kissing her father on the cheek.

Her father and brother had stood up, identical in shape, both twice the size of her mother. 'Hi, Elle, love,' John said. He gave her a strong hug. 'Lovely to see you.'

'I'm sorry I'm late.' She hugged him back. 'I got caught up at work, I was editing—'

'It's fine.' Rhodes gestured for her to sit down. 'You're here now. We'll get you a drink. So this –' he stepped aside, as if he were making a big reveal with a cloak, 'is Melissa.'

Elle leaned forward and shook hands with Melissa, who stayed seated. 'Hi!' she said, smiling to reveal perfect white teeth. 'It's such a pleasure finally to meet Rhodes's sister. He's told me so much about you!' Her grey cashmere cardigan slid off one slim shoulder. Melissa gracefully slipped it back into place, and put her hands back in her lap.

'Waiter?' Rhodes called. 'Elle, what do you want?'

As Elle looked for a seat, her parents moved so far apart that she had no choice but to sit between them. She put her bag on the floor, and glanced blankly at the menu. 'Oh – er –' she said.

'Elle?' Rhodes said again.

'Oh – I'll have a vodka Martini please, with a twist,' said Elle, and then instantly wished she hadn't. She had wanted to seem sophisticated, and it looked quite the opposite, ostentatious and stupid, and besides, lately, she had stopped drinking when Mum was around.

'Mum?' Rhodes said. 'Another drink?'

There was a pause. 'Oh, I'll stick to the orange juice, thanks!' Mandana said. She raised her glass. The hand that clutched the tumbler shook slightly.

Having taken the rest of the order, the waiter moved off and there was a silence.

'Sorry I'm late,' Elle apologised again. 'I have to go on somewhere afterwards, and I was in meetings all day.'

It was the wrong thing to say. Rhodes's nostrils flared.

94

'Melissa, you should know we're lucky Elle's been able to drop by, even for a few minutes—'

Melissa cut in, smiling again. 'Wonderful that you're here, anyway!' she said. 'And wonderful to meet you all.'

There was another silence. The last time her family had been together was when Elle had graduated from Edinburgh, over four years ago. Before that, God only knew. She stole a glance at her father, immaculate in his dark blue wool suit. He looked older than Elle remembered, but he always did. In her mind, he was ten years younger, around the time he'd left. It was strange, how ageing affected people. It was in his eyes, around his mouth. An expression; she couldn't explain it. Elle smiled at Melissa.

'So, welcome to the UK!' she said brightly. 'What have you been doing since you arrived? Have you been on the London Eye?'

'Actually, I did a Masters at LSE so I've spent a lot of time in London', Melissa said, one slim, perfectly manicured finger fiddling with the pearl earring in her finely scrolled ear. 'And I just love it. It's my favourite city, you know? So I've been catching up with some old friends, and we saw the Tate Modern, and Rhodes took me to Jamie Oliver's new restaurant on Sloane Street, which is truly amazing.'

Next to Elle, Mandana nodded politely, the tiny circular mirrors on her fabric waistcoat flashing as they caught the light. Elle could tell she wasn't really listening though; neither was her father, nor, in fact, was Rhodes.

'So you're missing the US election!' Elle said, aware that, like her mother, her voice was slightly too loud. 'That must be weird.'

Melissa gave a tinkling laugh. 'You know what? It's crazy, my girlfriends all think I'm insane for being here instead of there, but I told them, you know what? I have to meet Rhodes's family, I just have to, and there were reasons – well!' She smiled, and leaned forward to finish her drink.

'How wonderful,' Mandana said automatically.

'So Elle, Rhodes tells me you work at a publishing house,' Melissa said, smiling in a friendly way. 'That's so fascinating! What do you do there?'

Elle thought back to the book she'd been editing that evening, *Romance with a Soldier of Rome*, a time-slip erotica novel. Time-slip erotica novels were all the rage at the moment. 'Well, I started there as a secretary, and I'm now an editor,' she said.

'Wow,' Melissa said. 'That is amazing. So, you edit the books? What does that mean?'

Elle said, 'Oh, I'm just a junior, it doesn't mean very much. It's our romance list. Doctors and nurses, sheikhs and girls lost abroad, Regency heroines and dashing dukes. All that. A couple of werewolves, sometimes.'

'Romance!' Melissa laughed. 'Oh, wow.' Then she realised Elle was serious, and her expression changed. 'That must be fascinating.'

Yes, fascinating, Elle wanted to say. *I spent two hours on the phone to Regina Jordan listening to him whinge about sales and how he wasn't going to change a scene in which a girl is chained up in a Gothic dungeon for two weeks and repeatedly has sex with the sinister Duke yet orgasms every time.*

'What do you read in your spare time, then?' Melissa asked.

Elle didn't want to say that she was currently rereading *I Capture the Castle* for the seventh time. 'Oh, manuscripts,' she said.

'Elle's done very well,' her father said, as the drinks arrived. 'I'm very proud of her.'

'So am I,' said her mother softly, beside her, and Elle felt a pain in her chest. 'They've promoted her, she's obviously very good.'

Elle picked up her drink. 'Not really,' she said, not wanting to sound rude but also not wanting to look like a vain bitch. 'They made me junior editor last year, just so they could offload some work. My friend Libby was offered it but she left, so they gave it to me. I've been there over three years, they sort of had to.'

'Libby?' Rhodes, who had been looking bored throughout this exchange, sat up. 'What, that girl I met? You . . . lived with her, something like that?'

'I didn't live with her, but yes, the one you met.'

'Where'd she go?'

'She's gone to work for Eyre and Alcock, it's a literary imprint at a massive publisher's. Part of Bookprint.'

'I've heard of them,' Mandana said. 'Well, Libby, I only met her once or twice, but you could tell she was a very ambitious girl.' She said this as if it weren't a good thing. Elle wondered again why you never heard men described as being 'very ambitious' in a pejorative way. 'Well, it's great, love. How's Karen?'

Rhodes clinked his glass. 'Actually – hurr.' He coughed. 'We've got an announcement.'

John and Mandana looked up, as Melissa raised the left hand she'd been hiding in her lap.

'We're engaged!' she said. 'Look!' She flashed a diamond at them. It sparkled in the dark bar, along with her teeth.

'Oh!' Mandana said, leaping up. 'That's – well, that's wonderful!' She gave her son a clumsy hug. 'And Melissa, welcome! Oh, welcome to the family.'

As she was hugging Melissa, who was holding her as much at arm's length as she could, Elle caught her father looking at Mandana, and almost blanched.

My God. He really loathes her, she thought. Elle bit her lip, then stood up.

'Congratulations,' she said, hugging Melissa. 'That's such great news. I'm – so happy for you.' She patted Rhodes's shoulder. 'Your diamond is so beautiful. And I love silver.'

There was a shocked pause. 'It's *platinum*,' Melissa said. 'From Tiffany. Rhodes chose it all by himself!'

Rhodes shrugged, his eyes half closed, and then he turned to Melissa, and kissed her briefly on the cheek.

'Well,' John said, as they all sat down. 'This is great news. Have you set a date?'

Melissa and Rhodes looked at each other and laughed, in that infuriating way couples have when they want to impart what they think is fascinating news. 'Well, yes, we have!' Melissa said. 'Next autumn! Maybe in September, my birthday's in October and I definitely want to get married before I'm thirty!' She stopped, and looked at Rhodes. 'Shall I ask her?'

'Go on.' Rhodes smiled at her, and Elle nearly reared back in shock, she hadn't seen her brother smile since the mid-eighties.

Melissa said breathlessly, 'Elle, I would love it if you'd be my . . . bridesmaid?'

'Me?' Elle said, trying to sound delighted. 'I'd – wow, I'd love to!'

Melissa clapped her hands. 'Really? Oh, gosh, that's so great. I really felt it was important to have Rhodes's family involved too, and I want to get to know you better, you're Rhodes's sister!' Elle opened her mouth, but Melissa went on, 'My best girlfriends are Hayley and Darcy and they're going to be my other bridesmaids along with my sister Francie, which is four, I know it's not that many for a bridal party, but I just really don't want it to be too confusing for the guests, and I can't wait for you all to meet!'

Elle was touched. 'That's so sweet, Melissa,' she said. 'How exciting!'

'Yes!' Melissa said. 'And I hope you'll come over for the bachelorette party, it's going to be so much fun! Do you have a boyfriend?'

'Um –' Elle was blindsided. 'I – no, I don't.'

'Elle doesn't have time for a boyfriend, do you, Elle?' John said, and Elle realised there was pride in his voice. 'She's a Career Woman.'

'The two aren't mutually exclusive, Dad,' Elle said. 'They don't make you sign an agreement at the Career Women's Coven, you know.'

'OK. That's OK,' said Melissa, ignoring this exchange. 'But hey, maybe you'll meet someone before the wedding!'

'Hey!' Elle said, holding up crossed fingers. 'Maybe I will!' She stared into her Martini glass. 'Um . . . I might get another one of these, actually.'

A waiter shimmered into place beside her and took their order again. Mandana said suddenly, 'Rhodes, love – where's the wedding going to be?'

Melissa and Rhodes looked at each other and clasped hands again.

'Well, we're moving back to the UK after Christmas,' Rhodes said. 'I'm being relocated, I don't know how long for.'

'Which means it's going to be *so great* you're here to help me!' Melissa turned to Elle.

'Oh,' said Elle. 'Yes!'

'Anyway, we want to get married in the States, so we get the chance to go back and see our friends and family,' said Melissa. 'My father has a place in upstate New York. It's near Woodstock, it's got beautiful gardens, right next to an old coaching inn. We'll put a rose bower up at the bottom of the lawn, by the stream, and we'll have the ceremony there. It's *very* romantic.'

Elle's mother sat back against the seat. 'Oh.'

'"Oh"?' said Rhodes, turning to her aggressively. 'What the hell does that mean?'

'Don't be rude to her,' Elle was quick to defend. She hated the way Rhodes would side with Dad, act like that to Mum. They were so similar, they looked the same; so unapproachable, convinced of their own rightness, with a definite place in the world, never wrong.

Mandana was twisting her small, shiny paper napkin into

a spiral between her fingers. Her big brown eyes were sunken smudges in her pale face.

Elle's father crossed his arms and turned to Mandana. 'Go on. Tell them.' It was the first time he'd directly addressed his ex-wife since Elle had arrived.

'Tell us what?' Melissa smiled.

Elle felt an oiling trickle of discomfort, like sweat rolling down the back of her neck. Something was wrong. She didn't know what. The alcohol rippled on her empty stomach. This was so unnatural, all of it, the four of them were never together as adults, and these words like family, engagement, bridesmaid, romantic – the Bee family didn't use them. They didn't do this kind of stuff.

Mandana swallowed. 'I – oh, God. Love – Rhodes – look. I – can't come.'

'What?' Rhodes said sharply. 'What do you mean, you *can't come*?' John sat back against the banquette. 'Go on. Tell them, then,' he said, with something like satisfaction in his voice.

'I can't come . . . if the wedding's . . . in . . .' Mandana looked up, her eyes flicking from her ex-husband to her son, her thin fingers wrestling in her lap. She cleared her throat. 'I can't come if the wedding's in the States. I'm not allowed back there.'

Melissa's eyes grew huge and tendons appeared on the sides of her neck. She made a sound in her throat. 'Mmm?'

Mandana glanced imploringly at her ex-husband. 'Ah – well, when I was – when I was twenty-five, I was in California. In Haight-Ashbury. I got – ah.' Her voice was so soft Elle could hardly hear her. 'I was arrested. For dealing . . . for dealing pot. Just pot, a tiny bit, nothing else,' she said, pleading. 'I was convicted. Given a fine. I got a record. But my visa had expired too, and both those things together mean – well, I'm not allowed back in the country.'

There was a long silence.

'I'm sorry – what?' Rhodes said. His voice was light. 'You *what*?'

Mandana didn't say anything.

'Mum, is that true?' Elle asked, disbelieving. 'Why didn't you tell us?'

'She didn't ever bother to tell *me*,' John said.

'John, don't,' Mandana said, a flicker of impatience in her voice, like the furious, rollicking Mandana of old, not this timid woman terrified of making a mistake. 'Just don't.'

'What, I'm the one who shouldn't say anything?' Elle's father didn't even look at her mother. 'I always wanted you to know this, you two,' he said, looking from Elle to Rhodes. 'Now you understand why she didn't come to Disney World. I didn't find out until we actually arrived at the airport.'

The Disney World holiday. Instantly, Elle's palms started sweating at the memory. The journey to the airport, both parents in a terrible mood, but Mandana worse than usual. She'd be fine for months, then suddenly she'd go mad, and this was one of those days. Queuing up to go through, Elle holding her Dumbo toy, making him fly along the fabric tape separating the queues. Then something happening, and Mandana screaming at John, him shouting back, in front of everyone, but they didn't care: that was how it was with them. Rhodes and Elle, eleven and eight respectively, had stood to one side, silently watching and holding each other's hand, not understanding how this holiday – which was basically the best thing that had ever happened to them, which their dad had booked as a surprise and only told them about a week ago – was now, suddenly, going so horribly wrong.

Their mum had left, not even said bye to them. John fussed with passports and pieces of paper, as if nothing had happened. Elle had watched her mother walk away, her shoulders hunched, head bowed, and the further away she'd got the faster she'd walked, as if she was glad to be free, till she was almost running down the long grey terminal building, no

101

one else paying any attention. Elle gazed at her till suddenly she turned a corner and was gone.

'Where's Mummy?' Elle had asked, as they were sitting in Wimpy a little later, eating burgers and chips, trying to recapture the excitement they'd had earlier.

'She's not coming. There was something wrong with her passport,' John had said, and they'd left it at that, and the holiday had been great – children are selfish, it was Disney World, after all – but when they'd got back home a week later, it had been bad. Very bad, because Mum wasn't good on her own. Curtains closed, a meaty, musty smell through the cottage, everything in a mess, Mum most of all, till she saw them and burst into tears. That was the first time Elle realised she drank too much. Not like Emily from Brownies' mum who had three sherries and then started singing music hall songs. That was sort of funny. Different from that. This wasn't funny. But she and Rhodes could boast about their Disney World holiday at school and things went back to normal, sort of, until the next time, and the time after that for a few years more, and then the holiday in Skye, which somehow was the final tipping point.

Elle glanced at Rhodes, wondering if he was thinking the same as she was. But he was watching their mother, and the look on his face was enough.

'I'm sorry,' Mandana said eventually. She looked up, her eyes full of tears, her cheeks hollow. 'I am so awfully sorry. It was a stupid mistake when I was young. I've paid for it, but it's – it's so awful that you're suffering too. Of course, you must have the wedding where you want. I'll be so happy for you, wherever you do it.'

Rhodes spread his fingers out on his knees. 'That's not the point, is it?' He looked at his mother. 'How will it look, Mum? You're always going on about that bloody San Francisco trip like it was so pure and free and everything else is crap by comparison and it's bollocks. You're full of shit.'

'Rhodes,' their dad said sharply. 'That's enough.'

'Rhodes, no,' Melissa said. She gave a fixed smile, her bottom lip pushing her top lip up, her cheeks puffed out. 'We may well relocate to London in any case. Perhaps we should think about having the wedding here.'

'Or in a castle in Ireland like Posh and Becks,' Elle said, in a misplaced attempt to lighten the mood. The four of them looked at her oddly. The drinks arrived, the waiter putting them gingerly down one by one, and there was complete silence at the table.

'Well, it would be wonderful if it was, if it was, if it was here.' Mandana's stuttering voice was still barely audible. 'I am so sorry. For everything.' She stared at her orange juice.

'No,' Melissa said suddenly, putting her hand on Mandana's knee. She swallowed. 'Um – it's no problem. It's good we found out now, so we can do something about it. It's going to be great. If it's in the UK, I'll need Elle's help even more. Thank goodness!'

Mandana nodded gratefully and Melissa smiled at her, and Elle found herself warming to her, though she didn't think this was at all how Melissa had expected the announcement to turn out. She picked up her Martini, and drank half of it in a swift gulp. She'd known it was going to be a long night, but it already was.

JUST BEFORE NINE Elle left the Savoy and, dodging the rain and the churning buses, crossed the Strand. She passed the entrance to Lion Books and remembered, as she always did here, that terrible interview with Jenna Taylor where all she'd been able to say was, 'I'm passionate about reading . . . I love books, I love them.' She'd seen Jenna at a party about a year after she'd started at Bluebird and, gauchely, bounced up to her and said hello, but Jenna hadn't recognised her. At least, she'd pretended not to. Elle had been in publishing for over three years now, and she knew enough to know that bouncing up to people and saying hello was not what you did. Sometimes she missed being gauche, though. She felt as if she'd grown up, but not necessarily learned anything.

Elle hurried up Bedford Street, past the big windows of the Garrick where you could see the walls lined with identical paintings of old white men, then past the diamond-leaded, brightly coloured panes of the Ivy. In the American diner on the corner of Cambridge Circus they were celebrating the US election with a special red, white and blue menu, and different seating areas saying 'Gore' or 'Bush'. When she got to Dean

Street, she pushed open a nondescript black door and went inside.

'Hi,' she said uncertainly to the man behind the black reception desk. 'I'm here for the Eyre and Alcock party?'

'Great,' he said. 'Sign here. It's upstairs, to the back. The TV's on but the announcement hasn't been made yet.'

'Thanks,' Elle said. She gave him her coat and glanced in the mirror. Her hair wasn't too wet, her black lace choker was still in place, her mascara hadn't run. She cleared her throat. For the second time that night, she wished she wasn't nervous, and again, she didn't know why, she should be used to it all by now.

This was what you were supposed to do if you were in publishing, wasn't it? Go to cool Booker Prize parties at media hotspots, hang out at Babington House, get a table at Nobu? As she climbed the narrow stairs, from the main room below she could hear guffaws of laughter, a piano playing. Who was in there? Keith Allen and Meg Mathews? Chris Evans and Blur? On the first floor there were two doors. Both had signs, printed on A4 paper and stuck to the door with sellotape. The first said:

BOOKER PRIZE PARTY: PRIVATE

The second:

PUBLISHING PARTY: PRIVATE

Feeling a bit like Alice in Wonderland, Elle pushed the first door open, and went in.

The room was full of people, and everyone seemed to have their backs to her. They were all talking intently, and in the corner was a smallish TV with the Booker Prize ceremony transmitted live from the Guildhall. Elle helped herself to a glass of wine, looking around for someone she knew and trying not to feel like a spare part. She caught sight of a flash of dark blonde hair, disappearing between two suits. 'Libby!' she cried, and the hair turned around.

'Oh, Elle. There you are!' Libby embraced her enthusiastically, her face breaking into a big smile. 'I thought you might not come.'

Elle smelt Anaïs Anaïs and cigarettes, that familiar Libby smell, and closed her eyes briefly, it was so powerful. 'I had a shocker—'

'Hold on,' said Libby immediately. 'I'm just getting a drink for Jamie. I won't be a sec.'

She disappeared into the throng. Elle took another large sip of her wine, and remembered she was two Martinis down already. But she didn't care, to be honest. She was happy just to be out of the Savoy. She couldn't even begin to process how strange the earlier part of the evening had been. The incongruous memory of the four of them around the table – five, now, of course five. Melissa was going to be part of her family. Elle smiled to herself: how could you join something that didn't exist? She knew that at some point she had to talk to her mother. Go and see her, maybe this weekend? She knew she was free. These days, Elle was always free on the weekends, just in case.

Libby had totally disappeared. Picking a handful of nuts from a passing waiter, Elle looked around the crowded, noisy room. 'Well, my money's on Atwood,' she heard someone behind her say. 'But I saw Simon on Saturday at Mark's, and though he was keeping his cards *pretty* close to his chest I got the feeling that *Passengers* might just steal it.'

'You went to Mark's?' his companion asked him, running her fingers through a thick beaded necklace. 'I did so dreadfully want to go, but we were at Paul's for the weekend and we just couldn't drive back for it.'

'Ah. Well. Did you know—'

Elle moved through the crowd, feeling totally invisible. She could hear snippets of conversations. '*Paid over five hundred*

for it — I know. They'll never make the money back. . . .' 'She's
moving to another publisher, you know. She's just had enough, and
who can blame her.' 'I said to him, "Sir Vidia — enough is enough.
Let sleeping dogs lie."'

Elle felt even more of an outsider, now she was in the thick of the party. Why had she said she'd come, when she didn't want to?

She knew the answer perfectly well, and it made her even sadder. She heard a voice and looked up. Libby was standing by the window, laughing with someone. Elle paused, not wanting to interrupt, but Libby saw her and beckoned her over.

'Sorry, Elle,' she said. 'So rude of me to invite you and then abandon you!' She tucked her hair behind her ear. 'This is Tom Scott, Tom, this is a dear friend of mine, Elle Bee — oh, it always sounds so stupid when I say your name like that. Eleanor Bee.'

Elle nodded up at Tom. 'Hi,' she said. 'I'm Elle. I work at Bluebird.'

She wasn't sure whether to refer back to their only, rather unfortunate, meeting at the sales conference, two and a half years ago. Of course he won't know me, she told herself.

'I know,' he said. He stared at her. 'We have actually met before. At the Bluebird sales conference. Your hair was a different colour.'

'Oh,' said Elle. 'Sorry — well, yes, I do remember you. Just I thought you wouldn't remember me.'

'Really,' Tom said drily. 'That's kind of you.' He obviously didn't believe her. Libby laughed.

The scene at the Savoy, the Martinis, the walk through the rain, a loud room full of people she didn't know and feeling dog-tired suddenly all overwhelmed Elle. She had one last look around and put her hand up to her cheek, to stave off the tears she was horrified to feel rising within her.

'Um, I think I'm just going to go,' she said. 'Sorry, but I'm really tired, and I've got loads on tomorrow.'

Libby watched her through narrowed eyes, and then put her hand on her arm. 'Oh, I'm bloody crap,' she said. 'You had that drink with your parents, didn't you. Was it awful?' Elle shook her head, unable to speak, then nodded. 'Oh, man. I'm sorry, Elle.'

Miserable and embarrassed, Elle glanced at Tom, but his expression was unreadable.

'Here.' Libby whipped a plate off a passing waitress. 'It's for my friend, she's feeling faint,' she said. Someone behind them half turned. 'Typical Libby,' he said to his companion, and they laughed. 'Oh, shut up, Bill,' Libby said flirtatiously, tossing her hair. She handed Elle the plate of canapés. 'He's our MD. He's so annoying! Here, have some food,' she said, waggling the plate under Elle's nose.

Elle ate a mini-samosa as Libby watched her intently. 'So, it was grim then. Did you meet the American girlfriend? What's she like?'

'Like an Appleton sister,' Elle told her. 'The mean-looking one. They're engaged.' She picked up another samosa. 'And they're getting married in the US, only it turns out Mum can't go because she's got a criminal record in the States.' She threw the samosa into her mouth.

'What?' Libby said, gaping at her. She glanced at a woman passing behind them. 'Hiya! Yeah! See you in a bit!' she mouthed.

'Excuse me,' said Tom, making to move off. 'Libby, I'll catch you—'

'Oh, don't go,' said Elle, hastily swallowing the samosa. 'I don't want to drive you both off. It's just my family. My parents hate each other and my brother hates us all.' Mad as it sounded to say, as she said this out loud, she felt much better. 'Yep. I was just meeting my brother's fiancée. It's over now. Done.'

Libby nodded intently, then turned to Bill and started chatting, offering him the plate of canapés. Elle's face fell. Tom moved a little closer, so he was standing next to her.

'Wow.' He raised one eyebrow. Elle was impressed, she'd always wanted to be able to do that. 'Your parents really do hate each other?'

'Yes. Well, my dad definitely hates my mum. And I don't think she likes him much, if I'm honest.'

'That sounds like my parents.'

'Really?' said Elle, not knowing what else to say.

Tom nodded. 'You're not alone. I mean, I don't want to sound competitive, but it's true. Maybe they should get divorced.'

'They did,' Elle said. 'So it's OK.' She tried to sound breezy about it, as if it was all fine, but she couldn't do it. She thought of her mum's sad eyes, her dad sitting so upright, so tense, the distance between them as they sat on the same sofa.

'I'm sorry. When?'

'Oh, ages ago now. I was sixteen when they got divorced. It's just – I can't explain it. I don't ever see them together, we're never all together, and tonight we were, and it made me see – see things I hadn't noticed before.' Her mother's shaking hands, the orange juice, the Disney World trip, the ring flashing on Melissa's finger, her brother and father, how they were so angry with Mum, how Mandana just let them be, as if she deserved it, like a dog being kicked by a gang of boys. 'Sorry,' she said, simply. 'I don't normally think about it much.'

Tom watched Elle. She looked up at him. His jaw was angular, dark with six o'clock shadow, and his grey eyes were kind. He said, 'Well, that's something at least. My parents never got divorced, and then my mum died, so my dad was denied the opportunity of cheating on her any more. He was never quite the same again.'   .

'Wow,' said Elle. 'You win.'

Tom gave a little nod of the head. 'Glad to hear it. I can play one-upmanship on the sad families any day. The dead mum means I usually win. So cheer up.' He saw her expression tighten, and said, in a low voice, 'Hey, I'm sorry. I was only joking.'

'I know,' said Elle, shaking her head. 'It's just – too many Martinis and no food, after a day editing romance novels. It makes you – a bit nuts.' She swayed slightly as she stood in front of him.

'Have a burger,' he said. He put his hand under her elbow. 'Here.' He smiled at the waitress and gestured at the plate. 'Can I keep this?'

The waitress shrugged. 'Go crazy.'

'Eat up,' Tom continued. 'Let's make ourselves really gloomy. Tell me which songs make you cry, childhood pets you've lost and the closest you've ever come to death.'

Elle laughed. 'My dog Toogie attacked an otter in a stream and got put down.'

'That is a depressing story.'

'Yes. The otter was fine. Not the dead dog. Gosh, I was upset.'

He laughed too, and she thought how nice his face was when he was smiling. How nice he was, in fact. It was strange, being able to chat to blokes without worrying that they might think you fancied them or were making a play for them, because she'd never be interested in them, and she couldn't ever explain why.

Tom changed the subject. 'So, you're editing MyHeart books, then? Do you enjoy it?'

'Enjoy it?' Elle was slightly fazed. People never asked her if she actually enjoyed it. 'It's great. I do enjoy it. But you can have too much of a good thing, I suppose,' she said in a rush. 'Are you – how's the – are you still agenting non-fiction?' she asked awkwardly. 'I should know, I'm sorry. I don't deal with a lot of agents yet, not unless they specialise in love stories about doctors and nurses.'

Tom shook his head. 'Ah, that's a shame. I do have a

submission ready about a doctor and his love for the first female Beefeater, but I guess – not one for you?'

Elle made a mock-sad face. 'No, sorry.'

'What about a man with a scabby face and a doctor specialising in skin disorders? Called . . .' He trailed off, biting his lip in concentration.

'*Scabs and the City. Pick Me, Scab.*'

'No. *I've Got A Flaky Boyfriend.*'

Elle gave a snort of mirth, catching wine at the back of her throat. She choked and then coughed, then swilled some more wine. He smiled again. 'You OK?'

'Scabs? Beefeaters?' At the sound of their laughter, Libby turned eagerly back to them. 'What are you guys talking about?'

'I was just about to tell Eleanor Bee,' Tom said, 'that I'm not an agent any more.'

'You're not?' Elle said.

'No. As you may have noticed at the sales conference, I was a crap agent. I love books, but I'm no good at looking after authors. I hated evenings like that. I've got a bookshop instead.'

'That's so great. Where?'

'Richmond. Just back from the river. It's quite big, on two floors, and the location's good, we get passing trade.'

'Tom's shop is wonderful, Elle. You should check it out one day,' Libby said. She put her hand on Tom's arm. 'And of course, Tom set up the Dora Trust.' She nodded at Elle, as if to say, *Pretend you know what I'm on about.*

'Oh . . .' Elle said weakly. 'Of course . . .'

'You've heard of it?' Tom asked.

'Yes . . .' Elle nodded vigorously. 'It's an amazing . . . trust.'

'Well, well well,' came a voice from behind her, 'what have we here? Number one traitor, Libby Yates, defector to the world of the literary wank? Black-and-white photos of stubbly young male authors a must? Covers with huge block type printed sideways on? Eh?'

'Oh, go away Rory,' Libby said, but her eyes lit up and she grinned, and gave him a big hug. 'How are you? Is it true what they say, that we're about to buy Bluebird? Will I be your boss this time?'

Rory smiled and pretended to ignore her. He waggled his glass in his hand and looked around, as if noticing Elle for the first time. 'Hello Elby, where've you been? Working the livelong day, eh?'

'I had . . . a drinks thing,' Elle said. He nodded vaguely.

Tom reached out and took Rory's glass. 'Hi, Rory,' he said. 'Shall I get you a refill?'

Rory looked shocked, as if Tom had tried to mug him. 'What? Oh, hi, Tom. Thanks, thanks a lot.'

As Tom walked off and Libby turned back to Bill, her boss, Elle whispered to Rory, 'Rory. What's the Dora Trust?'

'Oh.' Rory rolled his eyes. 'It's some prize in memory of Dora Zoffany. Old Ambrose there set it up earlier in the year. It's to raise the profile of *women* writers.' He pronounced it 'wimmin'. 'Very PC. He got loads of press for it. And Bookprint's sponsoring it, guess that's why Libby's so keen on him.' His smile became politely fixed as Tom reappeared.

'Thanks, mate,' Rory said, taking the glass off him. 'Was just telling Elby about the Dora Trust, very exciting, etc. etc. How's it all going?'

'Good,' said Tom. 'We had a meeting with a PR agency last week. And we're getting a website, though I've no idea what we'll actually put on it. It's Greek to me at the moment.'

An agent, a young, wiry guy called Peter Dunlop, plucked at Rory's sleeve. 'Rory, hey. How are you?'

Elle scrunched up her nose. 'Well, we set up a MyHeart database, you'd be amazed how many people have the Internet at home now. Or they just give us their work addresses. We email them once a month to let them know what the new releases are and give them special offers. I know it's silly, but—'

'No,' Tom said. 'No, that's not silly at all. It's great. Why would you think that?'

Elle was embarrassed to find herself blushing. 'You know, romances, all that. It's not on a par with –' She waved her arm round the room. 'You know.'

Tom smiled in amusement. 'Are you indicating the Groucho? Or –' He looked out over the rainy street below, streaked in yellow from the lights. 'Or the district of London? Or the amazing literary wonderment that is the firm of Eyre and Alcock?'

She laughed 'I suppose the latter.'

'They were going out of business before Bookprint bought them up, don't forget. Bluebird's still making money, it's practically the only old independent left.'

He stopped, as Peter Dunlop nudged him. 'Hey, Tom, what are you saying about Bluebird?'

'Just singing its praises,' Tom said. 'Especially its excellent MyHeart imprint. I hear the books on that list are brilliantly edited.'

Peter said, 'You heard the rumour it's up for sale? Rory says it's rubbish.'

'It *is* rubbish.' Rory was smaller than both of them. He craned his neck up and said firmly, 'It's absolutely not true. We're doing great.' Elle watched him, trying not to smile; she found Rory at his most hilarious and strangely adorable when he was trying to play with the big boys, she didn't know why.

'That's not what I heard,' said the remorseless Peter. 'I heard the cousins, Harold Sassoon and that lot, want to get more money out of the company. They think Felicity's losing her touch. Sorry, mate.'

'Again,' said Rory, shifting his weight from one foot to another and smiling patiently, 'it's not true. Everything's fine. These stories only come up because people are jealous, they want to see us go under, just because we're the last of the old school. You know Felicity. She'll buy some book for two K tomorrow and it'll sell a million.'

Peter Dunlop shrugged. 'Bluebird turned down *Polly Pearson* because of her, we all know that. That's what I mean about losing her touch. No offence.'

There was a short pause. The success of *Polly Pearson Finds a Man* and the subsequent two follow-ups, *Polly Pearson's Big Drama* and, released only last week in hardback, *Polly Pearson Gets Married* – with combined worldwide sales of well over a million copies – was an extremely sore point in the Bluebird offices.

'Headline deserves that success, they did a great job,' Rory said, after a small hesitation. He patted Peter on the back and said graciously, 'Sorry I don't have better gossip for you, Pete. Give me a call and let's have lunch. You too, Tom, love to catch up and hear about the shop.'

'Oh, he's good,' said Libby, who'd been listening to the latter part of the conversation, as she and Elle watched him.

Elle was used to her boss. 'Yes, he is. But he sure knows it.'

An hour later, an air of drunken despondency hung over the party. They had crowded round the TV, and had seen Margaret Atwood win, to the disgust of those in the room (the agents and publishers from other companies politely agreeing that of course, their man should have won). Elle was chatting to Lucy, Bluebird's publicity director, who in the way of all publicity directors had scented out the best party and attached herself to it, when Tom Scott came up to them.

'I'm off now,' he said. 'It was lovely to see you again. Good luck with the job.'

'Thanks,' Elle said. 'You too.'

'And thanks for the emails database idea,' he said, raising his glass. 'That's really interesting. See you – soon.' He scratched his head and walked out.

'I'm going in a minute too,' Elle said, watching him. 'I'm done.'

'Oh, are you?' Loo Seat slammed her glass down on the side. 'I might come with you.' Her eyes followed Elle's, watching Tom leave, and she flung her mane of hair from one side of her head to the other. 'He's cute, isn't he? So . . . grrr. Geeky and moody, I don't know if he'd ravish me or make me a cheese soufflé, you know? Mmm.'

'Er – yes,' said Elle, not really listening. She rummaged in her bag. 'I'm just looking for my TravelCard.' She rummaged around. 'Dammit. I hope I haven't . . .' She looked over to the coat rack. 'Don't wait for me, Loo— Lucy. I can't find my TravelCard, I'm just going to look over there.'

'Go and ask Rory while you're there, you know you've got a crush on him,' Loo Seat said. She laughed, too loudly.

Elle laughed too. 'Good idea. I'll see you tomorrow. You'll be all right?'

'Sure, sure,' said Loo Seat, tying her trench coat tightly round her slim waist and sashaying tipsily towards the exit. 'See you tomorrow. Adios.'

Elle went over to the hanging rail in the corner of the room and took her coat. She tapped Rory on the shoulder.

'I'm off now,' she said. 'Was looking for my TravelCard, but I can't find it.'

'Ah, right,' said Rory, briefly, turning around from his conversation with a man in a bow tie. 'See you tomorrow then.'

'Sure,' Elle said. She opened her mouth to say something else, but then just said, 'Right. Have a great evening.'

She walked down the stairs, putting on her coat as she left. Halfway down, she remembered she hadn't said bye to Libby. She stopped, but knew she couldn't go back. It wouldn't work if she went back. It had gone wrong when that had happened before.

She walked up as far as St Anne's Court and stood there, waiting. She didn't have to wait for long this time.

'Hey.' Rory was running after her. She stuck out her hand for a passing cab. 'I found your TravelCard. It was on the floor, right where your coat was.'

'Oh, my God!' Elle said loudly. 'Thanks! Here, do you fancy a lift back?'

They climbed into the cab, and it headed up to Soho Square. The moment they were on Oxford Street, clear of traffic, they moved towards each other and started kissing. He pushed his hand up her thigh, she pulled him towards her, feeling his tongue in her mouth, the muscles under his shirt . . .

Warmth spread through her, lovely, sliding, gooey warmth. *This* was what she'd been waiting for, all through the interminable day, the long night, his hard, solid body against her, his hands on her, his skin underneath her fingers.

'That worked well,' Rory said, pulling at the buttons of her new shirt. 'But we'll have to get a new system. The TravelCard routine's been done twice now.'

'Who cares,' Elle said, her eyes shining in the dark. 'Kiss me again.'

SHE'D FORGOTTEN HER toothbrush again, and her shirt was still slightly damp; she didn't have a spare, or any clean knickers. Elle thought of her tidy, tiny, cosy room in Ladbroke Grove, where her books were, her pyjamas and her totally unsexy bedsocks. She shook her hair out, frowning at herself in the mirror. How ridiculous to long for things like bedsocks when she was here. She walked back from the bathroom, holding her stomach in; the thought of Melissa's tiny arms and flat tummy had made her feel like a sumo wrestler.

'Rory. Can I ask you something?' She climbed into bed.

'Mm.'

'Darling – why do we always stay at yours?'

'Hm?' Rory was reading a Minette Walters, his legs splayed, his penis slimy and slack against his stomach. Elle pulled the duvet over both of them, and lay against his chest, where she could hear his heart beating. She loved being with Rory after sex most of all, when he would hold her, kiss the top of her head, make her feel safe, that everything was going to be OK. And until recently, it had been.

Something had to change. She didn't know what came next, but something had to.

'I said, why do we always stay at yours? It's a pain in the neck for me. I forgot my toothbrush, and some spare underwear, and I'm running out of clothes here and I'm the one who needs more things, you know,' Elle said, her voice muffled. 'I need make-up, and a different outfit every day. I have to look presentable. You just wear the same suit and a different shirt.'

Rory patted her head, absent-mindedly. 'I know. Hmm.'

Elle was silent for a moment, and then she sat up. 'Are you listening to me?' she asked mildly. 'Did you at all hear what I just said?'

Rory put his book down and sighed. 'Yes, I heard you. The answer is, I don't like your flat, it's miles away, and Sam might see us. Plus I need to be in work early. I thought you were OK with it.'

'I was,' Elle said, hurriedly. 'But – it's been a while now, Rory, I just thought –'

He leaned forward, and kissed each of her nipples in turn. 'You can bring some more clothes over at the weekend, and as for your underwear . . .' his hand slid between her thighs, 'I like it when you don't wear underwear, darling. I like it when you're as naked underneath your clothes as possible. I like,' he said, whispering in her ear, and kissing it gently, 'I like it when I think I could just grab you by the hand, shut my office door, pull your skirt up and fuck you on the desk.' His hands were on her breasts now, stroking them softly, insistently. 'Don't you agree?'

He knew exactly what to say. He always did. Elle breathed in, shuddering slightly. 'I'm not just a . . . a toy for you to play with, Rory.'

'I know you're not, darling.' He licked her nipples, buried his face between her breasts. 'You're much more than that.' He looked up and kissed her on the lips. 'Are you upset?'

'No, no, I just –'

'All I wanted was you tonight, you know.' His green eyes

bored into hers, and he clutched her hands in his, the pads of his fingers softly stroking her palms. She could feel the heat of his skin, as though it was branding her. 'Just you, it nearly drove me mad.'

'Really?' Elle loved hearing this, though she didn't wholly believe it. Why had he spent twenty minutes talking to that agent Emma Butterworth, then flirted outrageously with Libby during most of the TV announcement if he was tormented by unquenchable lust for her, Elle?

'God, yes,' said Rory. 'Seeing you with Tom Scott, talking away . . . he reminded me of that loser you went out with who used to turn up at the pub. I hated him.'

'Fred?' Elle laughed. 'Rory, that was over three years ago. He turned up at the George MacRae once, by coincidence. Anyway, I was still your secretary then.'

'And I never laid a finger on you. Apart from once or twice. We knew there was something going on. But I waited till you were a woman. Like a dynastic marriage.'

That was one of their jokes – that what they were doing wasn't wrong, because he'd waited until she'd been promoted before they'd actually slept together. Elle wasn't often entirely sure if it was a joke or not.

'We snogged and then we barely discussed it, partly because both of us were so drunk we could hardly remember it,' Elle said, trying to sound reasonable. She smiled at him, feeling a flush of love spread over her. 'Don't romanticise it.'

They gazed at each other, still and silent.

'I like romanticising it, Elby. Because one day it's the story we'll tell our grandchildren.' He lay down again, and she put her head back on his warm chest. 'Anyway, I do remember it. Every little detail.' He picked up his book again while she lay with his other arm wrapped around her. 'Doesn't matter now, does it?' he said. 'You're all mine. All mine, for ever and ever, happily ever after, the end.' He squeezed her tight, and she smiled to herself, flushed with love. Everything was OK now. It always was, when she was alone with him.

It was always OK when she was alone with him. It was funny, really, how easy it all seemed, because when she thought of the ramifications of it all, it became rather scary, so she pushed that aside and just thought about how much she loved him. Other things were difficult, but when it was just them it was simple, because it was just amazing, because it was so right.

It was true that she barely remembered that kiss in the cab after the sales conference, two and a half long years ago. The next day she was mortified, and nearly hadn't come into work, but Rory had made it all right. He'd caught up with her on the way out to lunch, and they'd laughed quietly about it as they both walked towards Tottenham Court Road, agreed it was silly and embarrassing but hey, no harm done. They joked about their respective hangovers and parted, smiling, and when they returned to their desks, they grinned and it was all OK. Elle liked him all the more for that, the way he could make it into a joke between them, and at the same time not make her feel stupid.

That July they kissed again. It was after a drinking session in the George MacRae following the annual Bluebird summer day trip to Eastbourne. In hindsight, Elle thought they'd both known it was going to happen – they'd gone outside ostensibly for a cigarette, and snogged in one of the side streets off the British Museum, unseen by anyone except tourists and students. Then again the following January, in a booth at Kettner's after a dinner with some Ottakar's booksellers.

It was strange in that it didn't feel strange. It felt like a totally separate part of their relationship. They'd see each other at work the next day and it was as if nothing had happened, but she kept it inside her, a secret that sometimes made her smile at her desk.

The sales conference was Thursday 12 March 1998.

The trip to Eastbourne was Friday 24 July 1998.

The evening at Kettners was Wednesday 20 January 1999.

Oh, Elle remembered every date, every single one. It was as if something had lit up inside her, a switch turned on; though months would go by and nothing would happen, it was OK, it was in her head until the next time. Work was like a stage. People kept commenting on how good she looked, how thick her hair was, had she lost weight? Elle, who paid such great lip service to swearing she didn't believe in true love that lasted for ever; Elle, who liked the fantasy of romance novels because they were between two covers, and nothing like real life – when she looked back now, she realised she had been ripe for the picking. She should have seen it coming. Because when she fell, she fell hard.

In October, Libby handed in her notice, to go to Bookprint. Felicity, Posy and Rory tried to keep her – Libby was brilliant with authors, fantastic at copy, always coming up with new ideas, never ruffled. But she said no, she wanted to work at a more literary outfit, always had done and so, much to her surprise, Elle found herself promoted. She wasn't exactly commissioning bestsellers and flying off to Frankfurt, but she wasn't sending faxes and doing the filing any more either. People asked her opinion, sometimes. Felicity, once, gave her the first few chapters of her precious Victoria Bishop to read, wanting to know if she thought it was pacy enough. Even Posy let her talk in the editorial meeting, about a new contract for Abigail Barrow.

And Rory . . . she felt Rory's eyes on her, as the days went by, and as she grew in confidence, as she stopped wearing short skirts and started coming in earlier; she felt him smile with pleasure when other people agreed with her, praised her, noticed her. She knew he was watching. She knew it. And it wasn't a surprise, therefore, to either of them when, after a drunken night at the George MacRae celebrating – oh, something or other, there was always some reason to decamp to the pub – Elle went back to Rory's flat and slept with him for the first time. He lived just off Myddelton Square, in Clerkenwell, 'only a five-minute cab ride away, come on'. It was almost as if that was what they were supposed to do next. They even laughed about it the next day, as she was scrambling into her clothes, rushing home to change before work. *We're such a cliché.*

But Elle played it cool. It was as if he was willing her to, wanted her to be the sophisticated, together girl he knew she was about to be, not the prawn-sandwich-in-filing-cabinet, disastrous dye job she had been. So she grew up for him. She smiled at him briefly at work, and just went about her business, but that glow was there, the sparkle in her eyes, that . . . something.

She was glad Libby wasn't there any more. She couldn't have hidden it from her.

At the Christmas party they slept together again, and this time it seemed to stick. Sam was staying at the conference hotel to clear up and Rory came back to Elle's and somehow, letting him see her flat meant she was letting him into her life. He seemed to acknowledge that, too. They had sex that night, in Elle's IKEA-furnished room, with old film prints Blu-tacked onto the walls, and it was more intense than ever. It was intense because, in her tatty, homely flat, this thing now felt real. He was her boss, he was sleeping with her, and she had totally, utterly fallen for him. When he came, that first night, she cried.

They were glorious, those first few months. He made her laugh, he made her feel safe, she could ask him anything and he'd tell her, about how things worked, about books and book people, about life in general. She'd read more than he had, and he loved that. He was older and more experienced; she was the wise one, the one who'd calm him down, advise him not to ring up X and tell them to fuck off. They fitted together perfectly; she looked up to him, and she looked after him. He was so easy to be with, so charming and funny and moody and silly, so gorgeous, with his kind eyes and handsome face, his sweet sticking-up hair. She couldn't believe he was hers; he reminded her of Anthony Andrews in *Brideshead Revisited*, slightly aristocratic, languorous and handsome.

She adored him, and she couldn't believe she was finally allowed to. At the start, she used to literally skip along Amwell Street, the morning after she'd spent the night with him, to catch the bus. How strange that it was possible to feel like this, like the sun was always shining on you, that you had been born to love someone, that the world only made sense when you were with them.

They met up once or twice a week, usually on Tuesdays and Thursdays, nearly always at his flat, when Sam would be staying with her new boyfriend (Dave having long disappeared), and Elle could be away without arousing suspicion. Elle found it funny sometimes that her love life was meticulously arranged around the fact that Sam's boyfriend Steve had football practice on Mondays, the game on Wednesdays, and that he liked to go out with his mates on Fridays and was usually in Hertford on Saturdays and Sundays. It didn't bother Rory, in fact he liked the compartmentalisation. If she ever talked about the next stage, or moving things along, he freaked out. *We have to be careful. We have to find the right time to tell people. Not yet.*

For most of that year, this was fine with Elle. She didn't want to talk to anyone else about it. It was just the two of them, watching videos, making love, cooking together, dancing to the Stones on his old record player, sneaking into dark corners in restaurants. This was romance, a big, grown-up, full-on romance. One day, she told herself, we'll look back and laugh at the time when we couldn't tell anyone. She felt, by keeping this secret, she was paying for the relationship that meant more to her than anything else ever had. Sometimes, when she thought of Felicity's face when she found out, or what people in the office would say – Sam, or even Libby, how she could have hidden it from them for such a long time – she quailed at the thought. Anyone who has been through the same thing will know what it's like. But then she told herself she knew he loved her. That certainty gave her strength, as summer faded into a cold, wintry autumn.

She didn't realise that it would all have to change at some point, that it wasn't in her nature to live like this. She didn't notice what was going on around her, or the storm clouds gathering around the two of them.

THE MORNING AFTER the Booker Prize, Elle was eating toast up at the breakfast bar as sunshine flooded through the large French windows of Rory's sitting room. Rory was getting dressed in the other room, listening to Radio 4, where the news was all about the undecided result in the US election. Bush had been declared winner but that had been withdrawn and a recount announced in Florida.

'They'll never elect Bush,' Elle said loudly. 'There's no way!'

Rory appeared in the doorway to the kitchen–diner, fiddling with his tie. 'Oh, come off it, of course they will. It's a done deal. His brother's Governor of Florida, they've got the Secretary of State in their pocket, saying the vote's on their side. It's terrible. This is a guy who's been arrested twice. I mean, I don't even know anyone who's been arrested *once*, let alone twice.'

That's because you still haven't met my mother, Elle wanted to say. Rory turned back to the bedroom, and Elle, suitably quashed, finished off her toast, wondering if it would be OK to turn the radio over to Capital FM. She was all for staying abreast of current affairs, but she didn't see why she had to engage with those current affairs at 7 a.m. when her mind

125

was waking up. She wanted cheery pop music and light banter at that hour of the morning, not John Humphys haranguing someone about Chechnya or rail safety or what was going to happen to the Dome.

Feeling brave, she got up and turned the radio over, just as someone said, 'And now, back to the terrible floods that have wreaked havoc over the past two weeks. In Sussex—'

There had been bad flooding near her mum's. Mandana had mentioned it last night at the Savoy, she remembered. Those drinks . . . Elle stood by the radio, gazing out of the window and reliving the previous evening. It wasn't her mum's conviction that shocked her; that wasn't a big deal. It was the atmosphere. The fact that Rhodes's engagement had starkly exposed how the Bee family as she knew it simply didn't exist any more. They didn't know how to be together, even in a civil way.

Little by little, she'd come to see how much her relationship with Rory had helped her to block out a lot of stuff. She didn't get as upset about her mum and dad any more, or wound up by her brother, or annoyed by Sam and her enthusiastic singing of Robbie Williams in the shower. And that was fine, except she increasingly wondered if, as with so many things, this curious half-life she led meant she just didn't notice what was going on around her until she was confronted with it, like last night. Elle decided to call Mum and ask to come and visit this weekend. Yes, that was it – she'd go down, help her with the house, spend some time with her.

'Rory?' she called, going into the other room. 'The weirdest thing happened with Mum and Dad last night . . . Wow! You do look smart.' She kissed him.

'Thanks,' he said. 'Can you turn that racket off and put it back to Radio 4? In case there's anything on the Booker.'

'Well, but we know who won, don't we?' Elle was always amazed at Rory's obsessive nature when it came to the World of Books. He could not stand to be out of the loop. Posy would say to Felicity, 'Did you hear Sue MacGregor on the *Today* programme interviewing Helen Fraser?' And Rory would be simply furious he hadn't heard it, as if this meant he was a publishing outcast, a leper.

'Listen,' she said, ignoring him. 'This awful thing happened with Mum and Dad yesterday. I didn't tell you.'

'What?' Rory asked. He turned to look at her. 'Is my tie straight?'

She ignored him. 'I told you Rhodes was engaged, right?'

'Right,' he said. 'To a skinny fearsome American. She sounds rather great. Can't I meet her?'

There was a silence. 'You could meet any of them, whenever you wanted,' Elle said. 'You know that, Rory.'

'Go on,' Rory said, ignoring this. 'I'm late.' His voice softened. 'Sweetie, go on, tell me.'

Trying not to show how much this wound her up, Elle went on, 'Well, they're saying they want to get married in the States, and we all say oh that's nice. And then Mum announces she can't go back there, because she's got a conviction for dealing pot in the seventies, and she's banned for life.'

Rory was looking in the mirror but he turned to her, an expression of disbelief on his face. 'Seriously?'

'Seriously. And all this stuff makes sense now.' Elle bit the top of her finger, thoughtfully. 'Like, why she didn't go to Disney World with us.'

'What?'

'It's a long story,' Elle said. Now wasn't the right time to go into it, she wanted to tell him properly. 'Too much for first thing in the morning. But all this other stuff too, like how she and Dad met, and why they got married so fast – it kind of makes sense now.'

'How soon after they met did they get married? If you see what I mean.' Rory slipped his jacket on, and brushed his shoulders, one side at a time.

'Oh, only six months,' Elle said. 'They met at a CND march. Dad wasn't on the march, he treated Mum when she got pushed over by a policeman and had to be taken to hospital.' Elle stared into the middle distance. 'I bet she was drunk. I never thought of that.' She shook her head. 'Oh . . . poor Mum. She was so . . . upset last night.' She gazed into the distance. 'Dad was pretty horrible to her.'

'Do you think she'll start drinking again?'

'She doesn't really drink any more, Rory.' A year ago, she'd told him about her mother's drink problem, and how it sometimes got worse, sometimes better. She now wished she hadn't; he was always telling her what to do about it, as though she was a little girl. And he was always using the word 'alcoholic'. Mandana wasn't an alcoholic. She was a librarian from West Sussex.

'You're always saying that,' Rory said. 'But it's a day at a time with someone like her. Didn't you say she got really pissed a couple of Christmases ago and that's why your brother left early?'

'Yes, but –' Elle sighed. 'Rhodes hates Mum. He blames her for them splitting up. He's older. It was harder for him.'

Rory gave her a curious look. 'Perhaps he remembers things you don't.'

'I don't know how that can be, when he was practically never bloody there,' Elle said.

'Well, perhaps you should make sure she's all right.'

'I'm going to try and see her this weekend,' Elle muttered. 'That OK with you, boss?'

'I'm being serious, Elle.'

'It's my mother, not yours,' Elle said angrily. 'She's fine. Don't you tell me how to look after my family. You've never met them, you make it clear you don't want to, you don't know them. OK?'

'OK, OK.' Rory came around to her side of the room and put his arms round her. He kissed her hair and she relaxed

128

into his embrace, feeling the scratchy surface of his woollen suit on her cheek, his warm, lean body against hers. 'I'm sorry, Elby,' he said. 'My poor girl. You're the one I care about, not them. I'm sorry.'

He held her still for a moment, then stepped back. 'Must be off now then,' he said. He stopped. 'I'll be in a bit later for the editorial meeting. I'm having breakfast with Paris Donaldson.'

'Oh, OK. Didn't you just see him last week?' Elle was looking for her cardigan, which had been thrown somewhere under the bed the previous night in the furious scrabble to remove their clothes. She looked up, suddenly. 'Hey. I just remembered something. Does Loo Seat know?'

He was by the door, fiddling in his pocket for his keys, wrapping a scarf round his neck. 'Know what?'

'About us. She was pretty drunk last night, but she said something . . .'

'Stupid cow.' Instantly his face darkened with anger. 'What did she say?'

Elle flinched in surprise. 'God, I don't know. Something about how it was obvious I had a crush on you and we should just get on with it and shag already. She was drunk, Rory, it wasn't a big deal.'

'Oh.' The frown lines in his face cleared. 'Well, that doesn't mean she knows anything. She's just talking drivel. Thank God.'

'Why?' Elle said quietly. 'Why would it be so completely awful if she found out?'

'It just would, and you know it would, darling,' Rory said. 'Look, Elby, I want people to know too. I want to celebrate it. I want to meet your parents, I want you to move in with me, I want this whole thing to be over. But now's not the right time.' He sighed. 'You don't seem to understand. This is hard for me, too, you know.'

'How? How is it hard for you?' Elle smacked her hand

against the wall. 'I hate sounding like a whiny little girl, Rory, but you can't keep saying now's not the right time, over and over again,' Elle said, her voice rising. 'When? When will it be the right time?' It seemed to rush upon her at this moment, a feeling of helplessness, of despair, that she was her mother all over again, a fool in love. She cleared her throat. 'Honestly, Rory.' Her voice, when she spoke, was shaky. 'It's been nearly a year, and I don't think anything's changed, except – I thought this was for ever.'

'It is for ever,' he said, his voice small. 'Elle, don't talk like that.'

'You don't get it,' she said. 'I just don't know if . . . if I can do this for much longer. I meant what I said in the summer. This has to change. And I don't think you're listening to me, I don't think you want it to change.'

In July, after a row like this one, Elle had walked out of the flat, told him she was never coming back, that she couldn't stand it any more. And it was true. She couldn't. She asked Sam to tell work she had the flu and went to bed, wallowing in her own greasy, unwashed filth, crying so much that every time Sam looked in on her, she was convinced by the red-rimmed eyes and streaming nose. After six days, Elle knew she couldn't go through with it. She rang him, crying, and he came straight over, his face ashen, clutching a bunch of petrol-station chrysanthemums. 'I missed you so much,' he said. 'I've been in hell. Don't ever leave me again, Elby.'

That was the moment, as she stared at him, standing on the threshold in the scuffed doorway, when Elle realised, for better or worse, that she was in too deep. She loved him, and he knew it, and she'd go back to him, and he knew that too. But for a while that autumn she just didn't care, when she loved him so much. She loved him for all sorts of reasons. He made her laugh. He made her feel like a mature, prudent person, for the first time, in a grown-up relationship, thinking about the future. They lived in the same world, she thought she knew him. And she wanted him, plain and simple. Elle had thought she'd been in love with Max, her university boyfriend, but that was nothing. She could not resist Rory's touch on her body. He knew her so well, and all she could do was ask for more. He controlled her in bed, could make her scream and cry with pleasure. Elle hadn't known what this was like, before. To want someone so badly you can concentrate on nothing else. To want to bring their name up constantly in conversations, no matter how spurious the segue, like a talisman, a test of devotion. Rory was seven years older than her, and he was far more experienced than she. In every way; lately, she felt as though he were outstepping her, outsmarting her and she couldn't explain why.

'Soon,' Rory said now, and he pulled her towards him and looked down at her, his clear, cool eyes searching her face, as if looking for her agreement. 'Look, we need to get through Christmas. The New Year will be a whole new start. I can't say why but I've got a surprise for you. You're going to love it, I promise. Trust me.' He squeezed her shoulders. 'Do you trust me?'

'I – I do,' Elle said smiling, meeting his gaze.

He hesitated again. 'Look, why don't I cancel my weekend plans. What are you doing?' He kissed her forehead. 'We could hang out here. Maybe go somewhere for the day. Go to Whitstable, get some sea air, have some oysters. Hey – we could even have a break away somewhere, if we thought about it.'

Elle felt her heart thumping in her chest; they'd been away twice for the night, to boutique hotels in romantic country settings, but otherwise they never hung out at the weekends. 'I'm sorry, I really can't do this weekend,' she said. 'I want to go and see Mum.'

'Of course.' He nodded. 'Next weekend. Let's do next weekend.'

'Darling, I can't. I'm away.'

'Where?' he asked quickly.

'I'm in Bristol. Visiting Hester.'

'Who?'

'Old friend from uni?' He looked totally blank. She tried not to be irritated; how could he know any of her friends if he wouldn't meet any of them? And indeed, as she said it, she wondered if she could get out of going. *No. You haven't seen Karen since your holiday in Greece, and she's your oldest friend; you haven't seen Libby for two months, and you know perfectly well why. Don't do the same to your university friends.*

'Oh.' He looked sad, and then his brow cleared. 'Another time, then. I'll take you to Whitstable and feed you oysters and ravage you as the wind lashes against the windows.' He put his finger under her chin. 'Are we OK now? Are you OK?'

'Yes, I'm fine,' she said, smiling. 'Go. It's fine. You look very smart and I love you. See you later.'

'I love you. I want you to trust me, too. Don't forget that. Just wait and see. See you later, my sweet girl.'

He picked up his keys and shut the door behind him, and she was left alone in the echoing flat.

THERE WAS A strange mood in the office when Elle arrived. She put her coffee down on her desk, untangled herself from her manuscript bag and turned on her ancient computer, looking around her to see who was in.

'Horrible morning, isn't it?' she said to Helena, Libby's monosyllabic replacement.

Helena nodded politely, and went back to her Dictaphone typing. Elle suppressed a sigh. She missed Libby, in all sorts of ways. She missed her friendship – they still saw each other, but it wasn't the same. They did things like going to the cinema now instead of ranting over cheap Valpolicella in musty Soho restaurants. She missed being able to tell her anything; and there was so much she couldn't talk to her about. Libby loved her new job and wasn't that interested in the life she'd left behind. She tried, at first, but it soon became apparent she didn't care about the drama over Elspeth's new typewriter ribbon, and though Elle tried to understand, she still missed it.

Elle took a sip of her coffee, waiting for her computer to warm up. She opened her day book and turned to a fresh page.

Wednesday, 8th November, she wrote.

As she did every day now, she was writing a list of what needed doing. Elle knew her working self, after three years, and it was different from her university or school self, different also, alas, from her bookish, dreamy self. It was strange that the more experienced you got in your chosen sphere the less you enjoyed what had made you like it in the first place. Her friend Karen, who was now assistant producer for the TV company she worked for, said she never watched TV any more. Elle hadn't read a book for pleasure in she didn't know how long. And *Venetia* remained on her windowsill, gathering reproachful, blackish polluted dust.

Elle was just writing *Phone Abigail Barrow* and chewing the end of her pen, wondering how she was going to tell her she had to drastically cut the eight-page sex scene in *Duchess, Mother, Mistress?* when emails started slowly popping into her inbox. There was something tantalisingly stressful about waiting for her ancient computer to load all its new messages. She stared at the first one and then peered closely. The address was unknown to her.

To: Eleanor.Bee@Bluebird-Books.co.uk

From: Mhoffman@Bloomberg.com

Subject: Bachelorette Planning!!

Hi Eleanor,

It was so great to meet you and your parents last night. Thank you for welcoming me so warmly into your family!

I am honoured to have you as my bridesmaid. I thought we should touch base about my bachelorette party. Did you have any thoughts or themes already you'd like to go with? I've gotten nowhere apart from a few basic ideas. I'm really relaxed about what we do, even though Rhodes calls me Miss OCD! I just want to plan everything carefully and get it right so that everyone has a great time, especially since we are now restricted by location in terms of where your mother can travel. Here are a few thoughts.

1. Weekend in New York? That way we can see my girlfriends, have some cocktails, and shop till we drop! Obviously your mother cannot be involved in this option.

2. Spa weekend? I have a very dear friend who did the same last year in Mexico and it was so special. Can your mother travel to Mexico?

3. Wine tasting in France, or even California? Bethany lives in Sonoma and I know would be happy to host us. I know this is not suitable for your mother.

4. Girls' weekend to Rome or Barcelona. Again, this might incur costs for my US friends, so maybe we should consider our options.

My preferred option would be a trip to New York. Let me know what you think! Look forward to talking with you soon. It's so truly exciting.

Melissa x

PS I would love your mother to feel she is still welcome to come along if that's appropriate.

Elle sat back in her chair and tried to breathe calmly. She earned £17,500 a year. She lived in the most expensive city in Europe, she took home just over £1,000 a month and she considered that a major achievement. Flights to New York, she knew from booking Rory's trips there, cost at least £300. Then there was the hotel, the cocktails, the shopping till dropping . . . And what did she mean about Mum? Miss

OCD, well, Rhodes was right about that, for sure. Twenty-four hours ago they'd never met, and this morning she was supposed to have come up with a four-point plan for Melissa's hen weekend?

Elle had been almost relieved to discover that, though her affair with Rory had turned everything else she believed on its head, she was still bewildered by most weddings. She wanted to be with Rory, always, for ever. But the rest of it – expensive once-worn dresses, thick, cloying cakes in icing like white cement, heavy, unscented flowers that looked like plastic, and this mysterious code of womanly behaviour around weddings she couldn't understand that used words like 'girlie', talked about garters and involved a lot of screaming – left her cold. Elle had been to a wedding of a school friend the previous summer, in Dorset. The hotel had cost £120, the train fare was £50, the present was £40, the hen weekend was £170, and she'd ended up eating Rice Krispies for the rest of the month till payday. She wouldn't have minded if it was Libby or Karen, or even Sam, but she didn't even *like* Charlotte that much, and she couldn't remember why she'd agreed to go except that it seemed you couldn't do anything involving weddings by halves. There was a moment when, sitting round the table listening to all these girls talking incessantly about their boyfriends and relationships and how he never washed his socks and what kind of wedding they'd have, Elle had understood why her mother who, after all, read fairy stories to children for a living, had said to her a couple of years ago, in one of her more expansive moments, 'Be careful before you settle down, love. It's the living with them that's hard, not the falling in love. Anyone can buy a big white dress, you know.'

She thought about this a lot now she was with Rory, and felt Mandana would approve. They were in the hard period now. The future would be brighter.

As Elle was typing him an email, just a silly thing to say

136

hello, she saw him dash in half an hour before the editorial meeting. He was dripping wet, the rain was still lashing the building and the square outside.

She had just written:

I know you're having a hard time. I love you. I just wanted to say—

'Elle?' a voice behind her said, and Elle jumped, and pressed Control and Tab instantly, praying they hadn't seen her. It was Posy. 'Have you got the figures for the new Victoria Bishop contract I asked you to print off?'

'Yes, yes . . .' Elle said, her fingers clumsily shuffling piles of paper in her in tray. 'Um – oh . . .'

'Everything all right?' Posy said, her cheeks slightly pink. She was always suspicious, convinced something was going on behind her back. Elle could feel her face burning. She nodded, mute. 'Look, just bring them to the meeting, Felicity'll go mad if they're not there. She's in a funny mood today. OK?' she added.

'Yes . . . yes! Fine. Sorry, you gave me a shock.'

Elle sat back and breathed out.

The wind that day was so high that even up on the second floor, leaves blew past the old windows, which rattled loudly as the various members of the company took their seats for the meeting. Elle sat down and passed the sales figures over to Posy. 'Here they are,' she said. 'Hope they're OK.'

Editorial meetings still made her nervous, even after all this time. You couldn't anticipate Felicity's mood, or her point of view. Posy didn't smile. She just nodded. 'Thanks,' she said. She was sitting in a row with Jeremy and Loo Seat, who was looking uncharacteristically sombre.

There was a muffled hushing sound as the door opened and Felicity, flanked by Floyd and Rory, swept into the room and sat at the head of the table.

'Good morning, everyone,' she said, shuffling her papers. 'Well, what a ghastly day. My morning has been enlivened somewhat by an article in *The Times* which says that—'

Elle groaned inwardly. Felicity loved a story. Why she thought it fostered company unity to hear a long tale about her childhood pet kitten, or the time she'd met Queen Mary, Elle had no idea. But she was always doing it, especially at the start of editorial meetings. Elle looked down at her To Do list. Already she'd been annoyed by an email from the agent of a chick-lit author Rory had bought (to try and emulate *Polly Pearson*) called Katy Frank, saying they both thought the type on the new jacket was disastrously tomato-coloured and this was a very serious matter. It had added, at the end:

> 'Katy's very worried about the takeover rumours and she's not the only one. Are they true? Give us a scoop!

'Anyway,' Felicity was saying, 'you may well have seen the article yourselves, or heard about it from friends. I can assure you there is nothing to worry about.'

Elle sat up. What was she talking about?

'The situation is this.' Felicity put her fingers together, her booming voice still slightly wheezy from the walk upstairs. 'Someone has offered to buy Bluebird Books.'

Elle looked at Rory, but his eyes were fixed on the table. Did he know? Then she bit her lip; she understood now. Of *course* he'd known.

'They are a much bigger company, a conglomerate. Briefly, their bid would only be successful were enough members of the board to agree to sell them enough stock that they could mount a hostile takeover. Now, I have spoken to all of the board –' Felicity gave a rattling cough, and Elle looked at her in alarm, but she seemed unperturbed – 'which is made up of relatives of my father's and relatives of his original investors. We have nothing to fear. The sale will not go through. My son and I will be here for years to come.' She looked over at Rory, who gave her a quick smile. The room watched, transfixed. 'Especially Rory! But you won't be seeing the last of me for quite some time –' she reached forward, and patted the old mahogany table – 'God willing.' There was a murmur of approval around the room, and she beamed. 'And so to business, but before we do – any questions?'

Joseph Mile raised his hand. 'I have a question,' he said slowly. 'Who are the board members considering the bid?'

Felicity gave a growling sound in her throat and stiffened slightly. 'The ins and outs aren't relevant, Joseph,' she said.

'They are relevant, if I may,' Joseph persisted. There was a tense silence. 'I ask so you can reassure us that the offer to buy shares is being considered by only a couple of members of the board, rather than the majority.'

Felicity closed her eyes briefly. 'Very well,' she said. Rory shot Joseph a look of anger. 'My father's cousins, Harold and Maud Sassoon, have the largest joint block of shares. They are considering the bid. I expect them, however, to reject it.'

'Why?' Joseph asked.

'Because I hope I have persuaded them that my vision for Bluebird has been and continues to be the right one,' Felicity said.

Joseph Mile nodded. 'Thank you,' he said, pursing his lips delicately, as if he had won some excellent debating point. Elle saw Rory shoot him a look of pure loathing.

'Rory,' his mother said. 'Do you have anything to add? You've been here through all this.'

'Not really,' Rory said. He turned to the rest of the room. 'Look, guys, this has been a big shock. We're one of the last independent publishers in London, and we'll show them – ah.' He paused and then gathered himself. 'Yes, we'll show them. Bluebird can carry on into the twenty-first century stronger and better than before.'

Felicity looked at him in delight. 'Excellently said,' she nodded.

'Lazy git just doesn't want to work for anyone else,' Floyd whispered to Elle, when the meeting ended and everyone filed out murmuring to each other, unsure of what to make of it all. 'Likes having the ideas and getting you to do the work. He'd sink like a stone in another company.'

'No, he wouldn't,' Elle replied loyally, her head spinning. Someone behind her tapped her on the shoulder.

'Elle.' She turned around; it was Rory.

'Hi,' she said.

'I left a manuscript on your desk. Paris's new thriller. Can you read it and make some notes, and we'll discuss?'

'Sure,' Elle said. 'I'll come and see you later –'

His eyes were expressionless. 'I said I'd get back to him with initial thoughts by the end of the week so—'

'OK, OK.'

He descended the stairs swiftly, not looking back. 'You edit his manuscripts for him?' Floyd said, in disbelief.

Elle wanted to call after Rory, to see him turn round, see his handsome, sad face, reassure him that everything would be OK. 'Yes, of course,' she said, after a moment. 'I do it for Posy, too. It's part of my job.'

'Bet Posy doesn't pass it off as her own work though.'

Elle ignored him. 'Floyd, can you tell me something? I love this company, but why would anyone want to buy us? Aren't we terribly old-fashioned?'

Floyd gave a short laugh. 'You're such an innocent, Elle. You know, we're a gold mine, to the right buyer,' he said. 'To a big company like Bookprint or Lion Books we're dead attractive. We've got regular authors, big brand names, a profitable reference list, and we've got MyHeart. We know what middle England likes. May not be sexy, but it's a damn good investment. Those ancient cousins have got umpteen greedy children who want the money. The takeover's going to happen.'

140

He walked off, and Elle watched him crossly. Jeff Floyd was the gloomiest man she'd ever known; he managed to make every piece of good news sound like a disaster. 'She's Top Ten again,' he once announced of Victoria Bishop. 'But it's the slowest week of sales for eighteen months. So she'd be dead in the water if she wasn't.' But his words echoed in her ears. Rory wasn't lazy. Elle knew she was learning more from Posy about how to edit a book, or negotiate a contract, than from Rory, who had a tendency to perch on the edge of her desk and say, 'You need to make a splash. Why don't you try and poach Helen Fielding?' or, 'Let's poach Jilly Cooper.' He wasn't the most diligent of editors, but he wasn't lazy. He loved big ideas, not the development of them. She loved him, but she wasn't blind to his faults.

She wondered what this meant. When the old independent educational publisher Edward Olliphant had been sold last year all but five people had been made redundant. She looked round the office, and noticed everyone else was doing the same.

'Is it true?' Helena hadn't been in the meeting. She hissed across the desk. 'What they're saying, that we're up for sale?'

Elle nodded. 'Someone's tried to offer for us, but I don't think you should worry. We're privately owned, and the family has to want to sell. According to Felicity, they don't.'

'But what if it happens? They're not going to want you and me, are they? They only take the big people. We'll be the first to go.'

'Oh, Helena, cheer up. It might never happen. And you never know, we might all die of the plague first.'

She kept her voice light, but she couldn't help feeling a cold chill, which she assumed must be fear, run through her body.

ON HER WAY to Sussex that Saturday, still panting as she'd overslept and nearly missed her train, hungover and clutching her coffee, Elle drew out her new Nokia 3660 and winced again. Though it was true that many a happy hour for her could be whiled away texting on her new mobile, she wished there were phone police patrolling the streets of London who would take your phone away if you were rolling out of the pub clearly having had too much to drink and about to climb aboard a night bus with no other distraction than the dangerous world of texting. As had happened last night with disastrous results. Elle clutched her coffee, shuddering at the memory.

Already the office was abuzz with gossip. People were nervous, eyeing each other up, speculating wildly at the pub. Elle could feel the change in the air, and she hated it. She had no idea what was going on; she hadn't seen Rory on their usual Thursday, had barely even spoken to him. He was either on the phone or absent from the office. On Friday, she and Sam went for Just the One at the George MacRae with some other junior Bluebirds. Halfway through their first glass of wine, Rory had appeared, with Jeremy. They had waved at their table, but gone to sit around the corner.

'Wonder what they're talking about?' Georgia from publicity said.

'Oh, probably how they'll carve the company up,' Helena said gloomily.

'If I lose my job I'm going travelling,' said Angelica from sales. 'Sam, didn't you hear Rory say something about how he was going to meet someone from the board this weekend?'

Elle's ears pricked up, as they always did at any Rory information. 'Who?' she said. 'Where?'

Angelica looked at her curiously. 'Don't know, why?'

Elle sat back. 'Nothing,' she said.

She hated this. If they knew, these girls who were her colleagues and friends, they'd think she'd lied to them, whereas she was as in the dark as they were, probably more so, because she didn't ever gossip or speculate. She wanted to sit in the pub with Rory the way Sam did with Steve, the way Matty and Karen had done last weekend with their boyfriends, to hold his hand as they walked down the street, to be able to smile in public at him, not this controlled, agonisingly formal behaviour.

Sometimes, she thought, she'd gone straight from being a white-wine-swilling short-skirt-wearing girl about town who fell asleep on night buses to a kind of geisha in a tower, waiting to be summoned, to be wanted. It had struck her, this week in particular, that she was completely isolated. She couldn't talk to Rory, she couldn't talk to her friends, and she didn't know when that would change. And she couldn't do anything about it; she was weak, because she loved him too much, not that that was weakness, but – she was powerless. Elle shifted miserably in her chair, and drained the last of her drink.

'My round,' said Sam, leaping up. She always tried to get the drinks in. Elle patted Sam's arm and said, 'No, it's mine, I'm sure.' She stood up and went to the bar, and as she looked up her heart leapt, for Rory was standing there next to her.

'Hi,' she said, looking round; the casual glance appraising the room, which she'd perfected over this past year. She let her eyes rest briefly on his profile, and for the umpteenth time felt her heart thumping. He was hers. He was so handsome, so grown up and wise, and he was *hers*. She wanted to shout it out loud to everyone, and she couldn't.

'Hey,' said Rory. He glanced at her. 'You OK?'

'Sort of. I hate this,' she said conversationally, as the barman fetched her order.

'I know.' Rory turned his head to her. 'Look, I'm sorry I didn't answer your email yesterday.'

'Or my phone call. Or the day before.' Elle folded her arms. 'I know you're busy, but you could just text me, Rory. I can't – it's very hard – it . . .' She trailed off, as her throat was closing up and she didn't want to make a fool of herself. She couldn't *force* him to see her.

Rory made a clicking sound under his breath. 'Look, Elle – I've said I'm sorry. Things are crazy at the moment, you know that. Plus the board are all so old each time one of them moves it's like a creaky pub sign, trying to work with them is infuriating. And Felicity is so outraged anyone would have the temerity to bid for her beloved company she can't even acknowledge there's an issue. I've honestly spent the last two nights with her trying to calm her down. That's all I've been doing.'

It struck Elle then for the first time that it was sort of strange that, except in times of extreme stress, he always referred to his mother as Felicity, never Mum. 'And you're caught in the middle . . . poor Rory,' she said, trying to sound sympathetic but failing. She was cross with him. She missed him. And she was scared, deep down, because she felt him pulling away from her, and even though he assured her he wasn't, she didn't believe him.

He looked at her suspiciously. 'I am caught in the middle, Elle. You have no idea.'

'What does that mean?'

His voice was low, urgent. 'It means what I said to you on Wednesday morning. Wait till Christmas is over, darling. Everything will be OK.'

Elle stared at the rows of spirits above the bar. 'Why do you keep talking about Christmas? What's happening at Christmas?'

Rory didn't reply. His hand was next to hers, on the wet glass surface of the bar. Slowly, he pushed it against hers, and very lightly hooked his little finger in hers. He rubbed the edge of her palm with his thumb, and breathed out, through his nose.

'Oh, Elby, I miss you,' he said. 'I want you so much.'

'I miss you too,' Elle whispered, swaying slightly at his touch. 'I'm sorry for being a witch.'

'You're not, you're not,' he said. His voice was fierce. 'Just hold on. This'll be over in a few weeks. But we need to keep an even lower profile than before. Mum heard me on the phone to you last Saturday. She knows I'm seeing someone. If she were to find out now, in the state she's in . . . I can't risk it.'

'That's eleven pounds eighty, please love,' the barman said, breaking into their low conversation.

Rory gave him £12.00. 'There you go.'

'You don't have to do that,' Elle said. 'It's fine.'

'Least I can do,' he told her. 'Just remember, if we don't speak, it's not because I'm not thinking about you, darling. I always am.' He looked round; Jeremy was reading the paper. 'I'm thinking about the next time we're alone, and I can peel your clothes off. One by one.' His voice grew softer, and still they didn't look at each other. She strained forward. 'Feel your soft skin against me. Mm? And . . .' He gave a little sigh. 'Slip my fingers inside you. So I can find out how much you've been missing me.'

Elle watched Jeremy over her shoulder as Rory's breath tickled her ear. Her eyelids were heavy, her body felt molten.

145

She blushed, wishing more than anything she could wrap her arms around him, feel him press her against the bar, feel his lips on her skin. She summoned all her strength. 'I'll speak to you later,' she said, and walked off, with her tray of glasses and a sudden desire to drink herself out of the way she was feeling.

As the train drew out of Victoria and crossed the leaden, churning Thames, some memory crept over her, and Elle had a thought, and looked in her 'Sent' folder.

There, in black type against the sickly grey-green background, were three texts dating from last night. The first read:

> To: Rory S
> I miss you so much. I know it's hard for you right now.
> I want you to know I will always, always love you. In
> fact, I want your babies one day. That's all. E x

Shit. Elle turned pale. She opened the next one.

> To: Rhodes
> I just have to say this . . . u were a real dcik to Mum
> last week. That's all. E

Oh, God. Elle swallowed. She reached for her coffee, her hand trembling. She opened the last one.

> To: Mum
> Can't wait to see u tomorrow Mum. I have to say this
> . . . I hate it when you get droiunk. I'm glad yr not
> drinking any more. E x x

The train was picking up speed. Elle stared at the rows of suburban houses, blinking fast. She thought she might be sick. WHY did she do this? She was a terrible drunk texter. All the things she wanted to say to people during the day came out at night, like a vampire. And the tone of them! It was so pompous!

She closed her eyes, and her head thumped. She wished she was back in bed in Ladbroke Grove, listening to the traffic outside. She would crawl out of bed, sit in the warm kitchen with Sam, drink black coffee and then possibly go downstairs in her pyjamas to the shop the other side of the pizza place, and buy a paper and some magazines, read the new *Heat* and *Hello!* and wait around for Saturday night TV to start. If only.

Elle blinked. Beads of sweat formed on her forehead. She started typing, slowly. Rory first.

Ignore that text. Was drunk. Super embarrassed. Spk tomoz. E x

Hi Rhodes. Ignore that text. Was drunk & am embarrassed. Sorry. E x

Hi Mum. On train. Ignore that text. Really sorry. Was v drunk.

She stopped. What next? *Was v drunk so thought would tell u I think u have drink problem.* She shivered. God, what an idiot. She deleted the last sentence and put:

Was out of order. See you v soon. E x x x

Elle closed her eyes. What a crap start to the weekend. As they sped towards the countryside, green and scrubby and still waterlogged from the recent floods, she felt herself drifting off. She was dreading seeing her mother now, although if she were honest she'd been dreading it all week.

After the divorce, Elle's father had said they had to sell the family home. He needed the money: it was a lovely house, not huge but with three small bedrooms, a big garden leading down to a stream, five minutes' walk from the London train. Mandana, who had loved the garden and being near her friends, was devastated. She complained vociferously, long after her move into a converted barn outside the village.

147

Everything that was wrong with the barn was John's fault; two weeks after the move, their old dog Toogie had run back to Willow Cottage and caught a pregnant otter, and then been put down, and Mandana rang her newly ex-husband in Brighton in floods of tears. 'Come and see what you've done!' Elle remembered her shouting. 'You killed the dog, you killed the dog.'

Elle felt sorry for her, but secretly she was glad they'd never have to go back to that house again. 'He's in Brighton, in his swanky new house with the fucking Aga – how ridiculous in a town house!' her mother had screamed once, early on at the barn as the wind howled round the isolated house, pulling open the front door, which banged alarmingly against the stone walls. 'He doesn't bloody care, you know that, don't you? He's off with his pregnant girlfriend in fucking Laura Ashley, why should he care about us any more!'

This was how Elle found out her half-brother Jack was on the way. Later, at university, she'd learned to make this into a funny story. It was so awful, it was hilarious, the way she told it. People would wince, laugh, and then nod, and go, 'Man, parents, eh? Wow.' And for a few moments afterwards, Elle would feel as though she wasn't alone, that there were other people who knew what it was like, how you felt when everything fell apart and no one seemed to know how to put it back together again.

Waiting outside the tiny station in the freezing damp fog, Elle stamped her feet and waved, as her mother's battered old Mini swung into view. Though the coffee and some water had done much to restore her equanimity she was still nervous. Through the grimy windscreen Mandana flicked a glance up at her daughter in recognition. Elle waved again, her heart thumping.

Mandana pulled over, on the other side of the car park. Then she leaned over and wound down the window.

'Get over here,' she shouted. The thin line of exodus from the train turned, curiously. Her mother shouted even louder. 'I'm OK to drive, you know. I've only had two bottles of wine today.'

Elle stood rooted to the spot in embarrassment. She looked around, then hurried over.

'Mum – I'm sorry –'

Mandana smiled at Elle's horrified expression. 'Oh, good grief, don't give me your worried Ellie face. Halley's Comet isn't going to crash into the house, that mole isn't cancer, and I'm not furious with you. I was, but I'm not now.'

'It was stupid, I'm sorry, I didn't mean to—'

'We all do things we shouldn't, darling. I should know. Get in and calm down.'

Laughing with relief, Elle climbed into the car and they drove off.

It wasn't till later in the afternoon that Elle began to feel human again. It was after three, but the light was already starting to fade, and the smell of wood smoke, the warm feeling in her stomach from Mandana's pumpkin soup, the tiredness from lugging boxes back down from the attic all contributed to a soporific sense of ease. The ground floor had been flooded but the flagstones remained intact and there was no lasting damage. Elle and her mother unpacked Mandana's precious children's books which she read at the library, plus the things that had been on the shelves till the flood warning came: a few snaps of Elle and Rhodes on holiday, a photo of her mother, their grandmother, her thin, anxious face almost cracking a smile, standing on a pier in the wind, and a small black-and-white snapshot of Mandana protesting somewhere outside a classical building, she couldn't remember where. The room was cosy with everything back in it, thoroughly clean for once, and for the first time in ages Elle felt at home in the barn. Her eyes were heavy.

149

As Mandana got up from the sofa to throw another log on the fire, she said, 'So darling, tell me about work. You said on the phone that you weren't sure what was going to happen.'

'Well, I hope it'll be fine,' Elle said, blinking to stay awake. 'They all have to want to sell. And apparently they don't. But Felicity and Rory spend a lot of time behind closed doors.'

'Felicity's the owner, yes?' Mandana said.

'Yes, sorry. Rory's her son. He's my boss.'

'Of course. You rather like him, don't you?'

Elle looked quickly at her mother, but her expression didn't convey anything beyond mild interest. 'He's great, yes.'

'I'm so proud of you.' Mandana leaned forward and patted her arm. 'You're doing so well. When do you think you'll move onto doing proper books?'

Elle laughed. 'What do you mean, *proper* books?'

'Oh, I don't know. Not romances, I suppose. You don't want to spend your whole life doing – what is it? Fairy tales, I suppose?'

Elle glanced at the row of battered old Ladybird Well-Loved Tales back on the bookshelf. *You're the one who read me every fairy story under the sun about twenty times, Mother.* 'I won't, Mum,' Elle said, trying not to get annoyed. Suddenly she saw herself at Elspeth's age, still editing MyHeart, still grovelling to a ninety-year-old Abigail Barrow, in an office draped with cobwebs, the same huge grey computer monitor and plastic in trays covered in dust, still waiting for an eighty-year-old Rory to announce their relationship.

'Any boyfriends?' Mandana asked suddenly. 'I never hear you talk about boyfriends.' Elle hated the way she'd do that, cut the conversational ground out from under her.

'No, nothing,' she said, looking down at her lap. 'I'm a black hole when it comes to romance.'

I wish you were the kind of mum I could talk to about it, she found herself thinking. *I wish you were calm and wise and I could sit next to you on the sofa and tell you everything.*

As she thought this she knew how unfair she was being. She couldn't tell her mother because she wouldn't know how to begin to talk about Rory now, after all this time. She had rewired her brain successfully to live in this secretive world that it occurred to her now must have changed her, permanently, in other ways she didn't yet understand.

Mandana stood over her, her arms crossed. 'I don't believe you!' she said, her tone betraying how pleased she was with this detective work. 'I think you're lying to me! Who is it?'

'It's nothing,' said Elle. 'Honestly.'

Mandana sat down next to her. 'Is it a girl?' she said, her brown eyes peering through her fringe. She stroked Elle's cheek. 'It's fine if it is, love. You know that stuff's fine with me.'

'What? No, it's not a girl!' Elle said. 'God, Mum! I don't have a boyfriend so I must be a lesbian? Isn't that a bit of an insult to lesbians, apart from anything else?'

'Don't be snappy with me, Ellie,' Mandana said shortly. 'I'm only asking because you're so closed off – it's like you don't tell me anything about your life and I worry that—'

'Mum,' Elle said, crossing her arms. 'I'm not a lesbian. I don't have a boyfriend. Everything's fine. You always want there to be something wrong. And there's not.' She knew it was the wrong thing to say as soon as the words had left her mouth. *And don't call me Ellie,* she wanted to add.

But Mandana didn't react as she'd expected her to – by flying off the handle. She pursed her lips and stood up. 'Sorry you think that,' she said. 'Listen, I couldn't care less if you're a lesbian, you know. I'm not your father. I don't mean that. I mean – I was in San Francisco just after the Summer of Love, you know. Half my friends were gay.'

One of Elle and Rhodes's few private jokes had always been about Mandana and her references to her time in San Francisco. When she talked about it, she'd always make it sound as if she'd been present at the writing of the Ten

Commandments. They never quite understood what was so amazing about it. They were children of the seventies. Hippies didn't interest them.

'Yes, I know,' Elle said, not wanting to sound rude about the golden months in San Francisco, especially in light of Tuesday's announcement at the Savoy. It occurred to her how little she actually knew about it despite her mother's tendency to make extravagant claims: for example, that she'd dropped LSD with Timothy Leary. She looked at the photo of Mandana outside the classical building again. 'Was that taken there?' she asked, interested despite herself.

'Could be actually, I think that's City Hall. We were protesting about the war. My friend Kathy was arrested.'

'How long were you there for, before the . . . before you had to leave?'

Mandana put her hands on her hips and stared at the ceiling. 'Ooh. Not long. About four months. Arrived in October.'

'Wasn't the Summer of Love over by then?'

'Well, yes. It was in '67. So, long over.' Mandana paused. 'I probably missed the best of it, if I'm honest. There were loads of people out of their heads, tie-dye everywhere. And it was freezing, too. I thought it was sunny all year round in California. Not in San Francisco. It snowed. I only had a mac. That's my main memory, the cold. Not very blissed out, man.' She smiled.

'You always make out you were there in the thick of it, Mother,' Elle said. 'So you're telling me you were two years late and it was winter, not summer. What a pack of lies you've fed us.'

'I know,' Mandana said cheerily. 'But it felt like something amazing was still in the air, even then. It was . . . special.'

'Where did you live?'

Mandana sat down on the sofa, and tucked her feet up underneath her. 'Oh, right in Haight-Ashbury, along with all

152

the other kids who'd run away to find the hippy dream,' she said, hugging herself. 'This old Buddhist guy owned the house. He didn't want rent, he just wanted us all to cook and clean, enjoy each other's company.' She sighed. 'It was a great place. Overlooked the Panhandle. Shared a room with a girl called Jackie, she was from Liverpool. Everyone else was American, and they loved Jackie's accent because of the Beatles. Jackie's sister went to school with Paul, you know. People used to come by just to meet her.' Her eyes grew misty at the memory. 'And they loved my accent too, it was much more Northern back then. I ironed it out afterwards. Later. A guy told me once I looked like Jane Fonda. From Liverpool. I mean, I wasn't from Liverpool, but I didn't correct him.'

Elle shifted on the seat. 'What did you do all day, though? I mean, didn't your parents mind? Grandma and –'

She'd never really had a name for her grandfather. Though they were supposed to call him Grandpa, they hardly ever saw him, and it seemed too – cosy a name for someone you didn't know.

'I'd run away. There wasn't much they could do,' Mandana said. She looked slightly ashamed. 'They thought I was going to secretarial college after university, and I was going to learn Spanish, they'd paid for my ticket to Madrid. I forged a cheque and changed the ticket to a flight to New York, then I hitch-hiked my way across the country. Just wanted to get as far away as I could.'

'Your dad – wasn't he furious?'

'I didn't care,' she said simply. 'I hated him. Hated Mum too, but him mostly. He was a horrible man.'

'Why?'

'He drank.'

'Drank? He was –' Elle didn't know how to phrase it. 'Badly?'

'Yes, badly.' Mandana gave a small smile and hurried on, before Elle could interrupt. 'Anyway, where was I? San

Francisco. Oh, yes. I'd been at home, in Nottingham, and I thought I'd never get out. All my friends were at college, learning how to do things. Dad wouldn't let me go, so I was working at Boots instead. Coming home every evening to that house, eating dry cardboard food, sitting in the near dark, listening to him, wishing he was dead. And I couldn't take it any more, so I made up the secretarial course in Spain and I just kept lying.' Her accent was stronger, as though she was nineteen again. 'Dad wouldn't let me leave the house without my hair all neatly tied back, I had it bouffant in a bow, you know? And always in these horrible court shoes, I hated them. God, I hated them. No sun, no one smiling, cracks on the pavements and weeds everywhere. Then a month later there I am, two blocks from the Grateful Dead, by the ocean, where no one cares if you wash your hair or wear a bra or any of that shit. They just want you to be yourself. There's no lies, no fakes, no society. Everyone's at peace.' Her eyes were glazed; she blinked slowly. Elle watched her, transfixed. 'I met Ken Kesey, you know. And I was at Altamont, that's my one claim to fame.'

'What was Altamont?'

Mandana came to, as if she'd forgotten Elle was there. 'Oh,' she said. 'Just – yeah. It was a free Stones concert out past Oakland. Big disaster. Some Hell's Angels stamped a couple of guys to death. People say it's when the love stopped, you know. December, yeah. And then it was so cold in January, and I was working as a waitress, but then I got busted –' She stopped. 'And that's when I got sent home. You know it all now. I'm sorry I didn't tell you before. About the arrest.'

'That's OK, Mum,' Elle said awkwardly. 'It's fine. You could have told us, you know. It's not, after all, for God's sake, not heroin or something. It's not a big deal.'

Mandana moved closer next to Elle. She took her hand. 'It was to me. I think it was like, here's this great life, you've tried it and now you're never, ever going back to it, you're going back to your shit world in Nottingham, and Dad'll still be drinking and Mum'll still be lying like everything's all OK, and that's your punishment, more than how angry they are. And I'm sorry. I sometimes think – anyway. But you see, I wasn't drinking all evening at the Savoy, now was I?' She knelt down and patted her knees, her brown eyes full of concern. 'It's fine, Ellie. I'm not like Dad.'

'Dad hardly ever drinks.'

'My dad, not yours.'

Elle barely remembered her grandfather. She knew her Grandma, who was quiet and meek, afraid of shadows, a door slamming, children running. She lived in a poky house on a dark side street in Nottingham. They hardly ever went there. She much preferred Granny Bee's house close to the Thames by Marlow, near *Wind in the Willows* country. She knew her mother did, too.

'So, he was . . . an alcoholic?'

'I suppose so. He was a drunk, for sure. We didn't really talk about it. He was either in the sitting room reading the *Express* and drinking his whisky or he was down the pub, and he was a thug, you got out of his way. I hated him.'

Elle put her arm round her. 'Mum, I didn't know any of that. Why didn't you say?'

Mandana shrugged. 'I didn't particularly like remembering it. I wasn't the only one, you know. There wasn't much money for years after the war, no jobs. He'd been injured in France. When he got back everyone was worn out, everything was different. He wanted to manage a picture palace, you know, something glamorous where the stars would come to visit. He didn't want to work in a shop. I think he was a disappointed man. But I still didn't love him. I couldn't. He wasn't nice. And that's the way it is.'

Elle didn't know what to say. 'But – poor Mum. Do you ever wonder if it made a difference . . . I don't know, to your life?'

155

'How so?' Mandana pulled away a little.

'Well –' Elle held her breath, and then she said, 'Why you drink so much, or why you used to. The bad times when Dad left, all of that.'

Mandana patted her knee. 'I know what you're like, and you shouldn't worry. Those bad times, they were ages ago.'

Elle swallowed. 'I just never know with you,' she said.

'I know I was drinking too much back then, and there's lots of things I screwed up. But he left over ten years ago now. And I've got it under control.' Her mother's brown eyes were fixed on her face.

'Have you?'

Mandana said, 'I promise I have.' She nodded.

Elle didn't realise she'd been holding her breath. She exhaled, trying not to let her shoulders slump with relief. 'OK.'

'I'm not drinking, there's lots to look forward to and everything's going to be OK. You mustn't worry about me. I can take care of myself.'

'I don't—'

'You do, you worry about everything, Ellie. And I can't stand you worrying about me, OK? I'm your mother, and I'm absolutely fine.'

Elle hugged her, smiling into her shoulder. 'I'm sorry, I won't. I don't. You're right.'

'In fact,' Mandana said, 'I wanted to talk to you about something, Ellie.' She jumped up and went over to the kitchen, picked up a cloth and started wiping down a surface. 'I want you to do me a favour.'

'Sure, of course, what is it?' Elle got up and went over to her.

Mandana patted her flat short hair with the hand that held the cloth, awkwardly. 'Well, I need you to email your father. Tell him I don't want his money.'

'What?'

'He sends me money every month.' Her jaw was set. 'I don't need his guilt payments any more.'

'But Mum – that's your alimony,' Elle said. 'He agreed to pay it till you were sixty. It's very generous of him. You shouldn't give it back.'

'I want to!' her mother shouted suddenly. She dropped the cloth in the sink, wiping her hands on her cords. 'I'm doing all right! I don't want any more bloody money from him! I want him to leave me alone! Just leave me ALONE!'

She used to say that all the time, when Elle brought her a cup of tea after she'd been crying, or when someone bothered her about something. *Leave me ALONE!*

'Mum,' said Elle, steadily. 'I'm only trying—'

'I've got a new life, you know. I want to put the marriage behind me. Things are going well with Bryan, and—'

'Oh,' said Elle. 'Right. Wow, that's—'

'It's not a big romance at the moment, love.' Mandana held up her hand. 'I just want you to know I've got other things going on. I've got more hours at the library, you know, that pays more. And Anita in the village and I, we're setting up a company, Ellie. You don't know anything about it. We're setting up an import company.'

'OK,' said Elle slowly. 'Right. That sounds interesting. What is it?' She checked herself, aware that she sounded like a disapproving teacher.

Mandana said proudly, 'Indian textiles. Mainly bedspreads. Anita goes to Rajasthan all the time. She's going to buy them and bring them back and we'll sell them here. We'll have open days, this will be like a – a very exotic warehouse. We've already sold three to people who are interested.' She went back to her cleaning, leaving Elle watching her. 'So it would be very kind of you if you could email your father. I don't like living off him, Ellie, a man shouldn't be the plan. I need to make it work by myself now.' She took a deep breath. 'It's time for me to start over again. Stop the bad behaviour. Forget the past.' She raised her head. 'He's obviously been poisoning Rhodes against me, and that American girl. So I want you to speak to him.'

'Did you mind, about last Tuesday?' Elle asked.

Mandana laughed quietly. 'It's my fault, all of it. It's just I feel so ashamed it happened. I didn't like the way she looked at me, either.'

'Melissa? Oh, I don't think she's so bad,' Elle said, hoping this was true rather than believing it.

Mandana shook her head. 'I hope I'm wrong. She looks at you like she thinks she's better than you. She just seems like trouble.' Her eyes narrowed. 'And it's pathetic, but I don't want to communicate with your father, especially not after the things he said to me at the Savoy.' She poured herself some more wine. 'I know we'll have to be civil at the wedding, if they do go ahead with it here, but in the meantime – well, I'd be very grateful. You do understand, don't you?'

'Yes,' said Elle, shaking her head. 'Of course I do, Mum.'

She picked up her tea mug, wondering what Rory was doing right now. He hadn't replied to her texts, and she was kind of glad. As she looked around the room, she tried to picture him here, chewing the fat with her mother, by the fireside. She couldn't see it.

'It's lovely to have you here, Ellie,' her mother said, interrupting her train of thought. 'Thanks for coming. Thanks for putting up with me.'

'Me too,' Elle said. 'I'm the one who should be apologising.'

'No, love, it's me,' said Mandana. 'But like I say, it's all fine now.' She looked out of the window and laughed. 'The future's bright. I just want you to believe me, Ellie love.'

They raised their mugs of tea to each other, in a silent toast. From outside came the steady hum of more rain, pattering on the roof, the path, the puddles.

BY MID-DECEMBER, they were 'definitely in the bleak midwinter', as Bernice, the lady who cleaned the phones and the computer keyboards, told Elle on her weekly visit. It was so cold, the sun barely appeared for days on end, and in Bedford Square especially, the tall buildings cast long shadows against the naked black branches in the square.

One particular Thursday morning, Elle was feeling especially bad. She had a cold, the kind that seems to muffle your brain so that everything appears to happen in slow motion, somewhere out of your grasp. She hadn't seen Rory since Tuesday; he'd been out of the office the day before, not in yet this morning, and she hadn't had a moment alone with him since the previous week. She had wanted to buy her first book, a spoof novel she'd read called *Regency Romance*, and both Rory and Posy had said no, dismissed her as if she were an irritant, like a fly. She was fed up. The phone rang and she sneezed loudly. Opposite her, Helena moved back a little, as if Elle had the pox. Elle wearily picked up the receiver.

'Hellouh, Edditoreull,' she sniffed.

'Hey, Bee,' said a voice. 'God, you sound awful. What's happened?'

'Nothing,' said Elle. 'Libs, is that you?'

'Yes,' said Libby. 'I was ringing to see how you are.'

'I'm fine.' Elle looked round her. It was impossible to have a decent conversation with someone in an open-plan office. 'Actually, I'm not fine, I've got a terrible cold. That's all.'

'Ohhhhh.' Libby sounded almost disappointed. 'Right then. Well, I was only ringing . . . to . . .'

She trailed off. Elle sighed. It was over four weeks since Felicity's announcement at the editorial meeting, and nothing had happened. In the office and out of it, rumour and counter-rumour still swirled around like heavy mist in a creaky horror film. It was exhausting. Every time Elle talked to an author they asked plaintively, 'Any news yet?' When she went for lunch with an agent, or had a meeting with anyone connected with publishing, they'd say, 'You know, I heard it's Rupert Murdoch. He'll strip the company assets and just use the name.' 'I saw Liz Thomson from *Publishing News* yesterday. She said it's definitely WHSmith. You're moving to the Euston Road.' 'Did you see that piece in the "Books and Bookmen" column in *Private Eye*? It's definitely Rory. He's trying to split the company up, sell it for cash.' This morning alone, Elle had had two different conversations about the takeover.

'Were you ringing to get the gossip?' Elle said flatly. 'There isn't any. I promise you.'

Libby said, 'Sorry. That's rubbish of me. It's just everyone at Bookprint's desperate to know. They think we're taking you over and you're all going to come in and make us publish erotic romances and sagas. I keep telling them that's not all Bluebird does, but they won't listen.' She cleared her throat. 'What are you doing this evening? It's been ages, Elle, can't remember the last time I saw you. In fact, I can. Booker Prize night, and I hardly saw you then, either. I've been rubbish. You around for a drink this eve? Just the one?'

'I'd love to, Libs, but I – I really can't,' Elle said. 'I'm knackered, and I've got to work late anyway. I think I'm just going to – yeah, go home and flop. If that's OK.'

'No, that's fine,' Libby said. 'Poor thing, have you got loads to do?'

'It's a nightmare at the moment, yeah.' Elle glanced round the office, not wanting to say more. She wished she could moan about *Regency Romance* but now wasn't the time, and how to explain that you were sick of your bosses, and you thought one of them didn't really know what he was talking about, even though you were sleeping with him? Besides, she couldn't entirely rely on Libby not to call up the agent and buy it herself. She was a bit like that, these days.

'OK, OK,' Libby said. 'Look, I'm going to go. I just wanted to – see if you were all right. You – you are all right, aren't you, Elle?'

'Course I am,' said Elle, astonished. She sneezed. 'Apart from the cold. I'm fine! Why shouldn't I be?'

'Nothing,' Libby said. 'It's – I worry about you sometimes. It's been ages and I hear –' She stopped. 'I just wanted to say hi. It's fine.'

It's fine. Elle was uneasy. What did she mean? 'Look,' she said. 'I'll call you tomorrow.'

After she'd put the phone down she wished, for the umpteenth time, that she could talk to Libby, ask her advice. But she couldn't.

Elle scrolled through her emails and, with a sigh, saw another missive from Melissa. Elle was already having grave doubts about her ability to be the kind of bridesmaid Melissa needed. Not only did she seem to want to book Elle in for every weekend possible in the New Year for dress fittings and 'planning sessions', she kept saying things which Elle found slightly alarming:

Should the bridesmaids start thinking now about the length of their hair come September next year? Because during my conversations with Darcy and my sister I conveyed to them that I would love if you all

161

had long straight hair in a chignon. In that eventuality, as your hair is short, perhaps you should start growing your hair now. Or in the New Year, I really don't mind! (But maybe now if it takes a while to grow as some people's does.) Melissa xoxo

Eleanor heard a loud crack, which made her jump, and only then did she realise she had snapped a pencil in half while she'd been reading. She tugged her hair, wondering at this parallel world she had somehow entered. What would the next email suggest? Plastic surgery so they all had the same size boobs?

'Blimey, Elle. You've got a face like thunder, what's up?' said Posy, dropping a cover proof on her desk for her to check.

'Bloody weddings,' Elle growled, before she could stop herself. 'I'm a stupid bridesmaid for my brother's wedding, and the bride wants us to –' she took a deep breath – '*start growing our hair* so we can all have the same style come September.'

'Oh, bloody *tell* me about it.' Posy sat on the edge of Elle's desk and crossed her arms. 'I was always being a bridesmaid. I did it for someone I was at school with, and on the morning of the wedding she asked me to stand behind the ushers when the photos were being taken because she said she'd been looking through photos of the hen night and I wasn't photogenic enough to stand with the other bridesmaids.'

Elle gasped.

'I know,' Posy said, with a smile. 'I can laugh about it now, but the thing is, I always just thought, "What a strange thing to be worrying about on your wedding day."'

Elle was amazed; the most personal conversation she'd had with Posy up till now had been about the death of Mr Collins, her cat. She nodded, not quite knowing what to say.

'I just thought, "I'd like to remember my wedding day

162

because I married the man I loved and my friends were all there,"' Posy said after a minute, examining a pulled thread on her pink cardigan. 'Not, "Oh, look at ugly Posy, I may have known her since I was eight but she's ruining all the photos, I wish I'd asked her to put a towel on her head."'

'Wow,' said Elle. 'That is incredible.'

'I'll tell you *another* thing I hate,' Posy said, hitching herself a bit more onto the desk. She looked up, as Rory came out of his office and went into Felicity's, slamming the door behind him. 'Oh.'

'It's a shut-door day,' said Elle.

'Never a good sign.' Posy stood up.

'It could mean anything.' Elle tried to sound upbeat. 'It could be good news. Perhaps we're all getting a big Christmas bonus.'

'Trust me,' said Posy, gazing towards Rory's empty office. 'I used to work for Robert Maxwell. It's never good news when the doors are shut. Never.'

At half past twelve, Elle was putting on her coat, slowly. She was meeting Nicoletta Lindsay for lunch, to tell her that she needed to stop trying to make her country-doctor-in-the-Lake-District romances into mystical screeds on prehistory and pagan topography and to that end, she would have to completely rewrite her new book, and think seriously about the direction of her future novels if she wanted another contract with MyHeart. Felicity had given Elle this speech yesterday at the editorial meeting, and Elle had written the salient points on Post-its which she'd stuck on the inside of her bag, ready to refer to surreptitiously at lunch if necessary.

Wrapping her scarf around her neck, Elle went over to the photocopier by Felicity's office, to copy the latest sales figures for Nicoletta Lindsay. Rory's office was empty; she hadn't seen him all morning. As she stood there pressing Copy and wondering if she could pop in for another word with Felicity to gee her up, she suddenly heard her voice through the heavy wooden door.

'How could you not tell me?' she was shouting. 'Rory – I don't understand.' Could she be crying? 'With *her*, as well. I don't understand it.'

Elle carried on mechanically pressing buttons, but her heart was thumping, and there was a lump in her throat.

Rory replied, but his voice was too low to hear. And then she caught the end of the phrase. 'You don't understand. It's going to be wonderful. I thought you'd be pleased when I explained –'

The worst bit of it all was Felicity's tone. It was half amused, half desperate.

'*Pleased?* Rory, you must have gone mad. Do you have any idea what you've *done*?' There was a massive, trembling, gasping sound. 'She's – so young! And she knows *nothing*! This isn't what I wanted for you, darling. All the plans . . .' She broke off. Rory started to say something, but she interrupted. 'You have to put a stop to it. End it. Now. She'll understand when you explain why, I know she will, Rory, she will.'

Picking up the pages, her hands slick with sweat, Elle clutched them to her chest, looking round the office to see if anyone else had heard. Helena was still typing, Joseph Mile was on the phone, two fingers smoothing down his ginger cowlick and, over in the corner, Jeremy and Loo Seat were regaling the marketing and publicity departments with the story of Jeremy stepping on Victoria Bishop's pet dog the previous week. It was just her.

Elle crept out, as the faint bellows from Felicity's office grew softer, and when she reached the stairs, she ran.

AFTERWARDS, ELLE WONDERED how she'd got through lunch. She couldn't remember a thing about it, what she ordered, what she said to Nicoletta Lindsay, how Nicoletta took the news, whether she'd made any sense at all. She knew that afterwards, as they'd stood on Charlotte Street outside the restaurant, Nicoletta had shaken her hand and said, 'You know, Elle, you've given me a lot to think about. Perhaps you're right, perhaps it *is* time for me to throw caution to the winds and write that time-slip novel.' And Elle remembered nodding and thinking, *That's not at all how that was supposed to go . . .*

She walked down Percy Street, looking in the windows of the galleries, not really seeing anything, and shivering in the bitter cold. Should she go back to the office? Would everyone else know by now? Would Felicity fire her on the spot, order her from the building? She couldn't do that, could she? Elle stood still, not knowing what to do.

She felt very small. She'd wanted this for a while now, and she'd known Felicity would be surprised, but the disdain, the horror in her voice! – that was something else. Once again, she wondered how she'd got to this place, where there was no one she could ring, ask for advice, someone who was a friend. She was basically alone.

165

And then Elle thought back to the last time she'd seen Rory properly, the previous week. They'd had glorious sex in his flat, loud, uninhibited, ripping each other's clothes off, the usual constraints that surrounded them gone. Rory had shut the curtains on the square, spread an old silk rug in front of the fire, while she knelt there, naked, waiting for him, and he'd reappeared with two glasses of champagne.

'Had it in the fridge,' he said, kissing her, as they drank. 'We should celebrate. Us. Celebrate us, baby.' And then he pushed her back on the rug, and they rolled around, till she was on top, her knees on the hard floorboards, one side of her hot from the fire, squeezing her thighs to feel the warmth of him between them, the thickness of him inside her. They couldn't stop smiling, either of them.

'I love you,' she said, suddenly, slowing down her rocking movements against him.

His teeth were clenched and his eyes shut, but when she said it his face cleared and he looked serious.

'I love you too. More,' he said.

The release when it came was overwhelming. She gripped his shoulders. The relief of being with him, feeling like herself again: this, here, the two of them, by the fire, panting, clinging to each other naked and without anything else to define them, this was what it was about, no matter what happened. Later, they sneaked out to the Charles Lamb pub and ate sausage rolls and Scotch eggs. They got hopelessly drunk on cider, laughing at each other on the way home as they weaved across the City Road back to the haven of his flat, and they fell asleep in each other's arms, his breath blowing in her ear, on her hair.

The memory of that night had sustained her the past seven days, and it did now. What came next might be terrifying but after that – they could get on with the rest of their lives together. Go for dinner with friends, meet families . . . in a way it *was* terrifying, though, to know she'd have nothing to hide behind any more. Part of her thought she wouldn't be up to it, that she should call in sick for the afternoon, go home and tremble under a duvet.

'No more lies. No,' she said softly to herself. 'Come on, Eleanor Bee.'

She had to go back, to face the music. Elle crossed Tottenham Court Road and picked up her pace, rummaging in her bag for her spare glove.

'Hey!' someone behind her called. 'Hey, you! You dropped something!'

She turned round. A man was running towards her, holding her errant glove. 'Tom?' She shook her head. 'Hello. What a surprise.'

'Elle!' Tom Scott said. He grasped her shoulder, and smiled. 'I wondered if it was you.'

'Oh. Thanks,' Elle said, smiling back. 'How are you?' She looked up at him slightly breathlessly. She always forgot how tall he was, how quietly he spoke, now against the roar of the traffic.

'I'm fine. Just been having lunch with an old publishing friend of mine . . .' He looked at her closely. 'How are you?'

'I'm good – yeah, I'm OK.' She gathered herself. 'Not really. I suppose you know what's going on with us.'

'I do,' he said. 'And I heard the latest, too.' He nodded. 'Big blow-out this morning, Rory and Felicity. News travels fast.'

Through her shock and fear, Elle was astonished at the speed with which rumours like this were spread. 'It's – it's rubbish. Don't listen to a word of it.'

Tom shoved his hands in his pockets. 'I'm sure you're right,' he said. 'I shouldn't be repeating gossip like that, especially to you. I'm sorry.' There was a pause. 'Look,' he said. 'I've been meaning to email you anyway, to say thanks. The database idea – it's brilliant.'

Elle stared at him. She had no idea what he was talking about. 'Database?' she said blankly.

'For the Dora Trust. You suggested – look, it doesn't matter.'
He shook his head impatiently. 'I'm an idiot. Don't worry
about it.'

'No, no, I remember.' Elle shuffled on her feet. 'Great.
Look – I'd better –'

' 'I know, I know,' he said. 'Can I just say something?'

'What?'

He cleared his throat, and took a deep breath. 'Elle, look.
I owe you a favour. And this is also probably none of my
business but –' His quiet voice was hard to hear; she leaned
forward to make out what he was saying. 'Don't trust Rory.
I know he's your boss, and I know you like him, but things
are going to get messy there. He's nothing like his mother.
He doesn't know what he's doing and he's dangerous as a
result. Be careful.'

She stared at him. 'I don't know what you're talking about,'
she said. 'I have to go.'

'Hey – Elle –' Tom shrugged his bony shoulders so that
they stayed up by his ears. 'Hey – I didn't mean to be rude.
I feel like I owe you. I just wanted to—'

But Elle was running down the street already, leaving him
behind her. How dare he. How horrible. She'd always thought
he was horrible actually, with his thin face and strange weird
manner. He was jealous of Rory, that was the trouble – darling
Rory –

She ran all the way back to Bedford Square. When she
touched the buzzer, Elspeth answered, and when Elle gave
her name, Elspeth said, 'We're all in the boardroom. Come
straight up, please.'

ELLE WALKED SLOWLY up the old, carved stairs, catching her breath, past the portraits of old members of the company, past the framed covers, past the Ladies where she'd screamed in horror at her yellow-dyed hair, the night she'd kissed Rory for the first time. As she passed the first floor she looked in at the empty office, newly decorated with Christmas lights and a tree twinkling in the corner. Her knees buckled slightly beneath her; what had happened? She walked up the second flight of stairs and knocked softly.

'Come,' Felicity's voice boomed.

Elle opened the door, and went in. The large mahogany table was folded against the wall, and virtually the whole company sat in rows in front of her, their arms crossed. As Elle stood by the door, her heart thumping, her eyes met Felicity's, which were bloodshot and puffy. Her hair was flat and untidy, her brooch slightly askew; Elle blanched with shock, at seeing her anything other than immaculately dressed.

'Come in, Elle,' she said, her voice thick. 'Sit down, please.'

'I –' Elle hesitated, looking for Rory. She couldn't see him. Someone opened the door behind her, and she jumped. It was Sam and Georgia.

169

'Oh, there you are,' Sam whispered. 'Been looking for you *everywhere*. Come and sit with us?'

It was then Elle started to wonder if she'd got it all wrong. 'Sure,' she said gratefully.

Sam looked at her. 'It's going to be OK, you know,' she said.

'What is?' Elle asked her.

'Everything. Never mind. We'll talk about it later.' Sam nodded. They filed to the back, past the rest of the company, sitting in silence or faintly whispering and then the door opened again, and Rory entered. Elle's heart jumped at the sight of him, as it always did. He looked so handsome and serious, in his smart grey suit.

He was with a thin, tall woman, with thin blonde hair, thin fingers and a long, strangely beautiful face, like an angel in a Flemish painting. She said something to Felicity, sitting in the front row, and then Rory clapped his hands.

'Hi, everybody,' he said. 'Look, I know you must have guessed something's going on by now. We've been wanting to tell you for ages, and it's been really hard, because it's exciting, but at the same time it's going to mean a lot of changes.'

The woman next to him nodded. Elle watched in confusion. She and Sam were so far back, they could hardly hear Rory, let alone see him.

'You know that Bluebird has had a wonderful and illustrious history. Well,' Rory said, 'it's time to take that history into the twenty-first century. Over the past few months we've been thinking about the Bluebird legacy. We've had a couple of offers, as you might know. What was difficult was working out how best to proceed. To do what's right for the company, and for the board, and the employees.'

He cleared his throat.

Felicity got up, her chair scraping the floor. It made the same sound as Rory's throat. She shook her head, and clasped her hand to her mouth. Her eyes were bloodshot.

170

'I'm sorry,' she said, her voice muffled. 'I can't listen to this. I won't.'

She walked out, slamming the door behind her.

The silence in the room was total. Rory looked at the closed door, and then pressed the bridge of his nose between thumb and forefinger. 'To that end,' he said, carrying on as if nothing had happened, 'there is a press release going out now that we wanted to read to you.' He took a piece of paper out of his jacket pocket.

'The board of Directors of Bluebird Books Ltd and Bookprint Publishers are pleased to announce that today, Tuesday 12th December, they have agreed to hasten the process of due diligence, expected to be finished within the week, which will complete the sale of Bluebird Books to Bookprint Publishers. Bluebird will become an imprint of Bookprint Publishers, the UK's largest publishing company.'

Rory paused and looked up, slightly, but only to the top of the piece of paper, as if he couldn't bear to look any further.

'Ahh. Er. He continued reading:

'At that time and with immediate effect, Rory Sassoon becomes Deputy Managing Director of Bluebird Books and will oversee the transfer of assets to Bookprint Publishers. Felicity Sassoon steps down from her role as Managing Director of the company with the board's grateful thanks for thirty-five years' service with the company. She will remain on in the role of Publisher-at-Large.

'As with any company restructure, there will be a period of consultation resulting in redundancies across the company. The board of Bluebird and Bookprint Publishers are in discussion about the number and range of these redundancies. These redundancies relate only to Bluebird Books and are designed to ensure, along with its sale to the UK's best and biggest publisher, that the brand has a long and successful future.'

When he finished, the only sound was that of the piece of paper, being folded up and put away again by Rory's clumsy, shaking hands. He looked up and – Elle couldn't quite see, but Sam swore later he did – shrugged his shoulders, sighing, and giving a small smile.

'What does that mean, "redundancies"?' Loo Seat put her hand up, her voice carrying loudly in the quiet room. 'How many?'

'I don't – know. Yet.' Rory shook his head. 'Look, guys. This is a shock, I know. It's been a shock to a lot of people. But the board agrees with me. We have to – um, look to the future.'

Elle kept staring at him, hoping he'd glance her way, but he didn't. *The board agrees with me*? What did he mean? What about Felicity?

'Right. So, you've sold us down the river, Rory,' Floyd said calmly. 'You've taken the money from the buyout and hung us out to dry. What does your mother make of it? Is that why she's gone?'

'Felicity agrees that this is for the best.' Rory stood on one foot, then the other. Elle stared at him. She nearly jumped out of her skin when, next to her, Sam stood up.

'Excuse me?' she said politely. 'I hope you don't mind me saying this, but she doesn't seem very pleased about it. I don't understand why she's not running the company any more.'

Elle wanted to hug her. 'Look,' said a calm voice. 'The legacy of Bluebird Books, it lives on. That is what is important.' The thin woman in grey had been so silent Elle had forgotten she was there; her voice was low, with a slight French accent. They all listened, mesmerised.

Rory flapped his right hand at her. 'Guys, this is Celine Bertrand,' he said. 'Sorry, I should have introduced her before. She's the MD of Bookprint UK.'

172

Celine nodded, watching them all, her slim hands clasped together.

'I look forward to getting to know you all. For some, it will be sad circumstances, others happy. But I promise Rory has acted in the best interests of the company, in persuading the board to accept our offer.' She turned to him coolly. He smiled at her. Elle stared at him, in his smart grey suit and short hair, flushed with excitement, like a little boy with a new toy. She bit her lip, hard; she barely recognised this Rory. Then she realised, as she tasted blood, that she did. Of course she did. She'd pushed this version out of her mind, only seen the one she wanted to see. But this Rory had been there all along. He was there in front of her now.

Back at her desk, Elle looked around the office. Everyone was in shock; Loo Seat was comforting someone in publicity, who was sobbing quietly in her arms. She saw Carl from IT's head, above the wall dividers. He was saying to Floyd, 'What am I going to do? My wife's ill, she won't be back at work for a year even if she gets better, and there's no way they'll keep me on. We're fucked.'

And Floyd, calm, practical: 'It won't be like that, mate. And the package is good. I've seen it. Promise.'

Elspeth was in tears, Posy patting her on the back. 'They – I've been here thirty years,' she was saying. 'What will I do now? I don't know how to do anything else.'

'We don't know who it'll be,' Posy said, her face grey. 'You mustn't worry just yet, Elspeth, dear. Rory wouldn't let us—'

'Wouldn't let us starve on the streets?' Elspeth said, her tone vicious. 'If he can stab his own mother in the back I should think he's capable of anything, wouldn't you?'

Posy said sadly, 'Yes, maybe he is.' Her face was haggard; she looked much older, all of a sudden. 'I thought I knew him. Funny, isn't it.'

Elle's phone rang, as she was watching this. She jumped. 'Can you pop into my office?' Rory's voice said, tersely.

Elle gathered her notebook – she didn't know why – and crossed the floor, shutting the door behind her. Her heart seemed to be thumping loudly in her throat.

'Hi,' she said.

'Sit down.' Rory rubbed his eyes, and then looked up at her. 'Hey.' He touched her hand; she looked down. 'So –' he said. 'This is it, then.'

'Yes?' Elle asked, not sure what he meant. Her tired mind seemed to be scrambling the information it received.

'I wanted to make sure you were OK. And I wanted to tell you I've sorted it with Celine. You're OK. Your job's safe.'

Elle stared at him. She didn't know what to say. 'Um –' she said eventually. 'Thanks a lot.'

Someone was shouting outside on the floor. 'Pub! Come on. Pub!' There came the clattering of bags and coats being gathered. Elle and Rory sat in silence, in his office, listening, their knees almost touching.

'Where's your mother?'

Rory shrugged. 'In her office. I think she'll probably go soon. It's for the best.'

'But – she's Publisher-at-Large, still,' Elle said, and hearing herself she realised how naive she sounded.

'That doesn't really mean that much,' Rory said quietly. 'That's what you give people when – well. She knows it. We all know it.'

'Rory – how could you do that to her? How could you betray her like that?'

His eyes flashed. 'I've done her a favour, Elle. You have no idea what you're talking about. We had to change, or else we'd fail. She was a brilliant woman in her day, but the truth is she's past it.' Rory drummed his fingers impatiently on the desk, watching her as if he expected her to

174

agree, reassure him he was right. She couldn't speak. 'This way, she and I have made a tidy profit from the sale, she can retire, and Bluebird can start moving into the twenty-first century.'

'You keep talking about the twenty-first century,' Elle said tiredly. 'But our best-selling books, the ones that actually make the money, are all about people living in the past.'

Rory looked as if he didn't quite understand her. 'Elle, this is business,' he said blankly.

Elle tried not to shout. 'It's people too,' she hissed. 'It's your mother, it's your friends, your colleagues, it's me!'

'I told you,' Rory said. 'You're OK! Promise.'

She stood up. 'You really don't get it, do you? Rory, I don't want a job because I'm screwing you.'

'You've got one anyway.' Rory's voice was cold. 'I thought you'd be pleased.'

'But I don't—'

'Shut up,' he interrupted impatiently, leaning forward. 'I've said I need transitional people who know the list. It had to be someone, so why not you? You'll be fine there, I know you will.'

'Don't you understand?' Elle's hands fell limply to her sides. 'Carl's wife's ill, Elspeth's never going to get another job, Angelica sends money home to her mum every month. They're people. And they're good at their jobs. You're making a mistake, you can't just wipe out a company like this. It's not about me.' Her voice was pleading, she was desperate for him to see, to understand. 'I'm not your –'

She was going to say, *I'm not your little bit on the side*. But that was exactly what she was, she saw it for the first time.

Rory was watching her, expectantly. 'Look,' he said. 'Celine is absolutely wonderful. I've got to know her these past few weeks. She'll see us through this, and it'll be great.' He sat up straight in his chair. 'When it's over, we'll look back and say, "Yup, right thing to do."' He tugged at his tie. 'Right thing to do. Elby?' He gave her a small smile. 'By the time Christmas is here, you'll have got used to it. I told you to trust me. Like I say, it's business.'

Trust me. She didn't know what else to say, so she turned around and left, not caring, for the first time since she'd known him, whether he watched her go or not.

THE DAY BEFORE the supposed 'Christmas Party', Elle got home late, weary and annoyed after Christmas shopping. She let herself in to find Sam sitting at the kitchen table, tearing a paper napkin into shreds. She was singing 'Good King Wenceslas' to herself.

'You all right, Sam?' Elle dropped her bags onto the lino and shrugged off her coat, grateful for the warmth of the small kitchen.

'Yeah. No, not really. Been made redundant. Got told just now,' said Sam.

Elle sat down at the table, her mouth open in shock. 'No. Oh, no,' she said. 'Oh, Sam. I'm sorry.'

Sam didn't look at her. 'Yeah. It's a pain. I thought it was all done by now.'

The past two weeks had been brutal. It became clear over the days that followed the announcement that everything had been planned in exquisite detail; one by one, most of the company fell. There were fifty people in the London office. Thirty of them were to lose their jobs. Carl, Elspeth, Helena, Angelica. All of publicity, including Loo Seat, had already gone. Sandy the post-room lady had left the afternoon they told her. Floyd and most of the sales team were made redundant. Even Posy, she'd heard last week. There would be no one left, beyond her and a few others, and no one knew the full extent of what Posy and Elspeth did. It was mad.

Elle swallowed. 'I thought they'd done them all. I thought you'd be OK.'

'I'm the last person they told.' Sam smiled. 'Nice, eh.'

Elle didn't know what to say. She reached out and took Sam's hand. 'Bastards. What do you get?'

'Six months' pay,' Sam said. 'Not bad. I'll be OK for a while. I might see what Steve wants to do. You know?'

'That's a good idea. Or you could take some time, think about if you want to try another career?' Elle hated the jaunty tone in her voice.

Sam wasn't really listening. She carried on gazing at the kitchen wall. 'It's just – I don't want to leave. I liked it. I liked what we were. Jeremy wants to take me with him, he said so. He's going to need someone, but they won't budge. All those campaigns I've sorted for March and stuff. He won't know where anything is. He'll screw it up.'

Elle winced. 'You're the one who runs that department. He's only got a job because he's a mate of Rory's. Everyone knows that.'

'Could you have a word with Rory?' Sam said, getting up. 'Tell him I should stay.'

Elle scratched her head. 'I don't think he listens to me, Sam, but I'll have a go. He's stupid.'

Sam carried on talking. 'I'll probably have to find somewhere else, or stay with Steve.' She cleared her throat. 'So I guess you'll be moving in with Rory then, will you?'

She looked at Elle. An ambulance blared outside, as the two girls stared at each other.

'Won't you?'

'What do you mean?' said Elle, mock-jokily, sticking her elbows out, as though she was an old-school comedian.

178

'Elle, come on,' Sam said. She pulled her top lip down over her teeth.

'How do you know?' Elle said quietly.

'I'm not stupid, Elle. I've lived with you for three years. I know we're not as close as you are to Libby, but yeah. I'm not stupid.'

Elle's throat was dry. 'Sam –' She pressed her hands to her burning cheeks. 'Sam – I'm sorry. I should have told you. No one knows, not Libby, no one. Then all this happened – the takeover –'

'You're going to Bookprint, aren't you.'

'Yeah,' Elle said. 'I think I am.'

'Thought so,' Sam nodded. 'I don't blame you, Elle. Honestly, I don't.'

Elle could feel a sob rising in her chest. 'You should.'

'It's OK though. You love him. I've always known it, from the way you look at him. And he loves you.' Sam rubbed her nose. 'I'm happy for you, it's weird but I am.'

Now that she could finally talk about it to someone, there was nothing Elle could say. She turned away. 'I'm so sorry,' she said again.

'Why? Don't be. I'll be OK, honest. We'll look back in a few years' time and laugh,' said Sam philosophically. 'We'll always be friends, won't we? Anyway, everyone always knew Rory wanted to run the company.'

'And that's fine except the way he's gone about it.' Elle stared at the wall again. 'I just don't understand it. I don't know who he is . . . I do but I can't . . . I can't . . .' she whispered. 'I don't think I can be with him any more.'

'Serious?' Sam pulled herself up so she was sitting on the counter. She opened a tin and shoved two biscuits in her mouth. She looked wiped out and Elle saw then that her eyes were bloodshot. In over three years of living with her, apart from Princess Di's funeral, she'd never seen Sam cry.

She kicked at the kitchen unit. 'I want to be able to look

179

at him and say, "I'm proud to be with you, I love you, you're a good person." I can't do that with him. Ever – ever again.' She'd never said that out loud before, she'd never realised it before.

She got up, went to the fridge and pulled out some sausages. 'I'll make you supper. Do you want supper?' she added, wondering if Sam was hungry. She wasn't sure she could eat.

To her surprise Sam said happily, 'Yes, please. Toad in the hole?'

'Sure,' said Elle.

'Can't remember the last time we ate together,' Sam said. She started singing 'Deck the Halls with Boughs of Holly'. 'I'll go down and get some wine.' She picked up her purse. 'It'll be like our Christmas meal.' She turned back to Elle. 'Honestly, I'm happy for you, if you're happy.'

Elle shrugged her shoulders. 'Thanks, Sam,' she said. She grabbed her hand and stared at her, there in the warm kitchen, where they'd made probably thousands of cups of tea, chatted for hours, spent more time together than Elle had with most people in her life, and now it was ending. 'Thanks for everything.'

'No worries,' Sam replied, and went out, whistling, leaving Elle alone.

THE FOLLOWING DAY, Friday 22 December, Elle and Sam journeyed in together, with heavy hearts and heavy heads, due to the amount of red wine they'd drunk the night before. Sam had come back with a mulling mixture from the dodgy off-licence and they'd sung carols and Sam had said she thought it was the most amazing evening she'd had in ages, which Elle thought was bizarre from someone who'd been made redundant that very day.

They were greeted with the news that the period of due diligence was over and the sale was complete. At one o'clock Floyd turned off his computer, stood up and shouted, 'I'm out of here. I'm going to the pub for the last time. First drink's on me.' He looked towards Rory's shut door; as ever, Rory was closeted with Celine. 'Bye, Rory,' he shouted. 'It's been great. Good luck running the place. You'll need it, mate.'

He slung his backpack over one shoulder, and strode out.

In five minutes, the office was virtually empty and Rory and Elle were the only ones left on their floor. When Celine finally left Elle put the last of her things in the removal box she'd been assigned and closed the lid. She turned off her computer and picked up her bag, then walked over to Rory's office, her legs shaking. She felt like a little girl, or like the girl who'd walked up those steps that day in May, so long ago, in her brand new pink Oasis jumper, so proud and apprehensive and excited.

She knocked on the door.

'I'm off to the pub now,' she said.

Rory looked up and, when he saw it was her, pushed some papers on his desk away. 'Elle, ah,' he said. 'I'll walk out with you.'

Elle shrugged; she could hardly refuse. Rory picked up his coat and they walked through the abandoned office together.

It was freezing in the square, too cold to snow as Granny Bee used to say. A heavy fog hung over the park, it seemed to creep into Elle's bones. She shivered. Suddenly she thought, she didn't know why, of the day she'd thrown coffee over Felicity, and how Rory had said, 'Don't take on so,' just like Granny Bee. It was so long ago. She looked up at the building and realised then she wouldn't go back inside again. Ever.

'Look, Rory,' she said. 'I just wanted to say, things are obviously weird between us at the moment, and that's fine, I know you've had a lot to . . . juggle.' She didn't know the right word to use. 'It's just, I've thought about it a lot, and I don't want to go to Bookprint. I want you to give Sam a job instead. You need her much more than me.' She nodded. 'Trust me, I'm not being noble, you really do.'

'This again?' Rory stamped his feet on the ground, to keep warm. 'Look, Elle – we made our decisions for commercial reasons. I'm not giving Sam a job. She's a marketing assistant, they're ten a penny. You, however –' He put his hand under her chin. 'You're unique. And I wish you'd understand that. This isn't a charity I'm running. It's a business.' She stood still, not blinking, and just looked into his green eyes. He stepped forward. 'Christ, Elle, this is a hard time for me too, you know – I've got Celine on the phone fifteen times a day, I've got Mum crying to every dinosaur agent in town and spreading rumours about me behind my back. I don't know what the fuck I'm doing. Can't you just, please, cut me some slack?'

She put her hands on his chest, not caring if anyone saw. She could feel the warmth of him under his coat. 'But Rory, that's the trouble – I agree. I don't think you know what the fuck you're doing either.' She swallowed, and stared at him.

Say it, the voice in her head was shouting. *Say it.*

Don't, another voice said. *Don't say it, Elle, you'll regret it for ever.*

'Aaaah . . .' Elle said, knowing she was going to speak, that she couldn't stop herself, and she didn't know where it was coming from, and part of her desperately wanted her to stay silent. 'Oh, God. Listen, Rory. I think it's over.'

'What?' he said sharply.

Elle inhaled deeply, the icy air stinging her lungs. 'I don't know you, that's the trouble.' She shivered. 'I thought I did.'

'You do,' he said, staring at her in disbelief. 'I know all this is a shock but I couldn't tell you, it wouldn't have been fair to you. But it's all over –'

'God, Rory, I'm not doing this because you didn't tell me. I'm doing this because – because . . .' Elle trailed off.

He saw an opening, and he said, quickly, 'Try me.' His voice was hoarse. 'Elle, come on, don't do this. I'd do anything for you, darling, you know I would.'

Suddenly, she knew what to do. It was so clear.

'Kiss me here, now, in the square,' she said. 'Just kiss me, like you did last week, like you do when no one can see.'

He hesitated. She carried on, looking into his eyes. 'Then call Celine. Tell her we're in love. Go into the pub with me, buy them all a drink and hold my hand, kiss me again. Now's as good a time as any, Rory, they hate you anyway. I'm the one they'll hate now, even more. They'll say it's not fair, that I shouldn't have kept my job, that I'm a conniving bitch.' Her face was inches away from his, and she said, urgently,

183

'I've got more to lose, but I won't care, if you'll do that for me, because I'll know.'

She clung onto the front of his coat, staring at his lopsided, cheery mouth.

'Just kiss me,' she said again, her voice catching.

He straightened himself and stood back a little from her.

'Wow,' he said. 'You're so different, these days.'

'What?'

'The girl you used to be, the one I first met with long legs and long hair, so shy and awkward you wouldn't say boo to a goose. You've changed. Grown up. Sometimes I look at you and I don't think I know you any more.'

'But I haven't been that girl for a long time.' She stood firm, biting her lip. 'I asked you a question, Rory. Yes, or no?'

He hesitated. 'It's not as simple as that.'

'It is,' said Elle, feeling her heart physically ache. 'It has to be. If you won't come with me to the pub, I have to go now, otherwise I'll change my mind, and that would be stupid. Very, very stupid.' She covered her face with her hands, breathing deeply. 'As stupid as I've been these past few years . . . Oh, God, no.'

It was so strange, to be saying these words yourself, not reading them in a book, or watching them on a screen. This was how it felt to have your heart slowly pulled out. To be ripping it out yourself, after years of secret dreams and plans. *You stupid, stupid girl,* she told herself. *You should never have hoped so much for it. Don't you know it always ends up kicking you in the teeth. Don't hope. Give it up.*

Rory caught her hands in his. 'Elle, you don't mean it. We'll give it the New Year. Start again – we'll be at a whole new company, think about how to do it then, it's a fresh start!' He leaned forward: she was still standing close enough for him to kiss her cheek, her neck, to clutch her shoulders and kiss her. 'My baby girl,' he said softly. 'Don't do this, darling. You need me, I need you . . . come on.'

It was the 'come on' that did it: as if she were a disobedient horse, or a puppy he was trying to train. 'I'm not your baby girl, Rory,' Elle said. 'I'm a grown-up, and it's not good enough,' and she walked away, her heel crunching slightly on the frosting, glittering pavement beneath.

'I'll change your mind. I will,' Rory called out, in the empty square. His voice sliced through the icy air. 'Take your time, Elle. I'm nothing without you.'

She nearly stopped. Wouldn't it be easy, wouldn't it be lovely, to run back towards him, just once more? To grasp his warm hand in the freezing cold? To know they were together again, them against the world?

But why was it against the world? Why did it have to be so hard? And why didn't she trust him?

Elle carried on walking.

'You're nothing without me, either, you know that, Elby,' he called. 'You know it.' She was astonished he was being so loud, but perhaps he had a point to prove. She'd forgotten how he hated to lose.

Just then the Bluebird front door opened, and Felicity came down the steps. She was in bright red, and she had three or four books under her arm. Next to her stood Elspeth, sobbing, clutching the painting of Maurice Sassoon that had hung in Felicity's office.

And someone must have told the others, because a knot of people streamed out of the pub, and stood on the corner watching her. Floyd stepped forward. 'Come for a drink with us, Felicity,' he called. She gave a small smile.

'My dear boy, I only drink spirits, and triples at that. I only dropped by to collect a few things. Another time.' She took his hand. 'Thank you for everything.'

She held out her hand and immediately a cab appeared. Elspeth placed the painting carefully inside, and then embraced Felicity. Felicity had her hand on the door of the cab. Posy gave her a big hug, and said something to Felicity, then pointed across the square. Felicity turned, as did Elle, and saw what was by now most of the company on the pavement, gathered outside the George MacRae.

Felicity looked over at them, her eyes huge, mascara on her cheeks, and raised her hand to them. Elle stared at her, seeing for the first time the woman she was beneath her own trappings, the big hair, the loud colours, the queenly gait. Her eyes were swollen, her rosy lips pursed tightly together and her face flushed, and for an instant she looked young, vulnerable, entirely human. The cab engine made a juddering, impatient noise. People were waving, nodding.

'Bye,' Elle said softly, standing behind them all. 'Thank you.' Felicity looked up one last time, and then climbed slowly into the cab. Elspeth shut the door and it drove off. Elle turned round, to see if Rory had been watching. But he was walking towards Gower Street, head down. The others were turning back towards the pub. Posy hugged Elspeth. 'Come for a drink, old girl,' she said.

Elle found herself backing away, her eyes blinded with sharp tears. 'Coming to the pub, Elle?' someone, she didn't know who, said.

'No, thanks,' she said. 'No – it's OK.' She clutched her stomach, trying not to sob out loud. The pub door opened, the sound of electronic 'Jingle Bells' floating out onto the square. The others went back inside, talking, patting backs, hugging each other. Rory turned the corner and disappeared out of sight.

It was quiet again. Elle looked around her, but everyone had vanished.

Jane Eyre, who had been an ardent, expectant woman – almost a bride, was a cold, solitary girl again: her life was pale; her prospects were desolate.

Charlotte Brontë, *Jane Eyre*

June 2001

'YOU CAN GET down now,' said the lady with the half-moon spectacles, her mouth full of pins. 'It's almost perfect.'

'Thank you, Margaret.' Melissa stepped off the pedestal, turning her head over her shoulder and admiring her reflection in one of the long mirrors. Elle sat on the cream suede banquette, watching her.

'Mm?' said Melissa invitingly, though Elle hadn't said anything.

'Oh, it's beautiful,' said Elle obediently. 'Absolutely gorgeous. You'll look stunning.'

'You think?' Melissa said uncertainly. 'You don't think it's too out there?'

'If it's good enough for Posh,' said Elle.

'Who?' Melissa said sharply.

'Posh Spice. I mean, that style – that's what she had. If it's good enough for her –' Elle was out of her depth.

'Oh.' Melissa turned away as Margaret reappeared.

'When's the wedding, remind me?' Margaret flipped open a notebook.

'Oh, sure, you must have so many to remember! It's Saturday September 29th ,' Melissa said, smiling, though Elle knew that tone well by now. *You should have that date tattooed backwards on your forehead, Margaret,* is really what she was saying.

'OK. So we'll see you back here for one more fitting. You'll lose more weight before the day. They all do.' Margaret licked her pencil, much to Elle's delight, and scribbled.

'*I* won't,' said Melissa decisively. 'I'm at my wedding weight already.'

'Trust me,' said Margaret. 'All brides—'

'I'm not all brides.' Melissa put her hand gently on the pad. 'I won't. This is how I want it. This is how I'll stay.' She grinned reflexively, as if a robot voice in her invisible earpiece was saying, SHOW HUMANITY BY SMILING. The white teeth and the big diamond ring glinted together. 'I'll see you in August then, Margaret. Thank you.'

'I assess the global risk of African nations totalling seven billion dollars every year,' said Melissa, as they were walking down Marylebone High Street five minutes later. 'I think I know what my weight will be come September. These people.'

Elle said nothing, just smiled. The sky was layered in thick grey-white cover. It was humid, the air thick with heat and fumes. She swallowed. She was dying for a drink, though it was only just gone twelve. 'Where to now?' she said. 'What's next?'

Melissa nodded. 'I want to check on shoes in Selfridges. Not for me, for you guys. They said they'd have more Carvela stock in today and I have to see if they have those sandals in Francie's size. She has such vast feet, like a boy's, you'd never know we were sisters.' She pushed her sunglasses over her eyes and sighed. 'There's so many things to think about. It's crazy.'

'But it's going to be great, right!' Elle said, trying to sound cheery. 'We should have a chat about the hen weekend too. Dad's paying for my flight, did I tell you? I can't wait, I've never been to New York, I'm so excited!'

Melissa was one of those brides who could only see everything leading up to her wedding through the prism of her own viewpoint. The thought that going to New York might be exciting to Elle was of no interest to her. She nodded quickly and said, 'Yeah, that's great. Wow, I'm so annoyed Darcy's making us do it in July because of the kids. Between you and me.' She shrugged. 'I'm such a bitch.'

'No, you're not!' Elle said automatically, though slightly hysterically. Melissa turned to look at her in the street. She ran her tongue over her lips, and paused, as if she were about to say something.

'Thanks, Elle,' she said eventually. 'I know this is work for you and you don't know me and it must seem like I'm totally obsessive. It's just I've known how I wanted my wedding to be all my life. And we can't have it in the States, and that's *so* fine, but if it can't be perfect in other ways I don't want to do it at all. And maybe . . .' She paused and looked around her. They were standing outside a tapas place just off St Christopher's Place. 'Hey, it doesn't matter. I don't know what's wrong with me today. Why don't we stop here and have some lunch. I'm hungry.'

She plonked herself down at a table outside and dropped her bags on the ground, fanning herself. Elle sat down next to her. She felt there was something Melissa wasn't telling her.

'Is everything OK?' she asked.

'Sure!' Melissa said. She nodded vigorously, as if she were confirming this with herself. 'Sure. Enough about me, anyway. Hey, I want to hear about you. How is your new job? You must be so relieved you kept your position. They must think you're amazing!' She smiled, and Elle smiled back. She knew Melissa was trying to be nice.

'Oh, yeah. It's OK,' said Elle. She pushed her napkin and cutlery away.

'Only OK?' Melissa folded her napkin neatly onto her lap.

'It's a bit hard,' Elle said. 'I miss the old company. It was – lovely. It feels like a long time ago. A layer that's just gone.'

'Why? Isn't this a better company?' Melissa asked.

'It's bigger, I don't know if it's better. It's strange.' Elle couldn't explain the hugeness of the Bookprint building, the fact that three times since January she'd forgotten what floor she was on, that each evening on her way to the lift she walked past row after row of desks and had no idea who the people who sat at them were, or what they did.

'Don't you have any friends there? Didn't anyone come with you? I thought Rhodes said you knew someone, your boss, someone?'

'My friend Libby works there. But she was there already, and we're – quite different.' She had to perk it up a bit, she just sounded pathetic. 'A couple of people from Bluebird, that's the old company. But it's not the same.'

She didn't know why she was talking to Melissa, of all people, about this, only that she had to tell someone. Her throat hurt from not telling things. Eight, nine months ago she couldn't wait to get to work, couldn't wait to live the drama and excitement of her life, the desperate longing for him, the happy certainty when she and Rory were together, the fact that the office was a stage where she could, every day, watch the man she loved and see him watching her, smiling at her, sharing their secret. Every morning Elle would wake up glad to be alive. She'd even got used to Sam singing in the shower. Now Sam was in Hertfordshire and Elle had moved, in March, into a tiny damp almost-bedsit in Kilburn. She worked in near-silence with people she didn't know and she had lost Rory. Lost him because she'd let him go. And she couldn't allow herself to regret the decision.

Perhaps it'd be different if she didn't see him any more. But she couldn't help thinking about him, how he was, whether he thought of her. Then, two weeks ago, he'd texted. And she had her answer.

I can't stop thinking about you. I miss you. Please, can we meet up and just talk? Somewhere away from the office? Nothing to do with business?

He wasn't her boss any more, so Elle didn't know why he'd say that about business, but she didn't know what to do full stop.

The following night at the Chandos, the Bookprint local, a tiny little pub off Carnaby Street, she'd finally crumbled and told Libby. Libby wasn't excited or seduced by the romance of it, as Elle had hoped she might be. She'd been pretty strange about it, actually.

'You dark horse! Eleanor Bee!' She'd stared at Elle appraisingly, as if she'd got her all wrong. 'Rory? Seriously? All that time?'

'Er – yes,' Elle had said, wondering if it sounded as though she'd just made it up. Had she? Had the last eighteen months been all some weird dream?

'Well, I never.' Libby shook her head. She gave a curious smile. 'The dirty dog. I don't believe it.'

'Oh,' said Elle. She narrowed her eyes. 'Well – er, it's true. And I don't know what to—'

'I thought you didn't like men in publishing,' Libby went on. 'You always said you weren't interested.'

Elle had tried not to sound impatient. 'I don't remember. That was ages ago. Look, I wish I hadn't told you. I wanted your advice.' There was silence. 'I don't know what to do. I don't know if I made a terrible mistake. If I'm still in love with him.'

Libby had said decisively, 'I think it's pretty crap of him, actually. Taking advantage of you like that . . . and he's *still* taking advantage of you. Don't reply.'

'I can't not reply,' Elle said.

Libby was suddenly furious, more angry than Elle had ever seen her. 'He's exploited you, Eleanor. He's totally taken you for a ride.'

'Well, maybe but –' Elle didn't quite agree. 'I mean, what was in it for him? It's not like I'm Celine or someone and he was trying to persuade me to buy the company. I was just his assistant editor. We were – I really thought we were in love.'

'You were easy prey.' Libby shook her head. 'He shouldn't have done it. Oh, Elle.'

Elle looked around the tiny pub and downed the rest of her drink, wishing she hadn't told Libby, wishing she was back at home. She fingered the book in her bag.

'What are you reading?' Libby demanded.

Elle didn't want to tell her that, either. She didn't want to give anything more away to her. She said, after a pause, reluctantly, '*Faro's Daughter*.'

Libby looked blank. 'Don't know it.'

'It's by Georgette Heyer.'

'Oh.' She shrugged. 'One of those Felicity books. Right.'

Now, Elle could feel her face reddening with annoyance as she recalled the conversation. Strange that it should have got to her like that, though: these days, she just didn't care much about anything, really. Her job, her flat, her love life, the summer weather, anything. 'Heigh-ho,' she said, taking a gulp of her Rioja. It was delicious, heavy, powerful, warming in her throat. She changed the subject.

'Oh, by the way, Melissa, I wanted to ask you if you'd thought any more about dinner with Mum, some time in August? The three of us, or maybe more if there are other people who can't go to New York for the bachelorette party? She mentioned it last week.'

This was also a lie; Mandana hadn't mentioned anything.

194

In fact, Elle felt she deliberately avoided talking about the wedding, a combination of childishness and shame about the fact that it was taking place here because of her. But since Melissa and Rhodes had moved back to London in February when Rhodes's job demanded it, the fact that they were more on the scene now only served to highlight how obvious it was that Mandana wasn't making any effort with Melissa. They were too different, it was the simple truth. Elle wished she'd at least try, though.

'Yes! Of course, now I wanted to talk to you about that.' Passers-by jostled past each other on the crowded pavement. Melissa studied them for a moment and then she said, 'What would your mom like to do at the wedding, does she want to be involved? I gave her my step-mom's email so they could exchange information and what colour they'll be wearing so they don't clash.'

'Oh, great,' said Elle, unsteadily.

'But is there something else she'd like to do? I feel like she's holding back, or perhaps she's just not that interested.'

Since this was the exact truth, Elle didn't know what to say. 'Oh, no,' she said emphatically, the glow of wine giving her conviction. '*That's* not true.'

Melissa smoothed her hair over her shoulder with one hand. 'Well, we're going down to see her in a couple of weeks. Rhodes wants to spend some time with her. Make sure she's doing OK. You know, ahead of the wedding.'

A warning light began to flash in front of Elle's eyes. 'What do you mean, make sure she's doing OK?'

Melissa said, slowly, 'I think he – well, just checking in. You know.'

'Right.' Elle didn't know why she felt so defensive. 'I think Rhodes sees things that aren't there any more.'

'I don't know that he does, sometimes,' Melissa said. 'Some of the stuff he told me about her when she was drinking . . .

Maybe she didn't show you all of it, maybe she waited till you were at college. He worries she's started again, or she'll start again. I don't know.' She shrugged, tentatively.

'He left as soon as he could!' Elle wanted to laugh. 'Melissa, seriously! I'm the one who spent the most time with her. If she had a drink problem I'd know.'

'My dad was an alcoholic for ten years before I knew,' Melissa said, matter-of-factly. 'I guess that's all I'm saying.'

Elle's mouth opened. 'Oh. I'm sorry. I didn't know that,' she said.

'It's fine. He still is.' Melissa took a bowl of olives proffered by the waiter and neatly moved the side plates out of the way. 'Doesn't go away, you know. He hasn't had a drink since '95. He gave up the day he woke up in the clink for the third time in a year. Drove into a tree, off Interstate 87. Wasn't hurt, but that was luck. He could have killed people.' She moved one slim finger slowly over one of the side plates. It left a streak on the gleaming white china.

Unbidden, the time Mandana had crashed the car into a hedge on the way back from school flew into Elle's head. But it was once and it had just started raining, that really wasn't the same thing. 'That's terrible,' she said.

'It was terrible waiting for him to get back from work, never knowing where he was. I'd bargain with God. *This time, just this once bring him back this time, I'll do my math, I'll eat my crusts, I'll even stop teasing Francie about her bangs.*' She smiled. 'My sister was too young to remember it. So now I'm grown up, you see, I have to have things the way I want them. Otherwise it's all wrong.'

She clutched her stomach, as if instinctively, and then was still.

'Well, I'll ask Mum – maybe we should go out, have a day at a spa, or something –' Elle said weakly, though the idea of Mandana in a fluffy white dressing gown having a mani-cure was incongruous. She'd scream with derisive laughter at the idea. 'I'll talk to her. Don't worry.' Then she said gently, 'I know Rhodes finds her difficult sometimes. But I promise, she just wants him to be happy.'

Melissa put her hand on Elle's. 'We're all like that, I guess. I should stay out of it. Happy families, hey. It's been so great, spending this time with you. I really feel like we're all getting closer. That's what family's all about, isn't it!'

She smiled her big smile and once again, Elle shifted, uncomfortable in its huge beam. She felt she was further away than ever from knowing her future sister-in-law.

'I'M BLOODY SICK of these books,' Bill Lewis, managing director of the BBE (Bookprint Press, Bluebird and Eyre and Alcock) division said, attempting to throw the submission letter across the room. It juddered ineffectually in the air and landed a few centimetres away from him, on the pale ash table. Everything at Bookprint was either glass or pale ash. 'They said it'd be a flash in the bloody pan, and it's been five years. No sign of it ending either. If I read one more submission letter about a girl who works for an advertising agency in London who loves shopping and her boss I'm going to go mad.'

'This one's different, though.' Annabel Hamilton (junior editor, Bookprint Press) looked peeved. She glanced at Libby, her heroine, but Libby was doodling on her minutes and didn't look up. 'She's a witch, the heroine, and she can't find a man?'

'Ha!' Bill Lewis gave a hollow laugh. 'There's always something. This one's different. She's Asian, she's gay, it's set in Bogota, it's set in a fight club.' His voice rose, till it was almost hysterical. 'But they're *always the bloody same*. I hate Bridget Jones. Hate them all! Bloody pink covers.'

No one said anything; they shifted awkwardly in the glass

meeting room. Elle, who had been reading surreptitiously under the table, came to at this last sentence.

'That's not right,' she said, mildly. '*Bridget Jones's Diary* didn't have pink on the cover. And it had a quote from Nick Hornby. And it isn't girlie. It's just very funny.'

There was a silence, and Elle blushed, wishing she'd kept her mouth shut. Editorial meetings here were so incredibly long, every book thrashed over and over even when she wanted to shout, *'No one, NO ONE here wants to buy a book narrated by a policewoman who enjoys holidays on nudist beaches. Why are we all sitting here discussing it for ten minutes, Bill, you massive perv? Why?'*

Bill turned to Rory. 'So, Rory, what do you think? Do you have an opinion?'

Rory had been staring down at the table. 'Um –' he said. 'I agree with Elle.'

'You would,' said Bill, crossly. Elle flicked a glance at Rory, but he was scanning the minutes. No one else met her eye. She knew they all thought she was a waste of space, the hangover from quaint, past-it Bluebird who could only talk about romance novels and sagas. She knew she should care but these days, she didn't.

'OK, still on new projects,' Bill said. 'Who's next?'

'I've got *Shaggy Dog Story* to talk about,' Libby said, next to Elle.

Bill sat up. 'Of course. Great. Libby, do you want to explain to everyone what this is?'

'Sure. It's a first-time author. Wonderful idea. I want you to imagine –' Libby launched into a crisp, concise pitch, and Elle drifted off again. It was a novel about a boy whose dog talks to him. Elle thought it sounded bonkers, but there was a huge auction going on and it was being compared to *Flaubert's Parrot* and *The God of Small Things*, so what did she know.

'So we'll be going to best bids later,' said Libby. 'We're at one-seven-five for one. That's for this room only, guys, OK?'

Everyone nodded. 'Sounds great, Libby,' Jeremy murmured. 'Yeah,' someone else echoed. Elle turned the page.

'Libby, do let us know if you want sales figures or anything that'll help,' Sally, the sales director of the BBE division, was saying.

'Great, Sally,' Libby said, smiling at her. 'Thanks!'

'That's exciting,' Bill said, nodding at Libby. 'Keep us posted, Libby. OK. What's next?'

1. Buy bin bags
2. Confirm time for bridesmaid dress fitting
3. <u>Book flights to New York. Today.</u>
4. Email Melissa about mini-photo albums, fake veil, cupcakes in New York.
5. Ring Mum.

And then, because she'd learned now that the only way to write a list was to finish with something you actually wanted to do:

6. Buy *The Reluctant Widow.*

Elle fingered the last few pages of *Frederica,* and stared into space until suddenly Libby nudged her and she heard Bill yelling, 'ELLE! ARE YOU LISTENING?'

No, Bill. I was writing out a To Do list because I am organising a hen weekend which, FYI, is practically a part-time job. Plus you are really boring and a pompous git.

The rest of the room was silent. 'Sorry,' Elle said. She glanced at Rory, but he was staring down at his pad. 'What's up?'

'Celine wants to see you afterwards.' Bill smiled evilly. 'In her office.'

'OK,' said Elle coolly, trying to channel Libby. 'Thanks, Bill.'

On the way out of the meeting room she and Jeremy paused at the door at the same time. Neither acknowledged the other; Elle kept her head down and scurried back to her glass office.

During her first few weeks at Bookprint, she had tried to say hi to the other Bluebirds there, not Rory, but the others: Jeremy, Nathan the art director, Joseph Mile – other than Rory the only editorial survivor besides her. But she'd soon found this was a mistake. You didn't flourish at Bookprint by talking about where you'd come from and saying things like, 'It's weird, getting used to it here, we were so close there!' Because no one cared.

No, you devoted yourself to the big new company with the gleaming glass offices in Soho, you swiped your security pass through the glass gates and walked along in clicking heels, carrying your coffee to the glass lifts as though you worked for Willy Wonka. No one smiled at anyone in the lift, but you were on time and you made money for the company. M.O.N.E.Y. The idea of there being a Bernice to wipe the phones and the keyboards with her soft cloth was laughable, as was the idea of Felicity's fresh hand towels in her office, the family portraits on the staircase, the annual day trip to the seaside. At Bookprint there were Eritrean cleaners who spoke no English and were polite and shy. No one talked to them, you carried on working as they appeared in the offices, like vampires, after dark, as the strip lighting above them buzzed and crackled. There was a vast canteen, endless cream filing cabinets and lots of dead spaces called 'break-out areas'. Sometimes Elle thought she'd stepped out of the eighteenth century and into *The Matrix*.

Elle shared a tiny office with Mary, the cookery editor. Just as she was sitting down, Libby poked her head round the door. 'You OK?' she said. 'You were miles away.'

'I'm fine,' said Elle. Annabel Hamilton hung behind in the corridor, waiting for Libby to finish up.

Libby frowned. 'Has he texted you again?'

Elle tensed. She rolled her eyes towards Mary, Elle's office partner, who was scrupulously ignoring the conversation, making tiny pencil marks on a manuscript.

201

'I'm a bit busy now,' Elle said, wishing Libby would go away. 'Fancy getting a sandwich at lunch? Or a drink tonight?'

'I can't. I've got lunch with Peter Dunlop. *Shaggy Dog* UK agent,' Libby said. Her face was flushed. 'Got an author drinks thing tonight so I can't do then. But we should, soon. Just wanted to make sure you were all right.'

'Libs, Libs,' Annabel mewled from outside.

Elle nodded. 'I'm good. See you later then.'

'Great.' Libby smiled at her. 'Laters!' She turned and skipped out. 'Hi, Rory!' Elle heard her call.

Elle shrank back, as Rory walked past the office. He turned and looked in, as he always did.

Not for the first time, she wondered how he was getting on here. All he seemed to do was walk up and down the corridor, or sit in his office reading manuscripts he never seemed to buy. At Bluebird, he'd driven them all mad, with his energy and over-reaching ambition but here, it was as if he was stuck permanently playing a small boy on his first day at school, not quite sure whether he was doing the right thing. Even Celine, his best friend back in December, ignored him now. Elle wondered whether he ever regretted the sale. For many reasons. But she didn't let herself wonder for too long. She had locked her heart up against him, and it would take something extraordinarily strong to break it open.

Rory carried on walking, in his aimless way, and Elle turned back to her screen, her heart beating fast. She started listing the characters in *Frederica* in her head, breathing evenly, trying to stay calm. This was the only thing that worked, she'd found. She had to have something else to think about, a list she could recite, otherwise she thought she'd go mad.

One long dark night in February, when she had thought her head might explode with thinking, she'd crawled over to the shelf, picked up Felicity's long-rejected copy of *Venetia*, turned to the first page and started reading. Reading the way she used to, before she'd become an editor. She'd turned one page, then another, till it was almost morning. The next day, she'd gone out and bought another Georgette Heyer and now, it was early July and she'd read sixteen. She knew it sounded crazy, but she was quite sure if it wasn't for Georgette Heyer she would have gone mad by now. It had occurred to Elle over the weekend that if she'd been a rapper she'd have got a tattoo to commemorate her idol. Perhaps she should. Where would she get it? On her thigh? Her hip? Above her left breast, in a heart shape?

The first tattoo ever with the name of an author of quality Regency romances, in curly writing, underneath your bra. Yes, she thought, that's definitely the way to ensure no one ever asks to see you naked again. You might just as well walk around with a big sign round your neck saying SPINSTER, and just as Elle was wondering if that was, in fact, a sign of madness – wanting to get your favourite author's name tattooed on your bosom – Mary, the editor Elle shared the office with, turned round and said, 'Keep meaning to ask. How are the hen weekend plans going?'

'Fine, thanks,' said Elle, grateful for the interruption. Then she frowned. 'Oh, except I had an email from my father this morning – he's very kindly paying for my flight to New York, but he's gone mad because it's a hundred quid more than I thought.' Elle shook a fist in mock-fury. 'This hen weekend, man!'

'But you're going to New York!' Mary said. 'You'll have a brilliant time!'

'I know,' said Elle, trying to sound enthusiastic. 'It's just been a lot of hassle. And I don't even know Melissa that well, that's the weird thing. We're flying over to New York together. I don't know any of her friends . . .' She hesitated.

'And?' Mary said, curiously.

'Oh, I don't know.' Elle felt a bit disloyal, but she had to talk to someone about it, and Mary was a calm, wise person. 'She's obsessed with everything being perfect. So two weeks ago she was making me do everything with her, calling me twice a day, asking me to go for fittings with her. I've seen her boobs *four times*. And she'd email three times a day. Bonkers stuff. Like should we have themed T-shirts?'

'What kind of themed T-shirts?' Mary said suspiciously.

'Like the ones Madonna wore saying "Kylie Minogue". She wants ones saying "Melissa" on the front and "Mrs Bee to Be" on the back.'

'Wow,' Mary said. 'My God, I thought my sister-in-law was bad, but at least she only made us embroider her napkins.'

'She did what?'

Mary shook her head. 'Too soon still. I can't talk about it. Goodness, where does it end?'

'I dread to think,' said Elle. 'I said no. I'm already growing my hair so it can go into a stupid chignon, and I don't even know what they are! God. You wouldn't ask a load of *men* to grow their hair if they want to be ushers. It's so bloody stupid. I can't see her boobs again. I mean, I know she doesn't know many people over here and she means well but . . . I'd never met her before November. It's crazy.'

'Quite right,' said Mary, sympathetically. 'Maybe you need to start keeping her at arm's length.'

'Well, but that's just the problem. Now I can't even get hold of her. She's gone missing. She won't return my calls, and I don't know where she is. I haven't heard from her for days. I spent all weekend making the badges she wanted with sticky-back plastic and nothing. Not a peep out of her. I've obviously done something to upset her, and I don't know what.'

She had been over the latest dress fitting and the lunch afterwards, ten days ago now, several times in her head. What had they talked about? Had she missed something? Maybe Melissa had been a bit strange – but then she *was* a bit strange.

'Course you haven't,' said Mary. 'She's probably just busy with everything.'

Elle wanted to agree. 'Yeah,' she said. 'Probably.'

'Still, the wedding sounds like it'll be lovely.' Mary smiled, and clasped her hands together. She had just got engaged, and liked wedding chat. 'Sanditon Hall is such a beautiful venue, we've looked at it ourselves.'

'Oh, really? Good,' Elle said. Between dress fittings for the dark purple silk sheath to be worn with green and grey fascinator that made her look like an aubergine and organising the hen weekend, she had barely thought about the actual ceremony. Her family didn't do big parties, or celebrations, never had. 'Oh, it will be, it's just – I don't know why I'm not looking forward to it.' Then she said, in a rush, 'It's the going-by-myself thing too. Maybe that's it.'

'You should have someone as your plus one,' sensible Mary said. 'She's American, Americans always have plus ones at weddings, don't they?' She looked excited. 'You could take a date! Ask her.'

'Oh, right,' Elle said. 'Who would I take?' She gave what she hoped was a hollow laugh, but it sounded a bit too hollow.

Mary looked round and smiled mischievously. 'Oh, I don't know. Maybe you should ask Rory. I always think he's rather keen on you.'

'Really?' Elle said. She gave what she hoped was a dismissive smile and changed the subject. 'Anyway, I hope she hasn't killed Rhodes and gone on the run.'

There was a silence; Mary laughed awkwardly, and Elle paused: what if something bad really *had* happened, and here she was, joking about it? She shrugged, embarrassed, as Mary went back to checking her page proofs, and Elle opened her emails. There was one from Celine's assistant.

Celine would like to see you when you have a minute.

Hell. She'd forgotten about it. Well, it could wait another half-hour, couldn't it? Elle looked down at her nearly finished Georgette Heyer and the assignment she had this lunchtime. It was nearly twelve thirty, it *must* be OK to go now. She picked up her handbag.

'Just going out to get a sandwich,' she said.

The Bookprint offices were housed in a large eighties glass building on Golden Square; on the other side of Soho, just off Charing Cross Road with all the other second-hand book-shops was Bell, Book and Candle and this was where Elle came, at least once a week, usually twice, either in her lunch hour or on her way back to her flat.

'You finished that one *already*?' Suresh, the elderly man who owned the shop, knew Elle by now. 'You want *another* one?'

Elle smiled at him and headed straight over to the shelf in the corner of the shop. She breathed in the old, mildewy smell of second-hand books, as instantly comforting as ever. 'Yes,' she said, scanning the shelves. 'I'll just be a minute.'

'OK, OK,' Suresh retreated, muttering to himself.

Left to herself, in the blissful peace and quiet of the darkest corner of Bell, Book and Candle, Elle breathed out, for the first time in days. She felt calm here. No 'ping' sound when an email appeared, no brides to chase or bridesmaids calling her, no answering-machine messages from mothers screaming and swearing, no fathers yelling . . . and yet also no lonely, echoing silence, like the evenings in her new flat. Just the beautiful smell of old books, like mildew and incense and paper, the shuffle of fellow browsers' feet on the worn lino floor, the very faint burr of traffic outside, and a shelf of unread Georgette Heyers for her to choose from.

Elle often wondered what Felicity's favourite was. She wished she could talk to her about them, find out what she was doing, even just say thank you. She'd seen her once, walking down Regent's Street, in what looked like a grey woollen cape. It was strange, watching her jostling with tourists outside Hamleys: Felicity was born to be inside, holding forth in a meeting room, not someone who mixed with tourists in T-shirts and trainers. She was too far away for Elle to say hello but Elle really wished she'd run after her. She just watched her grey stately form as it was blotted out, swamped in a sea of backpacks and denim.

Elle picked out *The Reluctant Widow* – her fingers lingered over *A Civil Contract*, but she moved away, she knew the rules were one a week, and one at a time, no more – and paid for the book. 'You enjoyed that one?' Suresh said, nodding at *Frederica*.

'Brilliant,' Elle said happily. 'A real good 'un.'

'See you next week then,' Suresh said, shaking his head, for he clearly thought Elle was a nutcase. Elle waved and walked back towards the office, clutching her bag happily to her side at the thought of another book to devour. There was absolutely no chance of Elle meeting a Max Ravenscar or a Lord Damerel, not at the Mecca Bingo on Kilburn High Road, and certainly not in the air-conditioned gulag of Bookprint Books Ltd, no, never there. She crossed Golden Square and the glass doors slid silently back for her.

'Elle?' a voice behind her called. 'Hi, Elle?'

'Oh,' said Elle, snapping out of her reverie, and turning round with dread. 'Hi, Celine. I'm sorry I didn't – I was about to come and see you – I needed a sandwich – it's –' She stopped, not sure why she was making up fifteen different excuses. 'Hi,' she said, pretending she hadn't spoken. 'I was about to come and see you.'

'Good, good,' said Celine. 'I'm glad to see you, Elle. Come with me?'

They walked through the light-filled Bookprint lobby together. Elle jabbed the button for the lift.

'Thank you,' Celine said. The tone of her voice was always

the same: the slight accent, even and modulated, just friendly enough. 'So. You have been here six months now?'

'Yes, I have.'

'You know that you come with such high praise.'

'Oh – thanks,' said Elle.

'Yes. Felicity, Posy, Rory, they all said you were someone to watch.'

You made two of them redundant. Elle frowned, to hide her blush of confusion. 'Oh – I don't know about that.'

Celine didn't get self-deprecation, Elle could tell.

'I don't feel we've really spoken since you joined. Have you settled in?' she enquired, as if Elle were a guest at her B&B.

'Oh, yes,' Elle said, hiding the plastic bag swinging from her arm with the Georgette Heyers in them. 'Life is . . . good. Just great. Really . . . great.'

'I am glad to hear it,' said Celine. 'So, I wanted to talk to you because I have a project for you. I want you to look after Dora Zoffany's backlist.'

Elle was genuinely flummoxed. She looked around, to see if Celine was actually talking to someone behind her. 'Dora Zoffany? Me?'

Celine impatiently tapped her immaculate pointed kitten heel on the shiny marble floor. 'Bof! These lifts. They are terrible, you don't think? I will forward you the email when I get back to my desk. We have to reissue them. All of them.'

'I can't believe her books were allowed to go out of print in the first place,' Elle said. Then she thought that might sound critical, so she added quickly, 'So, that's good then. Thank you!'

Celine crossed her arms and drummed her fingers on her elbow. 'Well, I don't want to do it. I think it's a waste. She sells . . . nothing. But Tobias Scott is a very important agent to us, three of our biggest authors are with him, you know. So we have to.' She said it *wee aff toooh*. Elle rather liked how slightly more French Celine became, the crosser she got. 'I thought it would be a nice project for you, something to broaden your range. From all the romances. Do you mind?'

'Mind?' Elle said. 'Honestly, that'd be brilliant. I really love Dora Zoffany.'

'Rory said you did. He said you should be the one.'

Rory said. He knew she did. He knew she'd had hardly any room for books in her Ladbroke Grove flat, and yet they'd piled up against the wall unevenly like medieval towers, leaning precariously to the side, and that the space on her one small shelf had been reserved for everything by Dora Zoffany, old fifties Bookclub hardbacks, cheap and small, their clay-red or royal-blue cloth frayed at the corners. She hadn't unpacked her books since she'd moved to Kilburn. She didn't see the point. It was simpler to just keep buying Georgette Heyers.

'Rory?' she said, after a moment's hesitation. 'Well – I'm glad he did. It's very kind of you, to think of me.'

'I'm not being kind,' Celine said flatly. 'I have wanted to give you a project for a while. So I can talk to you about it more.'

Elle watched her. She wondered if Celine had a boyfriend, or if she lived alone like Elle. Not in a flat like Elle's. A white and glass apartment like the Bookprint building, overlooking the river, filled with fresh flowers and modern art. An older boyfriend, a philosophy professor from Sciences Po. Was she different when she spoke French, did her eyes sparkle, did she glow when she smiled?

'Ah, here it is, the lift.' Celine stopped tapping her foot. 'So, you will do this then? I'll send you the information. Look the covers over and talk to the art department, get the agent in. It's not Tobias Scott you will deal with. It's his son. His name is Tom. He is looking after this for his father.'

'Tom? I know Tom,' Elle said, relieved.

'Good. Just do it right. They are very important to us, let me know if there's anything else.'

209

Celine nodded briskly. She got into the lift. 'You are coming?'

One of the worst things about Bookprint was the torture of the lifts with your boss. Fifteen seconds of small talk – Libby was brilliant at it. 'Morning, Bill! Saw Ian McEwan in Warren Street this morning, isn't that weird?' Whereas every time Elle just stared at the floor wondering how fifteen seconds could seem to last hours, wishing the lift would plunge into the basement, killing them all.

'Er, no, I'm waiting for someone,' Elle said mysteriously. She was aware this sounded insane. Celine looked perplexed. 'Thank you again,' Elle added, but the door had closed.

She waited a good few seconds to be sure, then called the lift again, chewing her lip and thinking. She still had five minutes left of her lunch break to finish *Frederica* and read the opening pages of *The Reluctant Widow* and she didn't want to waste any more. It was boiling hot and there was no one around, but as she sat down, Rory appeared around the corner, and walked past her office. He looked in and stared, his eyes searching hers, and this time, Elle looked back at him. She found her heart was racing. He slowed down, and she thought he might stop, but he didn't, and she was glad – at least she thought she was, she couldn't tell.

THAT EVENING ELLE wearily climbed the stairs, pushed open the door and wiped her aching forehead. It was stifling. She dumped her bag on the floor and opened the windows. The tinny radio from the corner shop spurted sharp snatches of pop music. She drank a large mug of water from the tap, flopped down on the ragged old mustard-coloured sofa and stared into space.

Her new flat was not designed for the summer months, and as she'd only lived there since March she had no way of knowing if it was designed for the depths of winter either. The owner had been a stage manager in the West End who'd retired to Florida. The place was cheap enough for her to just afford it as it was tiny, had damp, and was on the fourth floor without a lift. It hadn't been decorated for well over twenty years, and was covered in posters for seventies farces and signed photos of ancient actors: row after row of photos of people like Liza Goddard, Paul Nicholas and Hannah Gordon signing heartfelt messages to Billy, her landlord. Next to the fridge, so that she saw it every morning and evening, was her favourite, a lurid seventies head shot of a woman with huge blonde hair. *'Darling Billy boy always in my heart for ever, your undying friend, Jilly! PS Remember sunlight and botty babies!'* the long-forgotten Jilly had scrawled underneath. Sunlight and botty babies, what did it mean? Darling!

Billy had rented the flat furnished. He'd said she was welcome to take the posters and photos down, but they'd been there for ten years or more and when Elle tried she was left with acres of dark squares on the walls, and she didn't know what she'd rather have up there, so she hung them back up again, in the hope the posters gave the place more of a homely feel. Even if it was that of someone else's home.

Her previous flat had been furnished too, but it also had cutlery, plates and glasses. Here there was nothing. She kept meaning to buy stuff from the pound shop, so she could have people over, but she never got round to it. Sam had given her a mug when they'd moved out of the Ladbroke Grove flat. It said 'Best Flatmate in the World' and it was that which Elle usually drank out of, either water or cheap Valpolicella from the Costcutter round the corner. She had a vase that she'd filled with flowers every now and again, but the smell when they went off – and they usually did so remarkably fast – was more potent than the fleeting satisfaction of having flowers in her flat, so she stopped bothering after a while. The thick green shagpile carpet, and the boxes of books she'd never unpacked overwhelmed the room, anyway. She'd bought two cushions from Cath Kidston, one floral, one polka dotted, and this was the sum total of her housewarming efforts in four months.

Elle drank some more water, the pounding in her head worse than ever. She knew what she had to do this evening – create some traffic, do something. Ring Karen or Matty or Hester, see what they were up to, fix up a date for drinks. Text Sam – she ought to arrange to see her, though the couple of times since March had been hard work. Or maybe unpack some books, try and settle in, stop pretending this flat was a temporary stopgap. But first, she should start by calling

212

Melissa again. On Saturday, it would actually be two weeks since she'd heard from her. That was unprecedented.

She lay back and took out her phone and there was a text.

I need to speak to you. There's something we need to discuss. Promise, this isn't a ruse. Call me. X

No, Elle thought, staring at Rory's name on the screen. There was an episode of *Sex and the City* that for some reason she kept seeing on Channel 4, about the length of time it takes to get over someone. Half the amount of time you were with them, which was about ten months if you included the period of snogging and tension before they started sleeping together, which meant she still had till about September or October to get to before she'd stop feeling this rubbish. The trouble was, she didn't know what she'd do after that. She clung to her misery, like a safety blanket.

Elle's thumb hovered over his number. Perhaps she should. Perhaps . . .

No. *No.* Elle knew she was pathetic in every other aspect of her life at the moment, she had to hold firm on this. She took a deep breath, and called Melissa again. There was no answer so she got up, wearily, and padded through to the open-plan kitchen in her bare feet. She stared at Jilly and her sunlight and botty babies, and grabbed a bottle of white wine out of the fridge and some Pringles, trying to allay the feeling of loneliness that threatened to overwhelm her. She didn't know what she'd do without a cool glass of wine to welcome her home at the end of the day, the feeling of fuzzy numbness she got after the first. How had she ended up here? It felt all wrong. It was wrong, wasn't it?

Lately Elle thought she could hear the answer: the past few years were just a flicker of fun; this was how it was going to be.

She looked at her watch: just over an hour till *Big Brother*. She could read *The Reluctant Widow* till then. Right. A plan.

She pulled the book out of her bag, along with the folder on Dora Zoffany's backlist. At the top lay her email and the reply from Tom Scott she'd had that afternoon.

I'd be delighted to come in. Looking forward to seeing what you've done. And to catching up. Hope you're enjoying Bookprint. See you next week. Best, Tom.

By the time *Big Brother* started Elle was two glasses of wine down, feeling a lot better about everything. Her headache had almost gone with the second glass. She poured herself another, and deleted Rory's text.

The sky became streaked with pink, and soon the sitting room was half in light, half in black shadow. Elle looked around her in the gathering gloom, at the nearly empty wine bottle, the bent Pringles tube, the old posters silent on the walls. She didn't feel sad. She felt – numb. It occurred to her then that perhaps this was just how it was going to be from now on, and in a way perhaps it was for the best, living alone with no annoyances, no one to hurt you.

'THESE JACKETS ARE awful,' Tom Scott said brusquely, standing upright. He folded his arms. 'I don't understand what you're trying to do with them. Are you trying to sell her to readers of classic English fiction? Or eight-year-old girls who like . . . Princess My Ponies, or whatever it's called?'

Elle bit her lip. 'Well,' she said. 'I think they're beautiful, and all perfectly tailored to the women's fiction market. I think they—'

'But they're all *pink*,' Tom said. A vein was pulsing on his right temple. He put his jacket down on the table and gazed at the offending covers on her desk. Elle hovered behind him. She'd forgotten how tall he was, and how abrupt he could be. Why had she thought this would be an easy meeting? Why? 'Why?' he said, making her jump. 'I mean, why the hell are they pink? Why? I'd never pick that up.'

'Well, it's an extremely crowded –' *Can't say market, said market already. Um . . .* A trickle of sweat ran between Elle's shoulder blades as she looked at the covers, pretending to take them in again. The truth was, she didn't much like them either, but what was she supposed to do about it? In their two-minute lift-waiting conference Celine had failed to mention that the illustrations had already been commissioned and were under way by the time Elle had taken the project over. She got the feeling someone had passed the buck. Onto her.

'It's really important we keep her relevant,' Elle said, trying to pluck some momentum from somewhere, anywhere. 'If we want to sell Dora back into the bookshops it has to be with a new look.' She paused, and added, 'I'm sure you know what I'm talking about though; I don't need to explain it to *you*,' as though they were both basically in agreement. She had learned this at last month's 'Getting to Yes: Managing Authors, Agents and Expectations' course. Bookprint was obsessed with courses and improvement. Barely a week went by when she wasn't being invited to apply for a Job Exchange Programme in New York, or learn about Basic Finance, or Royalty Systems.

'I don't know what you're talking about,' Tom said blankly. 'Look, Elle, I can't force you to change the covers if everyone thinks they're right for the books. But –' He gave a small sad shrug, which Elle found heartbreaking. 'I really don't like them, and I don't think Mum would have either. That's all.'

She knotted her fingers together, helpless in the face of his transparency. 'Right.'

'Don't look so tragic about it.' Tom smiled. She had hardly seen him smile before. It suited him, made his dark, flinty eyes look less severe, his jaw soften. He cleared his throat. 'Look, why don't—'

Elle's mobile rang, buzzing loudly on her desk. She looked down. 'Oh,' she exclaimed. 'Rhodes!'

'Take it,' said Tom, gesturing. 'Don't mind me.'

The phone went dead. 'No, it's fine – he's gone. It's my brother. I've been trying to get hold of him or his fiancée for, like, two weeks. AWOL, both of them.'

'When's the wedding?'

'It's in September. But the hen weekend's next week, and I'm in charge of it. It's going to be nearly a hundred degrees in New York, and Melissa, that's my brother's fiancée, she wants to go shopping and have a picnic in Central Park, and I've never even *been* there before,' Elle said.

'New York's amazing,' Tom said. 'You'll love it.'

'People keep saying that,' Elle said impatiently. 'But I don't know where anything is, and . . .'

She trailed off, aware that there was no reason Tom Scott should be interested in her brother's fiancée's hen weekend.

'I had to organise a stag weekend last month,' he said. 'My best friend from school. We went to Berlin. It was . . . awful.' He blinked. 'There were forfeits. He got dressed up in a gimp mask and bondage outfit, and when he tried to change out of it two of his alleged friends chained him to a lamp post and chucked the key into a river.' He shook his head. 'Maybe I'm just a peculiarly joyless person. But it was – well, it wasn't my cup of tea.'

'I'm with you,' said Elle, on the verge of blurting everything out, but then Tom's phone rang, and his expression changed.

'Oh. Do you mind . . .' He stared at the phone. 'I have to . . . take this . . .' He snatched up the phone. 'Caitlin? Hi. No. Yes. Yes. No, I'm in a meeting.' He shrugged apologetically at Elle, and turned away from her. His voice was low, with a tone in it she'd never heard before. 'I can't talk now. I – I'm sorry. No, I'll call you later. Don't be like that.' He was laughing. 'No! Later!'

He said goodbye and put the phone back in his pocket, then turned around. 'Mobiles, eh? Curse of the modern age.' He smiled awkwardly. 'What did we do before them?'

'I suppose we survived somehow,' Elle said, thinking she'd gladly go without the texting, the desire to check her phone every few minutes to see if he'd texted again, angry when he had, confused when he hadn't. 'I'm bloody glad they weren't around when I was a teenager, that's all. Who's Caitlin, is that your girlfriend?'

217

Tom paused, while Elle screamed inwardly to herself, *Get a frigging grip! What is wrong with you?*

'Oh – her? Caitlin? That?' Tom pulled at his ear. 'No, no! God, no. She's my – we work together. At the bookshop. She's amazing.'

'Right,' said Elle.

'She's not my girlfriend, honestly,' said Tom.

'Hey.' Elle held up her hands. 'None of my business.'

'Well – it's complicated,' Tom said.

'It always is,' said Elle sagely. There was another, awkward pause. 'Anyhoo!' she went on. 'So the bookshop's going well? You don't miss publishing?'

'I don't miss it that much,' he said. 'Sometimes, I suppose.' He smiled, and glanced down at the covers. 'I don't know, I never really fitted in, like a meat eater at a vegetarian society. Scanning parties for the people to talk to, knowing who's who . . .' He ran his hands through his close-cropped dark hair. 'You like all that stuff, you see. I don't.'

Elle flinched a little. She felt it was an implied criticism. 'I – I don't really like all that,' she said. 'I like books, giving people good books to read.' She realised it was true, that she really did, and felt herself blushing. It was that simple, she'd never thought about it before. 'That first night we met – the sales conference? I thought *you* were that person, not me. You were really rude, you know.'

Tom frowned. 'Me? You were terrifying, you were so confident and in control—'

Elle laughed, more out of disbelief than amusement. 'What? You must be thinking of someone else.' She remembered the direness of that evening, how uncomfortable she'd felt, how she'd tried so hard to get Tom and horrible Tony Rooney to talk . . . how the evening had ended . . . *God*, it was a long time ago.

Right on cue, Rory walked past and looked into the office. A couple of times, when Mary had been out, he'd even hesitated, as if he was about to come in. Elle wondered sometimes if he just walked around their floor in a continuous circuit, hoping to bump into her or make eye contact with her. She was waiting for him to make his move.

He saw Tom, and gave a wave.

'It was Rory who was supposed to be dealing with this,' Tom said. 'But then you emailed me. I don't really get it. Though I'm very glad. I'd much rather talk to you than him.'

'Is that because he knows your real name is Ambrose?' Elle spoke without really thinking.

Tom laughed. 'Now I really will have to kill him.' He watched her gazing down the corridor for a moment, then his eyes scanned her face, as if he were making up his mind about something. 'Elle, can I ask you a question? Would you like to go out some time, get a drink?'

Elle was so taken aback she had to replay the sentence immediately in her head, to make sure she'd heard him right. 'Go out – on a date?'

'Well,' said Tom. 'Yes, a date.'

'Oh,' said Elle, unconvinced. 'Well – thanks. But no, thanks.' She shook her head firmly. 'That's really kind of you though.'

'I'm not asking to be kind,' Tom said lightly. 'I'm asking you out because I like you.'

'OK, well, that's kind of you to like me, is what I'm saying.'

'I don't like you to be kind either,' he said.

Elle smiled. She thought she should feel more freaked out than she was, someone just blithely asking her on a date out of the blue: this didn't happen to her. 'Look, that's – great, but I'm not really ready to date anyone. I'm sorry.'

'You're not ready?' Tom studied her carefully. 'Are you one of those fundamentalist Christians? Won't put out without a wedding ring?'

'God, no!' Elle laughed. 'I just broke up with someone. It's been a bit rough. I'm not – back in the zone yet. Sorry.'

'No, I'm sorry,' Tom said instantly. 'I didn't – of course. When?'

'Well,' Elle fidgeted. 'December.' He nodded. 'I'm fine,' she said. 'I maybe – yeah, maybe I should be over it by now. It just – it's too soon, that's all.'

She wasn't quite sure why she was saying no. But it was all so out in the open, so clinical almost, it didn't feel like the beginning of something. Tom didn't say, that's tragic, you should be over it by now. He just nodded, his jaw set, and then he said, 'Well, I hope you're OK. Getting over someone can take over your life, so don't let it.' He looked down at the covers. 'I really hate these. But, like I said, I don't know what I'm talking about, and I'm sure you do.' He picked up his jacket. 'Look, if you want a shoulder to cry on, or anything, or you're in Richmond, come and see the shop. It's great.'

'Loads of MyHeart books in stock, I hope?' Elle tried to sound jaunty.

'Oh, absolutely,' he assured her, a twinkle in his eyes. He stared over her shoulder and then looked intently at her. 'We've got a whole shelf of Georgette Heyers, too.'

Elle followed his gaze and saw a neat pile of three Georgettes on her desk. 'Oh.'

He nodded. 'Great to see you, anyway. Thanks.' He touched his hand to her shoulder briefly and then he was gone.

She watched him, her mind ticking over, and after he'd disappeared at the end of the long corridor, she picked up the printouts of the Dora Zoffany covers and threw them in the bin. He was right, she knew it. She'd get them changed, by hook or by crook, and she knew in a flash exactly how she'd do them. She'd seen a beautiful exhibition at the National Portrait Gallery of black-and-white photos from the thirties. Find something similar, crop them, add bright, citrus, hot type. He was right, his mother's books deserved better, everyone did. As she watched him go, Elle's phone rang again, just as Libby appeared in the door, breathless.

220

'I got it!' she said. 'I got the job swap placement! I'm going to New York! Four months, baby, can you believe it?'

Elle held up her hand. 'That's brill! Just a minute – it's Rhodes. I have to take this, sorry, Libs –' She snatched up the phone. 'Rhodes? Rhodes! Hi! How are you? I've been trying to get hold of you and Melissa for ages! Is everything all right?'

There was a silence, as Libby watched her from the doorway. Elle's face grew pale as she talked to her brother, and when she eventually put the phone down, she rubbed her cheeks and bent forwards, so her head was in her lap.

'No way,' she said, into her skirt. 'No freaking way.'

'What?' said Libby. 'What's happened?'

Elle sat up and swivelled slowly round, so she was facing her. 'They've cancelled the wedding,' she said.

'*What?*'

'The wedding. I *knew* something was up. Rhodes said Melissa's changed her mind, she wants to get married in the States after all.'

'Why though, I mean – wasn't she like some Bridezilla?' Libby looked up and down the corridor, and mouthed *Hi* at someone in the distance.

'She was, yes.' Elle shook her head. 'I don't understand it. I saw her two weeks ago. She was so into the whole thing.' Suddenly, she heard Melissa's voice, outside the tapas place. *If it can't be perfect I don't want to do it at all.* 'She's got slight OCD, I have to admit. But I – I don't know. I thought I was getting to know her a bit.' She remembered something. 'Mum won't be able to go, if they do it in the States.' Suddenly she wished Tom was still here, she'd like to tell him. 'I suppose it makes sense though, in one way.'

Libby sounded slightly impatient, as if she wished she'd taken her good news elsewhere. 'Oh, why?'

'Just – my family. Couldn't picture the wedding photos,' Elle said, and it made a little more sense to her then.

*

When she got back home, late that evening, the clarification she was looking for was waiting for her. Of sorts. There was a letter – she never got post unless it was bills – in turquoise ink. No postmark, no stamp. She opened it, her grimy fingers leaving grey smudges on the white watermarked envelope, as she trudged wearily upstairs, longing for the tiny womb-like room, the sofa, the TV, the bottle of wine in the fridge. It was a printed card.

> Due to circumstances beyond our control, we are cancel-ling the wedding for September 29th. We hope you will understand how greivously we regret this and any expense you have incurred. We are extremely sorry. We remain in love and committed to each other and will be married quietly at a later date. With our apologies once more, Rhodes and Melissa

Upstairs, the light on her answering machine was blinking. She *never* had any messages. She played it, her heart thumping.

You have two new messages. First message.

'Elle? It's me. Listen. Don't believe what they say, if they ring you. Jus . . . don't believe them. They lying.'

There was a crackle on the line and a fumbling sound.

'Listen to me. OK? OK. Mum loves you . . . she loves you, Ellie. So ring me, give me a ring, ring a ring ding a ring.'

Second message.

'Elle? It's your father. Hope you're well . . . Uhm, yes. I wanted to know whether, since the wedding's cancelled, you'll be able to request a refund for the flight to New York? Can you call me, please. Yes. Bye – bye then.'

Elle looked around for her wine mug, and headed towards the fridge. She heard her mother's voice, her old cry of 'Leave me ALONE!' She wished she could ring them back, all of them, and just this once, say the same thing to all of them.

TWO DAYS LATER, Elle woke with a raging, deadening hangover to the sounds of Kilburn on a sweltering Saturday morning and the smell from the rancid greasy spoon across the road.

Her head was pounding. Her mouth tasted like the bottom of a rubbish bin. She lay there with her aching eyes half opened. Someone was playing 'Life is a Roller Coaster' extremely loudly nearby.

Elle rolled over, feeling a wave of nausea hit her. It was hot, the room was tiny, the purple blinds cast a lurid glow into the raspberry-coloured room. She opened one eye and closed it again. The walls looked as if they would close in on her. She tried not to gag.

I have to get out of here, she thought. She had spent the last two nights in by herself. She wanted to talk to someone, and everyone was away. Eventually she'd tried Karen, even though she knew she was on holiday with her boyfriend in Greece, but it was hard to have a chat with someone when they were on their mobile in a restaurant eating meze. All Elle wanted was someone to reel with. She was still reeling from it herself. That's why she supposed she'd drunk so much. She hadn't meant to.

Elle stumbled unwillingly from her bed, the vice-like grip on her head tightening as she stood up. She ran the shower till it was steaming hot, even though the weather outside almost equalled it. She'd found lately that a hot shower was the best cure for a hangover. That, and peppermint scrub from the Body Shop. As she stood under the wonky shower head that bloomed with limescale, scrubbing her hair and trying not to taste the tang of sour wine at the back of her throat, she vowed not to drink today. It was having a bottle open, that was the trouble – it was there, it was cool, and the last forty-eight hours had been rough.

She'd spent the last two days fielding calls from irate brides-maids, icy hoteliers, and alternately defensive and furious parents. The woman at Virgin almost laughed when Elle rang to ask if she could simply get her money back on the cancelled flight to New York.

'Madam, that's not our policy,' she'd said.

Elle couldn't help feeling sad she wasn't going to New York. She'd been so looking forward to it. She would never have told her, because Libby clearly didn't think she cared about work any more, but Elle was secretly quite jealous of her and her job swap to Bookprint US, though of course she was pleased for Libby. Libby was so on edge lately, so desperate for . . . something, the opposite of Elle, who these days was content to float along, like a pathetic piece of driftwood in a river. Perhaps it was the heat.

Her father was furious at the cancelled flight, told her she should have tried to reschedule it for another time. 'Four hundred and sixty pounds, Elle, I spent on your air fare. I'm not saying I shouldn't have done it. I was glad to help. It's just – well, what a waste. When I think about what we could have done . . .'

Elle tried to never feel resentful of Eliza, Jack and Alice, her father's new family. It was so different from her life with her father that she tried to separate it out. But there were

224

times like now when she wanted to scream at him, to shout, *'I wish you'd never offered in the first place. I wish you had spent the money on Alice's bloody skiing holiday or Jack's sodding new clarinet that he'll play once and give up like he did the violin and the frigging piano. It's not my fault!'*

'I know, Dad,' she'd said, biting her lip. 'Hey, did you say you were thinking of coming up one Sunday to help me put up some shelves?'

'Yes, yes,' said John impatiently, then his voice softened. 'Yes, that could be good. I'll have a look for some dates. We can discuss it all then.' He paused. 'Have you spoken to your mother?'

Her mother denied all knowledge of it.

'I got the note too. Mad. I've no idea what they're talking about,' she'd said, sounding astonished, when Elle finally rang her the night after she'd got the card. 'I never liked her, you know. Always thought she was batty. Don't tell anyone that.'

'When they came to stay, did anything . . .' Elle trailed off.

'Did anything what?' Her mother sounded sharp. 'I didn't do anything. I thought we had a lovely weekend. I was out with Bryan and Anita most of the time, discussing the textiles business. It's very busy at the moment. You know we're going to India in October.'

'Oh, right,' said Elle, struggling to remember what she was talking about and not wanting to ask when her mother was in a mood like this. 'How's that going?'

'Good, but I'm very busy with it. So I suppose I didn't see much of them. Yes, we had a bit of rowdy conversation on Saturday night, but it wasn't a row. It was just what you do, over supper, you know?'

'About what?' Elle said.

'Oh, do you know I can't even remember? America, maybe. She was being so patronising, telling me why America was

225

so great. I think I put her straight on a few facts. Oh, maybe she didn't like it.' Mandana sounded uncertain. 'Elle, I don't want you to think I did anything – I wouldn't – Oh, dear. Oh, dear – I really think I must have upset her. And I don't understand how.'

'I don't know, Mum,' Elle said, realising she sounded genuinely upset. She couldn't bear to see her like that again, knitting her fingers together the way she did when Rhodes came up, desperately trying to please him, placate Melissa, do the right thing, be the mother everyone wanted her to be. She pushed the sound of her mother's drunk voice on the answering-machine message out of her head. It was a one-off, she was sure, perhaps she wasn't even drunk anyway, Elle was just looking out for it. 'Don't worry, Mum. I'm sure it wasn't that. I don't know what she's talking about.'

In fact, as she got dressed, she decided she had to put all of them out of her head. Let Rhodes and Melissa go off and do their own thing; she'd had enough of leaving multiple phone messages, sending emails, trying to track them down. Let her father rant down the phone at someone else. Let her mother hang out with bloody Bryan and Anita and drink herself stupid. She was sick of the lot of them.

Ten invigorating minutes later, Elle got out of the shower, and put on her new black long linen skirt, struggling to get the zip up – how could she have put on weight when she'd eaten virtually nothing but Pringles the last few days? – her duck-egg blue vest top with lace trim – a triumph from the Whistles sale – and black flip-flops. She threw a thin black cardigan over her tanned shoulders – she'd been sunbathing a lot lately out on the kitchen roof of the flat. It was dangerous to climb onto but lovely once you were out there, hours of lying in the sun like a cat, drinking chilled rose and reading whatever Georgette Heyer she'd got to. You could waste away a whole summer like that.

She slung her bag over one shoulder, shoved her book and her purse, her Walkman and her phone and keys into it, popped her sunglasses on, and headed out onto the street.

There is something about being on your own during boiling hot weather that is much worse than being alone on a cold winter's evening, when you can be snuggled up on the sofa with a hot-water bottle, a glass of red, a gas fire and some comforting TV. When it's 30 degrees out you should be lying in a park with all your friends or your boyfriend, drinking Pimm's and eating snacks from Sainsbury's. Elle walked down Kilburn High Road, feeling the oily, dirty heat soak into her freshly scrubbed skin. She wished she could inhale some sweet, clean air. The street was crowded with shoppers, piling into crap Primark and Peacocks, standing outside the pub laughing, pulling kids and shopping bags along. Everyone was with someone.

She bought a can of Coke and headed towards the train station. Without really thinking about it, when a train arrived she got on it. She sat on the sweltering, graffiti-laced carriage as it trundled through town, and when she got to Richmond she looked around her and realised she didn't know where she was going. Perhaps she should get on the train again and go back. No. She got off the train and scanned a map.

Five minutes later, still trying to channel the casual 'Yeah, I've just popped over here for a day out' feeling she'd persuaded herself into, she walked through the open door of a cool, dark shop. A young man was at the till, his dark head bent over, checking off a list.

'Hi,' said Elle. 'Is Tom around?'

'Sorry?' The young man looked up and Elle saw it was a young woman, with a gamine, chic bobbed crop. Elle fidgeted with her own messy hair.

'Oh. Sorry – oh. I was just wondering where Tom was? I'm a – I'm a friend of his.'

The girl – who was very beautiful, and wearing a floral

top, Elle saw now, how could she have thought she was a man, much less that a man could have shoulders as slim as that and be wearing gold earrings? – put two fingers in her mouth and whistled. 'Tom!' she called. 'Someone here to see you.' Elle stared at her, impressed. 'Cheaper than an intercom,' she explained.

Tom appeared, framed in a doorway behind the till. He had a pencil behind his ear, and his sleeves were rolled up. 'Elle!' he exclaimed, coming forward. 'What a nice surprise. What are you doing here?' He kissed her. She noticed the freckles on his nose, slight sunburn on his face.

'It's so hot, I thought I'd treat myself to a day out of Kilburn,' Elle explained, pleased at how normal this sounded, because now she was here she felt she'd made a mistake. 'Work off a bit of the hangover, have a walk by the river, you know.'

'Well, I'm very glad you did,' he said.

There was an awkward pause. 'I'll just have a look round, shall I?' said Elle, now embarrassed. 'Came to see the bookshop, get some books, it's my mother's birthday, you know.' In February. She shook her head. 'Um –'

'OK,' said Tom. He glanced at her again, with a strange look in his eyes. 'Well, that's great. Do you want to get a drink afterwards? I'm off this afternoon, done my shift. We could –' He hesitated, looked swiftly back at the girl behind the till. 'Look, let me know when you've finished.'

The girl said, 'Tom, if you're going to go, go now. Remember Mervyn Thacker's coming in around lunch to talk about his event.'

Tom winced visibly. 'Oh, my God, thanks, Caitlin.' He turned to Elle. 'Shall we go?'

'Let's,' said Elle gratefully. 'Thanks,' she said to Caitlin.

'Elle, this is Caitlin. She runs the shop. She's the reason we make any money at all.' He squeezed Caitlin's shoulder. 'Bye, C. See you later.'

As they left the shop, Elle turned to look at Caitlin once more, mesmerised by her dark, almond-shaped eyes, her low, husky voice. She was watching them leave.

'There was a lunatic author we published at Bluebird called Mervyn Thacker,' Elle said. 'He wrote this book all about the real message of the Rosetta Stone. He was mad. Kept ringing up Joseph Mile and telling him that there were runes on the Pyramids that reflected markings on the surface of Mars and why wouldn't anyone listen to him.'

'Well, you're bang on the money,' Tom said. 'He lives in Richmond. He's written a sequel to the book about the Pyramids and published it himself and he wants to have the launch party at Dora's.'

'You called the bookshop Dora's.' Elle had seen the sign outside. 'That's so nice.'

'Well, my mum loved reading, and it's a good name.' He smiled, and rotated his head around his shoulders, as if he were tired. 'Plus the publicity doesn't hurt. That's the terrible thing.'

'You're a true salesman,' Elle said.

'I love it, it's strange,' Tom said. 'When I was an agent I hated trying to get people to buy books I wasn't sure about. Even when my clients wrote books I actually liked I always assumed I must be wrong and they'd never find a publisher. It's much easier when you're selling books. You don't feel as much pressure. I've read this book, I love it, I can hand-on-heart recommend it, promise, money back if you don't agree with me.' He paused and gave her a curious look. 'Elle, I hope you don't mind me saying it, but you're practically green. Are you all right?'

Elle coughed, and then laughed. 'Thanks. I'm fine. I just need a hangover cure, that's all. Or maybe another drink.'

'Oh-ho,' Tom said. 'Big night last night?'

Elle shook her head. 'Well . . . sort of.'

He chuckled. 'So, tell me all. I stayed in last night and made some pasta. Make me jealous.'

229

'Um – there's nothing to be jealous of.'

'I see.' His eyes gleamed. 'You were out on the lash, what on earth did you get up to? Come on.'

She said, almost crossly, 'I stayed in and drank a bottle of wine by myself, Tom. That's what I did.'

'Oh, right,' said Tom.

Elle was annoyed, and she flushed. She added, 'That's partly why I came here, actually.'

'Oh, yes? Why?' Tom steered her down a side street.

'Well, I don't know why, but I wanted to tell you, it's probably boring, and –' It sounded so pathetic now. 'All my friends are away, you see. And I kept thinking you'd get it. Don't know why but that you would. After our chat about weddings.'

She couldn't see his face, he was looking down the street. 'What's happened?'

'The wedding's off. My brother's wedding, you know,' she added.

His face was blank for one second, and then it cleared. 'The one who rang you? To the crazy American? It's cancelled? No way.'

They emerged from the shady lane onto the river bank, lined with trees, a field in the distance, the beautiful white stone Richmond Bridge to the side. Boats and ferries slid slowly through the water, and on the bank people lounged outside the pub, holding glasses of Pimm's and chatting, laughing, the smell of cigarette smoke, barbecue and green grass in the air. Elle looked around, and drew in her breath.

'Oh, it's lovely,' she said.

'I'll get you a drink, and you can tell me all about it,' said Tom. 'What do you want?'

Elle took a deep breath, telling herself she should just have an orange juice. 'Think it has to be Pimm's,' she heard herself say. 'The fruit will do me good, anyway.'

'Very true,' said Tom. 'Grab a seat, I'll be back in a minute.'

*

There were swans on the river, the sky was blue, all she could see were pretty nice things, and there was something about Tom, Elle felt she could tell him anything. On their third Pimm's, she said, 'I didn't come here because you asked me out, you know.'

Tom choked on a piece of cucumber. 'Wow,' he said, coughing, as Elle handed him a glass of something. 'That's someone's beer. I'm OK.' He coughed again. 'You are a strange girl, you know that?'

Elle stared at her drink, holding the plastic pint in her fingers, wondering as she always did how tight you'd have to squeeze it before it cracked. 'I know I am,' she said.

'I don't mean it like that,' Tom said. 'Honestly. I wish I'd never done it. It wasn't supposed to be that big a deal, just more a – hey, let's go for a drink. I wasn't . . . asking you out.'

'Oh. Yeah, I know,' Elle said, turning her head away. 'Just wanted to make it clear it wasn't a problem.'

'Let's stop talking about it,' Tom said. 'I'm sorry, again.'

'Very good idea,' Elle said, with relief. She bowed. 'Good to sort it out.'

He bowed back. 'I concur.'

There was a pause.

'So, Caitlin seems nice,' she said, and then bit her lip.

'Er, yes.'

Elle was determined to remove any awkward date element of their . . . drink, she supposed it was to be called now. 'You like her, don't you?'

'I do.' Tom looked out at the river. 'But she's slightly crazy. I don't know if I can deal with it.'

Elle watched him, saw the curled vein at his temple begin to pulse, and thought how much younger he looked out of a suit.

'So there is something going on with you two, then,' she said.

The rather harsh lines of his face relaxed. 'She's – I've known her for ages. We've been – well, it sounds a bit rubbish, when I asked you out, but we were seeing a bit of each other, earlier in the summer.' He slapped his hand against one cheek, shook his head quickly, sharply. 'But there's still this ex-boyfriend, Jean-Claude, hanging around. I mean, they split up but she still sees him.' He smiled, and she wanted to pat his shoulder, he looked so young, so sweet. He shook his head. 'Forget it. I've said too much already.'

'It's fine,' Elle said. 'Go on, please.'

'She seems to like it, the drama, the games. I –' His face was rigid, his jaw set. 'I don't, I've never been any good at it.' He gave a mocking half-smile. 'So I'm sure I'll screw it up at some point soon. I just wish I knew more.'

'Knew more about what?'

'Whether it's the circumstances that are the problem, or whether we're just not right for each other. Whether it's just the working together that makes us closer.'

'It's not,' Elle said, her heart in her throat. 'You spend all that time together, but it's not real time, it's work time.'

'How are you so sure?'

'I –' Elle faltered.

'Oh,' he said apologetically. 'I remember, you just broke up with someone. Forget it. I just want someone who knows, to tell me what to do.'

'I'll tell you, I'll tell you you should be careful.' Elle swallowed.

'How do you know?'

She took a deep breath; she felt reckless, she couldn't go back now. 'I had a – I was with Rory.' She still didn't know how to refer to it. 'An affair.' It sounded so lame. 'I had an affair with Rory.'

'You and *Rory*?' he said sharply.

She nodded.

'Seriously?' They were sitting at two corners of a table,

facing the river, but he sat up and looked at her, and cleared his throat. 'How long? Elle, I didn't know, I –' He rubbed his head again. 'Jesus. That's who you were talking about, when you said you'd split up from someone?'

'It's OK.' She hugged herself. 'No one knew. No one really knows now. It was – over a year, on and off. Started before that. The first night I met you, actually.' Suddenly, talking about it like this, she felt she was going to cry.

'So when did you split up?'

'Um – just before Christmas. Yeah.' She drained her drink. 'When everything happened with the sale.'

'Because of the sale?'

She screwed up her eyes. 'Sort of. More the – the whole th-thing. The lying to his mother, to everyone. He stood there and told us there wouldn't be a sale, and then he went behind his mother's back, sold us all down the river. It's weird,' she said. 'I was so in love with him. I still love that Rory. And there's this whole other person he is, too, who it means I just can't be with. Sounds crazy.'

'No, it doesn't, I know what you mean.' Tom stared at her, his eyes searching her face. 'I'm sorry. Oh, Elle. Well, he's paying for it now, he's absolutely sinking without trace at Bookprint. I heard Bill's looking to get rid of him by the end of the year. Oh, Elle,' he said again. 'You're well off out of it.' He laughed, a short, angry sound. 'God, why is it lovely girls like you fall for total wankers like Rory?'

'You don't know him,' she said. 'I wasn't blind to his faults, but – there's more to him.' She thought of his smiling eyes, the way he'd tickle her feet, how safe she felt in his arms, with her head on his chest. She couldn't explain it, not to anyone. She hardly believed it had happened herself.

Tom took a gulp from his drink. 'Are you still in love with him?' he asked flatly.

'No.'

He raised an eyebrow. 'Seriously?'

'I don't know.' Elle turned away from him and stared out at the water. 'Maybe, yes.'

'I wish you hadn't said that.'

'Why?' she asked, not really listening, still thinking about Rory's face, the day before, in the covers meeting, as Bill had torn a strip off him about the new Paris Donaldson jacket. Tom was still looking at her, and she realised it and faced him again. 'Sorry, where were we?'

He got up. 'Hey,' he said. 'Doesn't matter. Shall we get some food? It's nearly three. You don't have to rush off anywhere, do you?'

'No,' she said, getting up and shaking her head. 'Absolutely not. I might even have another drink.'

He laughed. 'You said earlier you were never drinking again.'

'Well, I'm changing my mind.'

ON THE WAY to the train station much later that evening, after pizza and a lot of wine, sitting outside in a shady courtyard off Richmond Green, Elle realised something.

'It's weird, I don't know anything about you,' she said.

Tom stopped walking. 'What are you talking about? We just spent the whole day together.'

'Yes, but we drank loads and chatted about – I don't know what we chatted about,' she said. Her parents? His parents? Rory? Work? Books? They'd definitely talked about all of that, but she couldn't remember what they'd said, or why. They'd talked, and laughed, and the sun had set, and now she couldn't remember any of it.

'I like conversations like that,' Tom said. 'Much less hard work. With Vicky, my ex, it was like pulling teeth sometimes. We had loads in common but we just didn't see the world in the same way.' He stopped. 'Oh, that was good. I should write it down.' He got out his phone.

'You're writing that down?'

'Yep,' Tom said, fiddling with his phone. 'I'm going to text myself. Oh, I can't. I'll text it to you, can you text it to me?'

She stared at him, trying not to laugh. 'Wow.'

'Right.' Tom put his phone away, as hers buzzed in her bag.

'You are weird, do you know that,' she said. 'Most of the time you're almost normal, but occasionally your super-weird side comes out. Maybe when you're drunk.'

'That's nice to know,' he said equably. 'You too, if I may say.'

'I'm not weird,' Elle said defensively.

'I mean in a good way. All the best people are.' He swallowed, as if he was thinking carefully. Elle saw he was a bit drunk. 'You've got staying power. Like with the Georgette Heyers. Reading all of them, getting obsessive about them. And you know, much better to be obsessed with crummy romance books than, er – hard-core porn, or something.'

She looked at him. 'Well, yes, that's true. How about you?'

'Me?' Tom wrinkled his nose, and put his hands in his jeans pockets, rocking slightly on the empty pavement. 'Me? Nothing. Nothing. Well, I really loved Pulp. Loved them. Love them still. Got every album and used to keep a book with a note of where they got to in the charts each week.' He was grinning, but he couldn't look at her. 'Album and single. Still got it. And a chart of who was connected to who. Every record Jarvis makes. Or Richard Hawley. Got them all.'

'OK then,' said Elle.

'Let me see, what else. Oh, Sherlock Holmes? I've read every Sherlock Holmes story about ten times. Some of them more. I know everything there is to know about them. Test me.'

'I believe you.'

'Test me! Go on!'

'Oh. Right then. What was the name of the hound of the Baskervilles?'

Tom looked at her pityingly. 'He didn't have a name.'

'Anything else, then?' Elle said. 'Any other weird thing you do?'

'I used to throw things into waste-paper bins. When my mum was ill. Five, ten times a day. If it landed in the bin I'd say she'd get better. If it didn't go into the bin I had to throw something till it did.'

Elle nodded.

'She didn't get better. So it didn't work. I told her, she said it was good to try anything. I never knew if it was, though. I should have been doing other things, trying to make her proud, not playing these stupid mind games with myself while she was . . . so bad.'

She wished she could put her arms round him, give him a hug, but she was suddenly shy. 'Where are you going now?' she said, after a few moments. 'I don't even know where you live.'

'I'm only ten minutes' walk that way. Um –' Tom looked at his watch. 'Wow. It's late. I might –'

'Don't go and see Caitlin,' Elle said suddenly, and then wished she hadn't. His face froze with that old look of formal, cold distance she knew so well. He carried on walking, and then stopped and turned.

'Why? Don't you want me to?' he asked.

'No! I think she's using you. To make Jean-Claude jealous. That's all.' She nudged him. 'Hey, what's up?'

'I can't tell you,' he said. 'It sounds too strange. You wouldn't understand.'

He was looking at her with his dark eyes, his expression deadly serious. Elle felt nervous, and then he moved towards her and she suddenly panicked. He wasn't going to . . . was he?

Tom put his hand on her shoulder. 'I'm drunk, sorry,' he said, and then he leaned forward and kissed her. Elle felt his long fingers on her shoulders, his breath against her mouth. He smelt of something spicy, wine, sweat. His lips on hers were hard, yet smooth; the stubble on his chin rasped on her skin. He pressed against her, fiercely, gripping her, and then, after a few moments, released her, almost pushing her away. She had her hands on his arms, and she clung onto him, momentarily, before letting go, stepping back, breathing heavily.

'I shouldn't have done that,' he said curtly. 'Too much to drink. Sorry. I just –'

'It's OK,' said Elle.

He swore under his breath and she was mortified; he was obviously regretting it.

They looked at each other. 'Well,' Tom said. 'This is awkward, isn't it? Forgive me. I wish we could forget it. Taking advantage of you.'

Elle couldn't help laughing, even as she pressed her hand to her chest, where her heart was hammering. 'Honestly, it's fine,' she said. 'I'm a big girl, Tom. I'm not going to collapse in a dead faint. We're – we're friends, aren't we?'

She reached out and gently touched his hand. He took a deep breath and looked at her, his eyes searching her face, in the dark passageway.

'Aren't we?' she repeated.

When he spoke, his voice was light again. 'If you can get over this embarrassing solecism on my part and the fact that I collect Sherlock Holmes memorabilia, then yeah.' He nodded. 'That'd be great.'

'I wanted to go and see *The Royal Tenenbaums* some time next week. You around, you fancy going?'

'That'd be great,' he said.

She looked at her watch. 'I'd better go, I'll miss the last train.'

They walked side by side, in silence, towards the station. Black cab engines juddered in the rank next to them, and a train pulled in behind them.

'Bye,' she said. 'I should go. Thanks for today, Tom, it was brilliant.' She paused, realising she meant it. She'd forgotten about her tedious, boring self for a good few hours.

'Yes,' said Tom. 'And Elle – look after yourself.'

He drew her towards him and put his arms round her. Elle leaned against him for a moment, the familiar scent of him, the comfort of another person. He squeezed her tight. She could feel his fingers, splayed out on her back. Suddenly she wanted to sob.

'Thanks for today,' she said. She cleared her throat. 'And for trying to be nice, you know, warning me off Rory. And for kissing me.'

'Thanks for warning me off Caitlin too, I can't talk either,' he said, almost flippantly. 'But – yes. I'll see you soon.' He laughed, and she turned and walked towards the ticket barrier.

On the train home, Elle took out her phone. She wasn't going to ring Rory but she might just text him. She unlocked the phone and there was a text, but it was from Tom, she'd forgotten.

We had loads in common but we just didn't see the world in the same way.

Even though it was after eleven, the night was hot and sticky as day. Elle sat on the rickety train staring at the screen, her head and heart pounding.

AUGUST IS SUPPOSED to be a quiet month, when everyone is either away or using the fact that everyone else is away to do nothing. Elle was looking forward to a few weeks of gentle stupor, no wedding plans, getting on with some more Georgette, sunbathing outside, doing not that much, when all of a sudden, several bombshells exploded.

The first – and second, really – was Libby. She burst into Elle's office, a couple of weeks after Elle's day in Richmond. Elle was chewing a pencil and supposedly editing a manuscript, though actually she was replying to an email from Tom about seeing *Moulin Rouge*. He wasn't keen, and she was trying to persuade him, without much luck.

> OK. How about we go to that Japanese place on Kingly Street FIRST, then you can drink all the sake you want and be pleasantly drunk by the time we sit down to MR?
>
> Oh, by the way, some new rough covers for your mother's books have come in and I think they're a vast improvement on the pinky cartoons. Can I bring them—

Elle was chewing her pencil because she and Tom had met up again, for a drink and a pizza, plus they were emailing and texting regularly. Now they were friends, it seemed weird to bring up work in an otherwise jokey email. It made her feel awkward, she didn't know why.

'Can you come outside with me?' Libby said dramatically.

Elle looked at her watch. She didn't want to cut into her *Devil's Cub* reading time. It was obvious Vidal was about to realise he was in love with Mary Challoner, even though she'd shot him in the previous chapter – but then she saw Libby's face, and stood up.

'Sure, what's happened?'

Libby mimed a zip across her lips and nodded in Mary's direction. They went outside, into the dusty street; Libby fumbled for a cigarette and lit it. Two Italian Goths walked past, chattering loudly, but otherwise the square was deserted. Everyone was away.

'Are you OK?' Elle asked.

'I can't go to New York any more,' Libby replied, inhaling smoke.

'What?' Elle was surprised. 'Why?'

'Well . . . Look, there's something I haven't told you.' Libby inhaled again, shuddering in horror like a thirties stage actress in her boudoir confronted with a sub-standard bouquet. Elle waited patiently.

'If I tell you, you mustn't tell anyone. *Anyone.*'

'Of course,' said Elle.

'It's Bill.'

'Who?' said Elle stupidly.

'Bill Lewis? Our boss?' Libby said furiously. 'The head of the division?'

'Oh, him. What about him?'

'We're having an affair.' Libby added, as if to confirm this, 'It's serious.'

Elle dropped her security pass on the floor. 'What the – what? But he's *married*!' she blurted, picking it up. 'He's got kids!'

Libby stared at Elle as if she'd just shot her. 'Oh, thanks. Like I didn't know that. You don't understand. It's *serious*. He's going to leave her. Like, soon.'

'What?' Elle was so surprised she barely knew what to say. 'Really?'

'Oh, my God, I wish I hadn't told you,' Libby said furiously. 'I knew you'd be all judgemental on me.' She inhaled again, and looked directly at her. Her eyes were red. 'God, Elle. As if you didn't do the same thing yourself.'

'That's different,' Elle said, and then wished she hadn't.

'It's not different.'

'He wasn't married!' Elle shouted. 'He didn't have children! A baby!'

'Right.' Libby blew smoke out, hissing maliciously, 'Course. It was fine. You didn't hurt anyone, did you? You didn't, for example, get a job out of it while everyone else with years of experience got left to starve in the snow.'

Elle swallowed, wishing for the umpteenth time that she'd never told Libby about Rory. She thought now that she'd been trying to draw Libby back to her, like a wife buying new underwear to thrill a straying husband. But their friendship had changed. She didn't know when it had begun but she suddenly realised the change could be characterised by Libby's reaction that night when she'd told her about Rory. An amused, almost annoyed detachment, as though she was trying to say, *'You're not the one who goes off with the MD, Elle. You're the one in the background. Wait and see. I am.'* Perhaps that was unfair. Elle remembered Tom's dark, sympathetic face as she had told him, his anger on her behalf, and turned back to Libby, biting her lip.

'Right,' she said. 'Look, Libby –'

Libby shook her head, her voice low. 'God, I'm sorry, I'm sorry,' she said. She pulled Elle towards her and hugged her. 'That's a horrible thing to say. It's not true. I'm a bitch. I'm a bitch, I hate myself, it's just it's not . . .'

She started crying and Elle hugged her back, trying not to sneeze at the cigarette smoke wafting up her nose. Libby was sobbing loudly, and Elle looked round instinctively, to make sure no one was watching. 'Sshh,' she said.

'I don't want to sshh,' Libby wept, phlegm gurgling at the back of her throat. 'Sometimes I think I hate him,' she added, and then she said, softly, as if to herself, 'How did I get myself into this mess? How?'

Elle felt a rush of sympathy for her; she'd never seen Libby this upset before, about anything. She was brutal with men; they were never good enough for her, right enough, important enough. And she'd always had a thing for men in power, men who were recognised at parties. They used to joke about it, when they were secretaries giggling opposite each other like idiots. *Oh, Libby. I loved you so much.* 'How long?' asked Elle, patting her shoulder.

'Eighteen months.' Elle tried not to look surprised. 'Ages really. And oh, you won't understand, but it's amazing. We're in love, properly in love, and it's just so hard –'

It was so familiar. 'So what's happened?' Elle asked, squeezing her shoulder. 'Why can't you go to New York?'

'Because Celine's found out about us.'

'How? Who told her?'

Libby bared her teeth. 'I don't know. If I find out I'm going to kill them. She just called me in to see her.'

'Wow. Scary.'

'She was scary. She says Bill put me up for the job-exchange programme because of our . . .' she hesitated, '*relationship*, and I said, no, that's not true, we want to spend every minute together, so why would he do that? Anyway, she says I've to stay here, that I can't go because it's not been done through due process.' Libby snarled, showing her tiny white teeth. 'She's such a bitch. I could . . . I could strangle her. Due process. I mean, what does that even bloody well mean? *I'm* the best! Everyone knows that. I should go.'

Elle nodded. 'Celine loves due process, though. She's a bit like Elspeth's more glamorous French daughter.'

Libby laughed, for the first time, and wiped her nose on the back of her hand. 'You're right. Only Elspeth didn't reckon herself and march around in tiny Agnès B size six suits, the bitch. Elspeth, eh. I wonder where she is now. And Felicity. I miss her.' She smiled. 'Gosh, Bluebird. It seems years ago, doesn't it? You and me, reading out the rude bits in the Abigail Barrows.'

Elle handed her a paper napkin from Pret she had in her pocket and Libby blew her nose, noisily. 'He says he's going to leave her,' Libby said. 'I don't know if I believe him any more though. But now Celine's found out, he says it takes time, we have to handle it carefully . . .'

Elle nodded sympathetically.

Libby's voice was soft. 'And he says . . . I know it's hard for him . . . but it's hard for me too, you know? And they're not happy, I know they're not. I just feel my life's on hold. New York was going to be a sort of fresh start. A chance for him to miss me.' She stared fiercely at Elle. 'He's got to miss me, then he'll realise that he can't live without me. He was going to come out and stay with me in my place, it'd have been the first time we were together properly . . . And that bitch has stopped it. I want to kill her.'

Elle felt so sad, though she knew that was hypocritical. It struck her again that's what had happened with her and Rory; she'd put her life on hold, and it was still going on.

We had loads in common but we just didn't see the world in the same way.

Libby took a long drag on her cigarette. 'I wasn't even that desperate to go, you know,' she said unconvincingly. 'But it's just the way she said it: "Yoo arrr not sue-tihbull for zis progrrammuh,"' Libby drawled, with an exaggerated accent. 'In such a nasty way, like I was an unclean woman and that if I went to New York I'd bring down the whole US operation with my foul cheating British ways. Screw her. It's for the best. Yeah.' She threw the cigarette on the pavement, and ground it with her Topshop flat that they'd bought together last week.

'That's the spirit,' Elle said.

'Right.' Libby rallied. Her shoulders rose. 'Like I say, actually it's probably a good thing. And Bill and I can work out what's going on.' She kissed Elle's cheek. 'Thanks, Elle. You're a good lass.'

An idea occurred to Elle. 'Libs – is the space free again? To go to New York?'

'Why, do you want to go?' Libby smiled. It wasn't a full smirk, but a sort of half-smile.

'Er, yeah,' said Elle, who hadn't really given it serious thought up to this point. 'Would you mind?'

'Of *course* not!' Libby said, but Elle didn't entirely believe her. It was probably a stupid idea. In any case, now wasn't the time to have asked. She nodded thanks and then gave her a hug.

'Wow, Libby. What a – good grief.'

'Do you hate me?' Libby said tentatively. 'I hate me. I – oh, it's all so awful. And I'm twenty-eight next week . . .' She sniffed, tears coming into her eyes. 'I feel so *old*, oh, God, so bloody *old*.'

Elle hid a smile; she didn't want Libby to think she was laughing at her. 'You're not old,' she said. 'Don't be insane.'

'Will you come for drinks next week? Promise? Because I was going to do something at the Crown and Bill said I shouldn't, and now I think I should. You know. Show Bill, Celine, all of them. *"Tell them, Julian, all, I am not doomed to wear / Year after year –"'*

'*"In gloom and desolate despair"*,' Elle finished for her. 'No, that's not the best bit. The best bit *is "And visions rise and change, that kill me with desire / Desire for nothing known in my maturer years –"'*

Libby joined in, clutching her hands to her chest. '"*When Joy grew mad with awe, at counting future tears*",' they chorused.

'Oh, Emily!' Libby said, leaning against the building. 'My favourite Brontë, my favourite. I'd forgotten that one. You know, my mum's from Haworth,' she mused. 'I sometimes think, perhaps her great-great-great grandad—'

'Saw Emily and Charlotte playing in the vicarage,' Elle finished. 'Yes, I know.'

'Or—'

'Had a sneaky tobacco chew with Bramwell,' Elle parroted. 'Yes, yes. I still prefer Charlotte, you know. She wasn't so intense. What about poor Anne?'

'You know I don't care about poor Anne,' Libby said, and sniffed. 'Aw, thanks, Elle.' She put her arm round her and gave a big, trembling sigh. 'I feel much better.'

Elle stroked her hair, remembering how much she missed Libby, how much she had once loved her.

'It'll be OK,' she said. 'You poor thing. I know it feels like it won't, but it will, one day. He's not the man for you.'

'He is,' Libby said weakly. 'Honestly he is.'

'OK, OK,' Elle said softly. 'Maybe he is. But I bet there's someone else just as wonderful out there for you. Don't let this flatten you, Libs.'

'Who, then?' Libby said.

'Don't know, but he's out there. You don't go into publishing to meet eligible men, that's the trouble.' She wondered about Tom for a second, whether he and Libby might work together? Could she see them as a couple? She shook her head, wishing she was the kind of person who could insouciantly bring people together over wine-splattered dinner parties from the *River Café Cookbook* with the Buena Vista Social Club in the background, and then dismissed the idea.

'Urgh.' Libby's shoulders slumped. 'I hate the fact that it obsesses me so much,' she said, sounding normal again. 'You know, I did my bloody MA on Elizabethan women who demanded to choose their husbands. It really annoys me, that it's basically the same thing today. Who're we going to end up with?'

'It's not the same thing today,' said Elle, shocked. 'Not at all.'

'It kind of is. It's a race, and everyone else is on the tracks, and I'm at the wrong venue, with the wrong shoes on.'

She looked so sad, Elle said again, 'That's rubbish. He's out there, I promise.'

'How do you know?'

'I don't,' said Elle firmly. 'I just like to kid myself that he is. And if he's not, well, there's more to life than just hanging around ruining your life waiting for him.' Perhaps she was starting to believe this. 'Much more.'

'WHAT ARE ALL these posters up for?' Elle's dad asked. 'They're not . . . *yours*, are they?'

He looked suspiciously at his daughter, as if she'd been hiding a thirty-year career in theatre management from him.

'No, Dad,' Elle had patiently. 'They're Billy's. My landlord.'

'They look awful,' said John.

'Oh.' Elle had stopped noticing them, for the most part. 'Well, we could take some down for you to put up the shelves. As long as I store them properly Billy said he didn't mind what I did with them.'

'Don't you have any nice book posters you want to put up?' her dad asked, rolling his sleeves. Elle watched him, transfixed, as he meticulously turned the two-inch cuff over and over again, folding it neatly above his elbow.

'Er, no,' she said. She looked around at the debris of the tiny room in the sultry heat of the late Sunday morning as the two of them stood awkwardly together in the cramped room. She had so rarely had another person there. Two people made it much harder to move around. Three days' worth of *Evening Standard*, two empty glasses and an empty packet of crisps, piles of books, a manuscript on the floor, *Heat* and

Hello! and – oh, God, a brown apple core, how had she not seen that?

But this was what divorced fathers did for their single daughters, they came up to London and put up shelves in their flats and had awkward lunches afterwards. Still, she saw it all through her father's eyes and was ashamed. He lived in Colefax and Fowler land, with an Aga in the basement kitchen of his elegant Georgian town house in Brighton and a black Labrador. When Alice and Jack, her half-sister and brother, were seven and five, only a couple of years ago, Elle had spent Christmas with her father, and on Christmas Day they'd gone to church. Alice and Jack had worn grey wool coats with grey velvet collars, like Princes William and Harry. Elle didn't know why, but somehow those coats summed up her dad's new life for her.

'Maybe I'll buy something new, after the shelves have gone up,' she said, trying to sound as though this was all part of a meticulous interior decoration scheme. 'Although, if I get the New York placement it'll have to go on hold.'

'Yes, New York,' said her father. 'So, what's that all about?'

'I don't know,' said Elle. 'The girl who was supposed to be going, my friend Libby?' she said, but he wouldn't remember her. 'Well, she's had to – er, drop out.' She hesitated; she still wasn't sure if Libby was OK with her applying for it. 'I wasn't going to do anything about it but they sent round an email saying they have to find someone else now, the person who's coming to us from the States has already rented out her flat and booked her flight, and I'm the right level. I talked to my boss yesterday about it, and yeah, had a quick interview in the afternoon. It's all quite fast.'

'And what do you do there?'

'Basically just go to the sister company for four months, observe how they do everything, widen your horizons a bit, I don't know.' Elle shrugged, trying to sound nonchalant. 'Have a change. Get to know a new city.'

John looked doubtfully at the shelves, which he'd brought up from Robert Dyas. 'Well, let's get started with this then. Hold this for me. Do you think you'll get it?'

'No idea. I gave it my best shot, so we'll see.'

Elle tried to sound breezy, but in fact, the job swap was suddenly all she could think about. As she'd sat in Celine's office that Friday, her hands crossed demurely in her lap, trying to think of what she'd want to hear, she'd realised she wanted to get out of here. She wanted to try, at the very least. This weekend had been almost unbearable, locked up here in the heat by herself, with nothing to do. She'd texted Tom on Friday, and he'd been out with Caitlin. She'd seen him only the day before, she knew she was pushing her luck, but he was the only one who'd understand – or was it just that he was the only one she felt like texting? It was pathetic, anyway, the hole she'd burrowed herself into. She'd finished *Devil's Cub* and she didn't know why, but all of a sudden she couldn't face any more Georgette Heyer. It was as though she'd eaten too much chocolate.

As she watched her father marking the wall with a spirit level, Elle grimaced.

'How's Rhodes?' she asked suddenly. 'Have you spoken to him?'

'Yesterday, actually,' her father said. 'I was going to talk to you about that. At lunch. They got married yesterday.'

Elle's mouth fell open. 'They got *married*?' she repeated. 'Where?'

'They're in New York for a few weeks. They went to City Hall. Just a couple of witnesses, her sister, her father, a quick lunch afterwards. They wanted to do it quietly. They asked me to tell you.'

Elle shut her mouth, then opened it. 'They're married,' she said, after a while. 'Just like that.'

'Yes. They felt it was for the best, a quick, quiet ceremony, but they wanted me to tell you. And – ah, if you could tell your mother.'

Elle stared at him. 'Why can't they?'

Her father turned back to the wall. 'I thought you'd be the best person,' he said, his voice cool.

'Can't they ring her themselves?'

Her father's jaw was set. He hated any disruption to his proposals. 'Like I say, they're in New York, and – Melissa's still very upset. I'm just going to drill a second.' He pressed the drill bit firmly into the plaster, and Elle watched his back, shaking her head in disbelief. *You're drilling, and Rhodes and Melissa are married, and no one's told Mum.* There was a *thud* as a chunk of wall fell out. 'Oh sh– sugar,' he said. 'Look at that.'

They both stared at the crumbling square of plaster on the green carpet. 'Never mind,' said Elle.

'I do mind,' said John. He stood with the drill in his hand, gently tapping it against his palm. He looked at the wall, then out of the window, then down at the floor. 'I should just use a smaller drill bit, that's all. So, can you—'

'Dad,' Elle said. 'You're making me really paranoid. Was it something I did? Was it Mum?'

Her father turned to her. 'I don't think it's for me to say. But all I will say is, they felt after the effort they'd gone to, to move the wedding from the States to accommodate her, and the care they were taking to include her, that Mandana had put them in an untenable position.' He turned back and drilled a small, neat hole in the wall. 'I have to say I agree with them,' he said, and the tone of his voice chilled her through. 'I wonder, to be honest, whether she'll have anyone left, soon.'

'But what did she do?'

'Let me finish this wall first, please, Eleanor.'

She took him to a gastropub and they made polite conversation along the way. 'So Alice is learning the flute, is she?

251

That's great.' After he'd squinted at the menu, chalked up on a board, Elle turned to him. 'It's so nice to see you, Dad,' she said impulsively. 'It's –' She didn't want to sound as though she was moaning. 'Sorry it's been so long.'

'No, it's my fault,' he said. 'I tend to think you're all right, you see. You always have been.'

Elle didn't know how to respond to this. She and Rhodes had never complained about not seeing John; like most children of divorced parents, they had just accepted, after a period of time, that that was the way it was. Of course he thought she was all right – how would he know any different?

She looked at him now – serious face, neat, greying cowlick, newly ironed shirt – he wore a proper shirt, even in August, on a Sunday, to do DIY at his daughter's, that's how correct he was. Elle wondered again, for the millionth time, how on earth he and Mum had ever had anything in common.

'What was she like?' she asked suddenly. She wanted to pick up the thread of the conversation again. 'When you first met her, Mum, I mean.' Her father's jaw tightened; he looked up at the menu board, concentrating hard. 'I'm sorry,' Elle whispered. 'Probably I should just shut up, it's ages ago, it's just –'

It's just I'm half you and half her. And that's scary. Will I end up like her? Or you?

'She was very different then, your mother,' John said suddenly. 'No,' he amended. 'That's wrong. She was the same in lots of ways. Just more carefree. She had a headscarf, and she used to have all this thick hair. After she had you two it was never the same. Very thin.'

Elle stared at him. John poured her some more wine. 'I won't have any more, I'm driving,' he said. 'Well, she was enormous fun. I was a very staid, boring chap. Chorleywood, Boy Scouts, studying medicine, not a spare farthing to rub together. And she – she just burst into my life, like a – well, she was like colour. Yes, an explosion of colour. She wore these long dresses, printed all over with flowers, these billowing silly shirts, like she was a Shakespearean actor, and these headscarfs, yes. She had her own megaphone. Can you imagine!' His eyes crinkled and he smiled. 'Your mother with a megaphone. What a terrible combination. And she was alive, passionate, she believed in things. She made me believe in things. She got so angry at the world—'

'Like how?' Elle asked.

His eyes flew open, as if he'd forgotten she was there. 'Oh – ban the bomb, the Tories, Mrs Thatcher the milk snatcher, the anti-Nazi League. If there was a cause she'd join it. We were so in love. It sounds like a cliché, but it's true. We were wild about each other. Crazy. Moved in together. It wasn't done in those days but we couldn't be apart.' He said it simply, and nodded. 'My mother said we should wait. But I wouldn't wait. And then she . . . she was pregnant. It was all very quick. Very jolly, very good news, that was your brother,' he said. 'And then you –' John reached out and touched Elle's chin. 'My little girl, you were then, and then, well . . .'

He put his hand on his chin and looked up. The clink of glasses, the banging of the door outside, the faint fumes from the High Road recalled Elle to where she was. She sat still and held her breath, hoping not to break the spell, that he would carry on talking.

'And then I really got to know her,' he said. 'The drinking. The lying. The selfishness. The childishness. She blamed me for her pregnancy, when she said she was on the Pill, so how was it my fault? She blamed me when the boiler broke and when she didn't get the jobs she wanted, when she got pregnant again, when people weren't nice to her, and it was always . . . *always* someone else's fault.' He sat up straight, clenching both fists on the table. 'When it wasn't. It was hers. Her, or the drink. The damn drink.'

'Mustard?' the waitress demanded brightly, springing up between them. John jumped. 'No,' he said. 'Er, no,' he repeated, blinking, as if remembering where he was, with whom, what he'd said.

'No, none for me, thanks,' Elle told her hurriedly, and she turned back to her father. 'Dad –'

'Ignore me,' John said. His face was grey. 'It was a long time ago. Everything happened too fast. And we'd never change it, because we have you two, so what's the point of complaining about it?'

Every point, Elle wanted to say. She chewed the side of her finger. If they'd waited a few years, they'd have had different children. Perhaps a nicer, calmer boy, and a brighter, better girl than the ones they'd got. They wouldn't have had to split up. Mum wouldn't be so sad. Dad wouldn't be so careful, so buttoned up. Everything would have been different if we hadn't been born. *Everything*.

'Mum might disagree with you,' Elle said. 'I sometimes think she wishes things had turned out differently.' She spoke carefully. 'Her life – it's – you know. It's been hard for her.'

To her surprise, her father put his hands on hers, a very un-Dad-like gesture. 'Forget about her, Ellie. You worry about her too much, always have done. I wonder sometimes, ah – well, I wonder if something is missing. Now this is none of my business –' A light perspiration glowed on his smooth forehead as he spoke. 'But I think New York sounds like a wonderful plan. And I think if they offer it to you, you should go. Why?' He held up one hand, forestalling her question. 'I think a change would do you good.'

Elle watched him carefully. 'I think Mum thinks it's a stupid idea,' she said.

John squeezed her hand. 'Your mother is selfish,' he said sadly. 'She is, Elle. She has problems, I know, but she's often not very nice.' The words were so simple, it was strange. 'I'm sorry to say it, but I think she's using you, and you can't see it.'

'She's got loads on,' Elle said. 'That's why she said she

doesn't want any more alimony, you know?' She wanted him to believe her. 'Things are going well with Bryan, and the textiles business, she and Anita have all these plans –' She hated the way her father was so hard on her mother. 'She's the one who's too busy to see me, Dad, honestly.'

He smiled. 'I don't believe everything she says, I've learned not to.'

'How would you know? You never speak to her,' Elle said hotly.

They were both silent.

'Do you want to know why they cancelled the wedding?' John said. He raised his head a little, like a general, the morning of the final battle.

Elle held her breath, bit her lip, and nodded. 'Yes,' she said quietly.

Her father said in a monotone, 'They went to stay with her for the weekend. She'd forgotten they were coming. They had an argument. She scratched their car with her keys. Ran around it scratching the paint. Then she was sick. Then she made them leave. Told them she never wanted to see them again. Some of the things she said –' He shook his head. 'To her own son. I can't believe it.'

It was very strange, hearing her father say those words, to her. Elle breathed in, and squeezed her eyes shut.

'Did they say – do they think she was drunk?'

John rubbed his face, his fingers tightly pressed together, a neat, furious gesture. 'She said she wasn't. I think she was. They weren't sure, they didn't see her drinking. She was always very good at hiding it.'

I think she was . . . 'You weren't there, though, you don't know.' Elle held up her hand, defensively. 'I know, but maybe they had a big argument and she – well, maybe it's worse than it sounds. Rhodes and Melissa don't make much effort with her, Dad.'

Her father's lips were set in a tight line. 'Elle –'

255

'She doesn't drink, Dad – she hasn't for ages, almost a couple of years now.'

'I don't believe it,' said John. 'She's done this before, too many times.'

'But even if she did – is that really a reason for the way they behaved?' Elle deliberately kept her voice quiet, her tone even. 'To cancel everything, leave everyone else dangling, run off to New York and get married there, just to spite her?'

'They weren't trying to be spiteful. I've spoken to Melissa. She wanted everything to be just right. I can appreciate that.'

'I don't think that's the way to deal with it. She's still our mother.' Elle took a deep breath. 'Look, Dad, I see Mum more than any of you. At least once, twice a month, OK?' She could feel herself going red. 'She used to drink too much, but that was because she wanted to forget about herself for a while. She was unhappy for a long time.' She stopped and looked at him. 'I know you didn't mean to hurt anyone, but neither did she. All I'm saying is, one falling off the wagon isn't the end of the world. She didn't kill anyone. She finds Melissa hard to talk to and the fact is, she finds Rhodes intimidating. I hear the way he talks to her.' She downed the rest of her wine and poured herself some more, aware of the irony of what she was doing. 'You know what, Dad, he talks to her like you used to. Like she's worthless, like she's a piece of shit.'

She found she was shaking. She took another sip.

John watched her. She stared back at him, genuinely intrigued to hear his reply. She never discussed these things with her father. She'd never had him with his back against the wall before either. He'd been either at work, or in the garden, or annoyed in some way, and then he was gone.

He cleared his throat. 'OK then. Maybe you're right,' he said. As if she'd told him it might rain tomorrow. He drew a finger across the wooden table. 'But if you ask me, if they offer it to you, I think you should go to New York. Leave your mum behind.' Then he paused. 'I think you're hiding behind all this, anyway. This isn't how I thought you'd end up. You're wasting your life. I think. That's all.'

She hated the finality of his tone, as though he was standing over the conquered enemy, nodding at his victory. Elle sat on her hands, wondering how to say all the things she wanted to him, and then he looked at his watch. 'Shall we have coffee, and then I should be off soon after, if I don't want to feel the wrath of the A23,' and she knew that was it, her slot with him had come to an end.

'I CAN'T BELIEVE you've never seen *The Godfather*,' said Tom, as they walked along the South Bank. He took a sip of beer from a bottle and inhaled the evening air. It was dark, one of the first slightly chilly August nights, a tiny sign that summer was coming to a close. 'How about we head to Gabriel's Wharf? There's a great pizza place, just by the river.'

'Fab,' said Elle. 'That was absolutely brilliant.'

'What was your favourite bit?'

'"I don't want my brother coming outta that toilet with just his dick in his hand",' Elle said, in her best 'fuggedda-boudit' voice.

'Wait till you see *Godfather Part II*,' Tom said. 'It's even better. We should rent the video one evening. It's pretty long. So maybe one afternoon.'

'Um – that'd be great.'

'How did your interview with Celine go then?' Tom said. He put his hand on her elbow, steering her out of the way of an oncoming rollerblader. 'When did I see you, Thursday? It was on Friday, right?'

'Yep. It was OK. I don't really know. It's just –' Elle hesitated. 'I'm never sure if she knows what she's talking about. She asks about books I've read and when I tell her, it's obvious she's never heard of them. I mean, she's heard of *White Teeth* and *Harry Potter*, but that's about it. So how does she know if I've given the right answer?'

'I bet you were great,' said Tom. 'Anyway, you love talking about books. It doesn't matter if she's heard of them or not, it's whether you sounded convincing. I bet you did.'

'Ready to fly the flag for Bookprint UK and not shag anyone,' Elle said. She shrugged. 'Oh, I don't even know if I want to go or not. I – well, I'll see.'

'Well, if you're going to go, go for the right reasons. Celine – well, I think she's mad, anyway. Just don't go because you're running away from stuff.'

Elle stopped, underneath some trees. 'What does that mean?'

'Nothing,' said Tom.

'I think running away from stuff's a very good reason to get away,' said Elle. She bent her neck back, staring up at the starry sky. 'To leave it all behind . . . That'd be great.'

'But it'll still be there when you come back,' Tom said. 'If you don't sort it out.'

Elle said, 'My family's never going to change. This job's never going to get any better. My love life's not going to improve. Libby's not going to stop winding me up. I feel like . . . I'm ossifying. And I'm twenty-eight in October. It's not right. I mean, I'm old, but I'm not that old.'

'Old! You're still a baby, Elle.' Tom dumped his bottle into a bin. 'Come on, hurry up. I'm starving.'

He was in a strange mood that night, Elle didn't know why. He smiled and laughed, and was as good company as always. But Elle felt he was distant. They sat outside in the sultry August night, a faint breeze from the wide, black Thames ruffling their napkins, Elle's skirt, her hair.

'Everything OK?' she asked him. 'You seem a bit quiet.'

Tom put a huge piece of pizza in his mouth, which

prevented him from answering. He nodded. 'Mmmmhmm,' he said.

'Good. Just – you know. If there's something you need to talk about. Buddy.'

'Buddy?' He said the word as though he'd never heard it. 'Right. Buddy.' He looked up, then down.

Elle was feeling reckless. 'We are buddies, aren't we?' She didn't know why she said it. She wanted to rock the boat.

'Course we are.' His eyes searched her face. He looked tired, she thought. The summer was dragging on, long, dry and too hot. She wished autumn was already here. 'You're – we're, well, this summer, the last few weeks, yes, we've become good friends.' He shook his head, then screwed his eyes shut, and swallowed.

'Is that all you think we are?' Elle asked.

'What about you?' he said, instantly. 'Is that what you think?' She held her breath. He looked as if he were about to say something, then he stopped. 'I'm really tired, sorry. I've had a bit of a rough weekend.'

'Is everything OK with you and Caitlin?' Elle asked, trying to maintain her calm.

'No, not really. We split up.'

'Oh.' Elle put her fork down. 'Oh, my goodness. Tom, I'm sorry.'

'It's OK, really it is.'

'When?'

'Saturday. It was mutual.'

'Really?'

Tom sighed. He was still wearing his glasses from the cinema, and he took them off, and rubbed the bridge of his nose. His jaw was rigid. 'Sort of. We realised it had to end, we both want different things. And I've been thinking this summer . . . about it all.'

She could feel the tension around them. It seemed to warm

her in the cold night air. Elle cleared her throat and said lightly, 'Are you being polite and saying you dumped her?'

Tom choked with laughter. 'I don't trash talk, Eleanor.'

'Is it permanent?'

Tom looked straight at her. 'Yes, it is. It is.'

They were both silent. His phone rang, reverberating on the table, and they both jumped.

'Shit, that's her,' he said. 'She said she might need to speak to me. Can I just –'

'Of course,' said Elle. 'Of course.'

He touched her arm. 'I won't be long, I promise. And I want to tell you something when I get back.'

He stood up immediately, and walked out into the horse-shoe-shaped piazza, lined with lights from other restaurants. Elle watched him, stalking across the concrete. Her heart contracted a little for him, and she tried to work out why. He was a curious mix of self-sufficient and vulnerable, and it was so transparent. He wasn't like most other publishing boys: Jeremy, smooth as you like, or Rory, boyishly charming, or Bill, aggressively laddish, all manipulative in their way. Tom just wasn't. That was why, she realised, she liked him so much.

After a few minutes, there was still no sign of him. Elle sighed. She thought he might be a while. Two weeks earlier, they'd gone for a drink in Chelsea, a small pub on a quiet street that wound towards the river. Caitlin had arrived, out of the blue, and tried to pretend it was a coincidence, though it was obvious it wasn't.

Elle picked up his *Private Eye,* which had fallen out of his jacket pocket and was on the floor. Inadvertently smiling at the cover, showing the newly convicted Jeffrey Archer on his way to prison, she opened the magazine and thumbed through to her favourite section, 'Books and Bookmen', and her eye was drawn instantly down, in that split second where you almost know you're about to see something before you read it. As she read, her jaw fell open, and it was only when she heard the crumpling crash of glass that she realised her wine glass had rolled out of her hand, onto the floor. When Tom came striding back towards her, shoving his phone in his pocket, he stopped as he saw her expression, the waitress beside her, sweeping up the glass, Elle putting shards into a filthy napkin.

She stared up at him, her eyes full of tears.

'You knew, didn't you.'

Tom looked down, and went pale.

LONG-TERM OBSERVERS of the goings-on at last-man-standing independent Bluebird Books were amazed when Rory Sassoon, son of The Old Gal Felicity Sassoon, outdid himself, even by his own slimy standards. Sleaze Sassoon shafted her back in December to sell out for ££££ to soulless corp Bookprint, run by The Gazelle, aka Celine Bertrand, worker bee for French megacorp BarQue. One might ask, given Sleaze's total lack of talent, why he was also promoted to the dizzying heights of deputy MD of the nebulous BBE division. But rumour has it he was more than The Gazelle's colleague for a good few months prior to the sale. Add to the equation his two-year affair with a junior member of staff, and you start to realise why he doesn't have any time for work. Current BBE MD Bill 'Groper' Lewis is also said to be none too happy, especially since he's just been rapped over the knuckles for his own 'dealings' with another junior ed. Rory spilled the beans to his Lady Boss on that one, and it seems the junior ed had taken her revenge by spilling the beans about his own goings-on in return, to anyone who'll listen! Heady stuff!

'Did you know?' Elle said. Broken glass crunched as she shifted her feet. 'You did, didn't you?'

He nodded. 'That they were having an affair? Yes, I'm sorry.'

'So Rory told Celine about Libby and Bill's affair,' she said. 'But who told them about me and Rory?' She jabbed the newspaper. 'Are they saying it was Libby?'

'It doesn't really matter, Elle,' Tom said. He took her hand. 'She probably told someone who told someone else . . . You know what publishing's like, it's all stupid gossip. I think everyone knows by now.'

She was still in shock. Rory – and Celine. How could she not have seen it earlier? She was so stupid. The whole thing: the idea that you were something to be grubbed over by people in a magazine, a nameless bit of totty. It was . . . bizarre. It was horrible.

'But he texted me,' she said. 'A few weeks ago. He texted me. I thought –' Her hands flopped to her sides. 'It doesn't matter now.'

Tom was still by her side. 'Do you want to stay, get a drink?'

The cinema, the meal, their conversation, it all seemed like another evening, before Caitlin rang and this thing appeared. She blinked, trying to transport herself back there. 'Not really,' she said. 'I'm sorry, Tom.'

He put his hand on hers. 'No one will remember it this time next week. Your name's not in it.'

She pulled her hand away and stood up. 'It's not the point,' she said. 'I'll remember. It's all so . . . grubby. Everything is. Nothing's about work, nothing. It's about who's sleeping with who.'

'Whom,' Tom said gently, trying to make her smile. She walked off, and he followed.

'I'm sorry, this evening's been ruined,' she said. 'Can we do something this weekend? Catch up properly?'

He faced her, as the wind came in from the river and whipped around them. 'I'd like that,' he said.

'WHY THE FUCK didn't you tell me?'

Elle stood in the doorway of Rory's office. He looked up, panic in his eyes, stood up and shut the door. Outside, Annabel Hamilton, hurrying along the corridor, stared at them curiously.

'You should have told me.' Elle moved towards him, shaking her head.

Rory sighed. 'Elle, I've been trying to, for the last month or so.'

'You didn't try very hard.' Elle wanted to laugh hysterically, go really mad. Smash his glass wall in with a baseball bat, tie that stupid novelty T-shirt from the sales conference round his neck and strangle him. She clenched her fists; she'd tried so hard not to let it all out, and now that she was talking to him all she wanted to do was lose it.

'I did!' Rory said loudly. He smacked his hands on his desk. Papers flew in all directions, floating gently down onto the grey carpet tiles. 'I kept texting you, saying I needed to see you! I needed to talk to you! And you never replied!'

Elle shook her head. She was so angry: at herself, for believing that she might be in love with him again.

'Sit down,' Rory said. 'Let's talk about this. I tried to explain –'

She waved her phone in his face. *'I can't stop thinking about you,'* she read, her voice dripping with scorn. *'I miss you. Please, can we meet up?'* She faced him. *'Nothing to do with business'?* That was less than *two months ago,* you wanker. You telling me you weren't still fucking her then?'

'It's only been a few times,' Rory hissed. 'And *never* when we were together, they've got that all wrong.'

'You're lying,' she shouted. 'You're bloody lying. You were cheating on me –'

He stood up and grasped her wrists. 'I wasn't. I swear to you I wasn't. It was Christmas, New Year . . . honestly, it was nothing. *Nothing!'*

'Christmas?' Elle's voice was withering. 'So you waited a few days till after we'd split up. Thanks, thanks for your consideration. I suppose I should be grateful, after all you fucked everyone else over, you cowardly, pathetic—'

'Elle, keep your voice down –' He flapped his hands at her. 'Now some shit's blabbed about it it's everywhere. She's furious. I shouldn't have been texting you, OK? OK?' He gestured for her to come closer, soothingly, like a lion tamer. 'It's just – I was missing you. I thought I should explain, and then I started thinking about us . . . I thought . . . I miss the old days. They were good. I – I made a mistake. I shouldn't have let you go.'

'I'm the one who ended it!' Elle shouted. 'I ended it! You completely broke my heart, Rory, and you treat it like it's not a big deal! It was for me, it was!'

Rory glanced behind her, and his mouth dropped open. Elle turned, to see Bill Lewis walking past, staring in open annoyance and curiosity at them. She didn't care. She flung the door open.

'Well, that's done it,' Rory said. 'As if I wasn't in enough trouble. Bollocks.' He put his head in his hands. 'Celine is going to kill me. She said she wasn't sure it was working out. What am I going to do?'

Elle gaped at him. 'I don't know,' she said. 'Is there someone else you can sleep with to keep your job? I don't know, ask Bill out for dinner.'

There was a curious liberation in it, in burning her boats like this. They all thought she was second-rate, absent, not much cop – well, let them think she'd gone mad now too. At least now they'd know the truth, know why she'd got the job here.

'I don't know how it came to this. It's all been a mistake,' he said quietly. He ran his hands through his hair, clutching his scalp. The familiarity of the gesture nearly broke her heart. All the things she'd been trying not to think about pulsed dangerously in Elle's brain. Had Celine sat with him on the big grey squashy sofa in his flat, watching the blossom sway in the square outside? Had she seen the mole on his tummy, the one that smiled when he sat up? Of course she had. What did they talk about, what were they like together . . . ? Elle put her hands over her ears, unconsciously mimicking him, trying to block out the voices in her head.

'I can't stand this . . .' she said, looking round. 'I – can't do it. I think I'm going mad.'

Rory's face was grave. 'Oh, Elle,' he said. 'I'm so sorry. I've made a huge mess of it, haven't I. I was wrong. Totally wrong.'

She didn't say anything, but shook her head, her lips closed tight together. She wished she could hold him, just one more time, just to remember what it was like, before she had to say goodbye again.

Then he said, 'But Elle. I'm serious. You mustn't tell anyone else.' His expression was urgent, his voice low. 'About us, I mean. I'm still trying to manage it with Celine. So –'

Elle couldn't listen any longer. 'Fuck off, Rory. Just. Fuck. Off.'

She walked out, slamming the balsa-wood door hard behind her, so that the office frame rattled.

'Elle, can you find the cover for—' Annabel Hamilton said, bustling up to her, trying to pretend she hadn't been outside earwigging the whole time.

'Not now, Annabel.' Elle held up her hand and strode in the other direction. 'I'm busy.'

She pushed open the door to Celine's office, knocking as she did.

'Eh?' Celine said, looking up irritably, but when she saw it was Elle smiled brightly at her. 'So – this is a bit strange, but Elle—'

'You knew about me and Rory, didn't you?' Elle said. She stood in front of Celine's desk, her hands on her hips.

'Yes, yes, I did.' Celine didn't cower, or avoid Elle's hard gaze. She nodded and patted the desk, indicating Elle should sit down. This coolness threw Elle slightly off. She was empowered with righteous anger and expecting Celine to grovel at her feet. 'This business is annoying.'

She said it 'beesniss' and Elle strained her ears, thinking she'd said 'bee's knees'.

'Nevertheless, it is not important, for the moment. I have heard from the Americans. They would like to offer you the placement.'

Elle laughed, shortly. She felt completely mad. She was glad she didn't have a gun. It was as though she was watching herself, standing there with her hands on her hips. 'What did you say to them to make them give it to me? Did you tell them you wanted me out of the way?'

'I made it clear to them that you would be the best candidate. For many reasons.' Celine smiled coolly and pulled at her earlobe.

'I'm not going, not like that,' Elle said firmly. Celine gave a little laugh. She pushed her hair over her shoulders and stood up, walking over to the big window, with its view over the rooftops of Soho.

'My dear girl, you are lucky I am giving you this chance at all. I am not trying to get you out of the way. If anything it is a risk for me.' She made a dismissive gesture. 'They don't know and they don't care, they only care if you're any good. It's a blank slate for you.' She drummed her fingers on her rosebud mouth. 'Hm. I do think you are talented, but you don't see it. Those new Dora Zoffany covers – they are much better. You were right.' Elle saw then that the proofed and printed covers were standing on Celine's shelf, behind her, an example of the best Bookprint could do. She smiled wryly to herself. 'That's why I picked you. You didn't do anything wrong. Libby did. Yes, Rory may have suggested it but – you and I both know what he says is often not to be trusted. Hm?'

Elle nodded. 'Yes,' she said.

A glint of something – was it laughter? – flickered across Celine's face. 'So I wish you could see I'm trying to help you.' Her tiny teeth flashed, and she turned back towards Elle. 'Really, can't you see that I am?'

Elle's shoulders slumped. 'Yes,' she said. 'Yes, I can.'

'So,' Celine said. 'I shall ring Caryn and tell her that you accept? Yes?'

They were both silent, and then Elle looked up at her and raised her chin. 'Yes. Yes, please.'

At six, they all went to the pub for Libby's birthday. Libby had been doing Libby PR for the last week, sending round emails, visiting people in their pods, practically begging them to come. With the appearance of the *Private Eye* piece, all eyes were on her, but Libby, as ever, flourished under pressure. The turnout at the Crown, a tiny pub behind Carnaby Street, was impressive, given that it was August and half the office was away.

Elle wasn't going to go. She was furious with Libby, convinced she'd told everyone the story of Elle and Rory's affair in revenge for Rory blabbing about her and Bill to Celine. But towards the end of the day the need for a drink overtook her, and the sudden realisation that, having not cared about so much this summer, she suddenly didn't really care about the whole fetid, gossipy, stewy mess any more. If she was going to New York, and she was, why burn any more bridges before she went? She got to the pub early, and took the seat next to Libby.

'Hi, love,' Libby said, her smile slightly too bright, though her eyes had bags under them and her normal bounciness wasn't there. 'You OK? Sounds like today's been rough.'

'No,' Elle said. 'Actually, it's been pretty great.'

She didn't say anything more, just gave the perplexed Libby a kiss and handed her a birthday card, then kept buying the drinks. Three vodka, lime and sodas weren't enough to take the edge off, so at about eight o'clock she had a large glass of wine, and things seemed mellower, even funny. It *was* funny, when you thought about it. Funny in a really fucking pathetic way. Libby shagging Bill . . . Bill married, Elle shagging Rory, Rory shagging Celine . . . Elle shagging absolutely no one. She looked around the table. It didn't really matter any more.

I feel nothing for these people, nothing, she thought. She drained her wine.

'You're getting through the drinks tonight,' Bill Lewis said. 'Drowning your sorrows?'

Elle didn't answer him, though it was one of the few times he'd ever addressed her directly. *I hate you,* she said under her breath.

'Elle used to fall over after one glass at Bluebird,' Libby said. 'Now she can drink us all under the table. You've really improved.'

Improved. The bottles at home that piled up every week, that she put in the bin rather than recycling, too embarrassed to let anyone see how much she drank. It took a bottle now before she felt any discernible difference.

'You've had a rough time of it,' Bill said. 'Mind you –' He paused, looked round the crowded table, which had fallen silent. 'I'd heard you were a girl with taste, Elle. What I overheard today proves otherwise. Seriously.'

Oh, yes, I hate you, Bill. You're the boss, you should be going over figures, or at home with your family, not sitting in a pub with a load of twenty-somethings pulling your macho shit, you idiot. Rage bubbled within her, and she reminded herself again. New York. She was going to New York. She had a chance. She'd mucked everything up, but she'd been given a fresh start.

Elle got up and walked out of the pub. She didn't say anything, didn't wave, just walked out. She walked into the warm summer night, through the crowds thronging the pavements outside the pubs, through the quiet back streets of Marylebone, holding her head up high. She had a shower when she got back. She wanted to scrub the alcohol out of her system, scrub the day away. I won't miss any of you, she thought. None.

Except Tom. She realised as she sat in bed, in her vest and shorts, that he was the only person in London she'd miss. She counted on her fingers the things they'd done that summer. It was only a month or so, but it felt longer. They'd seen *The Royal Tenenbaums* and *The Godfather*. They'd had pizza, sushi, tapas and Thai. They'd been to that awful bar on Wardour Street, the Ladbroke Arms and the place with the margaritas on St Anne's Court. She'd been to the Richmond bookshop to pick him up, a couple of times, too. And of course there was that evening at the Cross Keys when Caitlin had turned up halfway through, and Tom had tried to get rid of her, and then he'd turned to Elle afterwards and said, 'I'm really sorry. I wanted to see you, not her.'

Remembering his usually hard voice softening, his grey eyes looking straight at her, his light touch on her arm, Elle smiled, and lay back in the darkness of the tiny, hot room. They were meeting up on Saturday. Yes. The thought warmed her. She wasn't going to miss London, her family, or Bookprint, or anything else, but she'd miss him.

'WHAT DO YOU want to do, then?'

Tom stretched his arms. 'Nothing. I don't have to go back to the shop. I asked Benji to stay on a few more hours.' He lay back down on the grass. 'We can do what we like, what do you want to do?'

Elle looked around. They were sitting in Petersham Fields. The Thames flowed slowly in front of them, cluttered with the little ferryboats crossing the banks for 10p, and the pleasure cruises and yachts. It was a glorious Saturday, but again there was the feeling that the best of summer was over. Across the river, the trees in Marble Hill Park were pale, brittle green. There was no wind. Everything seemed still, poised on the brink of change.

'I'd like another drink, I think.' She looked down at her empty plastic glass. 'We should get another bottle.'

Tom gave a murmur of assent and shielded his eyes from the sun with his arm. 'I'm OK for the moment. Shall I get you a glass?'

'Oh. Yes, thanks.' Elle rolled over to get her purse. 'So, is Caitlin not working today?' she said, changing the subject. 'Is it all OK with you two then?'

Tom said, 'I don't know. She's upset.'

'Right,' said Elle. 'It's strange, she was so off with you, and you were so keen on her to start with.' She knew he didn't like talking about it, but she found Caitlin fascinating. 'It's like the roles reversed. We always thought she'd be the one to end it with you, didn't we.' *We. We always thought.* She blushed.

Tom shook his head. 'It was the other way round. Anyway, it's fine. We're fine. It's over.' He stood up. 'Let's walk back towards Richmond, shall we?'

They set off along the towpath, past the boat sheds and the pier, and the hordes of people lying out on the river banks.

Elle cleared her throat. 'So – I've got something to tell you. Some good news.'

'Hey? What?' Tom turned towards her.

'I'm going to New York.' She nodded. 'They offered it to me and I accepted it. I'm going in October.' She wished she wasn't nervous. 'Spoke to Caryn in New York yesterday again, she seemed really nice.'

'Oh. I thought when I didn't hear from you that you hadn't got it.' Tom carried on walking again.

'I'm sorry, I wanted to tell you today—'

He interrupted. 'That's OK.' He looked at his watch. 'I've had a pretty rough week anyway.'

'Oh no, what's happened?'

Tom jangled his keys in his trouser pocket. 'Oh – it's probably nothing. It is nothing.' He looked at his watch again. 'You're really going to New York then. Why?'

'Why what?'

'Why are you going? I don't understand, if I'm honest.'

Elle struggled to keep up with him, she didn't understand why he was being like this. 'Why wouldn't I go?' She peered at his face, then nearly crashed into a bench. 'It's going to be amazing, and I'm really lucky. I need a change.'

'Oh, right,' said Tom, cryptically. He shrugged. 'Won't you be missing out on stuff here if you go?'

'It's for four months!' Elle said, trying to give a natural-sounding laugh, though she felt as if she'd been winded. 'I'm not moving to Siberia to live for the rest of my natural life. Wow! I thought –' She shook her head, surprised at how upset she was. 'I thought you'd be pleased for me. You were pleased when we talked about it before.'

'It's different now,' he said angrily. 'I would be if I thought you were doing it for the right reasons, but I don't think you are.' They were in the middle of the green field, on the narrow path. People pushed past them.

'Why the hell not?' she said. 'Tom, what's up with you? Is everything OK?'

Tom shrugged, and cleared his throat, then he scratched his head. 'Well, I'm – I don't think you'll get Rory and the rest of them out of your system by running away to some identikit company a bit further away.'

'This isn't about Rory,' she said. 'Seriously, it's not.'

'Are you sure?'

'Yes, I'm bloody sure. And I'm not running away!' Elle didn't understand what he was talking about. 'I've been practically in hiding for the last six months, it's got to stop! It's going to be much harder, starting somewhere new. I have to prove myself – they wanted Libby, they didn't want me . . . I have to show them I'm good at what I do.'

He was silent. 'You are good at what you do.'

'Well, you're my friend,' Elle said, trying to sound patient. 'You would say that.'

'I want you to stay here.'

'*Why?*' Elle said. 'Tom, why?'

'You really can't see why I'd like you to stay?'

She knew what she wanted to think, but she couldn't trust to that, not when she'd been so wrong so many times before. She stared at him. In the cool of the trees behind them, a child screamed happily. Oars splashed in the calm water.

Tom had his back to the sun and she peered into his face, squinting. He pulled her round a little, so her face was out of the sun's glare. 'Look,' he said. 'Can I tell you something? I have to tell you, really. But I want to as well, I—'

'Tom! Tom! Hi! I'm here!' someone called.

He stared at Elle one last time. 'I'm sorry. I said I'd be here. I should have told her.'

'What?' Elle said. She looked behind him. Caitlin was marching towards them, her shiny black hair ruffled in the breeze. She was in cargo pants, fastened low around her slim waist, and a tiny polka-dot chiffon blouse. She looked stunning. Elle ran her hands through her half-grown-out hair, and looked down at her sweaty jeans, and the roll of what she thought of as wine-fat.

'Caitlin,' Tom said, going over to her. 'I said –'

Caitlin lifted a hand at Elle. 'Hi,' she said. She was thinner, paler than before, but Elle had forgotten how lovely she was; her dark, expressive eyes, her heart-shaped face. She tried not to watch her. 'Can I please, can I please just have a word with you?'

'Caitlin,' Tom said softly. 'No. Now isn't a good time. You must be able to—'

'Tom, please . . .' She tightened her grip on his flesh. 'I have to speak to you.'

'Can I come round later?'

Caitlin took a deep breath. 'It's just – I – I want to speak to you.'

'No –' Tom said. 'We'll –' He turned around, pointing at Elle.

'I got it wrong. It's yours.' Caitlin nodded. She gave a small smile of satisfaction, though she looked anything but happy.

Tom stepped back. 'What?'

'The baby's yours, not Jean-Claude's.'

There was a silence, broken only by the sounds from the river and some children shouting, far behind them. Tom nodded, the colour drained from his face. 'Are you sure?'

'Wow, what a reaction,' Caitlin said, licking her thin lips nervously.

'Caitlin, you know it's not like that.' He reached towards her, but she shook her head.

'What baby?' Elle asked. Though she knew the answer, but she thought she must be misunderstanding something.

'I'm pregnant,' Caitlin said. She pulled self-consciously at a lock of short hair. 'Found out on Monday, but I thought – er, well, I thought it was Jean-Claude's. I had the scan yesterday afternoon and I got the dates wrong. He was away – we weren't . . . together then. So it's Tom's.' She sounded as if she were reeling off facts from a list; but her face was pale, and she bit her lip as she stared at him, watching for his reaction. 'Yeah – um, it's Tom's. I told him I was pregnant on Monday but I wasn't sure if it was his. So I'm telling him – I'm telling him now.'

Elle hadn't really ever stopped to properly, honestly ask herself how she felt about Tom. It was only when he put his arm around Caitlin's shoulders and said quietly, 'No, that's great. That's really great,' that she knew. Caitlin rested against him, the tension in her taut body gone.

'Oh,' she said. 'Thanks.'

Elle stepped back. 'Congratulations,' she told Caitlin. 'That *is* great. I need to phone my friend Karen about this evening. Why don't you two talk.'

She walked away and sat on the grass, leaving the two of them behind. She held her phone up to her ear and pretended to be calling someone, and while she did she smiled, because she'd read somewhere that if you smiled things seemed better. Anyway, it was none of her business, it was between them now. She sat looking out at the water, until a light touch on her shoulder made her jump.

'Shall we carry on?' he said. 'Caitlin's gone home.'

They walked towards Richmond in silence, and as they got to the bridge, near the pub where they'd sat that first day together, he said, 'I can't say all the things I want to. I hope you understand that. I have to make the best of this. And

275

it'll be great, I'm sure. It's my mistake, I believed her when she said she was on the Pill. Now it doesn't matter.'

'Tom, I'm –' She didn't know what to say either. 'Are you going to move in together? Be parents together?'

He gave a small twitch of irritation. 'I don't know – we haven't discussed all that yet, Elle, it's – I need to get used to it. But I want to do the right thing, for her and the baby.'

Baby – only four letters, but it was such a big word. A baby. Tom was going to be a father, Tom and Caitlin would be parents. She'd got it wrong, whatever 'it' was, again. *He's not Rory*, a voice inside her head said. *He's different*. And this wasn't her business any more.

'I'm sorry,' Elle said. 'I was just – it's big news, that's all.'

'Yes. I know that, thanks a lot. Everything – everything's going to change.' He hit the side of his forehead with the ball of his palm. 'Jesus, Jesus Christ –' He looked around blankly, as though he didn't know who she was, where he was, and for a second, she thought he might just walk away. 'Anyway, you're off then,' he said, after a pause. 'That's great for you.'

His tone was ugly. As though she were skipping off to pick some flowers in a field and leaving him behind to go down the mines. 'Well, yeah. But I hope – do you think you'd come over, spend some time in New York?'

'I don't think so,' Tom said. 'Like I say, the summer's over.'

She was bewildered. 'I don't understand.'

'You're going, I can't change that. And I shouldn't.' He shrugged wearily. 'Doesn't matter what I think.'

Elle clenched her fists against her sides. 'It's four months. Tom, I know this must be weird, I can't imagine what you're going through. But it's two separate things, me going, you having a baby, you know?

'I'm not trying to keep you here,' he said, his jaw tight. 'Do what you like.'

'I want to go,' Elle said. 'I have to go – everything's –' She slumped her shoulders. 'Can't we get that drink? For God's sake, Tom, you must need one more than me.'

'That's the other thing, while we're at it,' he said. 'Might as well say it now. You drink way too much. Have you realised that?'

Elle scratched her arms, and then folded them. She shook her head, stuck her tongue in her mouth, and said, 'Wow. You're a real dick sometimes, you know that?'

'I know I am,' he said. 'I'm vile. I'm a coward in every other way. But someone needs to tell you, before you go, and I suppose it's going to be me. You drink more than anyone I know. Every time I see you you've had more than me and you always want more. Do you even notice? Last Monday you drank nearly a bottle of wine to yourself. I had half a glass of it. You didn't even ask, you kept refilling your own glass. Do you always do that?'

Something slimy, evil and mean was uncoiling itself within Elle. She could feel it, and it gave her strength. 'Have you ever seen me drunk?' Elle spun round on her heel. 'Have I ever made a big deal about getting a drink? No. I haven't because I don't – I *don't* drink too much, and Tom, wow – you are really a dick. I know it must be a shock, Caitlin appearing like that, but you don't have to go along with it, it's not your problem if you really don't want her to—'

'I don't run away from my problems. Don't try and deflect the issue,' he interrupted. His voice was cold, but he wouldn't meet her eyes.

'Why are you being like this?' She gazed at him, her eyes full of tears which she willed away. She wouldn't cry in front of him. 'I don't have a drink problem! I like a drink, but who doesn't?'

'I think you depend on it,' Tom said.

'Well, that's crap,' she said. 'Look, Tom, I'm going now, because this is a rubbish afternoon now and you need some time to . . . never mind. See you whenever.'

'Go home then.' Tom gritted his teeth, as if it was painful to speak. 'Go home and if you don't have an issue with it, don't have a drink tonight. Shouldn't be that hard, should it? If you really don't have a problem.'

She stared at him. 'I really don't understand you,' she said. 'I thought you were different. I thought you weren't like . . . like Rory. I thought we were friends.'

'Things change,' he said. He held her gaze for a brief, intense moment. 'That's why I'm saying this now. I think you don't like me much now anyway, so I might as well just burn my boats.'

'See you, Tom,' Elle said. She turned away, and walked up the steps towards the station, leaving the river and the sunshine behind her. Memories started flashing in front of her tired eyes. She thought of her mother's yellowish, angry face, of how she had had to mop up her vomit more times than she could remember, of the time she was at her drunkest when she hit her husband, slap across the face, and he, furious, hit her back, and they just carried on hitting each other. The time when she backed the car into the Dundys' fence, and Elle had to come and collect her, waiting for the bus to come for forty-five minutes, her mother's head lolling from side to side as she whispered, 'I so sorry, Ellie, I sorry, stupid me. Stupid me.'

You don't know what a drink problem looks like, Tom Scott, she said to herself as she reached the end of the path. She hadn't even said goodbye to him, hadn't hugged him, told him how much these last few weeks had meant to her, how much she was going to miss him, how she'd thought that maybe . . . No. She shook her head, turned, and took one last look at the river, where she'd spent such happy times this summer. It was over. Perhaps he was right. The summer was nearly over. Autumn was coming, she knew it, and everything was going to be different.

Where could she ever begin to attack a fortress like New York? She didn't even want to. She only wanted to stay there until she herself was part of it, one of those well-groomed, well-attended women, and she half realized that was a fantasy too.

Rona Jaffe, *The Best of Everything*

May 2004

'I BOOKED THIS place because I know you hate uptown,' said Mike, shaking his napkin over his lap. 'It's a two-week wait for a table, don't you like it?'

'Of course I do,' Elle said. She checked the strap of her pale rose shift dress. 'It's lovely, Mike, honestly. Just a little – grown-up. You know me.'

Mike waved to someone over her shoulder. 'I don't know you, no.' Mike liked to take a question literally. 'It's been three months, and I still don't feel I understand you.' Two glasses of champagne were placed on the table. 'That's why I wanted to ask you something tonight,' he said, raising one glass. 'Would you consider going exclusive with me?'

Elle shook her hair behind her shoulders, feeling it brush the bare skin on her tanned back. The windows were open onto the road, and a warm May breeze wafted through the restaurant. This was New York at its best, why she loved it here, why she never wanted to leave.

This May the city seemed especially perfect to her. She and Mike would walk back from Soho through the warm streets to her apartment in Perry Street, maybe stop off for a drink at her favourite bar on West 4th . . . Maybe she'd even get him to stay over, they'd had sex only a few times since they'd got together. Mike was a gentleman, which Elle found disappointing, because he'd been great in bed.

Marc, however, *wasn't* a gentleman. Maybe she could call him if Mike didn't stay. Elle shook her head. It would sound so bad were she to say it aloud. It was wrong to call your neighbour over for sex, especially your bi neighbour who worked in the same office as you. But since she'd discovered this American dating thing – you basically went out with who you wanted, and you had to have a proper chat to determine that you were seeing each other exclusively – Elle was reluctant to give it up. She'd come late to the dating game. And she liked the fact that, here, she was good at it. She was good at lots of things here.

Now she raised her glass and took a sip, buying time. 'Exclusive? Er – wow.' Mike looked at her gravely. 'Look, Mike,' Elle said, knowing she owed him a proper answer, 'I don't want to date hundreds of other people, it's not that. It's just – I'm not very good at relationships. Putting a label on things scares me.'

'You're nearly thirty,' Mike said.

Elle waited for him to expound on this: *You're nearly thirty, grow up*, or *You're nearly thirty, you're really old, everyone else is getting married*. But he was silent. 'Well, I know,' she answered, not sure how to respond. 'But – can't we just keep it as it is?' He looked questioningly at her. 'If it goes well, we'll know it, won't we?' Americans were so precise, that was one of the things she loved about them, but this was a downside. They liked a label; she didn't.

Mike sighed. 'Of course, that's fine,' he said, though it didn't sound entirely fine to him. He looked at his watch. 'We should order.' Immediately, a waiter stepped over. This was another of the things Elle loved about New York. There was no one working in a London restaurant, it seemed, whose job it was to be merely a waiter. They were all anxious to let you know they were psychology students or out-of-work

282

actors, as if being a waiter was beneath them. That drove Elle, with her newly acquired zeal for the work ethic, insane. Elle blinked and studied the menu, remembering that she had to call her mother, when she got home. Had to, but it was so hard to remember to do the things you ought to when it was warm, with the lights of the Village calling her and the last of the blossom lingering on the trees.

When they'd ordered, Mike leaned forward and took her hand. 'I'm sorry if I was being persistent,' he said. 'Maybe I'm being a jag. I like you, that's all. I want to spend more time with you.'

Elle scanned his face, his sweet, serious face, and squeezed his hand with both of hers. 'I do too,' she said again. 'It's my problem. I want to give you a get-out clause. While I'm back in England you might meet some hot Park Avenue Princess and stop wanting to slum it downtown with me. I'm just saying.'

'Never,' Mike said. 'I've met them all, and they're all awful. I'm going to miss you.'

'Don't you actually *know* someone called Bitsy?' Elle said. 'I thought people called Bitsy only existed in F. Scott Fitzgerald novels.'

Mike's gentle smile turned into a grin. 'Elle, she's eighty-four, I don't think it counts. Anyway, don't you know someone called Libby? Isn't that the same?'

'That cow? That's entirely different and you know not to mention her name to me.' She grinned back at him, happily, because she loved it when he showed some spark, took the piss out of her. That was the thing she missed most, here. On the table, her month-old BlackBerry flashed red and her eyes flicked instantly towards it. 'Oh –' she began, then stopped. 'Don't worry,' she said. 'I'll check it later.'

Mike said, shaking his head, 'Wow. They sure do get a good day's work out of you at that place. You put me to shame.'

283

Mike was a hedge fund manager. Elle had never heard of them when she'd met him at a launch in February for a book about the economic miracle of Wall Street. He'd been at Yale with the author, and was the only one of the Brooks Brothers *American Psycho* frat-boy lookalikes to break free from the pack. He'd introduced himself to Elle and her boss Caryn, who were chatting in the corner about the latest drama with their biggest author, Elizabeth Forsyte, and when he'd appeared by their sides and said, 'Ladies, may I join you?' Caryn had given him a swift appraisal, knocked back the rest of her Martini and said, 'Hey, Prince Charming. You're just in time. I'm off.'

Only, because she was more Queens than Park Avenue Princess, she said 'orrwff'.

And Mike had stepped back and said, in his mild, polite way, 'What a shame. May I see you to a cab?'

'No, thank you,' Caryn had replied, looking at him suspiciously. 'I think I can make it to the sidewalk from here. Tell you what, I'll yell if I need assistance.'

He'd smiled and nodded, and Elle had liked him even then, for the way he managed to be polite but not stuffy. Well, maybe a little stuffy, but his heart was in the right place.

Mike had an apartment on the Upper East Side, with a view of the Park: down a side street – he wasn't Brooke Astor – but you could still see the Park. Back in the mists of time his father had done something with whaling, Elle couldn't work out what or whether it was a good or bad thing; she kept meaning to Google him and find out, because that was what you did now, Google what you wanted more information on, that hot new restaurant, that sudden best-selling author who'd come out of nowhere and of whom you should have heard, the bit of Americana you didn't understand, and the source of the vast wealth of your date. The result of Mike's vast wealth was that his family had a house in the Hamptons, a ski chalet in Telluride, an island in the Stockholm archipelago, and Mike had one of those jobs that would only make him richer. He was bright, he worked hard, and he deserved to do well, but Elle found it strange, the calm, scientific way in which the Nordstroms accumulated money, having never had much herself, even now. She supposed that, one day, it would be all be passed down to Mike, his wife, and their future pack of little Nordstroms. It was interesting that not once had she even vaguely considered that might be her. Married to a millionaire, just like a MyHeart heroine.

She smiled at him now. 'I'll look at it later. I was waiting to hear from an author.'

'Check the email,' Mike said patiently. 'It's fine.'

'Sorry. Thanks a lot. I'll be one second.' Elle said. She opened her messages. Sure enough, it was the email she'd been praying for, from Elizabeth Forsyte.

My dearest Elle,

My most heartfelt thanks to you for the care and attention you have taken over getting this cover right. The Lord of Misrule is to me a very special story, one that I hope will bring my readers even more pleasure. I have been so very worried by the turn of events the jacket was taking, but now that you have been so gracious – that British charm again! – and the heart above my name has been removed, I have no hesitation in saying that we should go to press with this version, and God Speed us all the way to #1 on the lists!

Your friend,

Elizabeth Forsyte

Post script: Euphemia and Brunswick send you their thanks and love too, for releasing their story to the world.

Elle blinked: all Elizabeth Forsyte's emails were sent in tiny calligraphic script, on a lurid pink background decorated with Georgian pillars and other architectural features. It was so high-res that her emails frequently crashed the computer of whomever at Bookprint US she'd contacted, but no one would ever have dared to have pointed this out to her. *No one* said no to Elizabeth Forsyte. When you sold 600,000 hardbacks, and twice as many paperbacks, you could send child porn or videos of animal torture over the Internet to your publishers and they'd think very carefully before raising it as an issue.

'What's up?'

'Nothing, it's great news,' Elle said. Quickly she forwarded the email onto Caryn and Sidney, the overall MD.

We are GO, she wrote. **We can print tomorrow.**

'Done. I promise.' Elle put the BlackBerry in her bag and leaned back in her chair. Mike sighed.

'That woman,' Mike said. 'I sometimes think if she said, "I want you to eat fifteen raw eggs and ride the roller coaster at Coney Island," you'd do it.'

'Yes, I would,' Elle said simply. 'You know what it's like. It's business, and she's my biggest client. I wouldn't still be here if it weren't for her.'

'She's lucky to have you work with her,' Mike said loyally.

Elle shook her head. 'No, absolutely not. Without her I'd be a nobody back in London.'

'I know that's not true,' Mike said, smiling at her. 'You crazy girl.'

She closed her eyes briefly, as outside the new leaves juddered lightly in the breeze. She knew she'd never get him to understand. The waiter arrived, with a green salad for her and a soup for him. 'Cheers,' Elle said again, exhilaration sweeping over her; she couldn't wait to be in work tomorrow to discuss it with Caryn, hear if Sidney was pleased. 'Hurrah, this is a great evening.'

'Have a wonderful trip back to England,' Mike said, clinking his glass against hers. 'Don't stay there. Come back soon.'

'Believe me, I will,' she said fervently, taking only another small sip of champagne. 'It's in, out. Wham, bam. It's Wedding Supper, Wedding, Stay with Mother, Plane Back. No deviation, nothing. I'll be back before you can miss me.'

Mike nodded, pleased, and Elle realised this conversation could sound misleading. But she didn't care. Two days ago it had looked as though Elizabeth Forsyte wasn't going to let them publish with that jacket, and now it was sorted, and half a million copies could be printed, and they were all safe again, safe till the next crisis. While a small, very small part of her wanted to scream, *It was one tiny pink heart, you monstrous woman, get over it, do you realise how much time and effort has been wasted on this?* the other part knew it had Elizabeth Forsyte to thank for nearly everything. All because of Grammy Napper's brooch.

If Elle had known what the result of her innocent remark to someone in a Ladies' bathroom three years ago come November would have been she would have been amazed.

It had been her lucky day, she knew it now. She had complimented the rotund, mulberry-haired lady by the sinks on her pretty brooch – a tiny gold figure carrying a bunch of glass blue and red flowers – and the lady had turned around, with joy on her face.

'Brooch? What in the world is a brooch?'

Elle had explained.

'What a beautiful accent, mah dear. This pin was mah grammy's. How kind you are. I'm Elizabeth Forsyte.'

Elle had shaken her hand and said, shyly, how much she'd enjoyed the multi-million seller *Ladies Dance*.

This was good luck for several reasons: Elle really had

enjoyed it. Elizabeth Forsyte could write, and she knew how to tell a story. It wasn't another slim, derivative Regency romance, it was a big old-fashioned family saga, with lots of sex and intrigue; and the formula of a big fat beach read but with a tasteful jacket so the literati could devour it on vacation worked: it worked well enough that the book was on its way to selling a million copies in paperback, and ushering in a slew of rip-offs.

Secondly, little though Elle knew it, Elizabeth Forsyte and her agent were in that fateful day for a crisis meeting: they'd just told everyone at Jane Street that they were taking her next book to either Viking or Pocket, so badly, they said, was the publication of the follow-up to *Ladies Dance* being handled.

Thirdly, Elle had been in New York for two months. She had arrived in October, a month after September 11. The Stars and Stripes hung everywhere, 5th Avenue was a sea of them. Smoke from Ground Zero continued to rise; it hung in the air downtown. She was staying in Brooklyn, at the empty apartment of a friend of Karen's; every evening in the early autumn sunshine little boys ran around in the yard outside, wearing Superman and Spider-Man costumes. A lady in her building had lost her daughter in the South Tower. She hadn't even worked there, she'd gone in for a meeting. Morning and evening, Elle could hear the tramp of feet along the corridor to Mrs Bilefsky's apartment: friends, neighbours, reporters. The superintendent of the building brought her soup, even though the nights were still warm, long after Hallowe'en.

At Bookprint US, she was assigned to Jane Street Press, the imprint where Daria, with whom she was doing the exchange, worked. But everyone was still in a state of shock, striving to keep body and soul together for themselves, their families and friends. Daria was miserable in London and thought she might come back; every day she changed her mind, so Elle never knew whether she'd still be here the following week. People could not have been more welcoming but no one knew why she was there. She had no idea, either. They gave her some paranormal erotic romances to edit, she did a project on cover designs in the UK versus the US, but all the pent-up energy and good intentions with which she had arrived and which she was bursting to use were not appropriate, now.

She spent hours walking, around Midtown in her lunch break, around Brooklyn at the weekends. She buried herself in New York career-girl books, *The Group*, *The Best of Everything*, *The Girl's Guide to Hunting and Fishing*, even *Valley of the Dolls*. By December, she was actively looking forward to February, when her four months would be up and she could go back, though to what, she had no idea; she didn't want to go back. She loved being here, loved everything about New York. But it wasn't working out and she didn't know how to change things for the better, and perhaps it was wrong to try.

But then, one morning, Elle was sitting at her desk shuffling some submission letters around, when she saw Caryn storming towards her. Convinced she was after her for the cover copy she hadn't yet filed, Elle cravenly fled to the bathroom and, once the door was closed, blushed with shame at how pathetic she was being. Perhaps it was relief that made her lean against the door, panting and glancing apologetically at the lady reapplying her lipstick in the mirror, perhaps it was a desire to talk to someone, anyone.

'That's a lovely brooch,' she'd said.

The lady had put her lipstick down on the counter, turned around and laughed. Yes, somehow, she'd had the nerve to start talking to Elizabeth Forsyte, called a pin a brooch, and on the basis of this five-minute conversation, Elizabeth Forsyte decided she and she alone was the editor with the English charm and know-how to guide *The Marriage Game* through its delicate gestation period, and suddenly that was it.

For all that Elizabeth Forsyte was egotistical, demanding, passive-aggressive, she was a genius, in her way, and she had spotted something in Elle, and Elle never forgot that. Her work visa was magically extended; her salary was increased. Suddenly agents took her calls; in the great glass elevators in the mornings, colleagues nodded over their skinny lattes; when she had to present another book at the terrifying acquisitions meeting Sidney Levantine, the MD, peered over his half-moon spectacles at her and said, 'Ah, Miss Eleanor Bee. How very good it is to have you with us.' And when *The Marriage Game* went in at Number One that summer, smashing all records for a hardback, and Elizabeth Forsyte took out a full page ad in *Publishers' Weekly* to thank 'her friends at Jane Street Press', Elle's place at Jane Street was assured.

Elle changed, too. She all but stopped drinking: though she had pushed to the back of her mind the memory of those bloated, lonely last months in London, she reminded herself of them whenever she considered buying a bottle of wine. It was all too easy to remember the endless lonely nights in the Kilburn flat, the walls closing in, the alcohol in the pores, coming into the office hungover again and trying to hide it. Tom had seen that, he'd told her . . . But it was another life, that time, and she'd been given a second chance.

Besides, here, that wouldn't be tolerated. She didn't know how close she'd come to the tipping point, and she didn't want to know. She wasn't even sure if there *was* a tipping point, just that she'd walked away from whatever it was pulling her towards a dark abyss. She had to use this time to make a change, and so she did, and it was easier than she'd thought. She was walking everywhere and barely drank any more, apart from the odd cocktail here and there; she lost a stone without trying to. It was only when she saw the photo on her old Bookprint security pass that she realised how heavy she'd been getting, anyway. It was wine and Pringle weight, and she was viciously glad to be rid of it.

Like everyone else, she had a manicure each week, at the Korean walk-up next to the subway; her tights (pantyhose) were free of holes; she invested in a small, chic wardrobe from Banana Republic. She grew out her messy hair and had it cut into a glossy mane that hung behind her shoulders, light brown with buttery highlights. After a year, she rented a tiny apartment in the West Village, so small she had to go out, either to work or to dinner, and her possessions had to be organised, otherwise chaos would reign. But that was fine; it was small, but it was light and warm, cool in summer, with shelves already up for her books and besides, she liked being organised, now.

And, since she felt as though she'd been given a lifeline, she worked. It was almost her religion. She read everything, stayed late, never left an email unanswered. Every night as she left the office she was alone in the city once again, and she loved it here, she never wanted to leave. She felt as if New York loved her back, even the man by the subway who picked scabs off his elbow and ate them, even the smelly, frizzy-haired blind lady whom she always seemed to have to help across the road, who told her every time that she hated the British. Even when her air-con packed up and she lay sweltering in the heat, even when the traffic was awful yet again and her colleagues were terrifying . . . she just had to put on her trainers and walk back home as the purple sunset flashed between black gleaming towers at each corner, as the sidewalks filled with people talking, eating, laughing, back to the Village to feel that nothing, really, was that bad. Because really, nothing was.

She could barely remember her life in London now, didn't recognise the girl she'd been there. Here, she felt, she was the person she'd always wanted to be.

'SO, YOU'LL SPEND some time with your mom when you're back,' Mike said.

'Yes,' Elle replied. 'The wedding's in some plush stately home in Sussex, really near her. Sanditon Hall. It's funny, that's where Rhodes and Melissa's original wedding was supposed to be.'

'Is it going to be strange for you?'

'What, going back to the UK?'

They were walking up Bleecker Street, past yet another gaudy tattoo parlour, a divey, commercialised bar. Mike took her hand and squeezed it. 'Everything, I guess.'

She'd told him a lot, but not all. Elle watched a guy in a leather cap wrap his leg round a street lamp. 'Suppose so. I'm not massively looking forward to it, that's all.'

'Have you spoken to – what's her name? Melissa? – since those drinks last month?'

'No,' said Elle. 'I'll have to, though.'

'She sounds awful. I don't like the way she spoke to you.'

'Oh, I don't know,' Elle said. She didn't want to start talking about them now; it'd ruin the evening. They were reaching the nice part of Bleecker, with the Marc Jacobs and the Magnolia Bakery in the distance. People were eating out on the pavement, there was soft laughter from a nearby table, and Elle turned to look at two girls, around her age, with flowing blonde hair, in skinny white jeans, drinking gingerly from wine glasses. They were gorgeous, a ridiculous tableau of beauty, and she stared at them. 'Ah – do you want anything from London?' She didn't know why she was asking – what could she bring him that he couldn't get here? A biscuit tin with a picture of a soldier in a busby hat, a snow globe of St Paul's Cathedral?

'No thanks, Elle.' He smiled at her and took her hand. She held it tightly. 'Will you go into the office?'

'I might have to but I don't want to. I have a meeting with an author somewhere in town and that's it. I'm glad. It's kind of naff of me, but I don't want to – I don't like going back there much, I wasn't that . . .' She trailed off, realising she didn't know how to carry on.

'Naff? What's naff?' Mike said, and she thought he was probably just breaking the silence. She leaned up and kissed him.

'It means ridiculous and stupid and that's what I'm being so forget about it.' Elle ran her thumb over the ball of his palm. They were at the turning for Perry Street. 'Are you coming back with me?'

'Maybe I am,' he said, and he put his hand on her neck, pulled her towards him and kissed her lightly on the lips, so she could feel his smooth chin, smell his light, lemony smell, clean, calm and reassuring.

On Perry Street people were sitting out on their stoops, chatting and drinking beers. The newly leafy trees arched across the road towards each other. Marcy from next door and her boyfriend Steven were on the steps with some friends. 'Hey, Elle! Have a great trip,' Marcy called. 'Don't let your family drive you insane.'

Elle and Marcy had had cocktails the previous week – Elle

always forgot how even the most abstemious, triathlon-running New Yorkers could set about two Manhattans like they were ginger ale. Cocktails were a fast, efficient way of getting drunk, if that's what you wanted. You could control it, two was enough if you wanted to blot everything out, just once in a while. Much more straightforward than glugging back glass after glass of rancid white wine in a vile pub surrounded by City workers in cheap Next suits.

It pleased Elle that she couldn't take her drink any more, but all she remembered of the evening with Marcy was banging on the bar of the cocktail place and yelling, 'Bloody brother! Bloody mother! Melissa's an evil witch!' while Marcy applauded loudly.

Now Elle grinned at her, grimacing slightly at the extent to which she had unburdened herself. 'I'll call you when I'm back,' she said. She liked saying that. She would be back. It was only a few days. They couldn't make her stay, though sometimes she had dreams in which they did. She hurried Mike up the steps.

Marc was loitering in the hallway, as if he knew she'd be coming. He was ostensibly checking his mail but when Elle opened the door, he pushed it into his pocket, raised one eyebrow, and said, 'Hey, British girl. When are you flying?'

'Tomorrow night, the red-eye,' Elle said.

'Uh-huh?' Marc said, in the slightly evil, slightly camp way Elle found almost irresistible. They stared at each other, frozen for a second, and then the front door banged open and Mike, who had been tying his shoelace, followed her in.

'Hey, Mike, good to see you,' Marc said. (That was another thing Elle loved about New Yorkers, they remembered people's names and were polite. Also, they liked grammar and never said 'The Republican Party are etc. etc'. It was always 'The Republican Party *is*'.)

They shook hands. There was an awkward pause.

'Well, have a great trip,' Marc said. 'I'll see you guys . . .

later.' He smiled wickedly at Elle, pushing his pink lower lip down slightly, in a tiny pout. She watched him, amused and, as ever, slightly turned on, ridiculous as it was. 'Come and tell me all about it when you're back. Oi lahve—'

'Don't do the accent,' Elle interjected, desperately.

'—ah lahverlee Briddish cuhntree wodding,' Marc finished.

'I said *don't* do the accent.'

'OK, OK. And don't let that bitch of a sister-in-law get you down,' he said. 'Screw her bony Connecticut ass! OK!'

'She's actually from upstate—' Elle began, but Marc held up his hand.

'Don't ruin the moment, honey. Be cool. Remember, you have a Kate Spade matching bag and shoe set, as you keep telling anyone who'll listen.'

'I don't keep telling everyone!' Elle protested. 'Shut up.'

Mike pushed Elle towards her front door. 'Night, Marc,' he said firmly, and Elle threw one last look back at her neighbour.

'See you tomorrow,' she said.

He blinked lazily and mouthed, *I want you*, as Mike went in ahead of her.

Mike went over to the tiny kitchen, while Elle sat on the bed of the studio apartment and took off her heels, rubbing her feet. She put her earrings on the nightstand. The air-con cranked noisily in the window. She looked at Mike, leaning against the kitchen counter.

He rubbed his eyes, looking a little tired. 'I wonder if that guy is sometimes a little too much, when you're not in the mood. You want some water?'

Warwter. Wahdder. Warwter. If she said, 'Please could I have some *warwter*?' people looked at her blankly. Now Elle knew to say, 'Can I get some wahdder? Thank you.'

'He's OK,' she said, an image of her and Marc having sex on that very same kitchen counter only two weeks ago flashing through her mind, his jeans round his ankles, his firm, biscuit-coloured thighs pressed against her thighs, straining so she could open her legs wider, let him deeper inside her. Elle jumped off the bed, blinking, and went to the cupboard. She took down two glasses. 'Listen, Mike – about the exclusive thing –'

'It's OK.' Mike held his hands up, and then ran them through his short, dark blond hair. 'Let's forget it for tonight.'

'I like you,' she said. 'A lot.'

He smiled kindly at her, and she wished she didn't want him to be someone else.

'Tell me something,' he said. 'What exactly did Melissa say to you that was so awful? We never really talked about it.'

Elle turned away from him. 'Nothing. Forget it.'

THEY'D MET AT the Algonquin for drinks. It was March. Elle was late – a conference call with someone in LA had overrun. When she'd arrived, Melissa was one Martini down.

Since their cancelled wedding, Elle had seen Melissa and Rhodes three times. Once a year at Christmas. The first time, they'd met at their father's in Brighton. Elle had been dreading it, dreading what they might say, what she might do. When they arrived, she remembered instantly how *definite* both of them looked. Rhodes, beefier and larger than ever, aggressive, controlled energy bursting out of him, his hands big balled fists by his sides. Melissa, wiry, poised, smooth, always polite, never giving anything out, not to them.

In the end, it was OK: as ever with these situations, Elle hadn't factored in the random bombshell beyond her control. And theirs was great. Melissa was pregnant. 'The perfect Christmas present!' Eliza, Elle's stepmother, had exclaimed – but it also gave everyone an excuse to avoid talking about the cancelled wedding, the subsequent secret one, what had been said, and the one person who wasn't in the room. The elephant called Mandana.

(When her niece was born, Elle sent a toy elephant from Barney's, and afterwards she remembered and wondered if this was some weird subconscious link-up. But Rhodes and Melissa had moved from a flat in Battersea to Primrose Hill and Elle hadn't known. The elephant never arrived.)

The second year, she'd seen them at her mother's, and met little Lauren for the first time. They arrived for lunch and ate some turkey, and everyone fussed over the baby. It was so lovely to see her niece, who had curly hair like her father, and who looked like Mandana, Elle thought. They left straight after lunch, all very polite, but they clearly couldn't wait to get away, leaving Elle and her mother to flop in front of the TV with cranberry juices and Christmas cake, being jolly together. And that was it for another year.

The third year, Elle had seen them in Brighton again, and Lauren was eighteen months old and walking, and she said 'apple' and 'cheers', and she was very cute. And they'd sat round the large oak table in the big Brighton basement and pretended they were all one big happy family, even though, Elle realised afterwards, she hadn't had an actual conversation with either Rhodes or Melissa lasting more than fifteen seconds. They lived in London and she lived in New York, and she didn't miss them, because she barely knew them these days, her brother included. She just wished it could be different.

'It's so great to see you,' Elle had greeted Melissa, sitting down in the Algonquin bar, stamping her feet to get over the cold. 'How's Lauren, is she with you? Did she get the *Eloise* book OK? Why are you over?' Too many questions. Her voice sounded high and nervous.

'I'm visiting friends, and I'm having some conversations,' Melissa had said, draining the rest of her drink. 'We might move back here. Just thinking about it for the moment. Lauren's with her aunt. I'll give her your love.'

The bar was busy; she could hear various conversations burbling around her. 'I'm her aunt,' Elle said.

'Of course. No, her other aunt. My sister.'

Melissa was very beautiful. Elle always forgot that. She stole another glance at her. 'Right,' Elle said. 'That's great, can I maybe—'

Melissa interrupted. 'Elle, I have to go at eight. I wanted to see you so we could ask you something. You see.' She was fidgeting. 'We want to know how long you're planning on staying in New York,' she'd said, waving a finger at a waiter, who'd immediately slid into place beside her. She flicked an enquiring glance at Elle. 'What are you having? Martini?' Elle nodded, dumbly. 'Two Martinis please, you want yours with a twist? Great. Some more olives. Thank you.'

She turned to Elle. 'It's your mom. She needs help. We want to know when you're coming back.'

'Mum? She's fine. I spoke to her yesterday. She's – she was on her way out with Bryan.' Elle tried to divert Melissa away from the subject. 'Hey, where do you think you might live if you move back?'

Melissa said coldly, 'Elle, I'm not here to talk about the move. I'm here because I need to say this to you face to face. This isn't something that you can just sweep under the carpet any more.'

'What are you talking about?'

'Oh, come on. You know when I cancelled our first wedding it was because of your mother.'

'That's what I heard, you never actually told me why,' Elle said, biting her tongue to prevent her from saying more. She could feel a red mist of anger rising inside her. She remembered Mum's voice on the phone the previous night when she'd told her she was seeing Melissa for a drink. 'Oh, lucky you,' Mandana had said, deeply sarcastically. 'That'll be fun. Ask her to warn you before she smiles. I swear she's had her teeth whitened again. She nearly blinded me last time I saw her.'

Elle tried not to smile at the memory of this.

Melissa said, 'The reason I cancelled is I wanted everything to be perfect and it couldn't be, so I didn't wanna do it. You know that.'

'Melissa, you sent out a card a week before the bachelorette party, and that's all you ever said. Dad was the one who told me you'd fallen out with Mum –' Elle twitched, in irritation. 'God, it's not about me, it doesn't matter.' She looked up, suddenly desperate for her drink. 'It's just I never understood it. You were so into it, every detail was going to be perfect, it was this big expensive do, and two months to go you go totally silent and then cancel. It just didn't seem – I never understood – we didn't know –'

Having started off with some purpose, Elle ran out of steam. She sat back.

Melissa jabbed at a napkin with her cocktail stick. She said, 'I won't say I didn't regret it, because I did, actually.'

'Really?'

'Yes. Of course. But I couldn't go through with it after that weekend, worrying she might be like that. I've never –' She jabbed the stick viciously, piercing the wooden table beneath. 'I never saw anyone like that. Even Daddy, when he was at his worst. She was like Mr Hyde. Just – so angry. To me, but especially to Rhodes.' Melissa looked up then, over at the pianist, not at Elle. 'You know I think she gets mixed up sometimes, and confuses Rhodes with your father?'

Elle thought she was joking, but one look at Melissa's face told her she wasn't.

'They look the same. She looks at him, sees your dad, blames him, it's crazy. I couldn't – I couldn't face her doing that again, not on my wedding.' She gave a small smile. 'You know, I'm a perfectionist. I wanted it how I wanted it. It was all I could think about, I started having nightmares about what she could do.'

Melissa paused.

'I didn't even want to see her, to touch her, to have her there.'

Elle shifted in her seat. She realised she was still clutching her bag, her phone. She put them down on the floor. 'Melissa, I'm sorry, I—'

Melissa's tone grew hard. 'Rhodes and I don't want to have this conversation with you but we have to – I told him you have to tell us. When are you planning on coming home?'

'Not in the forseeable future,' Elle had said, hoping she sounded calm. 'Why do you want to know?'

'We just don't think we should have to look out for your mother all the time.'

'Why?' Elle said. 'Don't, then.'

'She's much worse.'

'Worse? No, she's not,' Elle said. 'She's doing really well.'

'Elle, for God's sake. She's drinking again. You must have realised that.'

Elle tried not to sigh. 'I—'

Melissa threw up her hands. 'Come on. She's an alcoholic, Elle. You're the one she tries to hide it from the most, and it's killing her.' Elle shook her head. 'Come on! She needs to go to a treatment centre. She needs counselling, she needs to go cold turkey. She is dependent on alcohol.'

The drinks arrived and Elle took a swig of hers, feeling the cool, thick, clear alcohol slide down her throat, hating how good it felt. She closed her eyes, briefly, marshalling herself, trying not to look at the hypocrisy of them with their vodka Martinis, condemning Mandana. 'Melissa – she doesn't really drink any more.'

Melissa gave a snort, something between anger and disbelief. 'You're – wow, you're just living in a fantasy land, aren't you?' she said. 'Of course she does.'

'Melissa,' Elle said. 'She and I talk about it a lot. I spent a week with her last summer when she came to visit. I know it's been hard for her, and she's relapsed a couple of times, but honestly. She doesn't drink any more.'

'She lost her driving licence in the summer,' Melissa said. Elle dropped her cocktail stick, and her mouth flew open. Melissa looked grimly satisfied. 'Come on, Elle, you didn't know that?'

Elle blinked. 'She – no, I didn't.' She remembered some story about Mandana not being able to pick her up at Christmas, but – Elle was resigned to it, Mandana was constantly changing her mind about things.

'She crashed the car the day after she got back from visiting you. She's lying to you, Elle, she's gotten really good at it. Come on! You're the one she doesn't want to find out. Us, she doesn't care any more.'

Elle ignored this. 'Has she done something, said something? She can be really vile, and I'm sorry if she's upset you.' Melissa narrowed her eyes.

'You don't know what you're talking about. You're running away from the truth, Elle.'

Don't know what you're talking about? Elle wanted to laugh. 'Look,' she said. She put her hand down on the table. 'It's not that I've run away to New York to get away from her. Seriously, Melissa. She stayed with me for a week last year and she was fine, more than fine. She's got the business with Anita now, she's got Bryan, she's doing the library stuff, when I talk to her she seems on good form. I want to believe she's telling me the truth.' She took a deep breath. 'And I do.'

'I've never met Bryan, have you? And you know how she crashed the car? You know what she did?' Melissa said urgently. Her cheeks were flushed. 'She got so drunk she tried to drive to your father's house. She crashed on some A-road. The police called us and when we got to the house there were three empty bottles of vodka. She'd drunk non-stop after she'd got back from New York. That's how she lost the licence, Elle.'

302

'But –'

Elle remembered the last night she'd had here with her mother, nearly a year ago. A few months after she'd moved permanently to New York, she'd paid an immigration lawyer to look at Mandana's case, and he'd found three other similar cases where visas had been issued, with certain conditions, and it proved to be the case with Mandana. Funny that three years ago Elle would never have dreamed of doing something so . . . bold. They'd seen *Henry V* at Shakespeare in the Park, then they'd had dinner on the Upper West Side at a tiny restaurant Mandana had wanted to go back to ever since she'd visited it in 1969, on her way to San Francisco. They'd laughed incessantly about the bohemian couple next to them at the play, who'd very obviously mouthed key lines. Mandana had been on such good form, ebullient, happy, flushed with laughter and the heat, how good a time they were having. Elle could hear her breathing next to her in the tiny double bed, and she'd listened to her that last night, watched her peaceful face, and felt that for once, her mother was, yes, OK.

And twenty-four hours later – really? Elle's left eye started to throb, beating a tattoo inside her head.

'Do you wanna know what she did when we told her we were having Lauren?'

Elle shrugged, and held it, her shoulders tense, her hands clenched in front of her, as if guarding herself from more blows.

Melissa ran a hand over her forehead, and her blonde fringe stuck up on end. 'We went to see her, the weekend before Christmas, to tell her our good news. Do you know what she did?'

'No.' Elle's voice was small.

'She was drunk when we got there.' Melissa breathed out deeply and closed her eyes. 'She said she pitied any child born into our family. She said she'd never seen any pictures of the wedding and for all she knew it would be a bastard. And she didn't care. She said that. Then she threw up. She's always throwing up, she's lost so much weight. She's sick, Elle. She threw up and she rubbed it all –' Melissa put her hands over her face. 'No. It was disgusting.'

'What did she do?' Elle thought she might be sick herself.

'It doesn't matter. It's enough. She was like – I don't know! God, like Quasimodo? Like an ape, a monster, lumbering round the kitchen, smashing things, these hands everywhere, and she was – man, she was so nasty. So nasty, like she was thinking all the time, What's the worst thing I can say now? And now?' Melissa paused, her face pink, her eyes wet. 'I was *pregnant*, with her first grandchild. This is your mother. This is what she's like. You think it's not your problem, somehow.' Melissa breathed out, her nostrils flaring. 'But it *is* your problem. I'm not responsible for her.' She looked down, and checked her phone and her watch. She drained her glass. 'We've tried our best. But Rhodes is sick of it, to be honest, and she needs help.' She paused. 'It's a cunning disease. You're the one she wants to be happy, and she's hiding it from you, and it's going to kill her. The doctor at the hospital after the crash told us her liver's fucked, but she discharged herself before they could do more tests. And she's fine now, God knows how she keeps on going.' She exhaled slowly, whistling through her lips. 'Like I say, you have to talk to her. It's your turn. She's only going to get worse. Someone needs to intervene.'

'Right –' said Elle. Suddenly, weirdly, she heard her dad's voice, that long-ago lunch in the boiling heat, the day he'd put the shelves up. '*I think you should go to New York. Leave your mum behind.*' She had. She'd done what he said. She'd done it for herself, and it had been the right thing to do. Except –

'Your turn,' Melissa said. 'You need to know it. When you're over you'll see what I mean, Elle. You Brits, you're in denial about putting a label on something that's a disease.'

You sound like a Woody Allen film, Elle had thought. Denial, labels. Instead she had said, 'Thank you,' which was the only thing she could think of. *Thanks for telling me it's my problem now, not yours.*

After their awkward goodbye Elle had gone home, walking back from the subway in the freezing slush, and she sat on the edge of her bed for a long time. She didn't know what to do; she felt totally alone. She couldn't ring Mandana and ask her if she was drinking, how she was; she wouldn't tell her. Elle knew her mother well enough to know how cunning she was, and in that she agreed with Melissa. She knew if she just turned up on the doorstep her mother would clam up. In the end, she RSVP'd to the invitation that had been staring at her reproachfully on the nightstand since it had arrived two days ago and booked a ticket. She didn't want to come back for the wedding. She had to come back, to see her mum. She'd see for herself then.

'SO ELLE,' CARYN her boss said, pacing up and down Elle's tiny office, her eyes snapping with excitement, cracking gum. 'What happens at an English wedding, huh? Hugh Grant making a speech? People in stupid hats? A panto?'

'A panto.' Elle laughed. 'Caryn, do you know what that word is?'

'Panto?' Caryn pronounced it *pintoww*. Her default English accent was worse than Marc's, worse than Dick Van Dyke's. Even though she was the head of a large publishing division that had many best-selling international authors, Caryn was Queens and always would be. Sometimes, Elle thought, she took a little too much pride in it. Elle didn't feel the need to let someone know within five seconds of meeting them that she came from a small village near Gatwick Airport, whereas Caryn would immediately say, 'I'm from Queens,' as if it would be rude to withold this information from a stranger. 'Oh, God, I never knew she was from Queens, I wish she'd told me,' Paul, the rights manager, had once said in a bar, and Elle had nearly fallen off her chair laughing, but also partly with shock: in New York publishing, you were professional, you didn't slag off your boss or take the piss, you didn't go to the pub and drunkenly rant, and you certainly didn't sleep with your co-workers.

'Panto. It's a stupid British thing British people do,' Caryn said, crossing her tiny, sinewy arms and smiling her glaring white smile at Elle. 'I don't know. Am I right?'

'Yes,' said Elle. 'That's completely right.' She thought of the pantomime they'd always gone to see when she was small, the year when Rhodes got picked from the audience to be shot out of a cannon by Lionel Blair, how she'd been so scared they really would fire it that her mum had had to explain it was a trick, just for fun.

'Are you a bridesmaid?'

'No, no,' Elle said. 'In the circumstances . . .' she trailed off.

'Thank God. I think you're nuts to even be going,' said Caryn. Elle didn't know if this was out of some tiny attempt to show she cared, or because in her absence Elle would miss the Fall Schedule Presentation and Sidney was particularly on Caryn's back at the moment about everything. 'But is it the crazy production it is here though? Like Judy's wedding last year? The doves dyed blue and the groomsmen having singing lessons to learn "When Doves Cry" a cappella as she walked down the aisle? Come on.' Caryn slapped her thighs. 'Nothing can be as heinous as that.'

Elle laughed. 'Not as much. Fewer bridesmaids.' She'd been to a wedding with Mike earlier in the month in New Hampshire, where there had been eight bridesmaids, with identical hair and dress, of identical height and weight, with eight identical groomsmen on their arms. There had been a wedding planner with a radio mic in her ear, a proper swing band, and on each table for the men there were cufflinks with the bride and groom's initials and for the girls, jewelled Melissa Odabash flip-flops to put on when their heels started to hurt. It was like a military operation.

Caryn looked at her watch. 'OK. What time's your flight?'

307

'Nine thirty, it's fine. I'll finish up and go straight from here.'

'That's great.' Caryn put her hand on the door. 'Did you speak to Molly Goodwin?'

'Sure, and I told her I'd go see her when I'm back to discuss a new contract.'

'How about Magnolia?'

'She's coming up from Georgia next month.'

Caryn shook her head. 'What else is there for me to worry about? You are the best, Elle. So, good work with Elizabeth Forsyte once again. It's going to be huge for you, that book.'

One of the things Elle admired about Caryn was that though she was a total workaholic, she belonged to the 'hire someone who wants your job' school of management: she actually liked the idea that the people who worked for her should do better than her. Elle had realised how lucky she was in her new boss when Bill Lewis, Libby's ex and MD of the BBE division, had come over on one of his US trips. Not only was she reminded sharply how little she liked him as a person, she saw how self-aggrandising he was – in meetings he took credit for books Elle knew other editors had bought – how pompous, concerned only with his own cause. Much like the way he'd treated Libby.

Libby . . . Elle shivered. Since she'd booked her flight back to the UK, she'd been thinking often of Libby, and wondering how she was. In a way, she owed everything to her, she'd never have ended up in New York if it weren't for Libby and her machinations. As she waved goodbye to Caryn and sat down again at her desk, Elle was sharply reminded, she didn't know why, of the week Diana died. That red-wine-soaked evening at the Dome in Hampstead, eating croque monsieurs and shouting about how much they loved art and literature and life and boys and life – oh, how cringeworthy. Coming home at two, Sam waking her with the terrible news. Sam – where was *she* now? Watching the funeral with Sam in their old flat, she and Sam sobbing, Libby trying not to roll her eyes. Little things, like Libby's blue sun dress, the crown of daisies she'd made the afternoon after the funeral as they lay in Hyde Park and talked about love.

It was not quite seven years, but it felt like a lifetime ago. Elle had to search hard within herself to remember being that girl. The girl who hadn't even kissed Rory yet. She had been thinking a lot about him too, these last few weeks, as the time of her trip grew nearer. She didn't want to forget how deeply she had loved him, how important it had been to her; she felt as if to discard the memory would be a betrayal of her younger self.

They'd had a drink the previous year in New York and it had been so strange, to see someone you knew and obsessed over so much, to hear his light, friendly voice again. His hair was the same, chaotic and floppy, his clothes were new versions of what they'd always been – low-key, dashing English bloke round town – but the lines round the eyes, the slight weariness of the face, the desperation with which he'd said, 'You're doing so well for yourself, I wish I had your recipe. You're so different, you look different.'

As she had left the bar of the Soho Grand – because of course he, like Bill, stayed at the Soho Grand – Elle had known he was right. She *was* different. She liked hearing it, because she wanted to recall just enough of it to remember that she never wanted to go back to being the person she'd been before.

At half past six, Elle shut down her computer and whipped out her suitcase, checked that her dress was still there, checked she had her passport, her BlackBerry, her shiny new blue iPod and her money, and shut her office door behind her, taking one last look at the sign on the door:

309

She trundled down the wide glass corridors, casting one look behind her at the glorious view over Midtown towards the Park. It was a beautiful evening, still bright. She fished around in her handbag for her sunglasses.

'Oh, goodbye, Elle!' Jennifer the editorial assistant said, smiling as Elle went past. 'Have a great trip, please do let me know if there's anything you need while you're there?'

'Sure,' said Elle. 'Thanks, Jen.' She raised her hand in a farewell greeting.

'Hey, let me get that for you,' Stuart Forgan, senior vice president, said as Elle arrived at the elevator, struggling with her bag, her case, her coat, her pass. 'So, you're off to merry old England, eh?'

'Sure am,' said Elle, in her best, but still terrible, American accent.

Stuart smiled and pushed his round glasses further up his nose. 'Are you going to the Bookprint offices?' he said, gesturing for her to go ahead of him into the elevator. 'I was going to wait till you came back but this is serendipity, in fact.'

'Oh?' said Elle, trying to look alert and interested but fishing through her handbag for her passport and ticket at the same time. She remembered how much she used to loathe lift encounters. Now she quite liked them. 'What can I do?'

'Yes, well, you might try and discuss Gray Logan while you're there. Even though they know he's a *New York Times* best-seller they do nothing with him. He says he doesn't want to be published by us in the UK any more, and that could affect our chances of doing another deal. Sidney says it needs addressing.' He folded his arms and looked at her over his glasses. 'I wondered if perhaps a solution might be to have you on board.'

Elle held her breath. Gray Logan was a giant of the New York literary scene, winner of the Pulitzer Prize, professor at Columbia, beloved by every reviewer, bookseller and book-buyer in Manhattan. 'What about Owen?'

Stuart pressed the ground-floor button and the doors closed. 'Owen's retiring next month, it's gonna be quiet, his wife's ill and he doesn't want a commotion. So, Elle, I wanted to talk to you about becoming Gray's editor. You could be the UK liaison point too, even though you're in the US. You could deal with Bookprint UK more effectively, make sure they don't screw it up again. We can't lose Gray Logan. What do you think?'

'I've never edited anyone like him before,' Elle said. 'He's . . . well, he's literary, isn't he?' They were on the twenty-fourth floor. That initial, first whoosh of the elevator made Elle's heart jolt, it always did. She swallowed. 'It's just – my friend Libby looks after him in the UK.'

'OK, so it's strange for you,' Stuart said. 'I'm sorry, this is probably inappropriate when you're about to catch a plane. Think about it. We'll discuss it when you're back.'

'It's fine,' said Elle. 'I'll do it.'

'You sure you don't mind? Your friend – it wouldn't be awkward?'

The lift doors opened. Libby's face, the daisies in her hair, receded into the background, as the glass lobby appeared before them, yellow cabs on Broadway flashing past them in the distance. 'I'm partly going back to see her,' Elle said, after only a faint pause. She gritted her teeth. 'You know, she won't mind.'

'HE THAT IS in a towne in May loseth his spring.' Elle remembered this long-forgotten George Herbert quote from her A levels as she negotiated the narrow lanes in her Polo hire car. She had had lunch off Dover Street with Heather Dougall, writer of cosy crime mysteries about an old lady and her cat (they couldn't give them away in the UK, but they sold like hot cakes in the States) and listened to her litany of complaints about Bookprint UK. After lunch, she walked through Mayfair up Old Bond Street towards Selfridges, looking at the expensive bags, the jewellery, the rich ladies and gentlemen in their smart cars – this was the London American people thought existed, the London of *Mary Poppins* and *Upstairs Downstairs*. She rather liked it, it was so far removed from her own experience. For a few more moments, she could enjoy being a tourist, rather than engaging with it all.

As she got into the car and switched the radio onto Capital, and as the sun shone through the heavy white clouds, she allowed herself to fall in love with London again, just a bit. She headed out down the Fulham Road, glancing at the floppy-haired posh boys ambling along the wide pavements, the pretty blonde girls with their huge handbags hanging painfully off their tiny wrists. A Maroon 5 song finished playing, and then 'Toxic' came on . . . Elle smiled, this wasn't too bad. It was going to be OK.

Her plan was to go back to Mum's later this evening, after the rehearsal dinner at the hotel. The rehearsal dinner was a stupid American tradition, she didn't understand why they all had to gather for a dinner the night before the wedding when they'd be doing the very same thing some eighteen hours later. This was England, the bride and groom were English, it wasn't a wedding in Ohio, where everyone had come from thousands of miles to be there.

She shook these thoughts out of her head, but she couldn't help feeling apprehensive as she sped out of London. She'd come back to bury something, to exact her own revenge by having a good life. To lay to rest the ghost of her tender years.

As she came off the main road and into the proper countryside, foaming with cow parsley and early honeysuckle, wood pigeons cooing loudly in the trees, hedgerows high with fresh new greenery, Elle felt nostalgic in a way only an English spring can make you. She couldn't help thinking about all the books that made her think like that, *I Capture the Castle*, *The Forsyte Saga*, even *The Wind in the Willows*. She had taken the train to Marlow once with her mother, and walked along the wide Thames peering into the rushes and riverbanks. There weren't any toads or otters in Manhattan. She hardly had time to read anything that wasn't a manuscript, anyway.

Sanditon Hall was badly signposted, a track off a small road, and Elle missed it and had to go back, so it was close to eight when she arrived. As she drove down the long gravelled lane, slightly dizzy with fatigue, she scanned the horizon for the hotel. She could see the horse chestnuts in bloom, the black iron guards around the trees in the park, rusty with age. Her heart was thumping in her chest.

'Come on,' she said out loud, but in a quiet voice. 'You're here now. Why are you nervous? It's all in the past. It's not a big deal.'

Elle got out of the car, pulled her hair out of her cardigan and shook it so it fell around her face. She reached into her bag to put some lip gloss on, and then she stopped. Why did it matter, why did any of it matter? She'd got this far without turning back and running away, she could go a bit further, and without lip gloss too. Elle walked up the steps of the Georgian house, the stone warm in the sunshine, and into the circular black and white vestibule, feeling a bit as though it was her first day at work again. 'I'm here for the wedding dinner?' she told the helpful man on reception.

'Of course,' he said, signalling right with his hand. 'The Friends and Family Dinner is taking place in the Orangery, madam. If you'd like to follow me . . .'

He took her bag and walked her to the end of a corridor, with a sign at the end.

YATES / SASSOON WEDDING
FAMILY AND FRIENDS DINNER

'Are you family or friend?' the polite receptionist asked, making small talk. The murmur of conversation came from inside.

'I'm –' said Elle. She had to think about it. 'Friend?'

'Well, they're all in there,' he said. 'If you need anything else?'

'Thanks.' Elle watched him walk away, and then pushed the door open. Her skin felt as if it was burning, there was a rushing sound in her ears, this was unreal, yet she was doing it, there was a dull damp mark on the grey paint of the door where her perspiring hand had pushed it open.

'Oh, my God, you're here!' A girl detached herself from the crowd nearest the door and rushed over to Elle, in a cloud of voluminous chiffon. 'Elle, I can't believe you made it.'

'Hi, Libby,' Elle said, hugging her friend.

'You're really here, I'm so glad you came.' Libby looked intently into her eyes, and grabbed her wrists. 'Thank you. Thanks. It means a lot. Darling, look. Elle's back.'

A man on the other side of the room turned round. 'Elle,' he said.

'Hi, Rory,' Elle replied.

He came forward, then stopped, a couple of feet between them. 'Elle, sweetheart. Thank you for coming.'

Libby was watching her, a little too intently, and Elle wished she'd cut her some slack. She hoped with all her might she wasn't blushing. She had to act cool. Not just for her, for them.

'It's lovely to be here,' she said.

Libby held Rory's hands in hers, over her billowing blue chiffon dress. Elle stared at it in surprise. She felt bad, but it was the truth: Libby had put on weight, and the best way to hide it wasn't beneath layers of flowing material. Elle chided herself for being horrible, and then stopped. *Come on,* she heard a voice in her head saying, one she didn't really hear that much these days. *You're at Rory and Libby's wedding. You're allowed to be horrible about them, just a bit.*

YES, SHE WAS here. And it was normal, she was behaving normally, they were talking. The bowels of hell had not opened up and sucked Rory and Libby into the earth's molten core. Elle had dreaded this day for months, ever since she'd heard about the engagement. She'd been amazed they'd invited her: but then she reasoned, why not? She was one of Libby's oldest publishing friends, and really, who actually knew about her and Rory? It might as well never have happened.

Elle had known they were together, of course, known for over a year now. She didn't know how it had happened, but then it was none of her business, and she didn't really want to know. She'd even had a drink with the two of them, when they'd come on a joint trip to New York the previous October. They'd had Manhattans at the Campbell Apartment, and Libby had oohed and aahed over Elle like a doll: 'You're so *successful*!' 'Your hair's so pretty, I love your *dress*!' 'You must be working so *hard*!' as if this was compensation for stealing Rory. She hadn't stolen him, of course, but Elle felt that she was acting as if she had.

They were the perfect publishing couple: it made sense, when you saw them together. Their talk was all gossip: who was sleeping with whom; why X author had left Y editor or agent for Z; who'd paid millions of pounds for some book that had tanked; what A had said to B at C's launch. They'd clearly forgotten they'd once betrayed each other's relationships – perhaps it cancelled something out, if Rory had blabbed to his boss about Libby's affair and Libby had given a story to *Private Eye* about Rory's? Elle had forgotten what it was like, over there, and she didn't miss it. She found it tiresome, as she did the fact that Rory left them twice, once to go to the bathroom and once to take a phone call about a book he was trying to buy, whereas Libby didn't budge, as if she couldn't risk leaving the two of them on their own.

Yes, that was tiresome, as was the way Libby spoke of their relationship as if it were a living entity, a mascot: 'I have to say,' she said with a girlish giggle – *Libby*, who despised cheesy romance, who'd told Elle Rory was a fool and that he was using her! – 'a lot of people in the publishing community are really pleased about our relationship, it's been lovely to hear.' Most of all though, Elle found Rory's blank eyes and quiet manner tiresome, as if he didn't want to unleash the full force of his devastating personality on her in case she burst into tears, ripped off her clothes and shouted, 'Take me now! I still love you, Rory!'

In the wood-panneled, reassuringly old-school New York environment of the bar, with Grand Central Station below with its practised rush of humanity, she'd felt safe, secure in the knowledge that she was on her patch. In fact, she'd felt more alive than ever, like the heroines in the New York books she loved so much. She was so fizzing with *something* that she'd caught a cab back to Perry Street, knocked on Marc's door and when he opened it, handed him a beer and said, 'Can I come in?'

'Sure,' he'd said, with his slow, evil smile, and she'd not left until the following morning. As she'd crossed the old parquet flooring in her bare feet and shirt back to her apartment, the morning autumn sun shining in on the honey-coloured wood, she'd thought, with a smile, yes. This is the life I'm supposed to leading. Leave them to their tedious publishing gossip, their endless connections, their wine-soaked evenings, their snobbishness and small-mindedness.

But now it was different, she wasn't on her own patch any more. She was at Sanditon Hall, where they should have had Rhodes's wedding, back in the day when Libby loathed weddings and was sleeping with Bill. She'd reconsidered a few things in the intervening years, that was for sure.

'Well, I am so glad you came,' Libby said. 'It means such a lot. I can't believe you came all that way!'

'Oh –' Elle began, then she stopped.

I have to check on my mother and I needed an excuse. That's how it works with her and me. So this is perfect!

'I wanted to be here,' she said, trying to look sincere.

'You look amazing. Amazing! Doesn't she, Rory?'

'You look like you're about to take over the world, Elle,' Rory said. 'Like a young Tina Brown. Or an old Gwyneth Paltrow.'

'Oh, shut up, Rory,' Libby said, pushing him, and Elle heard the Lancashire in her voice for the first time. 'Go and see if your mother's here yet. There'll be loads of people you know, Elle,' she said, turning back. 'Loads from publishing. We told the editor of the *Bookseller* we should send him a photo of the wedding! I'm joking, but it'd be funny, wouldn't it? Kind of a *Who's Who* of the Book Trade in 2004?'

Oh, God. 'Sure,' Elle said, looking around her to see who she knew, with a mixture of shyness and dread.

But when Libby suddenly stood back, and cupped her hand over her stomach, Elle realised the reason for the weight gain, the voluminous chiffon, the speed of the wedding.

'You're pregnant?' she said, hoping she wasn't wrong, that a hoary old sitcomesque scenario wasn't about to be played out.

'Yes,' Libby said simply. 'Nearly six months.'

'Oh, Libs,' Elle said. 'Why didn't you tell me?'

Libby blushed. She raised her chin, that curious mixture of pride and awkwardness. 'I'm sorry. I thought you probably . . . maybe sometimes you thought that it might be – that you might . . .'

It was just the two of them, suddenly. Elle put her hand on her friend's arm, noticing how white her English rose skin was. 'I never felt that,' she said. 'That's why it didn't work out . . . me and Rory.'

Libby nodded. Her cheeks were flushed. 'Mm-hm.' She smiled and breathed out. 'Thanks.'

'No,' Elle said, smiling at her, staring into her eyes. She and Rory both had green eyes, she realised. 'Libs, it's wonderful. I'm so happy for you.'

'Funny how it's turned out, isn't it,' Libby said. 'Role reversal. You, this – well, you're doing so well. Me marrying Rory, Felicity's going to be my mother-in-law. Imagine.'

Elle couldn't help but suppress a painful smile. The hours of sleep the younger her had lost, lying awake fretting over what would happen when the great Felicity found out she was having an affair with her son . . . Felicity. She seemed like a pharaoh, someone from another age. 'Where is she?'

'She's – she's actually coming down tomorrow,' Rory said, rejoining them. He nervously looked at Libby. 'She's staying with Cousin Harold tonight.'

'What?' Libby said sharply.

'She rang the hotel earlier and left a message. She said her car was playing up and it was best if she stopped at Cousin Harold's and got a lift with him.'

'Why couldn't she call your mobile?' Libby demanded.

'Darling, it's my mother,' Rory said, with exaggerated dry weariness. 'She doesn't believe in mobiles.'

'She said they were a young man's fad. You must remember that,' Elle said, though she felt a little sorry for Libby: weddings were a nightmare to organise at the best of times, and the last thing you needed was a notable no-show from your nearest and dearest. Elle wondered if the *Bookseller*'s diarist would note that, and the resident paparazzo record her arrival the next day, and suppressed a smile.

'Right, then, we should go in to –' Libby clapped her hands, anxiously. 'Hi, everyone! We should go in to dinner! Just through there!'

Her voice, unusually shrill, cut straight across the conversation, and the room fell still. 'Come on,' Libby said, taking Elle by the arm. 'Dinner, everyone!'

As she moved off Elle heard her say, 'I'll have to check the bloody seating plan again. We can't have any of my authors on your mother's table. I'm not risking her telling them a load of rubbish about me.' Her fingers were tight on Elle's arm. 'You're so muscly,' she said admiringly. 'Like a different person.'

'Oh – thanks?' Elle said quietly, but Libby had turned away, to greet another guest.

BY THE TIME Elle was back in the car on her way to her mother's, she was struggling to keep her eyes open. She hadn't slept during the flight, and she still had to get home, see Mum.

Tiredness washed over her, like an enemy trying to drag her down. The country lanes away from Sanditon Hall were rutted and narrow. So strange and weird, to be driving through the middle of nowhere in the dark, the occasional flash of rabbits' eyes catching the lights on the road ahead, the smell of freshly mown grass and faint blossom coming in through the window she'd opened wide, when twenty-four hours ago she'd been in the glass elevator with Stuart Forgan, discussing whether she'd mind taking over one of Libby's authors.

She'd grown cold, hard. It struck her now she was back. She'd had to, in order to survive in a new country on her own. She'd had to grow a thicker skin, learn a new set of rules, a way of being. She'd taken the one thing she had in New York that made her different – her Britishness – and used it. Used her English accent to charm Elizabeth Forsyte in the Ladies' bathroom, used it to set herself apart, so that she had a USP. Marc had made her watch *Gypsy* on DVD one rainy afternoon, and poked fun at her throughout, as they lay under the duvet. 'You gotta get a gimmick,' he'd sung, tweaking her nipples, his hands roving all over her while she squirmed with pleasure. 'You're Mama Rose, you dirty girl. You'll stop at nothing to get your way.' She'd screamed with outraged pleasure but, now, she knew it was true. In London, she'd always thought she was just one of a sea of mediocre pleasant girls – not the brightest, not the prettiest. She wasn't much at all, really. In New York, her gimmick was her Britishness, and her MO was the fact that she worked like a Trojan, so that no one could take anything away from her.

As it always did around this time, towards the end of the New York working day, Elle's mind started scanning over events, running through her To Do list. She had to call Caryn and pass on Heather Dougall's complaints about the UK company, call Jennifer and get her to fax Elizabeth Forsyte a message of greetings that she'd got there OK – Elizabeth loved to know Elle's movements, and she loved faxes, and Elle wasn't sure if her BlackBerry would work in the depths of Sussex, and thought it'd be nice for her to know she was still in touch. She had to think about how to approach the Gray Logan question – she wasn't even sure she wanted to edit him. His books were very literary, and although when she'd met him once he'd been very friendly, kind, rather handsome, even though he had to be nearly fifty, she was sure he was far too intellectual for the likes of her. Perhaps she should – she peered forward in the darkness, as a sign, *Shawcross 2 m, Torbridge 4 m*, loomed out of the darkness, and veered right.

'Come on, Elle,' she said, blinking hard in the darkness. 'Nearly there, nearly –' She paused. Home? It wasn't home.

Elle parked the car and walked up the path towards her mother's house. There was a chill in the air now. Dew was settling like a grey mist on the lawn. The kitchen light was on. She knocked, and opened the door.

She scanned the sitting room, and then saw her mother, under the yellow glare of a single bulb at the kitchen table. Her head was bowed. 'Hi, Mum!' Elle called, her voice bright. At the sound of Elle's voice Mandana stood up, slowly, and turned around. There was an empty wine bottle in front of her which she knocked over as she got up and Elle's heart sank. *Please no, please no please no.*

'Baby, you're back!' Her mother heaved herself up and came towards her, rubbing her eyes. 'I'm sorry. I had a glass of red wine, naughty me, and I must have fallen asleep at the table. How disgraceful!'

She hugged Elle, her arms holding her tight, and Elle felt her squeezing her, and she gave in to it, for one sweet moment. Then Mandana stepped back, and Elle saw, with a lurch, the cracked red-wine stains at the corners of her mouth, her out-of-focus eyes. Her hair was thin, wasn't it thinner than before? She could still remember Melissa's prim, harsh voice back at the Algonquin, every sentence of that conversation imprinted on her brain, she couldn't help it. *She's only going to get worse. Someone needs to intervene.*

Elle blinked. 'You drank that whole bottle?'

The bottle was, indeed, rolling in a creaking circular motion around the table.

'Of course not, don't be so rude,' Mandana roared, slapping her hands on her thighs and moving back to rescue the bottle. 'No, Bryan came over, and Anita. We had dinner in the garden. I wanted you to see them, only you're so late.'

'I'm not that late –'

'You were for them. I made dinner and then they left. Don't turn up here and . . .' She stopped. 'Oh, forget it,' she said, rubbing her hand across her forehead. 'Maybe I did have a bit too much, I'm sorry, love. Jesus, you sound like Melissa.'

Her skin was sallower, wasn't it? Was it usually that waxy, yellow colour? Elle stared at her, then she put her bag on the ground and moved towards the kitchen.

'Sorry,' she said. She glanced at the sink. It was certainly full: three, eight, ten people could have been there for dinner.

Mandana grimaced. 'Now, do you want a cup of tea? Or coffee? Hm . . . Let me see.' She looked around. 'I'm going to have peppermint, if I've got any . . .'

The rest of the kitchen was filthy. Elle's head droned with tiredness, like a softly humming cymbal, as Mandana chattered in the background. 'You remember Anita, well, she's going back to Rajasthan in September, and I think I might go with her, what do you say to that? I haven't had a chance to go, you see, yet. I went to India in '71, the year after I came back from San Francisco, and it was wonderful, you know, we stayed in these tents, well, Anita thinks we could bring some of them over too—'

'Excuse me a sec,' Elle interrupted. 'Mum, sorry to be rude, do you mind if I make a phone call?'

'Er . . . now?' Her mother stared at her. 'It's eleven o'clock!'

'It's to the States, it's only six there.' Elle flapped her hands, impatiently.

'But I haven't heard about how your flight was, your dinner – how's Libby? Love—'

'I'll be one minute, Mum. Then I can concentrate.' She dropped a kiss on her mother's forehead.

Turning towards the corridor, Elle scrabbled for her BlackBerry, her connection to the outside world. The connection was working; emails started filling up her inbox. There was a text on it from Mike:

Hi Elle. Hope you landed safely. Miss you already. Have a great trip. See you next week Sweet Pea. Mike x

What would Mike make of her mother, were he ever to meet her? The idea of Mike and her mother discussing stock prices or Rajasthani tents was totally alien to her. Back here for twelve hours or so, and Mike himself seemed totally alien. She scrolled through her emails.

Hi Elle,

This is probably odd after so many years, but I wondered if you were going to the wedding tomorrow? I've been invited, for some reason. I heard you might be coming back from Libby. Would you like a lift? I'd rather not turn up on my own and I hoped maybe you wouldn't want to either. Happy to collect you from your mother's, if L's right and that's where you're staying. My mobile number's below.

Hope all's well with you. Be nice to see you.

Tom

Elle stared at the screen for a moment, biting her lip. Then she called up Jennifer's direct line and while she waited for the call to go through she stood up in the stairwell, looking out over the cold, messy kitchen, and at her mother moving slowly about under the small circle of yellow light. She shuffled, touching one item then putting it back, standing warily in the middle of the room. Elle couldn't take her eyes off her. When Jennifer came on the line, Elle ran through a few things with her, then she typed a quick reply to Tom.

Yes please. I'd love that. 11? Torbridge Farm Barn, Near Shawcross, E Sussex.

It'll be good to see you again, she wrote, then deleted it. See you tomorrow. E

'Sorry about that, Mum,' she said, coming back into the kitchen. She sat down. 'Just needed to speak to my assistant and make sure a couple of things are OK.'

'Oh, no problem, you busy Eleanor Bee,' said her mother.

She smiled at her. 'Can I get you anything, love? Or are you very tired?'

She sat down next to Elle, and stroked her daughter's hair away from her forehead. 'You're so beautiful,' she murmured. 'All grown up, you are.'

Mandana's nails were yellow too; gnarled with ridges, cracked and bitten. Why hadn't she seen it, at Christmas? Because she'd hardly seen her at Christmas, Elle realised now. She took her mother's hand off her face, and held it in her own lap.

'Are you OK, Mum?' she asked. 'You don't look very well.'

Mandana squeezed her daughter's hand. 'I've not been that well, actually,' she said, sounding frank. 'Had a bit of a cold. It's been a terrible spring. Just got nice now.'

'Oh. Right,' said Elle. She took a deep breath. Enough head in sand. *Now. Do it now.*

She said, 'Are you drinking, I mean properly drinking?' Mandana made to snatch her hand away, but Elle held onto it. 'I'm not having a go at you, Mum,' she said, while inside she was screaming, *Yes, yes, I am, why do you do this? Why can't you see what you're doing to yourself, Mum?*

'Let me get some tea.' Mandana made to stand up, but Elle didn't move. Her mother sank back, reluctantly, into her seat.

'It's just I know you've had a problem with it, and there are things you can do to get help.' Elle put her other hand on her mother's lap, blinking hard, and she swallowed. She took some papers she'd put down on the table. 'There's a clinic not far from here, you know, and your local surgery's referred people before, I rang up and checked with them. Look, here's all the information. I printed it out before I came.' She slid the sheaf of papers across the table. They were held together with a big pink plastic paper clip; it was incongruous. 'If they won't refer you we can pay ourselves, Dad has said he'll lend me some money.' Mandana started. 'I said it was for home improvements, Mum, don't worry,' Elle said. 'He won't know any different. We just have to go to your doctor on Monday. I've booked an appointment at ten o'clock. That's all we have to do. Just tell her you need help, it'll be easy after that.' She knew that was a lie, but it had to sound true. Elle took a deep breath. 'And I'll be here, I'll do anything you want. I'll move back here, live with you, help you get better.' Mandana shook her head, weakly. 'I've thought about it, I'll give up the job and come back. I'd do it.'

Mandana twisted her hands away. 'No,' she said. 'No, never.'

'Or, Mum, I can come over for a couple of weeks each month, make sure you're sticking to it. I love you, Mum.' She cleared her throat. 'I want you to get better. You can, you know, I think you think there's no point trying, and there is, there really is.'

It was very quiet in the kitchen, no sound at all from outside, other than an owl, hooting faintly, far away. Elle didn't say more. She just looked at Mandana, her brown eyes meeting her mother's, terrified about what came next.

'It's too hard,' Mandana said, after a long pause. 'You don't understand, Ellie.'

'I know I don't,' Elle said.

Mandana looked at the floor. 'I don't want you involved in it,' she said after a while. Her voice was so soft Elle could barely hear her. 'I'm so proud of you. I keep thinking I can get back on track if I just sort it out myself, you know. I won't need it any more. I don't like – being this person.'

'But Mum, it's been twenty-five years.' Elle could hardly bear to look at her mother's thin frame, her papery hands, her cracked lips. 'I – you're going to kill yourself.'

'Who was it who said, "Life would be easier for some people if it wasn't such a big deal"?' Mandana said, with a small smile. 'I feel like one of those people. It's just hard, and it gets harder.'

327

'I know it must be –' Elle began.

'No, you don't.' Mandana tapped her hand lightly. 'Darling, you've no idea. It's black as night with me for days sometimes. That's why I do it, I guess . . . I don't want to be a burden to Rhodes, or your father . . .' She turned away. 'Or you. I always felt you saw the worst of it when you were younger, and I promised I wouldn't let you see it any more.'

They sat there, the two of them, nothing stirring. 'Mum, look at me,' Elle said gently. 'I'm not going till you say what you're going to do.' She held her breath, not sure how Mandana would respond. Elle's eyes filled with tears; she blinked them back, she didn't want her mother to see she was crying.

But Mandana saw. She frowned, her tired brown eyes clouding over, then she nodded, and muttered something under her breath. She took Elle's hand again and said, 'OK, I'll think about it.'

'Mum –'

'OK, on Monday. We'll go to the doctor,' Mandana said, in a quiet voice. She sounded defeated.

'Are you sure?' Perhaps unrealistically, Elle wanted her to *want* to go, not to feel forced into a corner.

'Yes,' said Mandana blankly. 'I'm sure.'

'Mum, it's going to be OK, you know,' Elle said. She tried to feel pleased, but she couldn't. It was cold in the barn, and she shivered.

'Let's go to bed,' Mandana said, standing up, moving away. She made a small, broken sound in her throat. 'Perhaps it's going to be OK, like you say.'

Suddenly she kissed her daughter, grasping her shoulder tight with one thin hand. 'Bless you, love,' she said, and then she was gone.

WHEN ELLE WOKE the next morning, for a brief moment she didn't know where she was. Her 'old room', as her mother called it, wasn't really her room, not the way her bedroom at Willow Cottage had been. She lay in bed, staring at the stone walls, listening for familiar sounds, and then she saw a pile of old Georgette Heyers, dumped here after she'd moved away, and slowly it came to her. She was in England. She was at Mum's. She and Mum had talked. It was Libby and Rory's wedding today. She pulled a cardigan on and went downstairs. Her mother was pottering round the kitchen, but she looked up as Elle appeared.

'Hello,' she called. 'Hello hello. I've been out to get a paper, it's a lovely day. Want some coffee?'

'Yes, please,' said Elle, smiling at her. She felt she had to mention their conversation as soon as possible. 'Feeling OK today?' she asked, sitting down. 'I hope I wasn't too bossy last night.'

'Oh,' Mandana said. 'No, not at all.' She sounded formal. 'No, that's all great. Yes, thanks, it was great.' She said with sudden energy, 'I was – I was going to make breakfast. Do you want some pancakes?'

Pancakes had always been Mandana's Saturday treat, when

Rhodes and Elle were allowed to pour as much maple syrup on as they liked, when there were endless rashers of bacon, sugar and lemon on the table. Elle held the record, still, of eighteen pancakes eaten, though it had come at a price – she'd been so sick their father had banned them from eating them for two months afterwards. Elle could picture Mandana so clearly, dancing round the kitchen to Radio 2's *Sounds of the Sixties*, in her blue-and-white striped apron, the wide floral skirts she always wore flying up around her, flipping the pancakes deftly with her special spatula and singing, while Elle and Rhodes watched, open-mouthed in admiration.

'Pancakes . . .' Elle wasn't that hungry, but she nodded enthusiastically anyway. 'I'd love some!'

'OK,' Mandana said. 'Great! Let me just . . .' She opened the fridge. 'I've got eggs . . . Oh, no.' She peered in. 'Is that? No, it's not.' She turned back. 'I need to pop out and get some things, so –'

Elle put her hand out. 'Oh, no, don't bother if you haven't got the stuff, Mum, I only—'

'No!' her mother said. 'It's fine!'

Elle said, 'Honest, Mum, please don't. I'm not that hungry anyway, I was just trying to be polite.' That was the wrong thing to say. 'I'll have cereal . . . or whatever you want.'

'No worries,' said Mandana, in the accent she used to do to annoy Elle when she was watching *Neighbours*. 'No worries, Charlene.'

Elle grinned, looked around and got up. 'I'll make some coffee.'

'What time do you have to leave?'

'Well, the wedding's at twelve. My friend Tom's coming to pick me up here at eleven, if that's OK.'

'Tom, eh?' Mandana said. 'Ooh, who's *Tom*?' She did a little wiggle.

'Oh, please, Mother,' said Elle crossly. 'He's a friend of mine, from back in the Bookprint days. Dora Zoffany's son,

I've told you about him before.' Her mother looked totally blank. 'We both needed someone to go with so we said we'd go together. If that's OK with you.'

The phone rang again. 'It's Piccadilly Circus in here!' Mandana said, pleased. 'Hello!'

Elle put the kettle on. 'Hi, Bryan. It was lovely to see you too, my love. Yes, of course you can come over later. Great. No, what's that? Oh, dear, Bryan, I can't hear you, you're breaking up . . .'

She cut the call and put the phone down, disappointed. 'He's gone.'

'So Bryan's coming over then?' Though she was never quite sure of Bryan's place on the scene, Elle knew he existed, if no more than that. She had met him once, at the village fete a few years ago: he was a bearded, waistcoat-wearing motorcyclist who liked pub quizzes, Captain Beefheart and hating cities.

'Yes, hopefully after lunch, at least I think so,' Mandana said. 'What a lovely day I have ahead of me, eh? You here, weather perfect, and it's the weekend . . . Lovely.' She sighed, and stretched her arms languorously above her head. 'Glad to be alive, that's what we say.'

Elle smiled. 'Me too.'

Elle had a slightly soft apple and some oatcakes for her breakfast, and then a long shower. As she was finishing her make-up in the tiny cream plastic mirror decorated with faded Hello Kitty stickers, she turned towards the window and her eye caught sight of a photo, one of several hanging precariously on the wall. It was in a simple clipframe, of her and Rhodes, the Christmas after she left university, 1996. They had their arms round each other – unusual in itself. Rhodes was floppy-haired and brawny in a suit and tie. Elle was – Elle was a mess, she realised, peering in towards the photo. That crop, the dark berry-coloured lipstick, the ghostly white face powder, it was awful! That vile silky cardigan from Kookai too – what had happened to Kookai, and why had she been so obsessed with cardigans? She turned and looked at herself in the mirror.

Last month on the first proper day of spring she'd splashed out on some Kate Spade coral-coloured heels and a matching handbag. It was the most money she'd ever spent in one go. As she'd handed her card over to the dewy-skinned assistant in the Kate Spade shop she'd told herself she deserved it. Unbidden, back at her apartment, came the sobering thought that in fact she had very little to spend her money on. She was only really interested in work. Flights back to the UK were her biggest extravagance, along with clothes, trips to the hairdresser and eating out. Last time she'd been back, she'd visited Karen and her new husband Graham, who had just moved into a two-bedroom garden flat in Belsize Park. Karen had told her it had cost £500,000, a sum so huge Elle could hardly compute it. And it seemed a million miles away for Elle, buying an apartment, putting down permanent roots. She liked the simplicity of her life. It gave her control.

'Elle!' her mother called. 'There's – Tom's here!'

Elle stepped into her indigo-blue linen dress, picked up the beloved Kate Spade shoes and handbag, and went downstairs. Tom was standing in the kitchen, hands in pockets, chatting to her mother. He turned as she entered the room, then did a proper, old-fashioned, double-take.

'Er – wow. Wow! Elle, is that you?' Elle laughed.

'Hello! Of course it is!'

'Seriously,' he said. 'What happened to you! You look bloody amazing!'

He hugged her. She hugged him back, remembering how lean he was. He looked down at her, his grey eyes smiling.

'You look exactly the same,' she said. 'And it's lovely to see you.'

'Well, you don't,' Tom said. 'You look – all glossy. Like

someone in a magazine.' Elle lowered her eyes, like a modest bride. 'Doesn't she, Mrs Bee!'

He turned to Elle's mother, and Elle flinched, as Mandana had once shouted at the woman in the post office, '*I'm not a fucking Missus any more, it's Mizz. MIZZ, FOR THE LAST TIME!*'

But, 'Call me Mandana,' was all that Elle's mother said, with a smile. 'Have you got time for a drink?'

Tom looked at his watch. 'Well –'

'I don't think so,' Elle cut in. 'We don't really—'

'I just meant a quick coffee?' Mandana interrupted. 'I've got some here.'

Tom looked from one to the other, quickly. 'Er – half a cup would be great. A wedding is a long day. Especially when you don't really know the bride or groom.'

'I don't really understand why you're invited, if I'm honest,' Elle said. 'No offence. I don't know why I am, either.'

'My parents were friends with Felicity, I suppose it's something to do with that. Who knows. I also think it's an "everyone in publishing come and witness our joyful publishing union" thing.' Tom put on a fluting voice and clasped his hands; Elle laughed. He did look the same, she told herself, just a little older. There were lines around his eyes, ones that hadn't been there before. But he was different, somehow. He was a father. She had to remind herself of that. She wanted to just stare at him, drink in the sight of him: he was there, in her mother's kitchen, talking to them as if nothing had happened. Tom.

'Last time I saw them,' he was saying, 'I told Rory he was a bit of a cock and I asked Libby why she'd published that dreadful Byron book.' Elle rolled her eyes in agreement, and Tom turned to Mandana. 'It was this book that came out last year, a fantasy poem about Byron going to Crete instead of dying in Missolonghi. It had no punctuation. Byron has a Mohican and likes punk. He calls himself Georgy. He sings the Sex Pistols while he's writing *Corsair*.'

333

Mandana laughed. 'Doesn't sound like my cup of tea. Or coffee.' She handed Tom a cup of coffee which he accepted gratefully.

'Dare I say I don't think it was. In fact, it was a load of pretentious rubbish. In my humble opinion. But it was very controversial. Got loads of publicity.'

'Sounds like Libby,' Mandana said.

'Mum!' Elle said. 'That's not nice.'

'Not nice,' Mandana mimicked, and her eyes flashed. 'Oh, she's a right madam, always has been. So patronising about my job, I always remember.'

'What do you do?' asked Tom.

'I'm a librarian, which is a dreadful occupation these days. No one cares about us, we're dinosaurs. It's full of idiots. Stupid. Having to work with pricks all day –' She opened her mouth wider, as if she was about to shout, or scream like a child, and then abruptly shut it. 'Anyway, I don't like it much. I used to read to the children three times a week, an after-school club, but they've stopped that now.'

'No, Mum, really?'

'Yes,' Mandana said. Her face fell. 'There weren't enough children coming. They'd rather stay at home and play video games. And I'm so bored of *Cinderella*. I've read it so many times I could scream.'

Tom looked quickly at her, and then at Elle, but he didn't say anything. Elle put down her mug, looked at her watch. 'We should go,' she said. 'OK, Tom?'

He took a swig from his mug and pushed himself away from the counter. 'Sure. Thanks for the coffee, Mandana. Great to meet you.'

'Well, you too, Tom. Come back any time!' Mandana said, and she gave him one of her gappy-toothed smiles, her eyes shining, and clasped his hand in her strong grip. Elle watched her, relieved and proud. Her hair wasn't really thinning, was it? She was imagining that, perhaps all of it. There was life in the old girl yet. Elle picked up her bag and touched her mother's arm.

'I don't know when I'll be back, Mum, but not too late. The bride's six months' pregnant, I can't imagine it's going to be an all-nighter.'

'Don't worry about me. I'll be fine.'

'You sure?' Elle said, in a low voice. 'Call me if you feel – if you need anything.'

'I'll be *fine*, Elle, love.' Mandana kissed her and smiled again. 'Like I said, I don't ever want you to worry about me.'

'Elle? We should go.' Tom's voice recalled her to the present with a start, and she tore her gaze away from her mother, shivering suddenly. 'What's up?'

'Nothing.'

'You look like a goose just walked over your grave.'

She hadn't heard that expression for years. 'No, come on, let's go. Bye, Mum. Hope you – have a great day.'

'Thanks, Elle,' Mandana said serenely. She picked up the *Guardian*. 'I might sit in the garden for a bit.'

She followed them outside and, as they climbed into Tom's car, waved them off. Elle watched her in the rear-view mirror. She waved energetically and then they rounded the corner and she was gone.

'I must say your mum's not how I imagined,' Tom said. 'From what you've said. It's weird, she's nothing like you, is she?'

Elle turned to him. 'Thanks,' she said. 'I'm glad to hear it.'

'Especially now,' Tom said. 'You're – well, I wouldn't have recognised you.'

'What does *that* mean?' Elle said warily.

'God, you're suspicious, aren't you? Are you like this in New York? Is that why people ask me if I know Eleanor Bee, New York's hottest editor? I only meant,' he went on, as Elle snorted, 'that you seem different. In a good way. You know. All – shiny.'

'That's the American way,' she said, in her best American accent, hoping he wouldn't notice how rubbish it was. 'I have a blow-dry every week and there has been no hair on my legs since two-thousand-one.'

'Glad to hear it,' Tom said. 'Hair on legs. I mean. That's disgusting. Urgh. Who'd have that?'

They were bowling along a sun-dappled country lane, probably one of the ones that had seemed so dark and difficult to her last night but now, everything was different. Elle's heart rose. 'It's bloody nice to see you,' she said. 'Thanks, for asking if I'd come with you.'

'No, thank you for saying yes,' he said. 'I'm sorry I haven't been in touch. I felt bad about how things were with us when you left.'

She turned to him, brushing a lock of hair out of her eyes. 'Me too. I still don't understand it, really.'

It seemed such a long time ago, she could say it now. She wouldn't tell him how bewildered she had been by what happened, how many times, those first few lonely months in New York, she had ached to call him, to tell him stuff. She didn't tell him Libby had wasted no time in passing on the information that he was back with Caitlin, that they had a daughter, that they were living together. That she'd even Googled him a couple of times, to see what it brought up – a couple of *Bookseller* articles about his shop and him, but nothing else – and it made her feel even more distant, somehow. He had a new life now, a daughter, a relationship. She'd known it would happen. And she had no right to stop it, of course. Then, somehow, things changed, her life picked up, communication with Libby slowed down, and she hadn't asked how he was, had been too proud to get in touch. But she still thought about him.

'Well, that was my fault,' Tom said, 'Elle, I owe you an apology. That summer was difficult for me.' He swallowed, and cleared his throat. 'But I treated you really badly, I said some things I shouldn't have. I want you to understand, though,' he said. 'I didn't mean them. I was angry.'

Elle hugged herself, and shook her head. 'It doesn't matter. How's your daughter? How old is she – two?'

'Yes, that's right. Well, she's great. Best thing that ever happened to me. So you see, that summer, when I'd just found out, I didn't know what I know now. I took it out on you and I'm sorry –'

She didn't want him to know how upset she'd been. It was all in the past anyway, what was the point? He had a daughter, he was with Caitlin. 'How's Caitlin?'

'We have a really good relationship,' Tom said. He swerved suddenly to avoid a lorry, thundering the other way down the road. 'Sorry,' he said. 'Caitlin, oh, yes. She put some great systems in place, and we've bought another shop, in Kensington. Might buy another one if a lease comes up in a place I've got my eye on. She's done all that, she had the background, the business degree. I don't know what I would have done without her to be honest.' He turned to her, quickly. 'Oh, and the Dora Trust just had its third awards ceremony. We're running a programme in ten inner-city girls' schools, which I'm very proud of. When all's said and done, things are good. You know, life doesn't always turn out the way you think it's going to and then you realise . . .'

He trailed off.

She prompted him. 'You realise what?'

'I was going to say it's for the best. Anyway.' He shook his head, his face falling into the hard mask of concentration she knew well, eyes fixed on the road. There was an uncomfortable pause. Elle changed the subject.

'Any vital publishing news I should know about, anything I've missed? Please tell me. You know what this wedding's going to be like. I have to be up to speed otherwise I'll be shunned, like an Amish who's left the fold.'

Tom laughed. 'Hardly. OK. Well, it's all about Richard and Judy, these days.'

'Who?'

He stared at her. 'You must have heard of Richard and Judy. The bookclub.'

'Oh – them. That. Sorry.' Elle nodded. 'I have. We've got Oprah though, she's much bigger.'

'Get you,' Tom said.

'What else?'

'Um – I don't know. Have you read *The Da Vinci Code*? I actually really enjoyed it. Or the new David Sedaris, I just finished it, it was hilarious.'

Elle said, 'I don't have time to read books any more, not for pleasure.'

'You? You used to read two books a week.'

'Well, things change. I read dreadful manuscripts and I look at book jackets instead of reading the books.' She cleared her throat. 'What else?'

'Bill Lewis got made redundant, but you probably knew that.'

'Yes,' said Elle. 'Not that sorry, to be honest. He was a crap boss. And he was horrible to Libby.'

Tom glanced at her. 'Yeah, I heard. He's not got another job. Last I heard his wife had chucked him out. Poor guy, though.'

'Yeah,' said Elle, thinking of Libby's tear-stained face, of how badly he'd treated her. 'Well, you plough your own furrow, and all that.'

'Wow, you're tough,' said Tom. 'I'm joking!' he said, as she swivelled round to stare at him. 'Don't worry about Libby, Elle. She's done all right for herself, as I think we're about to see.'

He turned off another road. Elle noticed for the first time what a calm driver he was. She'd been on road trips with Rory, sneaking out to places for the weekend, and it was always a nightmare, crumpled maps everywhere, swearing and shouting, like an Italian opera. She smiled at the thought, caught aback at a fond feeling for Rory for the first time in years. *Good,* she told herself. *It's his wedding day. It's right that you think well of him.*

'You're a very comforting person to be in a car with,' she told him.

'You too,' Tom said. There was silence. 'It is really great to see you, Elle,' he said after a moment. 'I think you're brave to come back. And I'm glad. I'm glad you did.'

She didn't feel brave, she felt cold, sneery and detached from it all and she couldn't seem to help it. 'Thank you,' she said after a pause. 'That's nice. I just hope it's – oh, it sounds horrible, saying I hope it's worth it, when it's someone else's day. So fingers crossed it doesn't rain,' she finished, unconvincingly.

'It'll be worth it, I promise you,' Tom said. 'At the very least, it'll be lavish, from what I hear. Rory's such a skinflint, he's never spent any of the Bookprint buyout money. Apparently Libby's gone mad with it and he's furious.' Tom pulled up in a quiet lane, and they got out. 'Oh, it's lovely,' said Elle, staring up at the church, the rolling green hills in the background, the last of the blossom on the trees. She wondered what Libby was doing, where she was.

Tom shivered. 'Weddings give me the willies,' he said, as they walked up the church path. 'I always think Grace Poole's going to jump out and try and burn the place down. Makes me feel trapped.'

'What a romantic you are,' she said. 'Grace Poole didn't burn the church down. She wasn't ever at the church, it was the brother. And name me one time that's ever actually happened.'

'Never, probably. I just –' he shrugged. 'I like the idea of being with someone for ever, being married to them, but all this – I mean, they've probably never even been to this church, it's all so fake.'

339

'Oh, come on,' said Elle. They paused outside, framed by the porch. 'I'm looking on it as a nice day out, like something from a mini-series they'd show on American TV. English country wedding, big white dress, posh people, marquees, you know.' She put her hand on his shoulder, and pulled her strap over her heel again.

'Come on then,' he said. 'Charles? Ready to face the enemy?'

'No *Four Weddings* quotes, please,' said Elle. 'Ready as I'll ever be.'

It was about thirty seconds before it became amusing. One of the ushers – a long, curly-haired guy who knew Tom – said, with some surprise, 'Hello, Scott. What the fuck are you doing here? Bride or groom?' before handing them an order of service and a leaflet.

> Please make sure you record your prescence at
> LIBBY AND RORY'S WEDDING!
> by visitng the photo booth, in the Orangery at
> Sanditon Hall to have your photo taken!
> We really want a record of all of you in your finery!
> Cheers
> Libby and Rory

'Bride, please,' said Elle, taking a leaflet and biting her tongue, as the usher led them to their seat. 'Wow, what a lovely idea.'

Tom put his hand on Elle's shoulder blade, gently pushing her towards the north aisle. She relaxed against him, glad she wasn't on her own. 'Here,' he said, stepping back to allow her in, and she sat down, relieved she hadn't seen anyone she recognised yet. The church was not big, a beautiful old Saxon building already full of people and vast floral displays, bright greenery and huge pink gerberas. Elle and Tom bent their heads, studying the order of service.

Tom said, after a while, '"Please stand for the Wedding Wows"? Who are they? A glee club?' He turned to the front page. 'Wedding Wows . . . Man. Look here! "The Marriage of Rory Sassoon and Lizzy Yates"? *Lizzy?* Did anyone proofread this?'

'Ssshh,' Elle whispered.

'Well, she's an editor,' Tom said. 'You'd think she'd have looked over it. Wow. Wedding Wows,' he said again, and Elle bit her lip, trying not to laugh.

On the bride's side she recognised a couple of Libby's old school friends; they stared blankly at her, and Elle realised perhaps they didn't know her with long hair. They were all in familiar wedding costume; LK Bennett suits, Hobbs and Whistles dresses, the men in morning suits. A few other people were vaguely familiar: there was a bloke called Noel she remembered snogging one drunken evening. Libby's birthday? Elle turned away and found herself staring directly at Rory.

He was looking around, nervously, joking with the best man, whom she didn't recognise. It struck her as appropriate that she'd spent so long in love with him and yet had never even met his best friend. He caught her eye and smiled, baring his teeth with an expression of mock-terror. She smiled back, giving him the thumbs-up.

So strange, to be here. A guest at his wedding. This was what she'd only allowed herself to dream of oh-so-rarely, saving it up as a treat for a birthday, after a terrible day at work. She, who had never liked weddings, had allowed herself this fantasy. Her wedding day to Rory. A pretty church in Sussex, festooned with spring flowers. Felicity, sitting in the row behind, decked out in green silk. Rows of ancient Sassoon relatives, and her, Elle, floating down the aisle in cream silk to 'The Arrival of the Queen of Sheba', with eyes only for him . . . Rory, slightly rumpled, slightly scared, her love, her only one.

But that wasn't how it had turned out. She knew she was OK, watching him, in fact she was happy for him, happy for

Libby. But she couldn't help feeling a pang of sympathy for the girl she'd been, who'd loved him so much. She was still dreaming somewhere, hoping this day would come.

It occurred to her as she looked around that when she'd wanted a big white wedding this really was the one she'd dreamed about. She couldn't help feeling slightly amused that Libby had nicked that, as well. Not just the man, but the county, the time of year, the setting . . . Ah, well. Elle shrugged. Time to leave the white dress behind. She breathed out slowly.

Tom said softly, 'You OK?'

'Sure,' she said brightly. 'Sure.'

Then Handel started playing on the tiny organ and everyone stood up to welcome the bride, and Elle turned towards the west door with a smile on her face, for her old friend, and for the old days too.

AFTERWARDS, ELLE WISHED someone could have told her in advance how mad this wedding was going to be. She wouldn't have dreaded it so much had she known about the slight surprised pause as the vicar called Libby 'Lizzy'. Or the 'Wedding Wows'. Or the Yateses' growling, furious bulldog, forced to wear a huge wine-red bow around his neck, or the fifty-minute wait outside the church for endless photos during which Libby's pitch got louder and louder as she yelled instructions at people and Rory looked more and more disconsolate.

Or, back at Sanditon Hall, the rickety photo booth, the 'book-themed' cocktails served at the reception, the six – SIX – bridesmaids, only three of whom Elle recognised, all in matching wine-red, a mean colour on blondes and brunettes alike, and Regency-esque straw hats which they all donned for the photos outside, including the obligatory slightly-fatter-than-everyone-else bridesmaid, who was probably perfectly attractive in a nice pair of jeans and Topshop top but, when forced to pour herself into a Pronuptia raw silk floor-length shift resembled nothing so much as a quivering pork chop, all dimpled fat and blotchy purple.

As they were shepherded into the Orangery, she and Tom

were handed a 'Great Expectations' (cranberry, orange juice and champagne).

'Cheers,' said Elle merrily. She clinked her glass against his. 'Here's to the happy couple. And the happy bulldog.'

'Oh, yes, Spot,' said Tom. He stepped closer, and said in a low voice, 'I take it back about not liking weddings. This might just be the most hilarious thing I've ever been to. I think Libby's gone totally mad, you know. Did you see the lobby? There are piles of Bookprint books arranged in a heart shape.'

'Hi, guys. Hi, there,' came Rory's voice. 'Hey, you! Hi!' He was pushing his way through the crowd, to where Libby was waiting by the door, at the beginning of the receiving line.

'Oh, man,' said Elle. 'I hate receiving lines. They make me—'

'Oh, I just remembered something. Excuse me a sec,' Tom interrupted, and suddenly disappeared. After a few minutes in line, Elle realised he wasn't coming back.

'Sod,' she said under her breath. 'Bloody sod.'

'I wondered who that was, swearing like an old navvy. Hello, old girl,' said a voice behind her, and a hand slid onto her shoulder.

'Jeremy!' said Elle with pleasure. 'Hey!' She kissed him. 'How are you?'

'I'm well, I'm well. You look great.' She blushed. Jeremy was exactly the same: tanned, gleaming white teeth, sparkling blue eyes. 'We hear great things of you from the States. You've done us proud.'

'Aw, not really,' Elle said.

'It's true,' Jeremy told her. 'I absolutely loved that *Diary by Design* book, you know, we hope Richard and Judy might pick it next year. Either way it's going to sell shedloads. Thanks to you we'll make budget.' As they moved slowly towards the front of the line, Jeremy hissed in her ear, 'Did you read that dreadful *Byron in Knossos*? Yet another Libby

344

special, all hype and no substance. It's sold about three copies, and we paid a fucking fortune for it – Hello!' he said, turning brightly towards the receiving line. 'Yes, I'm Jeremy, I work with Libby and Rory, have done for years. You must be Mrs Yates! Hi! Lovely to meet you, I love your hat, it's amazing.'

'Congratulations!' Elle said, as she reached the bride and groom. 'You look absolutely beautiful,' she said to Libby. 'You too, Rory,' she added, with a smile.

'Thanks, Elle,' Rory said. 'Thanks a lot.'

'Well, Elle,' Libby said, in a loud undertone, 'I know one thing for sure!' Her voice was too loud. 'If you'd been my bridesmaid, you wouldn't have missed those typos, that's for sure!! Bloody Annabel.' Her face was red, her lips contorted into a strange grin. Elle channelled all her acting energy, unused since a school production of *The Worst Witch* in 1988.

'What typos?' she asked. 'I love your dress,' she added, as Libby opened her mouth. 'It's so pretty.'

'Thanks,' said Libby. She narrowed her eyes, an old Libby habit Elle recognised with a jolt. It meant she was running down her mental checklist. 'Hope you like your seating position. Thanks again for coming,' she said, her voice softer than before. 'I really am so furious with Annabel about those mistakes. I mean, we're a laughing stock.'

'I promise you no one will remember it,' Elle said, squeezing her hand and taking this as her cue to move on. 'See you later.' She kissed her again, drawing her close. Libby's swelling bump pushed against her own stomach.

'Shame about the typos in the order of service, eh, Eleanor?' came a resonant voice. 'I'm sure you wouldn't have missed them!'

'Hello, Felicity,' said Elle. She couldn't kiss her, it'd be too weird, so she shook her hand instead. Next to her, her new daughter-in-law threw her a look of flustered annoyance, and Elle felt a stab of sympathy for her.

'Eleanor Bee,' said Felicity, in booming tones. 'Hello, dear.'

'It's lovely to see you again,' Elle said, suddenly shy. After all these years of thinking about her, to be standing in front of Felicity again was overwhelming. She was decked out in raw silk of a violent bright blue and looked exactly the same, even if her hair was a little greyer. She nodded briskly at Elle and arched her firm black brows.

'Yes. Lovely to see you too. I am Catherine de Bourgh, as you may have heard.'

'No,' said Elle, shaking her head. *Oh, dear,* she thought. *She's lost it.*

'Anyway, I expect we'll talk later.' She turned to Jeremy, saying, 'Whom have we here? Aha! Good afternoon, Jeremy,' with a great big smile, dismissing Elle with a nod.

That was the end of the line, and Elle was left on her own. She looked around, but couldn't see Tom, or anyone else she knew. She stood on one leg, then the other, and then she downed the rest of her Great Expectations, as a waiter hoved into view.

'What else have you got?' she said.

'Well, this is an Animal Farm –' said the waiter, removing a hand from the tray and pointing at one drink.

'What's in it?'

'Mint, vodka, something,' he said disconsolately.

'That'll do,' said Elle, taking a glass. 'Thanks a lot.'

There was a small sighing at her elbow, and she turned round. 'Oh,' she said. 'Hi, Annabel. Good job there.'

'Oh, hi, Elle, how's things,' said Annabel, tightly clutching her glass of champagne. 'I'm so pissed off,' she added, as if she'd last seen Elle yesterday, and not almost three years ago. 'Libby's been really horrible to me about the order of service, and it's so not my fault, you know?'

'Oh, dear,' said Elle sympathetically. 'Well, at least you've told her. It gave us a laugh, if that's any consolation.'

'Which one?'

'Oh . . .' said Elle. 'Well, Wedding Wows instead of Vows was pretty funny.'

'What?' Annabel cried. 'I didn't even notice that one. Oh, my GOD. This is fucking awful, Libby's never going to speak to me again. I hate myself.'

'Don't say that,' Elle said, resisting the urge to laugh. 'It's a lovely day and everyone's enjoying themselves. She's just a bit tense, she's in a delicate situation, you know.'

'So how are you?' said Annabel, ignoring this and sighing, so that her pig's-snout nose flared and her top lip fluttered. 'You're like, amazing over there, people keep saying you're like bloody running the company, it's so great for you.' She made this sound as though it was a criticism. 'It's really hard over here, you know, UK publishing's much harder, because of the . . .' She paused. 'You know, because the market's more sophisticated and all that, and the discounts are SO BAD.'

Elle thought of the front table at one of the biggest and best bookstores in Manhattan, the Union Square Barnes & Noble, which regularly had the most obscure literary books on glorious display so they were the first things you saw. She thought of the lovely little paragraphs, in the backs of her favourite hardcovers: 'A Note on the Typeface in This Text', the history of the font in which the book was printed, and why they were using it. The paper on US paperbacks was cut from sheets on the grain, so that the spines flopped open in a smooth, silkily satisfying way, instead of sticking up awkwardly and rolling over. These things, the care and attention that made her remember why she loved books.

She looked at her watch; it was, to her surprise, already nearly three o'clock. If she were in New York it'd be ten in the morning. She'd be up already, perhaps walking to meet Marcy and Steven for brunch at Lucky Strike or somewhere in the Village. Perhaps Mike would be with her. Perhaps afterwards they'd walk through Soho, and she'd buy a top in Anthropologie, and some cute new mugs at that homeware store on Thompson Street, and then she'd get a manicure at New Model Nails on Bleecker while Mike ran some errands, and then they'd queue for lunch at the Spotted Pig and wander up through Chelsea, as far uptown as they could go before she flaked out and got in a cab. Last month, they'd walked all the way from hers up to the Upper West Side and across the Park, to Mike's place on East 77th. She'd begged Mike for a rest in the Sheep Meadow, but he'd made her go on till they got there. Then out in the evening to Happy Endings, her new favourite bar in the East Village, so-called because it had been a massage parlour before. Or perhaps a film –

'Elle?' Annabel was staring at her. 'Did you hear me?'

Elle came back to the present with a thump, looking round the elegant Georgian room, filled with polite people decked out in pastels, the sun shining through the windows. 'Oh,' she said. The heavy scent of lilies and perfume flooded her nostrils. 'Sorry. I was miles away. Jet lag. Any more bridesmaid's duties you have to fulfil?'

'I've got to make a speech, and I'm just *really dreading it*? Because you know now Libby's furious with me and I really want her to be OK with it.' Annabel pulled the tight wine-red silk up and around her, wiggling into it. 'These dresses are really uncomfortable?' She stared at Elle accusingly, as if Elle had personally requested they be like this. 'I really like Elizabeth Forsyte by the way. Just wanted you to know.'

'Thanks,' said Elle. 'I'll tell her.'

'She's bloody brill.'

'Oh, thanks. She doesn't really have an editor in the UK because she's got me, but – I'll tell her.'

Annabel looked at her with a sort of disdain. 'I don't mean like that, actually. God. I was just saying I liked her.'

Elle flushed red, to the roots of her hair. She didn't seem to understand what her fellow countrymen meant any more.

She didn't get Tom's sarcasm, she didn't understand that Annabel was just trying to be nice. 'Sorry,' she said. 'I don't understand English these days.'

'Right,' said Annabel, clearly thinking she was being rude again. 'Look, see you later then,' and she stamped towards her fellow bridesmaids, who were also drinking champagne and looking terrified together in a corner. Elle was left thinking that while everyone else had stayed the same, she had changed. Someone cleared their throat, nearby; she turned round gratefully. 'Hello,' said a strange man standing next to her. She stared at him: he had a black suit and was wearing black gloves. 'Which card, miss, or should I say madam, is the queen of hearts? Don't know?'

He slid a pack of cards into a crescent fan and thrust them under her nose. 'Oh,' said Elle, staring at him distractedly. 'I don't know, no. Sorry.'

She turned, looking for Tom, but then the gong rang for supper, and a large, barrel-chested man in some kind of footman's garb said, in an awful, booming voice, 'My Lords, Ladies, and Gentlemen. The wedding breakfast will now be served, in the ballroom. Please consult the table plan to find out where you are sitting . . . and *who you are*,' he finished with a flourish, as people looked puzzled. The bridesmaids giggled with excitement in their bridesmaids' corner.

'Oh, get a grip,' Elle murmured, under her breath. The incessant theming was starting to get on her nerves. Someone touched her shoulder.

'I'm Frank Churchill,' Tom said, jabbing his thumb at the table plan. 'I can't wait for you to find out who you are.'

MARY BENNET. SHE was Mary Bennet, the sodding ugly plain know-it-all sister. As Elle sat down at her table – *Pride and Prejudice*, she was fuming. In fact, there were two tables called *Pride and Prejudice*, because there weren't enough Jane Austen novels to go around. The top table was *Pride and Prejudice 1*, with large name cards in sloping script denoting Libby as Lizzy Bennet (perhaps that typo wasn't a typo, then?), Rory as Mr Darcy, Felicity as Lady Catherine de Bourgh (so *that's* what she'd been talking about) and Libby's rather shy parents as Mr and Mrs Bennet. Elle was on the second-tier *Pride and Prejudice* table, with the Maria Lucases and the Mr Collinses. She realised now that Libby's dress was Regency style not just to hide the bump but because this was a themed wedding, like it or not. Everyone had a piece of paper and a prop on their table. The paper was a quote about their character from a Jane Austen novel, beautifully printed as if to be framed. The prop was, in Elle's case, some small antique glasses, about the size of a thumb.

'Can you explain to me what the point of this is?' she hissed, to the man standing next to her at their table, waiting to sit down. 'Who are you?'

'No idea,' he said unhappily. 'Well, I'm going out with

Amy –' He pointed at the large bridesmaid on the top table. 'My name's Joe. But in this, I'm someone called Mr Hurst. I don't even know what that means.'

'He's in *Pride and Prejudice*. He sleeps a lot, don't worry,' said Elle, holding up the eye mask to show him. 'This could come in handy.'

'Jesus, this is stupid,' Joe hissed. 'I hate this bloody fuss. Why can't we just have some food and some drink and go home, eh?'

'I'm with you, Joe,' Elle said with feeling. 'I. Am. With. You.'

'Hello hello,' said a voice behind them. 'Good-o, I'm next to you.'

She turned around again. 'Oh. Jeremy. It's you.'

'Don't sound so over the moon to see me,' said Jeremy.

'Sorry,' said Elle. 'This is Joe.' She stepped back. 'Joe, this is Jeremy. He used to work with the happy couple.' *The happy couple. They're married. Libby is married to Rory. Jeremy is sticking a thin moustache on because we are at their themed Jane Austen wedding.* 'Mr Wickham?' she guessed.

'Oh yes,' said Jeremy wolfishly.

'Who's he?' asked Joe. 'I'm an idiot, I don't know any of them.'

'The villain,' said Elle. 'And don't feel bad. It's showing off and it's really duff. And ridiculous.'

'She's just jealous they've stolen her idea for her own wedding,' said Tom, stroking his sideburns with pleasure as he sat down next to Jeremy. 'Hi, Jeremy, nice to see you again.' He turned to a girl on his other side, a friend of Libby's from home who Elle guessed must be Jane Fairfax, by the fact that she was next to Frank Churchill and had been given a miniature piano.

'Hi, I'm Tom, nice to meet you,' he said. He looked at her place name. 'Hi, Maya.'

'I fucking hate Jane Austen,' said Maya. She ground her teeth. 'This is fucking stupid.'

351

Pretending to be putting something in her bag, Elle covertly watched Tom's profile, as he talked politely to Jane Fairfax, smiling as he poured her some water. His hair curled, just slightly, behind his ears, at his neck. He was so different from the cold, distant man he'd been, the first time she'd met him. He was more relaxed these days, happier, more himself, she supposed. But there was still something about him that meant he held her – and everyone? – at arm's length. She wished she knew what it was.

The footman reappeared.

'Please, raise your glasses . . . Mr and Mrs Sassoon!'

Everyone clapped and cheered, and Libby and Rory stood up and bowed. Libby gave a small wave, smiling at them all as she did. Elle clapped politely, but the rest of the table – the most disgruntled people in the room, it was obvious – could barely muster a single clap between them. Maya clutched one arm with the other and stood like a moody teenager. Jeremy was checking his phone and half-clapping. And next to her, Joe snorted. 'Who does she think she is, the bloody Queen of England?'

Tom raised his eyebrows and smiled across at Elle. She smiled back, each knowing what the other was thinking. She chewed her finger, trying not to laugh.

'Please take your seats,' said the Master of Ceremonies. 'Before the wedding breakfast is served, Mrs Sassoon will now read a poem she has written.'

'More champagne,' said Jeremy hastily, reaching down and producing two bottles from underneath the table.

'. . . THE OTHER THING about Libby that's so wonderful is that she really cares about people,' Annabel intoned, crushing the pages of her speech again so that they crackled loudly against the microphone. 'When I have been down, she has been amazing to me as a friend, you know? She's a really special person. And that's why she and Rory are going to be so great together?'

A polite round of applause rippled slowly across the airless ballroom. Annabel licked her lips and swallowed, turning another page of the speech. She bent over and took a sip of water.

From their position in the corner at the back, craning right to see the speeches, Joe – who was practically Elle's best friend by now – turned back to Elle and whispered, 'What's up with this one, then? Is she in love with the bride or what?'

'Yes,' said Jeremy smoothly. 'Got the hots for her. Follows her round like a puppy.'

'It's an amazing day for them and for us to be a part of,' Annabel went on, both hands clutching the speech. 'It's also a great day for the book trade to have two people so passionate about books joining together as one to continue their love affair with themselves and with books – er –' she faltered, 'with books.'

'God help me,' Jeremy said, sotto voce. He nudged Elle in the small of the back. 'Check out Felicity's expression.'

Felicity was ramrod straight in her chair, one side of her lip curled up, totally still.

'Those of us who were on the epic hen weekend in Newcastle –' here Annabel paused, clapped a hand over her mouth, and giggled again, like a geisha, 'have sworn ourselves to secrecy! About the teddy bear we will say no more!' The other bridesmaids, apart from Amy, laughed hilariously. Elle gritted her teeth, then noticed Felicity was doing the same. 'All I *can* say is, "Hammertime"!!' She held her hand over her mouth until her nervous hysteria had died down. The guests waited, mostly stony-faced.

Annabel looked down at the rest of the speech. 'Anyway, so – Libby, I'm really really happy for you, and look I'm so so sorry? About the mistakes in the order of service?' she said in a rush. 'Here's to the happy couple, Libby and Rory, yay, cheers!'

'I'm going out for a fag,' said Jeremy, standing up, as the rest of their table clapped, and Annabel plumped herself down next to a stony-faced Libby. 'Come with me?' He jerked his head towards the open door, not three feet from where they sat. Elle looked round nervously. Would someone notice?

Over at the top table, Rory stood up, and tapped the microphone lightly. 'Hello?' he said.

'Sure,' said Elle, getting up. She caught Tom's eye as she did. He looked at her, questioningly, and she paused.

'In the time-honoured tradition of these things,' Rory began, 'let me begin by saying that my wife and I . . .'

'Let's go,' she said, and she and Jeremy slipped away.

Outside, Jeremy handed Elle a cigarette, and Elle, who didn't really smoke but who enjoyed one occasionally – and now was as good a time as any – accepted it gratefully, still aware that she was being rather naughty.

'Here you go,' said Jeremy, leaning against the wall of the building. He lit Elle's cigarette. 'Thanks.' Elle inhaled deeply. Rory's voice, amplified by the microphone, crackled in the silence of the hot afternoon.

'The first time I met Libby, I . . . well, I don't remember it, I confess,' he said, to laughter and applause. *'The great love story of Rory and Libby is that we began as friends. We worked together for several years, though I must also confess that I always found her extremely attractive. But the truth is, I was too chicken to do anything about it. I felt, and rightly so, that she was too good for me.'* There was a pause. *'I'm sure many of you would agree.'*

Elle stared into the distance, at the newly green oak trees lining the edge of the park. She scrunched up her eyes in the sun, and bit her lip. Inhaling the cigarette had given her a head rush. She realised she must be a bit drunk. She couldn't take it like she used to.

'I know about you two,' Jeremy said.

'Oh,' said Elle.

'Know it's in the past. Jus' was thinking this must be weird for you,' he said, and Elle knew he was a bit drunk too.

'I am happy for them,' she said quietly. 'It's only . . .' Stinging tears sprang to her eyes. 'It's strange, hearing some stuff. I was . . . I did love him. Big part of my life, it was. But he and Libby are perfect for each other,' she finished.

'Too right they are,' Jeremy said, and he laughed sardonically.

'It's just odd being a guest at the wedding. When you dreamed about it for so long, even if you were a different person, and it was years ago. Sounds so stupid. I was stupid.'

'No, it doesn't.' Jeremy tapped his cigarette ash onto the smooth flagstones. 'You were pretty adorable back then, you know, Elle.'

'Hardly,' said Elle. 'But thanks.'

'S'true,' said Jeremy. 'I had a bit of a thing for you, with your crop and your long legs, head in the clouds but always looking so worried about everything. And you got pissed really easily. It was cute.'

'*You* had a thing for *me*?' Elle grinned, wishing her younger self was here to hear this.

'Oh, yeah,' said Jeremy. 'For about a week, yeah.' He nodded seriously.

'A whole week?' said Elle. 'That's pretty long for you.'

'I know. I even thought about making a move, when we went over to Bookprint, but you were all silent and weird by then. Makes sense, I suppose. Then you were off. Pooff!' He raised his hands in the air, showering himself with ash. 'Shit,' he said.

Rory's voice floated into the pause that followed.

'*She has made me the man I wanted to be . . . the person I think I'm supposed to become . . .*'

Elle shook her head, trying to block out Rory's voice, and stubbed her cigarette out, feeling a bit sick. 'Jeremy, I had a crush on you that you wouldn't believe. We all did. If you'd tapped me on the shoulder and asked me to . . .' She trailed off. 'I don't know. But I would have done it.'

Jeremy raised one eyebrow. 'Very interesting indeed,' he drawled. 'And you and Tom? What about him?'

'What do you mean?' Elle was blindsided.

'Well, what's going on with the two of you? You arrive together, you're all buddy-buddy.'

'Nothing's going on, seriously,' Elle said. She shook her head.

'I thought he was living with that hot Caitlin girl and the baby. I dropped them off in their road last year after an event at his bookshop.'

'What?' Elle scratched her neck, trying to look casual. 'Oh, yeah.' Tom had said they were living together, hadn't he?

'Yeah,' said Jeremy. 'Remember it 'cause it was a weird

address. Yorkshire Road, Richmond. And there's a Richmond in Yorkshire, too. You see, it's confusing.' He nodded, his head almost lolling.

'Oh,' said Elle. 'I didn't know that.'

She shrugged, helplessly, trying not to seem concerned. 'Well, that's good. Strange, eh! Yorkshire Road, Richmond!' she said, keeping her voice level.

'We should go back in,' Jeremy said. He patted her shoulder. 'You're lovely.'

She stared at him. 'Gosh, you remind me of someone, and I can't remember who it is.'

'José Mourinho, some people say,' Jeremy said promptly, trying to look modest.

'Who?'

He stared at her in horror. 'God, you vile American girl. Go back to New York. José Mourinho? Only the greatest manager we've ever had.'

'Who's we?'

'Good grief.' Jeremy stubbed out his cigarette. 'He's finally finished, you can go back in.' He pushed her towards the door and Elle followed him gratefully, realising what he'd done.

As they re-entered the ballroom, people were clapping and they slipped back into their seats virtually unnoticed, Elle squeezing Jeremy's shoulder as they did. She looked up to see Tom's eyes fixed on her as she sat down.

OK? he mouthed.

Sure, she mouthed back, shortly, annoyed at his concern and feeling childish for being annoyed. She wasn't the hysterical ex-girlfriend at the wedding, she had this under control. He had Caitlin and their daughter in a nice flat in Richmond. And she – she was fine. He nodded, and turned away.

AFTER THE MEAL came the disco. Elle looked for Tom, but she couldn't see him anywhere. By now it was after nine, but it could have been three in the morning; Elle had lost all sense of time. Her glass kept getting refilled. At some point, she and Jeremy started dancing, and she danced through the pain of the beautiful Kate Spade coral heels. Then suddenly 'Beautiful' came on, and ten couples leapt onto the floor, as if they'd been hanging around for a slow song. Jeremy held out his arms, and Elle walked towards him.

'Come here,' Jeremy said, and she swayed with him, knowing she must be pissed – she'd never swayed to a slow tune on a dance floor before, not unless you counted the leavers' disco at her primary school when she was ten, with her and Imran dancing to 'Careless Whisper'.

'It's so good to see you, Jeremy,' she said, into his neck. 'You're so nice. Always was.'

'You too, Elle,' Jeremy said. 'Lovely.'

He had his hands on her waist, and he moved one onto her bottom. She did the same, and they danced like that for a minute, turning round and round. Elle started to feel a bit dizzy, and she was aware from some of the dirty looks they were getting that they were intruding on other couples' dancing areas. She patted Jeremy's back.

'I'm going to get drink,' she said to him. 'See you in a minute.'

'Sure,' said Jeremy, and with one arm he reached out and grabbed Annabel Hamilton, and started dancing with her.

Elle walked off the floor, twisting her hair up to let the cool air onto her neck, and stood at the bar. The sun had almost set outside, flooding the room with blood-orange light. When she took her glass of wine, the barman said, 'It's a pay bar now. That'll be four pounds fifty.'

'Oh,' said Elle, embarrassed. 'My bag's over there, hold on, I don't have any—'

'Let me, dear,' came Felicity's voice behind her. 'Here,' she said, proffering a five-pound note to the barman. The ornately set diamonds in her ears glinted in the setting sun.

'Thank you,' said Elle, blinking to try and sober up, and thinking she probably shouldn't be having that extra glass. 'That's very – kind of you.'

'How long are you here for, Elle?' asked Felicity, taking her change and dropping it precisely into her purse.

'Tuesday, off first thing.' She remembered her promise to her mother. The doctor was on Monday. 'I hope.'

'You wouldn't have time for a drink on Monday evening?' Felicity asked. 'I have something I'd like to talk to you about.'

'Me?' Elle said, then tried not to sound so surprised. 'Um – I'd love to. But I'm not sure yet when I'll be in town.'

Felicity watched her, pursing her lips slightly as if weighing something up. She said, 'Posy and I have started up a new publishing company, did you know that?'

'No,' Elle said, shaking her head, rapidly sobering up. 'Gosh, no. When?'

'The company's going to be called Aphra Books,' said Felicity. 'First professional female writer, Aphra Behn. We've got some interesting people coming up.' She clenched her jaw, looked about her and leaned in again. 'In fact,' she said, 'I wanted to talk to you about joining the team. There. What do you say to that?' She screwed her eyes up and stared at Elle.

'Me?' Elle said. She looked around, just to make sure Felicity wasn't talking to someone else behind her.

'Yes,' said Felicity, with the air of one conferring a great honour. 'Yes, you. I know it's a long shot, but both Posy and I think it could work out. We'd have to get you in for an interview, of course.'

Elle shifted uncomfortably. 'I'm really happy in the States,' she said, not wanting to say, *Are you mad, do you realise how well I'm doing over there? Do you really think I'd leave it all behind to come back and work for Bluebird, mark 2?* 'It sounds wonderful, what you're doing, but I'm not in a position to move back.'

Raising her eyebrows, Felicity said nothing for a moment. Then she cleared her throat. 'Are you really happy over there?' she said. 'You always seemed such a London girl to me, loved living there, loved the trade and the people and all of that. Always thought of you when I'd see these girls on the Tube, with their short skirts and their manuscript bags, laughing away at something. You're quite different, now. Very poised, all grown up. All –' she waved her hand up and down at Elle, 'this.'

Elle wished she hadn't drunk so much. She could feel a hot flush creeping slowly over her and tried to concentrate. 'I'm really pleased with the way things have turned out. It was the right thing, going to the States.' She sounded as though she was repeating something, a poem she'd learned by heart.

'But are you happy there?' Felicity asked again.

'You have no idea how much happier I am, actually,' Elle said. 'I'd never come back. Sorry.' Why was it suddenly so hot? She had to get outside, get some fresh air. 'Anyway, lovely to see you again. I'd better –' She gestured. 'Go and find someone. Sorry again about the drink.'

'Of course.' Felicity nodded. 'You may well change your mind. Let me know, Elle.'

Elle wanted to laugh, this was ridiculous, who did Felicity think she was, her fairy godmother? 'Thank you.'

She pushed her way through the bar, out through the French windows onto the terrace and stood there breathing hard, unsure as to why she felt so unnerved. *Felicity's a dinosaur*, she told herself, thinking of those unblinking dark eyes, the heavy scent, the firm, be-ringed hands dropping change so steadily into their pouch. *She's only doing it because she doesn't have enough people to boss around any more. Don't worry.*

Elle looked up at the full moon, hanging low above the trees, huge and yellow. Across the fields and lanes towards the moon was her mother, and Elle drank in the relative silence, letting herself wonder how she was getting on. She'd said she was going to do some gardening, maybe meet up with Bryan, sort some clothes out. And it occurred to her suddenly, in the still, sudden calm, that something didn't ring true. Was it Bryan? The gardening? A spasm of worry about her shot through her body, and then she rolled her eyes, laughing at herself. She could hear Mandana's mocking laugh, as if she were right next to her. *Stop being such a worry-wart.* There were hundreds of nights when Elle wasn't nearby and she didn't worry about Mum. It was the height of self-obsession to do so when she was only a couple of miles away. But still, she wished she was at home, right now, chatting to her in the warm night air, not here, hot and drunk and –

She turned, to go and find her bag. Perhaps it was time to leave, anyway.

'Ladies and gentlemen,' Rory's voice called from inside. He was standing on the dance floor, mic in hand. 'We're going to be leaving in a minute, so everyone, make your way to the front entrance for the throwing of the bouquet!' He looked over, through the door, at Elle. 'Single ladies especially!'

Elle looked desperately around her, like a rabbit trapped

361

in headlights. She considered flattening herself against the wall and moving, crab-like, towards the driveway like Tom Cruise in *Mission Impossible*. Perhaps she should try it. Someone strode through the doors and she jumped.

'It's only me,' said Tom. He was breathing heavily. 'I thought I'd come and find you. Thought you might need rescuing from the bouquet throwing.'

'God,' said Elle. 'I don't need rescuing.' She knew she sounded churlish. 'This isn't a bloody MyHeart novel, you know.'

Rory passed by the two of them. 'Come on, you guys? Elle, you have to catch that bouquet!' He nodded. 'Libs'll really want to see you.'

'Wow,' Elle said, suddenly sick of it all.

'Wedding wow,' said Tom, but Elle didn't laugh. As she watched the guests troop out Jeremy went by, his hand on Annabel's bottom and his arm draped over her breast, and this only incensed her the more.

'Why didn't I see it? What he was like?' She drained her glass. 'Men. You are so good at it. You're all the same! You seem different and you are all the bloody same.' She shook her head, feeling the blood rush into it, making her dizzy. 'I just don't get it. I thought I did after all these years and I just don't see how I could have been so stupid. And English men are the worst. I'd forgotten! All these years and I'd forgotten.' She nodded violently, as if in agreement with herself. 'Supposedly charming, pretend to have good manners and sound like Hugh Grant and you're actually weak, pathetic, lying—'

'Hang on, we're not all like that,' Tom said.

'Yes, you bloody are, Tom!' Elle exclaimed. 'Rory, he's just like Max, my college boyfriend, and Bill and Fred and Jeremy, and . . . all of you!'

'You're the one who's been off flirting with Jeremy all day, Elle, you can't have it both ways.'

'That's got nothing to do with it.'

'Oh, really,' Tom said, curtly. 'I don't believe you.'

Elle carried on; it was as if a light had gone off in her head. 'I can't believe I never saw it before. You say one thing and you mean something else altogether, and women get the rap for being the inconsistent ones! If I go on a date with someone in New York it's just a date. We don't have to get paralytically drunk to snog, and if it wasn't any good we don't see each other again.' She thought of Mike, cool kind Mike, with his Brooks Brothers blazer and his direct, quiet manner. She hadn't thought of him for hours. 'We just – it's good.'

'Right,' said Tom. He stood still, staring at her for a moment. Then he said, 'On behalf of my people – sorry.' He stepped back. 'Well – I'm going inside too.'

'Fine,' Elle said. She didn't know why she was so angry with him, but she had to take it out on someone. 'I'm going in a minute, anyway, I think.'

'Right,' Tom said again. 'So, I guess – I'll see you around, Elle.'

'Yep.' She crossed her arms.

He turned to go and then looked back, and said, 'No. You know what? You've been so odd today. I don't understand it. Is it New York?' He took a step forward, so he was only a foot away from her, and lowered his voice. 'I know this is a difficult day for you, but you're so different. So . . . I don't know, hard to talk to . . .'

'What?' Elle hissed. Another couple turned and stared at them. 'I mean – that's rich coming from you, the most socially awkward person I've ever met. Who are you to say that to me?'

'Who am I?' Tom had followed her, onto a dark terrace around the corner. The moon cast a greyish purple light onto the flagstones, but the park beyond them was dark, and the noise from the wedding party, by this time on the other side of the house, was all but inaudible. 'I'm – I'm your friend. Well, I was.'

363

'We're not *friends*,' Elle said, shaking her head in fury. 'We're not bloody friends. We hung out for a summer a while back, until you – you made it clear it was over. That doesn't make us friends, Tom. Anything but. You have no idea how much –'

How much you hurt me. She trailed off.

'You're right,' Tom said, smiling a strange smile. His hair was ink-black in the moonlight, his face dark, and he towered over her, even in her heels. 'I absolutely adored you once, Elle. 'Cause you were adorable, that summer. But you have, you've changed.'

'I HAD TO CHANGE,' she shouted. 'You don't understand!' She was shaking, she thought she might faint with fury. 'You're the one who told me how crap I was! How I drank too much, how stupid I was to moon over Rory! You're the one who played around with me all summer and then went off and did happy families with your ex-girlfriend! I had to make myself into a better person, be the hardest working, the most organised. I can't go back to the person I was. Who I am now, I'm . . . people think I'm great.'

'Oh, get over yourself,' Tom said impatiently. 'You're confusing success with importance. You might have done well but that doesn't mean we should all bow and scrape when you enter a room. If that's all you're interested in, then yeah, you're right, perhaps you did have to change.'

A tear rolled down Elle's cheek. 'I shouldn't have come.' She yearned to be back home with a strength that nearly felled her. The miles of land and ocean that separated her from Perry Street, from her beloved New York, from her office with Senior Executive Editor, Jane Street Press on the door that she could shut, bury herself away with a manuscript, making everything clean and clear, making the people in the manuscript do what she wanted, have everything the way she liked.

And then Tom leaned forward and kissed her, just like

that. She inhaled, quickly, with surprise, made a little noise in her throat.

'Maybe I'm wrong,' he said. He took her hand, and kissed her again. 'Maybe you should have come. Elle, I'm real, I'm standing in front of you now. I have a question, and you don't know what it is. You can't take a pencil and cross it out.'

Her lips were still tingling from his kiss. 'What is it?' said Elle, leaning back away from him, so she could see his face.

'Come back to my room, Elle. Let's forget this horrible wedding. Admit defeat, come back with me.'

'No,' she said, and she caught hold of his wrist. 'Didn't you just hear what I said? Tom, that's a terrible idea.'

'It's not,' he said. She could hear his breathing, heavy and rapid. He kissed her again. 'It's one night, Elle, you're going back soon. Come with me instead.'

There was a reason she shouldn't do it, she knew there was. 'I told Mum— '

'Your mum told you not to worry about her and have a good time. I heard her.' Her hands were still on his wrist; he gripped her elbow. 'Let's not let this be like last time. I screwed it up that day you left. I wanted to tell you then – but . . .' He stopped. 'Let's not go into it now. Are you coming with me?'

She knew it was almost certainly a bad idea, but she didn't care. 'Yes, OK,' she said, suddenly bold. She moved one step to her right, and he followed her. 'Let me see your face. I can't see your face.'

Tom laughed softly and moved to his left. She stared at him for a moment, and then kissed him, wanting him more than anything, wanting this. Her eyes glittered in the dark; her heart was thumping, blood and adrenalin were pumping through her. He tasted sweet, of wine and something else, she could smell the faint scent of sweat on him. He pulled her against him, furiously for a second, and then took her hand.

'Come with me,' he said.

THEY ESCAPED THROUGH the dark, deserted corridors of the hotel. Tom held Elle's hand as they walked for what seemed like an age. It felt strange, they'd never held hands before. They got in the lift, and she pushed herself against him, sliding her tongue into his mouth. He stiffened in surprise, and then pushed back against her, holding her head in his hand. She liked kissing in lifts, it felt bad, naughty, reckless. And this was what this was – a reckless thing to do, and she liked to do it, now and again.

Elle had had several one-night stands in New York. The first time she'd stayed on in a bar talking to a guy after Megan, a friend from Jane Street, had left, and she'd ended up going home with him. He was called Ryan. He was a nice guy with floppy hair; floppy everything else too, unfortunately. But she had found the experience itself thrilling. It was only the guy that needed adjusting. Now, Elle tended to go for the ones with the glint in their eyes, the ones that said, I want what you want, and let's not complicate this with anything else. She took them home to her place – she always kept a pack of condoms in her nightstand – she threw them out the next day, she knew what she was getting into, so that then all there was left to concentrate on was . . . sex.

Sex, sex, sex. She wasn't the chubby loser who drank rosé till she passed out in a smelly, dirty rented flat, she was in control, slim, busy, in charge of her own life.

As they emerged onto the second floor, Elle remembered Yorkshire Road and the flat with Caitlin, and she almost stopped and turned back, and then she hardened herself against it. *It's his problem if he wants to sleep with someone and he shouldn't,* she told herself. *It's a one-night thing. I'm in the clear. It's sex, nothing else.* She heard cheering. 'Is that them?'

'Don't know,' said Tom, pulling her by the hand. 'Come on.'

She stopped, and looked out of the window. There, in the front courtyard, were the groom and his pregnant bride, climbing into a grey Bentley as the guests cheered. Libby threw the bouquet, in an explosion of camera flashes and confetti. Annabel jumped high to catch it, the car door shut and they were gone.

'Elle.' Tom wrapped his fingers around her upper arm, stroking the soft skin on the inside with his thumb. 'Are you coming with me?'

'Yes,' she said, and they hurried along the long corridor, their feet silent on the carpet. Tom fumbled with the card key and pushed open the flimsy door so hard that it banged against the wall. He shut the door and then pushed her against it, kissing her again, and she ground herself against him, almost mad with wanting him. He was tall, and slim, she knew that; what she hadn't known was the sinewy, hard muscle on his body, his strong, smooth arms that wrapped around her, the things he whispered in her ear as his hands pushed her skirt up around her hips, things that made her groan against him, throw her head back, hold him tighter.

'Are you sure you want to do this?' Tom said.

'Sure?' Elle came out of her reverie. She stared at him, blankly, her tousled hair falling around her shoulders. 'Of course I'm sure, Tom.'

He pulled her onto the bed, with a smile, and they faced each other, kneeling. He unzipped her dress, kissing her all the time. She tried to undo his shirt, but her fingers fumbled with the small, hard buttons and he pulled it off over his head at the same time as her. She had a coffee-coloured bra on and matching knickers, she pulled them off too, and as he bent down and kissed her bare breasts he looked up at her, and smiled, a sweet smile. Already, his cock was jabbing against her knee; she held it and caressed it, hard.

'You're lovely,' he said. 'You're so lovely.'

He began to stroke her, touching her between her legs, and then he lay back and she climbed on top of him. He carried on stroking her, his other hand caressing her nipples, licking her, murmuring disgusting things to her. Elle could feel warmth swirling over her, blood rushing fast through every vein. She took his cock in her hand; he gave her a condom and they slid it on together.

'Come inside me,' she said, almost wild with wanting to feel him.

Tom shifted and she lowered herself slowly onto him. His hands were on her hips. She closed her eyes, and he suddenly thrust up hard from the bed, so that her eyes flew open in surprise. He was big, she could feel him despite how wet she was.

'I can't believe it,' he said, through clenched teeth. 'Elle . . . Elle . . .'

She looked down at him, sobering up. Tom Scott. She'd almost forgotten how well she knew him, and now she didn't know him at all any more: his eyes, staring up into hers, his hands, on her tits, his beautiful long muscly body . . . Tom Scott was inside her, grinding against her, touching her and she . . . he gripped her hands as she rose and sank on him, feeling him high up inside her. The moment had gone for her, gone for ever. It wasn't a one-night fantasy, wild and dangerous. It was Tom, he was real, she knew him, he was

with someone else, she lived miles away and there was Mike
. . . She wished they could start over, but that was too terrifying, she couldn't go back now. She ground against him,
hard, and he came soon afterwards, crying out in a low roar,
his hands on her hips, holding onto her as if he had to, like
a drowning man.

Elle found it hard to sleep with someone else in the bed; she
always had done. She woke up several times as Tom snored
lightly beside her, then fell back into a dream, where she was
living the wedding in reverse, kissing Tom, talking to Rory,
drinking at the bar with Felicity, dancing again. Soon after
dawn broke, she fell into a heavy sleep, only to be woken
by the sound of the bathroom door closing. She lay in bed
staring up at the ceiling. Her head was pounding, and her
mouth tasted sour. Through a gap in the heavy striped curtains
the sun pierced the room. She could hear birds singing, the
sound of pipes clanking, a conversation somewhere, with
someone . . . where was it coming from?

The door opened and Tom emerged. He scratched his head.
Elle closed her eyes. He climbed back into bed with her, still
naked, and put his arm around her. She turned over, so they
were spooning, and he pulled her against him. She could feel
his breath on her neck. His skin was warm. She was cold.

'Are you awake?' Tom asked softly.

'Mmm,' Elle said. 'Sort of.'

He rocked against her, and she could feel his erection.
'Morning,' he said. 'How're you feeling?'

'Not great.' Elle liked this, she could talk to him without
having to look at him, because it was going to be embarrassing. She pushed against him a little more, feeling his chest
against her spine.

'Anything I can do?' Tom said. She didn't answer, and he
said, 'It's nearly nine o'clock, that's all. If you—'

Elle sat up immediately. 'Oh, God. I didn't let Mum know

I wasn't coming back,' she said. Nausea overwhelmed her; her head spun dangerously.

Tom's eyes flicked to her breasts. 'Text her now,' he said. 'Say you'll be back in an hour or so, stay and have some breakfast.'

'I can't . . .' Elle scrambled out of bed.

'Come on,' he said. 'You'll feel much better after some breakfast and a shower.'

His voice was reasonable, as if they were discussing the weather, not how to exit this drunken shag situation into which she wasn't quite sure how they'd got themselves. 'OK,' she said. She called her mother's mobile, but there was no answer, and so she called the landline, her fingers dialling the number as fast as she could.

'Good morning,' came an old man's voice.

'Hello?' said Elle. 'I'm looking for Mum, is she there?'

'Mum?' said the voice. 'My wife died several years ago, I'm afraid.'

'Oh –' Elle clapped her hand to her mouth, suddenly realising. 'Mr Franklin, I'm so sorry,' she said. 'It's Eleanor – Mandana's daughter. I've – I've rung our old number.'

'Ah!' said Mr Franklin slowly. 'I wondered who it was. Still remember your first phone number, eh? How strange. I could have sworn I saw your mother, you know, early this morning, outside the house. Looking up at the windows.' Elle smiled; Mandana hated the salmon pink roses the Franklins had planted outside Willow Cottage. 'So fucking tacky. Like Margo in *the Good Life*,' she used to say, glaring at them whenever they happened to pass their old home. 'I'm positive it was her,' Mr Franklin said. 'Is she well?'

'Er – yes, she's fine. I'm so sorry to bother you –'

She said goodbye and rang off. 'Mum's out and about this morning already.'

'Great,' Tom said reassuringly. 'So you've got some time, anyway.'

She turned to face him, suddenly aware she was still naked. 'Er, yeah – thanks,' she said.

She texted Mandana, quickly. 'Come back to bed,' Tom said, pulling the duvet back. 'Just for a minute.'

'Um – OK,' Elle crawled back in next to him.

He took her in his arms, but her shoulder hurt, pressed up against him, and it was cramped and uncomfortable, though she didn't say anything. They lay there, blinking together, looking at the elaborate cornicing. Elle was suddenly restless, her mind alert and awake. She started remembering things. Caitlin. His daughter. What was she doing here? But if she asked, then it'd be a thing, and she was going back on Tuesday . . . It wasn't a thing, it couldn't be, she was here for two more days . . . She leaned against him, smelling his dry, warm skin, wishing she could just fall asleep against him, trying and failing to seem relaxed. After a minute, Tom gently stroked her arm.

'Hey.' He kissed the back of her neck. 'How about some breakfast?'

While Elle showered, Tom ordered room service and a cab for her and they ate bacon and eggs together, in fluffy dressing gowns by the window overlooking the park. It was a glorious May day, the sky a deep blue. But Elle couldn't eat; she'd thought she was starving, but her hangover kept changing, so that when the breakfast arrived the eggs were horrifically gloopy and the bacon rancid and fatty to her. She chewed on some toast, trying not to stare at Tom. They heard voices along the corridor from time to time, breaking into the silence of their room, as they tried to make polite conversation; the weather in New York in May, the age of Sanditon Hall, the best route for Tom to take back to London. It was awkward. *It's a one-night thing, don't worry about it, you're going back on Tuesday, and you'll probably never see him again.*

When the call came that the cab was here she was relieved. 'I'd better go,' she said, standing up and pulling on her clothes. He watched her.

'Last night was fun,' he said. 'You were amazing.'

'Oh. OK, thanks,' said Elle. 'You – you too.'

'Thanks,' said Tom. He carried on eating his eggs. She wanted to hit him, for having the appetite.

'I'm just prolonging an awkward moment,' Tom said. 'Just pulling it out for as long as possible, to maximise the awkwardness.'

Elle put her BlackBerry into her bag and pulled on her shoes. 'Job done,' she said, smiling at him. 'I'm sorry to rush off –'

'It's totally fine.' Tom stood up. 'Look, are we OK?'

'We're – yeah, we're great,' said Elle. She stopped, one hand holding her shoe. 'Yes,' she said, more calmly. 'It's all good.'

'I'll email you,' he said. He swallowed and scratched his chin, rough with dark stubble. She thought how sexy he looked, how unconscious he was of it. 'Elle, it was great, maybe we could—'

'I really have to go,' she said. 'I'm sorry, Tom – I need to get back to Mum, you understand, don't you? And you need to get back to –' She added it casually. 'Is it Yorkshire Road, where you live?'

He nodded, looking slightly puzzled. 'Yorkshire Road, Richmond? Yes, what a good memory you've got.' Then he took her hand. 'Don't worry. Speak soon, yes? Or – sometime. This is – I'm glad, anyway. Have a good trip.'

'You have a good – yeah, thanks,' she said, unable to articulate what she was feeling, and she shut the door, her last image of him standing there in the fluffy white dressing gown, black stubble on his chin and a worried expression in his dark grey eyes.

THE TAXI DRIVER was local, and knew the lanes well, so though he went too fast for her delicate head, it was quick, and the journey back through roads heavy with blossom and bursting with life was almost pleasant.

When she arrived back at the barn and paid the driver, she stared up at the old building, sunshine warming its old stones. A window was open; the geraniums in pots by the door looked bright and welcoming.

But then Elle heard something, a rocking, tilting sound, mixed with something dripping. She strained her ears as she walked to the front door. There was no answer when she knocked, again and again. She checked her text and her mother hadn't replied. And so she went over and peered through the kitchen window.

The old record player was on but it had finished playing and was looping round and round. A tap was half-running, dripping loudly into the sink. Mandana was at the kitchen table almost exactly as she had been before, only there was stuff all over the table, red and orange, and it stank, it stank, and when Elle shouted at her, screamed through the window, she didn't hear her.

And when she finally hitched her dress about her hips

again and climbed through the window, and shook her mother, soaked in wine and blood and vomit, she still didn't hear her, and she didn't move, not at all. It was only when the ambulance came and they moved the bottles out of the way that she saw the large piece of paper on the table with two words written on it, in looping, italic writing:

SORRY ELLIE

EVEN WHEN SHE was very old, Elle could always recall them in perfect detail, the days after she found Mandana. The drive to the hospital every morning that began to feel like a routine, as though she'd started a new job and that was the way her life was going to be from now on. It was a lovely drive, too, through the countryside. That was partly when she started to realise she really couldn't come home again. For ever in her mind, early summer would be associated with that time. The cow parsley in the hedgerows, the early flowering honeysuckle, the heavenly scent of wild garlic everywhere. Then parking in the vast, empty car park, going in through the massive portico stuck onto the eighties building. It was of fake marble, and it always made her wonder why it was there. To reassure people? *We've got a marble portico. It's OK, your mother / husband / child isn't going to die*. The feet squeaking on the rubber floor, the huge metal lifts, the way women always clutched their handbags to their sides and looked down, at the floor. Then Mum's room, just her in there and another lady. The other lady left after two days, Elle didn't know where she went.

Mandana lay on her back, her face tipped up to the ceiling. She would have hated that, Elle knew. Her mother slept with three pillows, practically upright, always had done. She loved sitting up in bed, reading, listening to the radio, chatting to herself, to whoever was there. Not lying flat, as though she was already a corpse on a trolley. Elle had asked a nurse if they could put some pillows under her head, but they'd said no. Mandana's face was yellow, her hair stuck to her forehead and neck, greasy and limp. Her hands were always in the same position, the left one clutched into a fist except for the index finger pointing, her right arm splayed out on the edge of the clean white sheets. It was virtually useless, the right arm; they told her the drink had cut off most of the circulation to it, over the years. She'd hidden that, too, using the left arm, asking other people to unscrew a jar, always keeping her right hand in her pocket, on her hip. Elle could see it, now it was too late.

One day Elle came in and the index finger had curled up, like the others. 'She moved,' Elle told the doctor. 'Her hand wasn't like that before, it was like this,' and she'd shown them.

But they hadn't listened, because it didn't matter, and they were trying to get her to see that; none of it mattered.

On the twelfth day, her breathing grew more ragged and her pulse got weaker. Rhodes had been in again to see her, and he was with Elle in the cafe, just inside the marble portico, when they called Elle back up again, but it was too late, and she'd gone.

Elle was glad Rhodes was there. Then he went home, back to Melissa and Lauren, and Elle went back to the barn. It was still light, though it was after nine. She called some people, her father, Bryan, Mandana's boss at the library, her best friend from school, but actually, there weren't that many people to contact. She spoke to Caryn, and told her what had happened. Caryn asked when she'd be coming back. Elle never forgot that, even though she loved Caryn and owed her so much. She would always remember that, on the evening she rang to tell her that her mother had just died, Caryn said, 'When do you think you might be back in the office? Only because I spoke to Elizabeth Forsyte today and she was wondering.'

When Elle got off the phone, she'd looked round the big, lonely barn, at the blue-grey twilight outside, then she went to the kitchen, got some bin bags, and went upstairs to start clearing up. What else was she going to do? Sit there and cry? She'd tried to, and no tears would come. Better to be doing something, she had to do something. She couldn't just stay still. She'd start to think about it then and she couldn't. So she went through the house swiftly and methodically, sorting everything into piles – keep, charity, rubbish – and then went through the 'keep' pile and divided it into three more piles – solicitor, Rhodes, me, sell. Two days later, she'd finished, and there was nothing left for her to do. By mid-June she was back in New York. Nearly a month to the day since she'd left. The BEA (BookExpo America) was just starting, and for three days she made the trip to the huge, faceless Jacob Javits Center on the edge of the city, walking past the stalls filled with publishers gossiping, greeting each other. *SORRY ELLIE SORRY ELLIE SORRY ELLIE.* Three days there, and that, too, started to feel like a routine after a while, so she told herself, in the long, hot, sweaty nights in her tiny apartment, that she'd just replaced one routine with another, and that was the best way to function.

Only later did she discover that grief doesn't look like anything resembling sanity.

On the last stroke of midnight, the carriage and horses, the coachman and footmen vanished. Cinderella found herself, in her old grey dress and wooden shoes, in the middle of a dark, lonely road.

Vera Southgate, *Well-Loved Tales: Cinderella*

September 2008

'OH, BY THE way.' Elle poured herself some more coffee. 'I have to go to London next month. For one of those Building Bridges conferences. I thought I'd see Rhodes and Melissa and Lauren, spend some time in the office.'

Gray lowered the news section of *The Times* and looked at her. 'When?'

'Not sure.' Elle pulled her iPhone towards her. 'It's here – yeah. It's Monday 20th to the Wednesday and I'm flying out on the Sunday, coming back Wednesday p.m., I think.'

'So your flights are booked already?'

The sun was streaming in through the huge open windows, another perfect September day. She blinked, thinking it through. 'Yeah – sorry, honey. We got told about it ages ago, I just kept thinking it might not happen. Seems ridiculous when the world's in freefall financial chaos to be jetting over to the UK to sit in a dimly lit room and talk about improving margins, but there you go.'

'I'll miss you,' Gray said. He took her hand and kissed it, his flat, nail-bitten thumb caressing the diamond that had only been on her finger for a couple of months; it still felt strange, too huge, to Elle. She kept catching it in things, her clothes, her hair. She had caught the side of Sidney's cheek with it at his belated retirement party, and nearly taken his eye out.

'I'll miss you too, honey,' she said, smiling at him.

'Are you used to it yet?' Gray said, reading her thoughts. 'Being engaged? It suits you, you know.'

'I don't know if I'll ever be used to it,' Elle said. This was one of the things she loved about him, that he always wanted honesty before flattery. 'It's such an unnatural state to be in, neither one thing nor the other. And I just – well, I never thought it'd happen to me.'

Gray said drily, 'Well, I'm glad to make all your dreams come true.'

They were holding hands across the breakfast table; she laughed, and pulled hers away, picking up the manuscript she'd been reading again. 'Oh, definitely,' she said. 'You have, promise.'

On Saturdays Elle and Gray usually had a late brunch in the apartment, and while Gray caught up on The *Times* and the *New Yorker*, Elle skim-read manuscripts, and answered emails she hadn't got to during the week. In the evening they often had dinner with friends – Gray's friends, the academics, liberals and writers that made up his circle. Saturday morning was one of her favourite times of the week, sitting on the couch in the Soho loft, listening to the people below and the faint rumble of traffic on the cobbled streets, for though she was working, she was undisturbed by phone calls, office visits, her BlackBerry vibrating. She had time to herself, so she could start the following week ahead of the game. The Frankfurt Book Fair was a couple of weeks away, and though she wasn't going there was the usual rush of insanely hot scripts to read, the usual fevered brow to mop of the editor who wanted to bid millions of dollars, and the merry-go-round of dinners, drinks and meetings to endure. When you ran a division and had a team of twenty-five, and when you were (relatively) young and successful and engaged to one of New York's most respected authors, you rarely spent time at home, which was why these Saturday mornings were precious to her. Dinner with Gray's friends meant old Italian restaurants, discussions about European cities she'd never been to, and reminiscences of people she'd never met because they were dead. And, kind as they were to her face, she knew what they were thinking.

This Saturday, curled up on the couch in her pyjamas with her laptop on her knees, Elle was typing so furiously she didn't hear Gray come in again from his shower. 'I'm heading out to pick up some supplies,' he said. 'Do you need anything?'

She shook her head, blew him a kiss and carried on typing. 'I'm OK.'

Gray paused by the door, then came over. He sat down slowly next to her on the sofa. Elle moved her legs, so that his body rested against her limbs. The lines on his handsome face were more noticeable in the bright morning light.

'I've been thinking,' he began.

'Always a dangerous sign. Go on,' said Elle.

Gray's eyes twinkled. His hand stole under the blanket and stroked her foot. 'I might come with you, to London. My French publishers want me to go over to Paris before the election, in any case, to appear on a panel, and I've been putting them off. I could stay with you and then take the Eurostar. Would that be OK?'

'Oh –' said Elle. She closed her laptop, put her hands on top of it. 'That's great. It's just I won't have much time for you, you know.' She silenced him, as he howled in outrage. 'I'm serious! Those conferences are eighteen-hours-a-day things, we're in a hotel all the time, and I'll be busy, seeing people . . .' She paused. 'I do want to go to London with you, it's just now's not the best time. I'm literally flying in and out again, there's a board meeting back here and a big presentation, I have to be back for Thursday anyway.' She was gabbling.

'Sure, sure,' said Gray. He didn't move. She looked at him, at his craggy, clever face, the Adam's apple above the check shirt, the baggy navy jumper. 'I know how busy you are. But Elle, I really do have to meet your family some day, you know. And I want to go to London with you. It's a city I love. I want to explore it with you. Have you show me your old places and all of that.'

She hesitated, and he moved seamlessly into the silence. 'I know you don't like going back there. I understand why. I won't make a big deal of coming over with you. But I love you, Elle, we're going to be married. I want to know that part of your life.'

It was so comfortable underneath the blanket, nestling against the cushions, safe and cosy and fine. Gray was here, Dean & Deluca was one block away, and she had two old episodes of *30 Rock* TiVoed to watch later. She looked at him, and clutched his hands. She knew him so well, and yet they were sometimes total strangers.

The truth was, she was terrified at taking this step. Much more than any other, in their relationship so far.

When Elle started editing Gray Logan people were quick to sneer. Gray Logan! He'd been shortlisted for the Pulitzer, his last two books were *New York Times* Notable Books, he wrote for the *New Yorker*, Philip Roth himself was a fan. And he was going to be edited by the English girl who did Elizabeth Forsyte and romance novels? Ridiculous. She had one agent, Bunny Friedman, ask her pointedly at lunch if there'd be any jobs left for older editors if the younger ones were going to snap up all the good authors.

'What experience do you have, editing someone of Gray's calibre?' Bunny had asked, in the icy cold of a steak place on 6th Avenue, surrounded by bloody meat and corpulent businessmen.

'None, none whatsoever,' Elle had said truthfully. 'It could be a disaster, but we all feel he needs a fresh direction and I'm honoured to be working with him.'

She'd learned this tack on a course she'd just taken, with the unintentionally hilarious title of 'Understanding People: Ten Tools Every Manager Should Know'. The truth was, she was as scared as she'd ever been. This was uncharted territory for her: an author who won prizes and gave lectures and taught American History at Columbia. Who was she, to tell him what to do to make his books better? But the success of her taking over of Miles O'Shea and the follow-up to *Shaggy Dog Story* had convinced Caryn, Stuart and Sidney, her bosses, that she would be the right person to look after him. Since she'd started publishing Miles his sales had doubled. And *Diary by Design*, a self-published book she'd picked up in a tiny bookshop in the Village and had fallen in love with and bought for Jane Street had sold over half a million copies and been nominated for the National Book Award.

So when Gray's first book with her, a follow-up to the Pulitzer-shortlisted (but zero-copy selling) *Bethan and Judy*, the much more ambitious *Gold Standard*, about a Jewish Upper West Side family whose son marries out of the faith, had hit *The Times* best-seller list and had sold over 100,000 hardcovers, no one was more relieved than her. There was even a rumour – 'It's a rumour but oh, my freakin' God, what kinda rumour!' Caryn had shrieked – that Oprah had read it and was considering mentioning it . . .

When Sidney retired, and Stuart and Caryn were bumped upstairs, at the age of thirty-three Elle was asked to take over Jane Street Press, and sit on the executive board. She now had a team of twenty-five people, a turnover of 20 million dollars a year, and an assistant all to herself, someone who did stuff like pick up her dry-cleaning, and book her lunch appointments. Elle couldn't imagine life without her, though Courtney was as unlike Elle at her age as it was possible to be. Demure, whip thin, friendly and efficient to within an inch of her life, she was almost too good to promote. In her idler moments – which were rare – Elle compared herself aged twenty-two to Courtney. Courtney would never address authors as Shitley, or order cabs that took her boss to Harlow instead of Heathrow, or leave agents waiting in reception for thirty minutes. It was a far cry from Bluebird to her job at Jane Street, but Elle didn't ever analyse what made a book work, what that magic formula was that ensured its success. She stuck to two principles: publish books you love, and treat the authors well. In fact, she'd treated one of her authors so well that now here she was, living in his loft apartment, in the heart of the preservation district, with his ring on her finger, and her future assured.

Gray had laughed when she'd moved in, the week before Christmas. All her possessions fitted into one cab.

'You're thirty-three, and you have three boxes, a little table and one lamp. That's all you've accumulated over the years?'

'Yes,' Elle had said. 'There wasn't room to swing a cat in Perry Street, and the flats I had in London weren't worth buying trinkets for.'

She had a few books, a couple of posters and the lamp, from a shop in Chelsea, a few pretty bowls from Anthropologie in which she kept her jewellery, and apart from her clothes that was it. Most of her books were in storage. But she still had with her, she didn't know why, Felicity's copy of *Venetia*. Perhaps she meant to give it back one day. Perhaps it was comforting to have it near.

'You haven't put down roots anywhere,' Gray had observed, taking out the lamp and putting it carefully on the sideboard. 'And now you are. Don't you think that's interesting?'

'No,' Elle had said, putting the few Christmas presents she'd wrapped already by the small tree. 'Don't get analytical on me.'

She hadn't meant to fall in love with Gray; she had never set her cap at him. He was nearly fifty, for goodness' sake.

386

All his female friends let her know in different ways how lucky she was; that he was an enormous catch. But he wasn't to her, he was way too old. That was why she didn't realise it, for a long time, and it wasn't till they were having dinner in the Village one evening – they lived close to each other, and had met up a couple of times – that he said something that she found funny and she looked at him and thought, Yes. I know you. *I know you.*

He was brilliant, he was interesting and held in high regard, all of those things. But he was also funny. He made her laugh, and no one had done that for a long time. And she made him laugh, in a way no one had, he said, since his wife died. It was the friends and the wives who referred to Julia, his dead wife, constantly, asked her how Rachel, his daughter, was doing at Stanford, as if Elle was responsible for her happiness, or rather her unhappiness. Elle didn't care. Gray had a good relationship with his daughter, they saw her all the time when she was back in New York. And Julia was part of his past, he'd loved her, if she were alive they'd still be together, but she wasn't, so why shouldn't he have someone else in his life, now? She hadn't stolen him from anyone. But Gray's friends seemed to think she had, from the arms of an older woman, someone who could complain about creaking knees with him, or talk about the good old days at Studio 54, Warhol and Basquiat and Bianca. After a while, she didn't mind that he was older, in fact she liked it. It gave him a past, one that he sometimes wanted to forget. They both wanted a new start.

When Gray returned, an hour later, from running his errands, he was clutching a Dean & Deluca cloth bag brimming with produce and a Starbucks iced coffee.

'I ran into Hana and Joel at the market,' he said, heaving the bag up onto the black marble breakfast bar. 'They're going to Joseph's party next week. And they saw a preview of *All My Sons* last night. They said it was great.'

Elle looked up from the new manuscript she was now reading, which was yet another *Kite Runner*-esque story about a boy in a small village, this time in Turkey. 'Oh, wow.' She shifted up on the sofa and stretched herself. 'What was Katie Holmes like?'

Gray looked blankly at her. 'Who?'

'Katie Holmes?' Elle said. 'Come on. She's married to Tom Cruise? He jumped on Oprah's sofa about her? It's her Broadway debut, it's huge.'

'Of course.' Gray smiled. 'All I know about it is it's a wonderful play by Arthur Miller and John Lithgow is one of our best actors. I'm a cultural desert, forgive me.'

Elle sank down into her blanket again, and turned another page of the manuscript. When Gray was like this she wanted to throttle him. He handed her the coffee.

'Did you think some more about the London trip?'

'Thanks,' said Elle. 'Sure. Let's go in the spring, next year, shall we? It's best if I just fly in and out this time. Is that OK, honey?'

'Yes,' Gray said, dropping a kiss onto her forehead. 'Of course it is.'

She watched him walk back across the huge room to the breakfast bar, and she wondered, once again, what she'd done to deserve him, and when he'd find out what she was really like.

GRAY'S SECOND ATTEMPT came a few days later. They had arranged to meet at the Regal off Union Square, to watch *The Duchess*. Gray taught classes on Revolutionary American Politics and the American Revolution and its Legacy at Columbia, and he had been impatient to see it, though Elle couldn't stand Keira Knightley and would have preferred almost anything to it, even *Transformers*.

It was extremely hot outside, the kind of heat you never got in London in September, and the traffic coming off Broadway was bumper to bumper, hazy fumes rising into the empty lavender-blue sky. Elle was waiting for Gray in the air-conditioned foyer, already shivering under the intense, icy blast from the unit above her. It occurred to her suddenly that that was the only thing she missed about London. Windows you could open that let fresh air in, air that wasn't either 10 or 90 degrees Farenheit – last summer on 4th July, the tarmac at JFK Airport had actually melted, when the thermometer hit 100 degrees. There were definitely several days of the New York year when Elle wished – not that she was back in London, of course not, but for a mild, foggy, temperate day, the kind of weather that London enjoyed for half the year.

As she stared at the picture of Keira Knightley in a wide-brimmed hat, her mind wandered back to Libby and Rory's wedding, she didn't know why. Perhaps it was because she'd spoken to Annabel that morning, on a video conference call; Annabel had waved to her and shouted, 'Hiya, Elle! Long time no see!' Elle, nonplussed, had raised a hand in silent greeting, and then turned to Celine. 'So, Celine. Where are we with the pitch for Zara Goodman?'

She knew she was being a bitch. Had Annabel kept that bridesmaid dress with the shepherdess hat? Did she still see Libby and Rory? Last time Elle had heard from Libby, she was pregnant with baby number two and they were living just outside Tunbridge Wells. It's a really lovely village, proper countryside, a real community, she'd emailed – of what, Elle had wanted to ask. Bankers and accountants commuting in to Charing Cross every morning? She'd promised to go and see Libby when she was over next. If I have time, she'd written, just what she'd said to Gray. You know what these conferences are like, you don't have a spare minute to yourself.

Sure, sure! Libby had emailed. Any time! I've got my hands full here with Scarlett! Life as a mum is way busier than my job as an editor, I hadn't realised! Elle hadn't replied.

Rory was still at Bookprint, by the skin of his teeth; Elle had found herself defending him, of all unlikely things, to her US colleagues. 'Who is that guy?' Stuart had once asked her. 'He's no good.'

'Him? I had an affair with him for over a year, actually. He was my boss.'

She hadn't said that. She'd said, 'They got him when they bought Bluebird, as part of the deal.'

'Bluebird?' Stuart had said, wrinkling his forehead.

'The Sassoons' company,' Elle had told him. 'Last of the old independents.'

'Oh,' said Stuart vaguely; he dealt in big-picture stuff, not nuance. Why would he have heard of it? It was very nearly eight years ago now, the sale. 'I remember. Kinda.'

She hadn't said she worked there. She didn't really know why.

She was lost in thought in the lobby, drifting aimlessly from one memory to another, delicately prodding, like a tongue on an aching tooth in case too hard a touch was painful, when Gray appeared.

'Honey, I'm so sorry,' he said, slightly out of breath. 'I had to see Morgan, he was late, we had a great meeting, but it overran – I'm sorry.'

'Don't worry,' she said, squeezing his arm.

He kissed her. 'Did you get popcorn?'

'Not yet,' Elle said. Gray loved popcorn. She leaned against him, inhaling the smell of him she loved so much: spicy aftershave, the faint buttery scent of his skin. 'Mm,' she said softly. She closed her eyes and took a deep breath, feeling the stress of the day flow out of her. 'I love you,' she whispered.

'I love you too,' Gray said, squeezing her to him. He kissed her ear. 'Honey, are you OK?'

'Fine, I'm fine,' Elle muttered, straightening up. 'Let's get in line then.'

'Sure.' Gray pulled a roll of bills out of his trousers. 'Oh, by the way, you booked your tickets for London, didn't you?'

'Well, not personally,' Elle said. 'The office did it, ages ago.'

'Hm, hm.' Gray made a great show of putting his cellphone away in the pocket of his battered old blazer. 'I do think I'm going to come to London, in fact. Morgan and I were discussing it today. There's some research I can only do in the London Library. They have a fantastic collection of topography, and there's a diary written by a housemaid in Benjamin Franklin's house in 1774. Would you mind, honey? I might as well come at the same time as you – although I could always go the week after if you don't want me there.' She stared at him. He leaned forward, squinting at the menu above them. 'Large tub of salted, please, and two Cokes. Honey, you want a Coke? Elle?'

She hesitated. She knew Gray's methods of old. Once again, she had to bow to his superior handling of the situation. What could she do but say yes? Elle bit down on the inside of her cheek, red mist hazing in front of her.

'Actually, I wish you weren't coming, I said so already,' she said. 'You know I'm going to be busy.'

'I know,' Gray said. 'I know you are. And –' He took a deep breath. 'I know you hate going back to London. I know you hate seeing your brother. But it's four years since it happened.'

'Sshh,' Elle said. She wanted to put her hands over her ears.

Gray said softly, 'It's four years since your mom died, Elle.'

She nodded, her lips clamped tightly together.

'We've been together for two years, we're getting married soon, and I've never met your family, I don't know anything about your life there.' He took her hands and looked into her face, his kind hazel eyes gazing at her. 'It's six years since I lost Julia, and when it happened I thought I'd never get through it, but I did. You've got the rest of your life ahead of you, Elle, honey. It might be time to start moving on.'

She hated the implication of what he was saying, the way he said it. *You should be over it by now.* He'd never understand. Julia died from a brain aneurysm, there was nothing he could have done. Elle pulled her hands away from his, grabbed her Coke and stalked away, towards the escalator. She said, 'I wish you weren't coming. But fine.'

'I'm coming anyway,' Gray said, behind her. 'And I don't understand why you're being like this, Elle.'

She hated when he spoke to her like a naughty child. 'You don't get it, do you.' She stopped and turned around, and

392

gave a short laugh, the incongruity of the red and yellow lobby, the muzak in the background, the sound of explosions coming from the screen next to them.

'No, I fucking don't,' Gray said. 'You won't talk about her, you won't mention it, you say it's not my business, you don't ever—'

Elle interrupted. She said robotically, 'I killed her, Gray.'

'That's ridiculous.' He stopped her with his arm. 'No, you didn't, Elle.'

'I did.' Elle pulled furiously away from his grip. 'May I have your tickets,' said the laconic woman by the screen door, chewing gum and staring over them into space.

'Let's go in and talk about this later,' Gray said, his jaw tight, and Elle saw she had pushed him too far. She loathed how she could do that, push him so far till he snapped, and Gray snapping meant he was cold and moody for the rest of the evening. He hadn't been like that when she'd first met him. She sometimes wondered if it was the only way he'd found to get through to her: just withdraw communication till she cooled down and begged him to forgive her for behaving like a silly child. It was so clichéd, that: as though he was a father figure to her, just because he happened to be sixteen years older than her.

She followed him into the movie theatre, feeling her way in the sudden darkness.

THAT NIGHT, ELLE woke up at three, wide awake. As if a light had been switched on. She turned onto her back and stared at the window. There was a gap at the edge of the blind; she could see the fire escape of the building opposite. The sound of someone kicking something – a can? – floated up from the silent street.

The image was back again. It was all she could see.

She crept out of bed, pulling on a robe, and tiptoed into the huge main room. It was cold, spooky, unfriendly in the dark. She opened the fridge door, quietly, and took out some milk. Tears were running down her cheeks. She batted them furiously away, as though insects were flying at her face.

It had happened all the time, after she'd come back to New York, at least twice a week. At first, she'd tried to go back to sleep, but it was useless. In fact, it was worse, because she would lie there and things would occur to her. What she should have done. What she hadn't done.

There was no ritual for grieving, not here in the States, not back in England. You didn't wear black any more, you didn't tear your clothes and wail in a group, you didn't visit the grave on the Day of the Dead, have a picnic, tell stories about the one you'd lost. No one gave you a manual about what to do when your mum died. You were just unhappy, desperate, and alone. People were kind to you, or they avoided you, as though you were tainted with something they didn't want to catch.

Elle sat on the couch and tucked her feet up under her. She'd tried reading, at first, but it didn't work, reading didn't really give her that much pleasure these days. She couldn't concentrate when it was like this, the image of her mother on the table covered in bloody vomit, those two big black words on the piece of paper dancing in front of her eyes, blinding her. *SORRY ELLIE. SORRY ELLIE. SORRY ELLIE.*

She usually watched TV. She flicked it on now, to try and make the image go away, rocking softly back and forth and breathing deeply. She found doing this helped her, it was her own ritual, when this happened. Because when it came it hit her as though she'd run into a wall, and if she really gave in to it, after all these years, it would flatten her, so the best thing to do was just ride it out, steer a path around the wall, watch something mindless, removed from what she was thinking instead, get that image to go away, stop haunting her. She flicked through the channels. There was a debate about the election on CNN, a group of white men in thick blue and red ties around a table talking about Obama and Palin. She stared at the screen, running through the names of senators she could remember in her head, and then the US states, in alphabetical order, till the ball of hysteria inside her lessened, just a little.

But the image was still there. The one image she kept coming back to, again and again. It was a little thing, but it was everything. Her mother's friend Anita (the one who imported textiles from Rajasthan, and who wasn't in business with Mandana, never had been, never would have been, it was a pack of lies, like so many things Mandana had told Elle over the years) told Elle she'd seen her, that last night before she died. They'd been to the pub. Mandana had stuck to Coke all evening. She'd left her purse behind and returned after closing time. She'd cycled along back towards the village and there, outside Willow Cottage, kneeling on the ground crying, semi-conscious and making no sense, was Mandana. Anita (she said), had stood her up, asked her if she was OK, and Mandana had told her to go away, and leave her alone. And she'd stayed there, for God knows how long. Anita had left her there – a fine friend, Elle thought, though it turned out they weren't really friends at all, and she was the one going out with Bryan, not Mandana. Mandana had never even been on a date with him. It was all a lie.

How she got back to the barn, a mile away, Elle didn't know, but she had, and she'd drunk herself to death there. Vodka, whisky, tequila. Half a bottle of each was enough to kill her. She died of massive internal bleeding, but already she had chronic liver failure, cirrhosis of the liver, had done for years, only no one knew apart from her, and the doctors. She'd been hospitalised in February; no one had told her, or Rhodes. When Elle asked why, the doctor sighed tiredly and said, 'They probably tried. But you're dealing with someone who'll tell several different lies to different groups of people in order to conceal the truth, so they can carry on drinking themselves to death. She told you one thing, she told us something else, your brother something else again.'

'A cunning disease', that's what Melissa had called it, and she was right. It explained so much: the yellowing skin and nails, the thin hair, the confusion, the paranoia. Her liver had stopped working, it couldn't break anything down, it sent ammonia to her brain, fluid to the legs and still she went on hiding it, using everything in her power to melt into the background, stop anyone realising so she could carry on drinking. Even Rhodes and Melissa hadn't known the full extent of it. No one had. Except Mandana.

It was the image of her mother, kneeling in the darkness in tears outside their old family home, that Elle couldn't stand. It was what woke her up, this picture, and it was crystal clear in her mind, every single time. How desperate she must have been, how lonely, unhappy, and no one had done anything to help, for years and years. Not Rhodes or Melissa, not her ex-husband, not her friends in the village, and most of all, not Elle, who had simply got up and left her, run away to make her own life. She had said the same to Gray earlier and it was still true: instead of going home to her mother, Elle had gone back to Tom's room, had sex with him, spent the night with him, out of some needy attempt to assuage her own sense of isolation at being back. She knew Mandana had done it deliberately. Couldn't face telling her daughter how far she'd fallen, couldn't face life without alcohol, didn't think she was strong enough to try. But if she'd got back that night instead of staying with Tom, perhaps it wouldn't have been too late. Elle never knew why Mr Franklin thought he'd seen her that morning. Perhaps he'd seen the old Mandana, a ghost, a vision from the past.

She knew she'd killed her, as sure as if she'd stuck the knife in herself, first by forcing her to confront it, then by abandoning her when she needed her. And people could tell her that was wrong, it was a terrible disease, alcoholism, it made people monsters who lied to those they loved best, and Elle knew it was all true. It didn't change things though. It should have been different and she would have to live with that for the rest of her life.

'The *New Yorker* editorial said this week, "The Presidency of George W. Bush is the worst since Reconstruction",' said the news anchor. 'What I wanna know is, what do you think of that statement?'

'Well, what I wanna know, Chuck, is, are they living in the same world as me? Where the hell do they get off referring to a man who's a patriot, a God-fearing man who loves his country and his people, in terms like that?' A perfect blonde in a red suit thumped a tiny fist on the table. 'I honestly think sometimes people don't see what's right under their noses, Chuck. Makes me real sad, real sad.'

'What's going on, honey?'

Gray was standing in the doorway, in his old T-shirt and boxer shorts, with his arms crossed. He peered at her, still half-asleep.

'You can't sleep?'

Elle shook her head.

'Did you see her again?'

Elle nodded. He came and sat down next to her on the sofa.

'You have to see your brother when you're back, talk to him, you know. You need to talk to someone else about it. Do you still have the number of the grief counsellor?'

'I don't want to go to them again,' Elle said. 'It's been four years, I can deal with it on my own.' She shut her mouth again.

'OK.' Gray looked at her, then at the screen. 'I can't stand that woman. Let's turn this off.'

'No!' Elle said, grabbing the remote off him. 'I need it. Leave it on. It's fine, I just need to . . . let the stuff go. Leave me alone. Why can't you just leave me *alone*?'

As she said it, she heard her mother's voice, and realised how like her she sounded.

Gray didn't move. He said, tiredly, 'Honey, I'm done on this with you.'

'You're *done*?' Elle said. 'What, you're sick of me being sad about Mum dying? I've had my time, now it's up?' She laughed, clutching her knees tightly under her chin. 'Wow, that's good to know. Just – leave me alone, Gray. I'll come back to bed soon.'

Why did she feel so angry with him all the time, when it wasn't his fault? She looked at him through her lashes, at the handsome, distiguished face with the kind smile. She thought of their second date, when he'd taken her up to

398

Martha's Vineyard for the weekend – 'away from prying eyes, honey, I don't want anyone else to know about us, I want you all to myself' – as though she was his precious prize, a reward for something. She loved it, loved feeling like that. That he – Gray Logan, *the* Gray Logan – had earned her, because she was worth earning.

She didn't feel like that now, in fact she couldn't remember what that feeling was like.

'I mean,' he said, sighing gently, 'you're less and less like the person you were. And that's not good. I don't want you to change, I love you and I will always love you. But I want you to be happy, and I want our lives together to be happy, and I'm done pretending it's all OK and you're fine, when you bury yourself in work and thrive on conflict and you're not fine. That's all.'

Elle nodded. Suddenly she felt very, very tired. A wave of it swept over her, as a chilly gust of wind blew in from the street and she wished for a moment she was in England, with all her heart. She didn't know why. Just that now and then, the smell of wet leaves or the rain on the Manhattan pavements made her think how subtly different autumn was back in London, how you felt the misty chill seep into your bones, into the damp spaces of old buildings, where pale yellow light shone from lamp posts onto white stucco and red brick. Usually she pushed the thoughts away, but now she didn't have to, because she was going back.

'I'll send you my flight details tomorrow,' she said quietly. 'I'm only there for three nights. I'll email Rhodes, too, and ask if we can come for supper. I suppose you should meet him.'

'Yes, I should,' Gray said. He opened his mouth to say something and then shut it again. Instead he leaned over and kissed her, his hands warm on her cold skin. She leaned back against the sofa as one hand ran over her body, under her vest, squeezing her breast. He kept his hand there as he carried on kissing her. She stroked his cheek and kissed him back. It was strange, but with Gray, it was never his experience that intimidated her, as it had been with Rory, when she'd been so young, so desperate to please, such an eager young thing. She was sorry Gray's wife was gone, and she was uninterested in his ex-girlfriends: it was the truth. Because when they were together it was about only the two of them, hand in hand, walking through the streets together, and the rest of the world receded into a blur, and as they kissed in the dark room, the TV flickering in the background, Elle clung to that image, and that one alone because perhaps, just perhaps it might work.

BUILDING BRIDGES CONFERENCE, 20th–22nd October 2008

> **Day 1: Schedule**
> **Delegates to gather in the Oak Room.**
> **9 a.m.** Coffee / mingling
> **9.30 a.m. Introduction** by joint CEOs **Celine Bertrand** and **Stuart Forgan**: Building Bridges and Bestsellers
> **10.30 a.m. Whither the printed book in the age of digital?** Panel Discussion with **Eleanor Bee** (Publisher, Jane Street Books), **Rory Sassoon** (Publisher-at-Large, BBE Books), **Tom Scott** (Owner / CEO Dora's Bookshops)

'WHAT ON EARTH?' Elle said, staring at the schedule in her hand. She flicked her BlackBerry out of her suit pocket, and then realised it was 9 a.m. in London, 4 a.m. in New York. Courtney would still be asleep. Someone said, 'Hello,' to her, as she stared at the tiny screen.

'Oh. Hey.' She looked up and, seeing who it was, tapped Celine's arm. 'Celine, I appear to be on this panel this morning. I didn't know anything about it.'

'What?' Celine stopped, and frowned. She looked up and

down the schedule, then at Elle. Elle felt as if she were four-teen again. 'That is most extraordinary. We emailed, your assistant assured us that you were up to speed. I even spoke to her myself, to make sure.'

'Well. She didn't tell me. That's –' Elle shook her head. She could feel her stomach churning. Never, ever in her life had she ever blamed a mistake on someone else. Well, there was a first time for everything. She'd had no sleep on the plane or last night in the hotel either, just that annoying state between sleeping and wakefulness, staring at the ceiling. Tonight was the dinner with Rhodes, she had umpteen unread emails already to deal with, and on top of it all she now had to sit in front of two hundred people with two of her ex – what, lovers? discussing ebooks.

Wow! she thought to herself. *I really am being punished for something.* 'Look,' Elle said hastily. 'Don't worry about it. I'm sure she mentioned it to me.' She was sure Courtney had, but she hadn't been listening. 'Funnily enough –' she took a deep breath – 'we had a digital-only board meeting a couple of weeks ago, so I'm up to speed from our point of view. I'm pretty sure I can muddle through –'

'Muddle through?'

'It'll be fine,' Elle said firmly. 'Don't worry.'

Celine nodded curtly and moved on, and Elle breathed in and leaned against the wall, looking around her. The conference room was in a faceless international hotel in Mayfair. Cream draped blinds hung at each window, blocking out the view of London; you could be in Singapore, Sydney, Berlin, anywhere. The walls were covered in oat-coloured fabric, the ceilings were low, the furnishings were minimal. Knots of people stood around the huge room, drinking coffee, murmuring. You could tell the Brits from the Americans straight off: they were slightly larger, they were wearing colours, their hair wasn't as good. Feeling guilty for thinking this, Elle waved to Caryn and Stuart, who were deep in conversation in the corner of the room.

A disembodied voice said, 'If you'd like to go in please, and find your seats. We'll start soon, thanks.'

Elle picked up her bag, holding her BlackBerry in one hand, and strode towards the conference hall. She looked at her watch. She hoped they wouldn't start late. She'd agreed to meet Felicity for lunch, for some reason, and she wanted to go to Waterstones and Smith's beforehand, check out some bookshops.

'Hi, Elle!' Annabel Hamilton was bouncing up at her side. Her hair was frizzy, and she had some kind of stain on her cardigan. 'How are you? It's been so long!' she said. She kissed Elle on the cheek, and Elle reared back in surprise at the unexpected physical contact. 'Do you want to sit with me? Us Brits should stick together, eh?'

'We have assigned seating,' Elle said. 'But I hope to see you later, Annabel.'

As Annabel strode ahead of her, huffily, Elle caught herself, as she did occasionally, and laughed. 'You're being a complete tool,' she whispered to herself as she went into the room. 'Get over yourself.' She took her seat, and looked at her watch. 9.30. One hour to go. Two girls walking past looked at her and then down at their feet, picking up the pace. 'Oh, my God, Tors – that's Eleanor Bee. The one from New York,' the first one said, in a perfect middle-class publishing girl's accent, the kind Elle used to be surrounded by and which she hardly ever heard any more. Elle pretended to be studying her BlackBerry. 'She used to be Rory's secretary.'

'Oh, my God, didn't she –' the second one began, before lowering her voice and scurrying on. Elle strained her ears, but she couldn't hear, which was probably a good thing, though she wanted to grab them and say, 'Solidarity, young women!', like an ancient suffragette. She smiled, for the first time since she'd got to the conference.

*

403

'Nice to see you,' Rory whispered, an hour later, as he joined Elle on stage. He kissed her on the cheek. 'Should I bow and call you madam?'

'No, sir,' Elle said, kissing him back. 'How are you? How's Libby?'

Rory drew breath. 'She's good, really good, she loves Tunbridge Wells, it's great, we have some great friends, and number two on the way, very exciting, it's another girl, I was hoping for a boy so we could complete the double act and call him Rhett, but hey, that's great.' He rocked on his feet, eyes crinkling at the corners, the old expression she knew so, so well. 'Yep, it's great.' He turned to Tom. 'Our daughter's called Scarlett, you see.'

'Yes.' Tom nodded politely. 'Hi, Elle,' he said. He kissed her and sat down. The room was filling up, delegates filing back into their seats after a coffee break and looking up expectantly at the platform.

'So,' said Rory, rubbing his hands. 'We should have talked about this before, I suppose, but that's the way of these things! Any pointers, anything you think we should focus on?'

She remembered his hail-fellow-well-met, I'm-a-nice-chap, jovial-jester act. You had to hand it to him: Rory was a survivor, against all the odds. In the eight years since Bluebird had been sold he'd seen off better men and women, and somehow hung onto his job, a mixture of nepotism, cunning and charm. He was just clever enough.

'Pointers? No, nothing,' said Tom. 'Just that – ebooks are rubbish and you should all carry on buying proper books from nice independent bookshops?'

Elle sat down next to him, with Rory on her right. The platform was insanely small. She wished she could space herself out instead of being trapped between the two of them.

'You've got four shops now,' said Rory. 'You're practically a chain, Tom. A corporate sell-out.'

Tom ignored him.

'Four?' Elle said. 'That's brilliant.'

He smiled at her, looking pleased. 'Thanks. Yes, the original one in Richmond, one in Marylebone, Kensington and Hampstead. I'm fighting to bring books to the liberal elite. The struggle goes on.'

'Where's the next one?' Elle asked. 'Don't tell me.' She held up a finger, as if testing it in the wind, for divination. 'Bath.'

He laughed. 'Spot on. You know your onions.'

'And shallots.' Elle felt mildly hysterical.

'And scallions. Isn't that something in New York?' Tom said. 'Something onion-based?'

'Anyway.' Rory was drumming his fingers, as Celine emerged from the side room. 'What about ebooks?'

'I don't know, let's make something up.' Elle felt reckless. This was the first meeting for which she hadn't minutely prepared for in she didn't know how long. 'We know what we're talking about, Tom, even if you think publishers are evil and booksellers are the oppressed masses.'

'Oh, be quiet,' said Tom cheerfully. 'You ghastly corporate sell-out.'

She shrugged, and held her hand out, as if to pat him on the shoulder.

'You're *engaged*?' Rory said, looking at the diamond on her finger.

'Oh.' Elle looked down, as if to verify this. 'Yes. Yes, I am.'

'To Gray Logan?' Rory shook his head. 'Wow, I heard you were seeing him, but – that's great, Elle! Massive fan of his. We must have you both down to Kent for lunch!'

'Oh,' said Elle. 'Yes, that – we really must.'

'Congratulations,' said Tom. He looked up at her. 'I'm really happy for you.'

'Thanks,' she said. She could feel her skin flushing red. 'It's not a big deal.'

He turned to her, and she wished she'd never said anything. 'Why?'

'Oh –' Elle waved her hand, suddenly conscious of her ring like never before. It was so *big*. Like a bauble. She had bought rings like this from Hamleys with her Christmas pocket money. 5p a time, they'd cost her, big glass diamonds, gold with green emeralds. The thin gold or silver paint always wore off, leaving a greenish-black mark on her finger. 'It's just – I didn't think I'd be the sort of person who got married, that's all.'

'What, you don't want a Jane Austen-themed wedding with six bridesmaids in massive hats?' Tom said. 'I'm surprised. I thought that was your kind of thing.' Elle glared at him, but Rory was checking his BlackBerry, his chin sunk into his chest, and didn't hear them. 'That was the last time I saw you.'

There was a pause.

'Er –' said Elle. 'Yes.'

He leaned towards her. 'Elle, I'm so sorry about your—' he began, but from the side, Rory suddenly said, 'Hey, Tom, how's Dora? Mum was asking.'

'She's very well,' Tom said. His knee was against hers; next to her, the arm of Rory's battered navy suit was pressing into her arm. 'She's very into *Hannah Montana*, I'm sorry to say.'

'Who's Dora?' Elle asked, feeling stupid.

'My daughter,' Tom said. 'I called her Dora too. I shouldn't have done it. Very confusing.'

'How old is she now?'

'Six –' Tom said, and then he leaned forward. 'Elle –'

Next to them, Celine tapped the microphone. 'Good morning,' she said, covering it and turning to them. 'We are starting in a moment. Please let's have a good, robust discussion. No holds barred. Any questions?'

Each of them shook their heads, mutely. 'Good morning again,' said Celine to the rest of the room. 'We are now lucky enough to be about to enjoy a debate with three key people in the publishing sector about ebooks. Rory you will know as he works here and has responsibility for them in the BBE division at Bookprint UK.' She shot him a disdainful look. *I love Celine*, Elle found herself thinking, staring at her perfectly poised head. 'Tom Scott is owner of the UK's fastest growing independent book chain, facing many challenges, including digital publishing. And Eleanor Bee is the Publisher of Jane Street, one of Bookprint US's most successful imprints. She started out in the UK and moved to the US seven years ago. She took over Jane Street last year and has added five million dollars to their turnover already.'

Yeah, Elle thought, scanning the room for someone to be impressed by this. But they were all listening politely, and she realised the majority of them didn't know or care in the least that she'd once been a scruffy talentless mess in too-short skirts with a tendency to burst into tears and lose prawn sandwiches in filing cabinets. It was her story, not theirs.

There was a shout from the back, and Celine looked up. Someone from the IT team whispered something to her from the bottom of the stage. 'We have a slight problem with the sound, so it'll be another minute,' she said coolly.

The panel sat back again, and Rory once more began tapping away at his BlackBerry.

Tom cleared his throat. She gave him a tight, polite smile.

'I wanted to say I was sorry about your mum,' Tom said quietly. 'It must have been very hard.'

Elle nodded firmly. 'It was. Thanks for your lovely letter. I'm sorry I didn't reply.'

He shook his head. 'Of course.' He looked almost angry, his jaw rigid, the way he always did when he was upset about something. She remembered that, too. 'You should have called me. I wish I could have helped.'

'Helped?' Elle said, blinking as the audience receded. How could he have helped, how could anyone, anyone but her have helped? She bit her lip.

407

I shouldn't have spent the night with you, she wanted to say. *If I'd come home she wouldn't have died. I'd have gone looking for her, I'd have found her, it would've been OK. But I didn't, I was with you, instead of with her, and that's why.*

Tom didn't try to coax anything out of her, in the way some of her other friends had done, convinced that if they didn't personally witness her grief through tears, then she wasn't properly grieving. He just nodded. 'It's stupid of me to say it. But I wanted you to know. She was lovely, I'm glad I met her. I am . . . really sorry.'

'Right, then,' Celine said, speaking into the microphone. 'Back on track. As you know, digital is the biggest challenge facing us . . .'

Elle had perfected an excellent 'focused and interested' face, and she assumed this while her mind drifted back to the days after she'd found her mother; she didn't know why, perhaps because she was seeing her brother tonight, perhaps because she so rarely allowed herself to mention it. She looked over at Tom; people didn't bring up her mother with her any more. She'd made it clear, soon after she got back to New York, that she wasn't going to talk about it.

She'd destroyed the note that said SORRY ELLIE. It wouldn't have mattered whether she had or not: it was burnt into her brain for ever. Often, afterwards, she thought she saw it, the two words jostling in the corner of her eye, in a meeting, on a screen while they were watching TV, while she was talking to Gray's friends over supper.

Everything else had been sorted out. Rhodes had sold the house and tied up the last of the loose ends, and she'd never been back to the village, not once, and she never would. Everything about her life now was designed to be as far removed from memories of Mandana as it could be. She didn't keep her mother's things around. Tried not to have anything obvious that reminded her too much of her. She didn't come back to England in the spring, either.

408

Just keep on going, don't stop, because then it falls apart. She'd learned that was the best way.

'. . . Yep, we do have a lot of ground to catch up,' Rory was saying. 'But I just feel . . . I just think if . . . good books will sell, and that's what we really have to focus on. Like there's this guy we're publishing at the moment, Paris Donaldson. Amazing guy. Been publishing him for years, never broken through, sells about—'

Elle looked around, and realised that she was in the middle of the panel discussion, which was now apparently in full swing. She had once, after a very bad night when the image wouldn't go away, driven to JFK to pick Gray up, and when she got there didn't remember getting in the car or any of the rest of the journey. The effect was just the same. She blinked; she wished she wasn't so tired.

'Paris Donaldson is not the issue, if you'll forgive me,' Tom was saying. 'The issue is that authors with real talent get overlooked in favour of commerce, and—'

'That's rubbish,' Elle said wearily. 'I get so sick of this discussion. The same thing was happening twenty, a hundred years ago. Look. I read about fifteen manuscripts a week, and those are the ones people think it's worth my while to read, and they're nearly always terrible. The trouble is too many people think they can write, and the truth is they can't, they shouldn't bother. If someone's good, they'll rise to the top. It may take a while but it'll happen.'

'Very Pollyanna of you,' said Tom. She turned towards him, effectively shutting Rory out. 'I'm on the shop floor, Elle. I see great books by brilliant writers come in and they've got no support, no money and then some pile of crap by some supermodel gets published and *that's* what you see on the side of the bus, it'll never make any real money for the publisher, they don't have a long-term career like the brilliant author, but it's shiny and glittery so fine, let's ignore the good authors and chase after the gold at the end of the rainbow.' He was breathing hard; his hand gripped his knee.

'If you didn't have the supermodel book making money for the company then you wouldn't be able to pay the "good" author, as you call them,' Elle said. 'And who's to say the supermodel book isn't good too? If I work hard all year and have two weeks' holiday in Greece I don't want some pale, worthy, boring book about middle-class people in London sitting round debating their stupid, self-satisfied lives. Sometimes I want a private jet and a hooker drinking champagne.' There was a ripple of laughter; she hadn't realised it would sound funny. 'It's true,' she said.

'It's fantasy,' Tom said. 'It's an illusion.'

She laughed. 'I have few illusions, believe me. It's escapism, it's what reading's all about.' She stared at him, her brow furrowed. 'That's what we all want. Don't we?'

'Not all of us—' Tom began, but Celine interrupted.

'This is fascinating, but I wonder if we could focus back on to the topic of the ebooks? How will they—'

'Guys!' Rory hissed under his breath, as Celine spoke. 'Include me in the debate, OK? I'm still here, you know?'

Elle realised she was almost facing Tom. He bent his head towards her and looked at her, so that only she could see his expression. His grey eyes were dark, his hands clenched on his knees. She shifted back. She'd forgotten how disquieting she found Tom, how funny he could be and then floor her with his intensity, with the way he'd look at her. Suddenly she was back in the hotel corridor, outside his bedroom, feeling his lips on hers, his hands on her body. Her palms were sweating. She wiped them on her black suit. Damn him. He seemed to know what she was thinking and to enjoy disagreeing with her, and it occurred to her then that it had always been this way. She looked helplessly, from him to Rory, her heart racing, and vowed to concentrate on what Celine was saying. *Snap out of it, Eleanor Bee.*

'I SHALL HAVE the steak tartare, and then the mussels,' Felicity said. She put down the menu. 'You?'

'Oh.' Elle scanned the sheet. 'The Caesar salad, please.'

'No starter, madame?' the waiter asked.

'Ah. The soup.' Elle was annoyed. She didn't have long, and she didn't want to get into a multi-course lunch with endless puddings, coffees and brandies, which she knew Felicity was entirely capable of. She liked a one-course lunch. Anything more made her bloated and drowsy in the after-noon. And she knew what this was about. Felicity was going to offer her some lame job at her publishing venture, and she'd have to be polite and sound interested.

She didn't know now why she'd agreed to come. A lingering sense of respect? Wanting to remember the old days, just briefly? But mostly she thought she'd not cancelled at the last minute because she couldn't wait to escape the thick-curtained, low-ceilinged confines of the conference suite. Tom was staying on for the sandwich lunch, and Rory seemed determined to keep her by his side, like a sort of good-luck talisman, and she wasn't about to tell him where she was going. She'd gone to the loo and then made her escape, hurrying out through the gloomy marble and granite lobby into the rain.

'I love it here,' Felicity said, looking around the panelled room. 'So *French*. Wonderful! One of the great things about working in Shepherd's Market, you know, the places to eat. Now,' she said, pushing her wine glass out of the way. 'You know I've invited you to lunch to offer you a job. You weren't interested before but I keep the faith. May I tell you about it?'

Elle, who was eyeing the bread basket longingly, jerked her head up and said weakly, 'Oh, no, Felicity – I'm not—'

'I know you live in New York, but I had heard that you might consider a move back to the UK,' Felicity said.

'Who told you that?' Elle asked. 'It's not true.'

'Aha,' said Felicity. She tapped one side of her nose with a large finger on which was an antique amethyst ring.

'That ring!' she exclaimed. 'It's the same!'

Felicity looked down at her hands rather doubtfully, as if she expected to see Brussels sprouts growing on her fingers. 'Why wouldn't it be?' she said. 'I've always worn it. Anyway—'

'Just that,' said Elle, trying to veer the conversation away from job offers, 'I used to see it every day; it's just strange, that's all. Long time ago.' She stared at the ring again; the memories were flooding back.

'Yes, it was.' Felicity's eyes flashed. 'I can barely remember it, if truth be told. So much has happened since.'

'Do you remember the day I threw coffee over you?' Elle said. 'It was the worst day of my life.'

'My dear, I remember it very clearly.'

'I thought you were going to sack me.' Elle gave in, picked up a piece of bread and slathered it in butter.

'How ridiculous.' Felicity smiled at her. 'I didn't recognise you at first, and then you started trying to wipe the liquid off my chest, and I saw it was you. I couldn't remember your name. And then after our chat I thought, "That's the one who's so good, but she's never read Georgette Heyer."'

Elle laughed, and then she said, 'I have a terrible confession. I still have your copy of *Venetia*. I never gave it back to you.'

'A book thief, goodness me. Did you read it?'

Elle said earnestly, 'Yes, and I loved it, I loved them all, it was the best recommendation anyone ever gave me, and I've never thanked you.'

Felicity shrugged. 'Well, isn't that why one lends a book? Isn't it wonderful, to know you've passed something good on?'

'I don't know that our sales director would agree with you,' said Elle. 'He likes people to buy new books.'

'Reading isn't just about sales, Elle.' Felicity waved to the waiter, for another glass of wine. 'You?' she said.

'No – er, no, thanks,' said Elle. 'Anyway – I'll send it back to you. I'm—'

Felicity waved this away. 'Please, goodness no. Now,' she went on, leaning forward. 'On to business,' she said, carrying on firmly. 'I want to offer you the job of Editorial Director, at Aphra Books. Here we are. You'll have two editors reporting to you. I want you to shape the list. You can be on the board if you'd like; I'd like that. To work with me and the team to take us to the next stage. It's entirely possible, you know. We've had two Richard and Judys and one book shortlisted for the Orange, and we've only been in business for four years. But we need more.'

'Of course,' said Elle. 'Everyone wants more. Our margins—'

Felicity put her hand on Elle's. 'No,' she said. 'We need more good books. That's all. Picked by someone who loves reading more than anything else, and that's why I thought of you.'

Elle smiled, and nodded. She didn't know why she felt so sad. Someone who loves reading more than anything else.

'Where's Posy?' she said.

Felicity took some more bread. 'Oh, she moved to Oxford

last year. She needed a change. Dear Posy, but she got so gloomy. She's working at a small publishers now, very happy I hear. Joined a choir.' She made a small conducting gesture with her hands. 'So. What do you think?'

Elle was torn between amusement at this dismissal of Posy and a slight feeling of annoyance that she wanted to suppress. She said, 'Felicity, I don't think you understand. It sounds wonderful, but I'm not looking to move, not at all. My fiancé's in New York, apart from anything else. We're getting married in March.'

'Congratulations,' said Felicity, looking up as the starters arrived. 'Ah. Wonderful, Pierre.' She started eating, leaving Elle staring into a bowl of anaemic-looking soup in silence.

It was a good tactic; after a few moments, Elle said, 'So I'm sorry, but it's really a no.'

'This steak is delicious. I don't think you've heard enough yet.'

Trying not to lose her temper, Elle said, 'Like what?'

'Well,' said Felicity. 'You'd be working in Shepherd's Market, after all. It's lovely.'

'Right,' said Elle. 'I was thinking more, what's the package like?'

'We'd be very competitive,' said Felicity. 'I know you're doing well over there.'

Elle bit her lip. 'Felicity, please don't take this the wrong way, but – er, I run a division.' She thought, not for the first time, that if she were a man she'd just say it, without apology. 'I don't really edit any more. I manage twenty-five people and I'm on the board. I have a budget of millions. I was hoping my next role would be to be running a company. A big company. Not –' She put her spoon angrily into her soup, and it splattered her. 'Not editing books at a tiny start-up. Please, I don't want to be rude, but I think I should just be honest.'

'You know what this all reminds me of,' said Felicity

414

cheerily, as if Elle hadn't spoken. 'It's rather like this business with the banks at the moment. I rather agree with those who think we'd be better off as a country if we weren't this huge global financial centre. If people went to . . . Geneva. Or Berlin. Or New York, for all of that. I'd rather we weren't as rich and everyone was more equal and we spent more time making good things rather than making money.'

Elle frowned. 'What's that got to . . .' she began, then she trailed off. 'Right. Well, point taken, but I like things the way they are.'

'No problem, no problem,' Felicity said, waving her fork at her. 'Try some of this steak tartare. Have you read *American Wife*? Did you love it? I thought it was marvellous.'

'No – not yet. I don't have time to read books for pleasure any more.'

'How sad.'

Elle ignored her, and took a forkful of the steak. It was delicious. She could feel the raw red meat in her mouth, tender and full of flavour, the egg and pepper coating it. She closed her eyes and let the meat melt in her mouth, then reached for another piece of bread. 'Maybe I will have a glass of wine.'

'Excellent idea,' said Felicity. 'Everything in moderation is good for you, my dear.'

'It's so funny, sitting here with you,' Elle said. 'If my twenty-two-year-old self could see me now, she'd be amazed.'

'You never know what's around the corner. When Bluebird ended, I was devastated. Thought my life was over. Now I'm glad. Best thing that ever happened, in fact.'

'Really?' Elle couldn't believe that was true. 'The end of Bluebird, the best thing that could have happened? I don't believe it.'

'Oh yes,' said Felicity. She nodded, smiling, turning the old ring around her finger. 'I run my own company my own way now, I can do things the way I like and it usually works out for the best. Most importantly, I found out before I needed to rely on him that I can't trust my son. I realised I had to look after my own future. And, Elle dear, the end of Bluebird meant the end of your relationship with him, and if only for that it was a good thing.'

Some bread stuck at the back of Elle's mouth. 'What?' she said, coughing.

'Oh, it's aeons ago now. Let's not dwell on it,' said Felicity. Elle gazed at her, half in horror, half in fascination. 'My dear, I'm not stupid. I thought there was *une affaire* but I hoped it was just a flirtation. I worried for you but what could I do? You were easily the kind of girl who'd spend her whole life mooning after someone who didn't love her, like Posy. He did the same to Posy, you know,' she said, as Elle shook her head, grimly fascinated. 'Two, three years and then he threw her over for a literary agent. Poor girl. Never got over it, never. Didn't want you to end up like that.'

'I didn't know –' Elle began. 'Well, it doesn't matter, does it? He's very happy with Libby.'

'Oh, Libby, of course. They're *perfect* for each other,' said Felicity, with heavy emphasis. She chewed some bread noisily, making a growling sound in her throat. 'That girl is the most competitive person I've ever met. Wasted her time trying to compete with him, with you, with everyone. Now she competes with other parents. Went into training for the mothers' race at my granddaughter's nursery last summer. Told me with pride she was the thinnest woman she knew who'd had children.' Felicity pursed her lips. 'Oh, well. What's sauce for the goose. If Bluebird hadn't ended, if we hadn't all had that awful time afterwards, well, all these good things wouldn't have come of it. So I for one am jolly glad. And I'm glad for you. I'm glad you had the presence of mind to get out.'

'I never thought of it like that.'

'It's true, isn't it?'

'It is. And thank you for, well, not saying anything. Only

416

I'm not the kind of girl to moon, honestly. I'm not the kind of girl who's sentimental about anything, any more. I used to be, that's really not me. Don't worry.'

The waiter took their plates away. Felicity nodded. 'Yes,' she said. 'It's a shame in a way.'

Elle said nothing. Afterwards, they stood outside the restaurant, in the chill autumn wind. She kissed Felicity on the cheek.

'Just think about it all,' Felicity said. 'All of it.'

Not quite sure what she meant, Elle thanked her for lunch and walked back to the hotel. She had barely been outside since she'd got here. It started raining again; it had been raining almost since she arrived. Elle walked through Shepherd's Market and past Heywood Hill bookshop, where Nancy Mitford had worked. She walked up to Berkeley Square and around, trying not to think too much, just letting London wash over her. Office workers late back from lunch scurried along the sides of black railings, early copies of the *Evening Standard* held above their heads. One girl stepped in a puddle and laughed, shaking her black-denier-clad foot out of the shoe while her companion watched, amused. Elle carried on walking, happy in her solitude. It struck her then that she didn't mind the rain. In fact, she'd missed it. It was cool and smelt metallic, the streets were beetle-shiny, clean and deserted.

'GABBY AND KENNETH live around here, but you know I've never visited this part of Primrose Hill before,' said Gray, as they walked up Kentish Town Road that evening. He swerved around a queue of people waiting for the bus. 'It's great.'

'This isn't Primrose Hill,' Elle said with a snort of derision. Gray's positivity was grating. 'Typical. It's Kentish Town. It's nice, but I don't know what they're going on about. Primrose Hill.' She laughed, as if Rhodes and Melissa had committed a hanging offence in describing their location thus. She picked her way past an overflowing rubbish bin and, taking Gray's elbow, steered him left. 'Off here. How was your day?'

'Wonderful. I went to the library, then I had lunch with Roger, and then I took a walk in Green Park, had a drink at the Stafford, it's my favourite hotel. Dropped into Hatchards. So I've done three of the things I wanted to do already.' He tapped a tree trunk thoughtfully with his umbrella. 'I'm very glad I came.'

'Good,' said Elle. She hunched her shoulders up around her ears and then released them, feeling the bones in her neck crunch. They turned onto a quiet side street, with pretty little houses, each painted a different colour.

'So today was no worse than you'd thought,' Gray said.

'Um . . .' Elle hitched her bag over her shoulder, struggling to recall the day. In the afternoon they had had a three-hour workshop on Synergy, where they'd been divided into groups and given a project (on Synergy) to complete. She had been in charge of a group that included Mary, her old friend from Bookprint UK, and Jeremy, that old, incorrigible flirt, who hadn't, she was relieved to discover, changed at all. It made a welcome, if tedious, contrast to the morning, and the lunch. 'In some ways, it was OK. In some ways . . . worse than I'd thought.'

'How so?'

She shrugged, and smiled at him. 'There are some people I don't like bumping into back here. Ancient history.'

'Oh, I get it.' Gray smiled. 'A woman with a past, that's what I've always loved about you. I have this image of you in your twenties in a hotel bar in Piccadilly somewhere, allowing men to light your cigarettes and buy you Martinis.'

'You make me sound like a prostitute, and no, it wasn't at all like that, believe me,' said Elle. 'Also, I was earning about fifty pounds a week after everything else was paid. That doesn't buy you many Martinis at bars in Piccadilly.'

'Well, I had a great afternoon at the London Library,' said Gray, seamlessly carrying on. 'I read the diaries, and I found a book on Paul Revere that's never been published in the US. Exactly what I needed, and I might submit an idea on Benjamin Franklin in France to the *New York Times* magazine when we're back.' He rubbed his hands.

'You like it here, don't you,' said Elle.

'Oh, yes,' said Gray. 'Like you with New York. I think I could live here.'

She thought of her lunch with Felicity, which had stayed with her all afternoon, Felicity's voice buzzing in her ear even through the maelstrom of discussion points and pie charts. 'Do you really?'

'Oh, sure. I absolutely do love it.' Gray took her hand. 'Hey, do you have time for a drink tomorrow?'

'Not tomorrow, no,' Elle said. 'The conference is all day and there's a big dinner in the evening.'

'Oh.'

I told you it'd be all work if you came, she wanted to say.

'Well, Wednesday, then? My Eurostar train isn't until five, and I want to revisit a delightful pub in Marylebone where I used to go with Adam. The Duke of York, it's wonderful.'

Elle marvelled at how easily pleased Americans were with British pubs. She knew the Duke of York, she'd met Karen there for a drink once on one of her previous trips as Karen was something high up at the BBC now and it was close to Portland Place. It was a totally featureless place, nothing interesting about it at all.

'What about the Windsor Castle, down the road?' she said. 'Much nicer, it's got loads of memorabilia and hilarious photos all over the walls.'

Gray looked disappointed. 'I wanted to go to this bookshop in Marylebone, on the High Street,' he said. 'It's called Dora's. Is it near? I can't be late for the train.'

'That's in Richmond.'

'No, there's one in Marylebone, everyone keeps telling me I have to go there, it's wonderful apparently.'

A six-year-old called Dora who loves Hannah Montana. 'Oh,' Elle said, remembering. 'Sorry, of course. I know the bloke who started them up.'

'Really?' Gray said. 'Dora Zoffany's son? What's his name? Tom something, not Zoffany. I hear he's a great guy. Passionate about good books.'

Elle looked down at the rainy street. She kicked at a cracked paving stone and said, annoyed, 'Why is someone only passionate about books if they're into literary books that win prizes? Why can't you be passionate about books and only read romance?'

'OK, OK,' said Gray, holding up his hands. He gave her a crooked smile. 'You're right. You can be. Everything's great. It's all great. Yes?'

'Yes,' she said, relaxing against him for a second. 'I'm sorry I'm such a cow.' He kissed the top of her head.

'You're not a cow,' he said. 'You're a porcupine, very prickly, but with a delightfully unusual scent.'

Elle pushed him away, laughing, and looked up at the house number on the door in front of them. 'Well, we're here,' she said. She went up the front path and pressed the doorbell.

EVERY TIME ELLE saw Rhodes these days, she was struck anew by how like their father her brother had become; a swarthier, bulkier version. She and her brother were very different, so different it was easy, in a way. They had nothing much in common. Rhodes liked running machines, John Grisham thrillers, the *FT*. Elle couldn't remember where he worked now – a rival to Bloomberg, she knew that much, doing the same thing, she thought. She should know, but she'd asked twice and to ask again would just be rude. Terrible, how hard it was to retain knowledge you didn't fully understand, whereas the first week's sales of all her authors and the name of every Georgette Heyer hero were imprinted in her mind for ever more. But their differences didn't upset her or bother her as they used to. She'd come to understand how relationships change. You get some people wrong. Some you get totally right. Some people are your best friends and then pass out of your life without a murmur.

She'd seen Mike, her old boyfriend, on 5th Avenue, a couple of springs ago, walking past the Banana Republic opposite the Cathedral. She was on her way to meet Gray in the Park. The pavement was busy; there was a girl next to him, a coral cashmere cardigan draped around her shoulders, a quilted Chanel bag slung across her chest. Elle's instinct had been to turn away and hide, but he'd seen her first. 'Elle?' he'd said. 'Hi, how are you? Come, meet Rose.'

She'd smiled at him. 'Hi, Mike,' and turned to Rose. But the coral-cardigan girl moved off, with a gaggle of her friends. Rose was on Mike's other side, every inch a Brooklyn hipster, vintage paisley shirt, black glasses, capri pants, cloth bag. The top had a stain on it. 'Hi,' Elle said, trying not to show her surprise.

'We just ate pizza, and I'm covered in marinara sauce,' Rose explained, gesturing at her top.

'How are you?' Mike had said. 'I saw your name in Gray Logan's new book, I meant to email you.' She'd nodded, unsure of what to say next. *Yes. We're sleeping together.* 'Well, it's great to see you.'

'And you,' she'd told him. There was an awkward pause.

'We'd better go,' he'd said. 'Good luck, Elle, take care.'

He'd squeezed her arm, lightly, and walked off. Because that was all you needed to do, you didn't need to promise undying friendship, you simply said, *Hey, our relationship ended, but I wish you well.* Elle often thought of that encounter when worrying what to do with ex-authors she'd bump into in the Village, or colleagues from the UK she'd come across over the years, or Libby, or even Sam. Funnily enough, she could envisage having a drink with Sam more readily than Libby, and that was strange. Too much water had flowed under their bridge with her and Libby, she knew. They'd been too close and become too different, whereas Sam was part of her past, but she was grateful to her for her years of friendship. Like Rhodes. She didn't have to ring him every week but she did have to see him from time to time. After all, it was strange to think it, but he was the only other person who'd been through what she had.

*

423

'Yes, it's a testing time, but we're all in it together, and we'll come out of it stronger.'

'Dad, I want some juice.'

'Go and ask Mummy. I'm talking.' Rhodes turned back to them. 'Where was I?'

'You were saying how Hank Paulson is a misunderstood man,' Gray said.

'Yes. Well, not misunderstood. Just that this is a bad time but we have to ride it out.'

'You're so calm,' Gray said. He put his gin and tonic down carefully on the polished mahogany side table. 'Every day I read in the paper how we're on the verge of total financial collapse, the Senate's voting for a bailout, countries, whole countries going bankrupt, and you think we have to ride it out?'

'Panicking only makes it worse,' said Rhodes. 'Believe me, these things pass.' He looked towards the corridor. 'Was that the door?' He stood up. 'Just one second, Gray. Hold on please.'

Melissa stood in the doorway. 'Rhodes, there's someone at the door,' she said. She looked at her husband accusingly.

'You're right by it, can't you get it?' Rhodes said, annoyed.

'I don't have my glasses on. I don't like answering the door to strangers.'

He nodded. 'Lauren, get off.' He prised his daughter's hand off his leg.

'Can I freshen anyone's drinks? Are we all doing OK in here?' Melissa asked. 'We should be ready to eat in a – Lauren, honey, what are you doing?'

'I want some more juice,' Lauren said. 'Daddy said he'd get me some.'

'Interesting. I think you've had enough, Lauren.' Melissa stroked her daughter's hair. 'I think you should go to bed. Do you want –' she bent down and whispered, but loudly enough that everyone could hear – 'do you want Elle to read you a story? She's your aunt, she's come to see you.'

'My aunt, like Aunt Francie who has the garden with the big slide?'

'Yes, just the same.'

Elle looked at the blonde, curly-haired child, who was her nearest relative apart from her dad and her brother, her half-siblings, too, she supposed. She looked just like Melissa. This was her family. These were her flesh and blood, her relatives in the world now, the little blonde girl and her beefy dad, scratching his chest and walking towards the door.

'No,' said Lauren. 'I don't.' She crossed her arms. 'I want Gray to read *Charlotte's Web* to me,' she whispered to her mother.

'You want Gray,' Melissa said. 'Well, honey, I'm not sure –'

'I'd love to,' said Gray, standing up. '*Charlotte's Web* is a fine choice. It's been a long time since I read it.'

'Gray is a famous writer, honey, you know,' said Melissa, smiling slightly at Gray. 'So you mustn't take up too much of his time. You're very lucky.'

There were footsteps along the corridor.

'I'm going to be your uncle soon,' Gray told Lauren, who stared at him. 'I'm marrying your aunt.'

Aunt, what a weird word. *Aunt. Aunt. Aunt.* It lost all meaning when you said it multiple times. Then Gray looked over towards the hall. 'Hello,' he said. 'I'm Gray Logan.' He held out his hand.

Elle turned her head and saw the figure standing in the hallway.

'Dad?' she said. Her eyes darted from her father to her brother. 'How – lovely!'

'I knew you didn't have time to come to Brighton.' John put his hat down on the table next to them and kissed Elle, squeezing her shoulders. 'And I didn't want to make you feel guilty. So when you said you were seeing Rhodes I invited myself up for the night. It's been too long and I wanted to see you,' he said in a rush, which Elle found comforting: like all the Bees, he never acknowledged the status quo. 'And

I'm dying to meet this chap.' He clasped Gray's hand. 'Good evening, sir, how very nice to finally meet you.'

Elle stared at her father, at his smooth blue wool jumper, immaculately pressed navy trousers, shiny shoes. He looked younger, as he pumped Gray's arm up and down. She stood on one leg, then the other.

'Can Elle read to me as well?' said Lauren, also standing on one leg and now giving Elle a toothy grin.

'No, Lauren,' Rhodes said, behind her father. 'You missed your chance. Elle wants to talk to Grandpa. She hasn't seen him for ages.'

They were in the tiny sitting room with the low ceilings, the sound of rain pelting outside, through the cream-coloured shutters on the bay window, and as Lauren started to cry the five of them, Elle, Gray, Melissa, Rhodes and John, all looked down at her, the fire casting huge shadows of them on the cream walls, as though they were giants.

'I'll take you up,' Gray said. He came forward and took Lauren's hand and she, out of surprise, stopped crying.

'Ah – I'll come with you, she doesn't like strangers,' Melissa said. 'Let's go.' She nudged him out of the room.

Left alone, Rhodes, Elle and their father glanced at each other.

'Well, well, here we are.' John sank into the chair Gray had been sitting in by the fire. 'Very nice.' He put his hands neatly on his knees. 'Well. Isn't this lovely.'

Rhodes said, 'When was the last time the three of us were together?'

'Mum's funeral,' Elle said automatically.

'I think,' John said as if Elle hadn't spoken, 'it was Alice's sixteenth, last summer.'

Rhodes pulled at his wristwatch. 'Dad, can I get you a drink? We have wine, a gin and tonic, there's beer, anything you want. What do you want?'

'Wine, I'd love a large glass of white wine.'

It was so strange, to sit here in this unfamiliar house with the sound of a strange child shouting upstairs, looking at her brother and her father next to each other, hands clasped between their legs, faces set in the same expression, so eerily similar, though Rhodes was bigger, more ebullient somehow. Her brother slapped his thighs and stood up to get the drinks. John brushed a speck of dust off his immaculate trousers. Elle watched him, remembering how much it used to upset her after he left them, when he'd arrive to take them on day trips, out to Brighton or Hastings for the day, and she wouldn't recognise his clothes. Every time he came back to Willow Cottage, before they had to move, something would always be different, and it simply rammed home what she tried to forget – that her father had moved on. He had a new life, and it invigorated him. He was happy in a way he hadn't been with their mother, while she stayed the same, and in the end it killed her.

Elle stared at his polka-dot blue tie tucked neatly inside his jumper, and blinked. 'It's lovely to see you,' she said eventually. 'I'm sorry – this is such a rushed work trip. Just not the best time to catch up, that's why I didn't suggest coming to Brighton. How's Eliza? How're Jack and Alice?'

Her father nodded ferociously. 'Eliza's good, though the surgery's very busy at the moment. And Alice is loving her A levels. We were worried when she chose Art History, but it seems universities will accept that, and she's still enjoying the flute, very much so. Yes. Oh, thanks, son.' He took a large gulp from the glass of wine Rhodes offered him. 'How's work, then? When will you be running the entire company? I tell all my friends about my daughter who's on the board, you know.' He smiled. 'They're all so surprised.'

'Surprised, eh?' said Rhodes, with a chuckle. 'That's nice, Dad. She runs a division, it's not a fluke.'

'Thank you, Rhodes,' said Elle. 'I didn't sleep my way to the top, you know, Dad.'

427

John looked shocked. He held up his hands. 'Of course you didn't, I know that. I'm sorry!' he said. 'I only meant, perhaps, that I always thought it'd be the other way round, with you two.' There was a pause. 'Not that I'm not very proud of you, Rhodes, too . . .' he trailed off.

The three of them were not a family, they were an uneasy coalition linked by blood and the unspoken tragedy that hovered just outside the room. Rhodes patted his father on the shoulder. 'I'll go and check on the supper, before you say anything really unfortunate, Father,' he said. 'Leave you two to catch up.'

Elle watched him go. *Do I actually like my brother?* she found herself thinking. *Is that actually possible? Strange.*

'What about Jack?' Elle said, turning back to her dad. She wished Gray was here. 'How's Jack?'

'Jack. Ha.' Her father sighed. 'Jack's still the problem child, I'm sorry to say. Very difficult at the moment.' He took a sip of his drink.

'Why, what's he done?'

John waved his hand. 'Oh, Elle, it's too boring to go into.'

He fell silent, and Elle was reminded of her lunch with Felicity. She had simply stopped talking, and suddenly, she realised this was her father's way of directing the conversation; using silence as a weapon, so someone else had to speak, to fill the gap. He'd done it all the time with their mother, letting her talk till she was screaming at him, and then he'd just cut her down with one sharp sentence.

He did that all the time, she thought. *How come I've only just noticed?* She didn't say anything, just nodded expectantly, waiting for him to begin the conversation again.

After a silence that stretched on for ever, her father narrowed his eyes and sighed. 'He's been excluded from his school. Yes. They handled it very badly, I must say. Foolish behaviour, on both sides, especially his.' He took another sip. 'Forget about that. How's work?'

'It's busy, it's challenging, blah blah,' said Elle. 'Come on, what did he do, Dad? Is he OK?'

'He tried to steal a car. One of the teachers'. When he was caught he –' John inhaled, through his teeth – 'insulted the teachers, kicked someone. So embarrassing, so stupid. But oh, yes, he's fine,' he said, with heavy sarcastic emphasis. 'His mother and I, however, are fed up to the back teeth with him. Yes, we've – we're reaching a crisis point. It's stay or go at the moment with him. We don't know where he is most of the time, what he's doing, where he's going. We've confiscated his computer, and I'm afraid the next step is to throw him out if he doesn't listen. A wake-up call. Hm.'

He shook his head, as if Jack's deliquency was only distantly connected to him, a vague irritant like a car alarm going off further down the street.

'Shouldn't you talk to him about it?' Elle said.

'Oh, don't be so American.' John smiled, but he was only partly joking. 'He needs to know he can't carry on like this. Passing out drunk in the hall, calling his mother names I've never even heard. He pushed me against a wall once. Bloody hurt. No, it might be time to force the issue.'

A shiver ran over Elle, and she rubbed her arms. She could recall perfectly how intractable her father was, how when Mum would get upset or behave badly he'd just shut off, as if it was nothing to do with him. The time a few weeks after they'd come back from Skye when they'd gone for a picnic concert in the grounds of a stately home nearby, and Mandana had been wandering around, chatting to people. To Elle it was obvious now: she'd been drunk. She'd staggered along, oblivious to the 'shhhhs' and hissed orders to sit down and shut up of the other picnickers, and John, instead of standing up, marching over, grabbing her by the arm and walking her off around the car park, had crossed his arms and ignored her, then taken the children, got into the car and driven off home without her. As if she were a total stranger, a down-and-out on the street.

Rhodes came back in, with a pile of books under one arm and a bottle of wine in the other. 'Elle, these are the books I mentioned to you, don't know why I've ended up with them,' he said. He tipped them into her lap.

Elle picked over them. '*Cinderella, Rapunzel, Ladybird Royal Wedding, Sleeping Beauty . . .*' she read aloud. '*Nursery Rhymes, Little Red Riding Hood* – Rhodes, where did you get these?' She opened the stiff cardboard cover of one. It was covered in her scribbles, some stickers, some random annotations.

'I've had them for years, since the clear-out,' he said. 'I think you meant to take them with you, but they were just left in the barn, in a pile on the table.'

'Yes,' said Elle, remembering. 'I did.' She clutched them to her. 'I must have left them behind. *Cinderella*!' she said, picking up the first book. 'I can remember drawing in this one. Look at Cinderella's dress.' She held it open at a scene from the ball, complete with extra felt-tip scalloping around the edge of the dress, an arrow and 'PRETTY' written in huge, mismatched letters.

'Is that how you edit?' Rhodes asked.

'Yes, and I always use green felt-tip,' Elle said. Rhodes laughed. 'Oh, look, the second dress was always my favourite, not the third one. She's in a blue, it's so lovely. It goes with her eyes.'

Their father and Rhodes watched her, in some embarrassment. 'Look, *Rapunzel*,' Elle said. 'Actually, that always annoyed me.'

'They all annoyed me,' said Rhodes. He picked it up. 'They're all a load of rubbish.'

'No, but this one's a cop-out. Because the prince loses his sight, and he's completely blind and wandering through the thorny desert,' Elle flicked through the pages. 'And she finds him – how does she find him for starters, it's a huge blimming desert. Anyway, her tears fall on his eyes and suddenly he can see again.' She shut the book with a snap. 'I always

430

thought it wasn't fair. In *Cinderella*, right, there's magic at the beginning, but in the end the Prince finds her by searching high and low through the land and getting everyone to try on the glass slipper. He works for it. This, they just have some magic tears and it heals him and makes everything better. Real life's not like that.'

'It's a fairy tale, Elle, dear,' John said. 'What did you expect?'

The squashy sofa covered in a pattern of green apples, by the fire at Willow Cottage, her and Rhodes huddled together as Mandana tucked her feet under her and read to them. Elle could suddenly picture it so clearly. She could smell the woodsmoke from the grate, feel the draft on her neck from the loose casement window, see the piles of books on the shelves, the cosy mess that had been their home. She stared at Rhodes. Did he remember it too? They had been happy once, a happy family of sorts, and that was because of Mum, not in spite of her. At the thought of her mother, tears sprang into Elle's eyes.

'I suppose I expected more,' she said. She put the books carefully in her capacious manuscript bag, looking down, not at her father.

ELLE HAD EATEN at some of the best restaurants in London on her trips back from New York, but she hadn't been to anyone's home in London for she didn't know how long. She was rarely in houses these days. Everyone in New York lived in an apartment and you never went there – you went out to eat or drink. Once, she'd been to Sidney's apartment for a drinks party for Elizabeth Forsyte's new book. And once she'd been to her assistant's apartment, when Courtney had been struck down with the flu and Elle had taken her some soup. It was a mess, full of girl's stuff, four different half-empty bottles of shampoo in the shower, tights hanging above the sink to dry, and when she went back to Gray's immaculate, sparsely furnished apartment that evening, she looked around and thought, *I live here. How nice.*

But as she was ushered into Rhodes's kitchen later that evening, it struck her that his little house was a home. It was cosy and tidy, full of toys and DVDs and cushions, postcards on the fridge, piles of washing by the machine, and upstairs a child sleeping in a bedroom.

'Hey, these are Mum's plates, aren't they?' she exclaimed. Rhodes turned round.

Melissa looked up from tossing the salad. 'Yes, yes, they are. We thought, since you had taken the sideboard—'

Elle cut her off. 'Oh, I didn't mean it like that! It's just – weird to see them here. Different context.'

'You have a sideboard?' Gray said, sitting down next to her. 'This is amazing, folks. When Elle moved in to my place she had nothing. A box, two boxes of possessions, that's it.'

'Haven't you shipped the rest over yet?' Rhodes said. 'It's still in storage?'

'Er, yes,' said Elle. 'I haven't – well, we didn't know if – we might not be staying there, after we're married – it's just never been the right time,' she finished limply, fingering the diamond on her engagement ring. It was sharp at the edges; she liked to press the pads of her fingers against it, see how hard she could push it.

'Elle never liked putting down roots, you know,' John said to Gray. 'Before she moved to the States she lived in this kind of studio – my goodness. I went to help her put up some shelves once. What a tip. Empty bottles everywhere. Pictures of old actors on the walls. Stained carpets.'

'Can I just point out the actors and the stains were nothing to do with me, they were there already,' Elle hastily interjected. 'Thanks, Dad.'

'Oh, you're welcome,' John replied. 'I said to her, Gray, I said, buy somewhere new! Put down some roots! But she wouldn't listen. She was off again.'

Gray rolled his eyes at John, the two of them bonding. Elle stared.

'That's rubbish,' she said, not wanting to sound like the bratty kid who shows off in front of her boyfriend by being rude to her parents. But she had to call him on it. 'Dad, you told me to go to New York. You were the one who said –'
She stopped.

'Said what? No, I didn't,' her father told her.

Elle tried to catch his eye. 'Well – OK.' But she couldn't

433

leave it, like a bite you can't stop scratching once you've started. 'You told me to leave Mum behind, you said I needed to make a clean break, that she was selfish and manipulative, she was using me.' He looked blank. 'You don't remember? I do, that's why I went, that's why I left her behind. And I shouldn't have gone.' She clutched her hands under the table, not looking at Rhodes or Melissa, standing next to each other with bowls of food in their hands, looking blank.

'Mandana was like that,' John said. 'It was best for you. You took the decision yourself.' He sipped his wine, and looked around him, as if the conversation was over. 'Well, this is very—'

Elle dreaded talking about her mother. She avoided any situation where it might come up. But now, she couldn't help the anger that bubbled up inside her. 'She shouldn't have died, Dad. She wasn't a bad person. She was a good person. She was my m-mum.' She could see her, smell her, hear her laugh, as if she were in the room. She was going to cry, she knew it.

Underneath the table, Gray's cool fingers stole across her lap and gripped her hand in his.

'Sorry,' Elle said. The rest of them were looking at her, frozen as if they didn't know what to do next. 'I just think we let her down.'

This is what I didn't want, this is what I was trying to avoid, this is what happens.

'You can't just come back here and start making these accusations,' Melissa said calmly. 'You weren't here. We tried. We had no idea how bad it was. We should have got her into rehab. A long time before.'

Elle thought of the night before she drank herself to death. 'I nearly did,' she said. It sounded so lame, she winced. Melissa looked at her.

'"Nearly"?' she said. 'Wow, Elle, well done. Nearly. Gosh.' Elle hung her head. Melissa said wearily, 'Look, I know—'

Rhodes interrupted. 'OK, Melissa. I think we're all to blame.' He looked at his father. John put his napkin on his lap, carefully smoothing the cotton, as if this conversation simply wasn't taking place. 'Dad?'

'Yes.'

'Are you listening?' Rhodes asked. Elle watched him.

'It's in the past now, Rhodes.'

'It's not, though,' Elle said. 'It's right now. It's stopping me from doing things, from moving on with my life. I know that sounds like a cliché, but it's true. 'Cause I blame myself for letting Mum die, and it just . . .' A lone tear plopped onto the table. 'It makes me doubt everything.' She took her hand away from Gray's. 'Rhodes, you know what I mean?'

'No,' said Rhodes flatly. He put the bowl down on the table. They all looked at it, as if food were an unexpected afterthought.

'I don't doubt myself and you shouldn't, Elle. I think she was selfish and mean. I think she was a monster,' Rhodes said. He took two serving spoons out of a Le Creuset jug by the Aga. Elle watched him, thinking how at ease he was. 'She loved drink, she didn't love us. She was embarrassing. If she'd loved us properly she'd have done something about it. Selfish, yes, like I say, selfish.'

'That wasn't her fault,' Melissa said. 'Rhodes, that's not fair, it was a disease. It is a disease.'

'She chose to have it, for fuck's sake,' said Rhodes, viciously chucking the serving spoons on to the table.

'No, Rhodes,' Melissa said. 'I wasn't her biggest fan, you know it. I don't think she liked me much either.' Rhodes nodded; Elle realised with a start that she didn't much either, but it struck her then that that was life, perhaps you just got on with it, sent birthday cards and presents for Lauren and tried not to let it bother you. 'But I think it was beyond her control. I saw it with my dad and he learned to control it, and now it rules his life, not drinking. She couldn't do it,' said Melissa. 'I just think her life didn't turn out how she wanted, and she used alcohol to help her deal with it.'

'Well. Like father, like daughter,' John said. He peered at the salad bowl. 'She always thought she'd killed him, you know. Ridiculous. This looks delicious. Is that goat's cheese?'

'What does that mean? "Like father like daughter?"' Rhodes asked.

'Yeah – what do you mean, Dad?' said Elle.

'Well, you know.' John cleared his throat. 'He was an alcoholic. He had a cerebral haemorrhage right in front of her. You must have known that.'

'We were kids,' Rhodes said, dangerously. 'How would we have known that?'

John sighed. 'Sorry. I thought she might have told you. She was drinking too much already. Always had done but it had got much worse. I'd given her leaflets, got her to a colleague of mine; she wouldn't listen. She went up to see him, her dad I mean. Had this idea all these things were all his fault; he'd knocked her and her mother around.' He looked down at his hands. 'Mandana always blamed him for all her problems, you know what she was like.'

Elle had the curious feeling their father had forgotten he was talking to them. 'Anyway, they had a huge argument. He told her she was out of order. He hit her again. The mother – well, she wouldn't say boo to a goose, ever – just watches. Mandana starts screaming at him. She hits him. He shouts and shouts. Then suddenly he collapses to the floor. Stone dead.'

He cleared his throat again and looked around, as if suddenly remembering where he was, with whom he was. 'You know, the holiday in Skye was only a couple of weeks later and by then she'd decided she was to blame. She was . . . It was like a switch just flicked.' He shrugged.

With a force that almost overtook her in its violence, Elle suddenly ached to slap her mild-looking, calm father, to shake him out of the wall of protective complacency that he'd built up, that stopped him from troubling himself about his ex-wife's problems or his teenage son's delinquency, or the lives and dreams of his older children once they were the slightest bit out of step with what he thought was proper.

'I didn't know any of that,' Rhodes said.

Gray's hand tightened around Elle's. She shook it off. 'Did you – know he was an alcoholic?' she asked her father.

'Oh, yes. He was a nasty fellow, really. Looked all right from the outside. Respectable. Beat her mother up. Spent what money they had on alcohol, spent all evening in his study drinking it. We hardly saw them, you know. M-Mandana went up on her own, from time to time.' He stumbled over her name. 'They disowned her when she got pregnant, wouldn't come to the wedding. Broke her heart,' he said, almost casually.

Rhodes and Elle looked at each other. 'I never knew that either, Dad,' said Elle, smoothing her fingers over the table-cloth. 'And he hit her too?'

'Oh, yes. A few times. Not regularly, but when he was in a bad way. That's why she ran off to the States the first time, when she was only eighteen. Then again when she was in her twenties, and she started doing stupid things like selling pot. She was pretty off the rails when I met her, I see it now.'

Elle realised her mouth was hanging open. She stared at Gray, but he was gazing at John too. Her eyes met Rhodes's, across the table. He shook his head slowly.

'And don't you think all that might have a bearing on the fact that she became an alcoholic?' said Melissa, in her clear, precise voice. She went over to the counter and fetched a water jug. 'You know alcoholics are three times more likely to have had parents who were alcohol dependent. You never thought to discuss it with her? You must have known that, you were a doctor.'

Elle wanted to hug her. John shifted in his seat. 'Melissa,' he said coolly, 'look, dear. Maybe I'm an old-fashioned sort of chap. But I don't care to discuss my first marriage with you. It wasn't a happy one. I love my children, but—'

'You can't airbrush her out like that,' said Rhodes. 'That's rubbish.'

Elle sat there, watching them. The images were stronger than ever now. Mandana reading to them; Mandana in the library, walking shy children in Clothkits pinafores around to the children's section; Mandana rolling around on the lawn with their smelly dog Toogie. And there it was back again; she blinked, it was horrible: the words SORRY ELLIE on that piece of paper, SORRY. *I'm sorry.*

Her father was slightly red in the face. She was glad, as if they'd got to him. 'We don't blame you, Dad, but – you mustn't do that,' she said. 'I wish we'd known. She didn't – what a waste,' Elle said simply, twisting her hands in her lap.

'It sounds like you do blame me,' said John.

'Well, you left her,' said Elle. 'You broke her heart, you went off with someone else and had a great life. And she didn't.'

'It wasn't like that,' said John. 'I never cheated on your mother. I was just . . .' He rubbed his face and looked up. 'I was just very tired, by then. Perhaps I should have done more. Things weren't right, I know, but after her father died, she changed. It was like a trigger, it was all out in the open. She drank and drank and I couldn't stop her. And then I'd stopped caring. I just wanted to get away.'

'But you didn't mind leaving us behind,' Rhodes said.

John bit his lip and then shrugged. 'I knew she wouldn't hurt you, you know. And you've turned out OK, both of you. She was a great mum.'

It was a neat speech; there was no way of undoing it without criticising the person they'd been trying to defend.

Elle wanted to say, *But she crashed the car twice with us in it*

438

when she was drunk. And . . . and I used to drink too, I nearly became an alcoholic, I can say it now. And it nearly killed me when she died. We aren't a family any more. She wished she could say it out loud. And then she wondered why she didn't.

She took a deep breath, and said, 'Dad, but she nearly killed us in the car, twice. I used to drink over a bottle a day and I nearly went the same way as her. I nearly went under when she died. We aren't really a family any more. I can't believe you knew all that, and you never told us, or tried to help her?' There was a pause. 'It's not all your fault, but some of it is.'

'I −' John said immediately, defensively, and then he stopped again. 'Well, I suppose some of it is. Sorry. I'm sorry.'

In the novels Elle read, whenever there was a reckoning between the family and the wayward son or parent or whomever, people hugged and cried and said, 'Forgive me, can we be happy now?'

Real life wasn't like that, and they weren't like that. Rhodes turned and glanced at Elle, and then he nodded, as if replying for both of them.

'Fine,' he said.

'Very good,' Gray said softly. He smiled at Elle. 'Very good indeed.'

Elle didn't know if it was good or not. It annoyed her that Gray was nodding, as though everything was OK now. She was very tired, and tired of trying not to give in and sob, because to think of her mother and how life had twisted and turned out of her reach so that she could never keep up with it made her feel totally hollow and angry, but she couldn't work out who to be angry with. Her grandfather, for drinking and hitting Mandana? Her dad, for leaving her? Rhodes, Melissa, Bryan, Anita, whoever saw her and failed to help her? Most of all herself, she, Elle, for believing her mother's lies because she wanted to ignore them, for burying her head in the sand. There was no neat answer, and she couldn't turn the final page and think, as she could with a novel, *That's the end of the story, all neatly tied up.*

She poured water into the glasses. 'Let's have a toast to Mum,' she said, desperate suddenly to change the subject, to move away from the past. 'Water, not wine, I don't care if it's bad luck. Wine wasn't good luck for her. To Mandana.'

The five of them clinked their glasses together, in the warm, quiet kitchen.

Damerel strode to the door, and locked it.
'And now, my love,' he said, returning to Venetia, 'for the
fourth time . . . !'

Georgette Heyer, *Venetia*

MY DEAR ELLE,

Thank you for your time yesterday. It was good to catch up and to tell you about our plans for Aphra Books. I know how busy you are; my thanks.

You said you weren't interested in a move, but I would ask you to reconsider. I don't know why I keep asking you. But you would be perfect for this job and I dare to say this as someone who has known you a while now, this job would be perfect for you. In this light and just in case it is of interest, I thought I'd break down the terms of our offer.

Editorial Director. £— salary plus — shares in Aphra books. Seat on the board with monthly board meetings. You would be expected to buy a minimum of 4–5 books a year and contribute to the overall shape of the list. You won't be managing anything unless you'd like; you'll be doing what you love best. You, more than most people, know the value of a good book.

It was delightful to see you again. I do wish you all the

best, my dear. I think you'd be happy in London, you know. To know yourself is to know where you're from.

Your friend

Felicity Sassoon

PS Keep the copy of *Venetia* for yourself.

The second day passed, as all conferences do, in a haze of strip lighting and expensive mineral waters. Elle couldn't remember anything about it; she shook hands, took meetings, answered emails, when all she wanted was to be alone, do some thinking, walk the streets. The final morning at the London conference was exhausting, and irritating: How to Increase Profit Margins. Bigger authors, bigger books. Regularity of delivery more important than delivery of quality, basically, endless discussions about post-*Twilight* and post-*Kite Runner* novels which were all going to sell millions of copies, of course.

She'd sat in the front of the huge conference room with her magnetic name badge pulling at her suit lapel, watching Stuart and Celine set out the ten-step plan to growth in 2009, with a PowerPoint presentation on a screen behind them, as though this was a political party conference. A hundred or so earnest souls sat behind her, scribbling notes. Three along on her row was Rory, nodding knowingly half the time and whispering gossip to his neighbours. Elle had just watched. She didn't want to write any of it down, instead she just wanted to shout, *People want good books.* She kept thinking of Obama's cock-up, last month, which people were saying could cost him the election: You can put lipstick on a pig, but it's still a pig.

'Great presentation,' she'd said, shaking Celine's hand, patting Stuart on the back when they'd come off the stage and she'd leapt up to congratulate them, coinciding with Rory. 'Great, very interesting, Celine,' he'd said. Celine had smiled, nodded at him. 'I'm glad,' she'd said. 'Thanks, Rory.'

Elle had felt herself shiver as the two of them jostled to congratulate the big chiefs. Was that it? Was she turning into him, someone who just went along in the slipstream, anything for an easy life? She'd looked down, embarrassed at catching herself momentarily like this, her fingers scrolling automatically over her BlackBerry, and that's when she'd seen the email from Felicity.

'It's just insane, but I love her bravado,' said Gray, chuckling over Elle's inbox half an hour later in the pub. 'She sounds pretty amazing, Felicity. I'd love to meet her one day.' He looked at his watch. 'Honey, do you want another drink?'

'Sure.' Elle was enjoying the cosy warmth of the pub; there was something deliciously indulgent about drinking whisky and ginger ale in the afternoon with the windows fugged up and the rain pouring down outside. She had – unusually for her – bunked off the post-conference debriefing session and come to meet Gray for a drink. She was terrified about saying goodbye to him, she didn't know why. London was changing her. Gray was the constant in her life, and it was as though she'd signed herself over to him: *Here, you. You look after me. You like it, I like it.*

'There's something about it I love, too,' she said, as Gray pulled out his wallet. 'Perhaps I miss it here more than I realise.'

Gray looked at her, and laughed, 'No way. You're not seriously thinking about it?'

'No – but – well, maybe, for a second or two,' Elle said. 'It's probably because I'm flying back in a few hours. There's nothing wrong with speculating, is there? Anyway, you said you'd love to live in London.'

'When?' Gray said with a faux-grimace. 'I never said that.'

'On Monday, when we were on our way to Rhodes's – you said –'

445

Gray leaned forward. 'Honey, I'm sorry. I mean, I love it here but – no way!' He sat back again, against the hard leather banquette. 'I couldn't leave New York. My job, my friends, my life – it's everything.' He looked as though he was humouring her in explaining.

'Rachel's coming over to Oxford for a year,' Elle pointed out. Rachel was Gray's daughter from his marriage, currently in her second year at Stanford.

Gray shrugged. 'So we'll visit her. She's in California most of the year anyway. It'll be the same.'

'I thought you liked it here.'

Gray drummed his fingers on the table. 'And I thought you hated it.'

She took a deep breath. 'I thought I did. Maybe I don't so much, any more.'

'Is this because of Monday, the big family showdown? Honey, I know it must have shaken you up, but I don't think you should start making judgements about your life based on some semi-closure with your father and brother.'

Elle looked at him, and didn't say anything. She put her BlackBerry back in her bag. 'It's OK, forget it,' she said. 'I just wanted to think about it. It's fine.'

'It is fine,' Gray said. 'It's more than fine, OK? Trust me. I know what's best for you.'

'You do, don't you.' She smiled at him, as the pub door opened and a blast of cold wind sent a chill down her back, and she shivered.

Gray looked at his watch again. 'So do you mind if we go now? I want to go to Dora's, and we won't have time if we have another drink.' Elle nodded, and stood up. 'You're a wonderful woman,' Gray said, gripping her shoulders lightly and kissing her hair. 'I'm really glad you're thinking that one day you could live in London, that you're rebuilding some bridges here. That's amazing. You know, even three weeks ago, you were in a bad place. Now, you're – a different woman.' He nudged a lock of her hair aside with one long finger, and stroked her cheek.

'Glad you think so,' said Elle, moving aside. She wasn't in the mood for Gray's Mend Elle Therapy Seminar, all of a sudden. She wanted to walk away, tell him to leave her alone, but she resisted the urge, as she always did. It was her, not him. 'What time's your train?'

'Five.'

'We should get going then,' said Elle. 'Drain your drink, come on.' She paused. 'You don't leave an empty glass in a pub. Charles II outlawed it. It's still not done.'

'Really? I hadn't heard that tradition.' Gray looked delighted, and swilled down the rest of his drink. She swallowed guiltily, feeling the whisky burning sweetly in her throat.

They left the pub. Gray put his umbrella up and his arm around her. She leaned against him, her head on his shoulder, as they walked along the wide, slick road. They crossed Harley Street, Gray chattering about whom he would see in Paris and why this was so important for his book. Elle said nothing. She told herself she was tired, the conference and the dinner with her father had taken it out of her.

Since she'd been back in London, everything seemed greyer, but clearer. She couldn't explain it. She'd been expecting it to be awful, and it wasn't. But the strangest thing was, she couldn't recall her New York self, the one who ran meetings and consoled employees behind closed doors and who had her assistant collect her dry-cleaning, who dined with Pulitzer Prize winners. She wanted that part of herself back, but she also couldn't remember what it was like to be that Elle. She would catch a whiff of it, like the snatch of a song that still won't lead you to the chorus, and then it'd be gone. She clenched her jaw and snapped her eyes open, as Gray said:

447

'Here we are. What a great place.'

Dora's glowed amber in the rain – it had rained non-stop since she'd come back to London, Elle realised then, and her umbrella was permanently soggy. Gray pushed open the wooden door. 'After you, my darling.'

It was funny, being in a British bookshop again. It was a lovely space. The shelves were wooden, there were old mahogany tables piled high with books of all kinds. In the centre of the room was the till, behind it were three steps and a children's area. Craning her neck, Elle could see the BFG painted on its wall, and the sound of a child screaming.

'Dora's has a fantastic history section, I've heard,' Gray said, his eyes alight with enthusiasm, touching her lightly on the shoulder. 'Here.' He bounded across the shop. 'Look!'

'I'm going to check out the Penguin Great Ideas, maybe get one for Rhodes,' said Elle. The sound of the child screaming grew louder as she crossed the floor.

'Hey!' she heard someone shout. 'Look, I'll – do you want a biscuit? Have this biscuit. And put a sock in it.'

Elle pulled out a paperback and started thumbing through the pages.

'Argh. Wretched child. What's wrong?' the voice said. 'Just tell me what's wrong, and I'll make it OK.'

'There's a cobweb!' the small voice yelled, shuddering. 'I don't like cobwebs! Scary!'

'Come out here then, let's go back into the shop. There aren't any cobwebs there.'

'I want to take Matilda with me.'

'Fine,' said the voice. 'Let's take Matilda, just stop bloody screaming. You sound like Alice Cooper.'

'Alice Cooper-Smith from school?'

'No. Alice Cooper is a singer. And a golfer, strangely. He wears a lot of black make-up. Here we – Elle? What are you doing here?'

Elle dropped the book she was holding. 'Tom? What are

you doing here, more like?' She stared at him, and the little girl holding his hand.

'I – er, well, I own the shop, remember?'

'Well, yes,' Elle said. 'I meant . . .' She trailed off.

'This is my daughter Dora,' Tom said. 'Dora, this is my friend Elle. She could hear you having a major freakout in the back there,' he told Dora solemnly. 'She was scared. Now she thinks you're a monster, not a little girl.'

Dora glared up at Elle from underneath a blunt black fringe. 'There was a cobweb,' she said.

'I hate cobwebs too,' Elle told her.

'I worry about them. I worry that they'll drop on my head and get catched up in my hair.'

'I worry about that too,' said Elle. 'But I'm nearly thirty-four and it's never happened, so maybe it never will.'

'There you go,' said Tom. 'You're not alone.' Dora picked up her book and opened it, extremely cautiously. Tom put a hand on Elle's arm. 'God. It's great to see you,' he said quietly. 'You left so quickly on Monday. I wish we'd had more time –'

'Elle? Come here, I want to show you –'

Elle turned her head. 'Gray, come over here a second.'

'No, you come.'

Elle sighed. 'No,' she said, trying not to scream with stress, fatigue, surprise, whatever it was that was making her shake, her vision blurry. 'Come here, there's someone I want you to meet.'

Gray appeared, holding a thick volume. 'This looks interesting,' he said. 'It's a new biography of George III. I didn't realise – hello. Gray Logan.' He held his hand out.

'Gray, this is my friend Tom. He owns Dora's.'

'It's my name,' said Dora. 'After my grandmother.'

'Your grandmother was a great woman,' said Gray, looking down at her. 'I had the privilege of meeting her once, in the late seventies. She spoke at my college, wonderfully. I loved her books.'

Tom's hard grey stare softened. 'Thanks.'

'So you know Elle –?' He left the question hanging.

'Oh, we worked together –' Elle said, as Tom said at the same time, 'We used to hang out, we were friends –'

'Yes, that's right,' Elle said, stammering slightly. She glanced again at Dora. 'So Dora, how old are you?'

'I'm six and a half, I'm seven in March.' She tugged her father's shirt. 'Dad, can I go back in with Matilda doll and play?'

'Yes,' said Tom. 'But you said you hated it in there and you were afraid of the cobwebs.'

'They've gone,' said Dora, stomping off towards the alcove.

'How nice to meet you,' said Gray. 'I'll buy this book, and then I should get going, sweetheart,' he said to Elle. 'It's later than I thought.'

He went over to the sales desk, leaving Elle and Tom alone.

'How was the rest of the conference?' Tom asked. 'Looked pretty grim to me.'

'It was OK,' Elle said. She couldn't stop staring at him. 'I'm sorry we didn't get to talk. Is – is Caitlin here?'

'Noo,' Tom said. 'She's in Bath, she's opening the shop up there. She has Dora on the weekends. Sort of.'

'Oh,' said Elle. 'So you're not –'

'We're not anything,' said Tom. 'Never were, really. We tried it, for about a year, but it was a disaster. So I bought a flat in Richmond, down the road from her, and we all lived on the same street. Then Dora sort of moved in with me, and that's how it is now.'

'Yorkshire Road, Richmond,' Elle said, as if in a dream. 'You lived on the same road together. That explains it.'

'Explains what?'

'I thought –' She remembered how angry she'd been with him – and herself – when they'd slept together, how she'd wanted it to be right, how she'd tried to make it into just another one-night stand. What had Jeremy said, all those years ago, at Libby and Rory's wedding? I dropped them off in the road, at their road, something like that. 'I didn't know,' she said. 'I knew you two were in Richmond – I thought you were still together.'

'No. Definitely not,' Tom said firmly. He looked across at Dora, who was hitting something on the wall with her palm and talking to herself. 'Caitlin and I – it was not meant to be, but I hated being apart from Dora. That's why I moved ten doors down.' He sighed, but he was smiling. 'We have a daughter, and she's really, well, she's the best thing that's ever happened to me, even if she can only speak in a loud bellow and is pathetically afraid of imaginary cobwebs.' His dark grey eyes looked into hers. 'It wasn't what I expected, but it all worked out for the best.'

'Sounds like it did. I'm really glad, Tom.' Elle didn't know what else to say. 'Look – I'd better go.'

He looked around and said softly, 'Elle – you know, I wasn't with Caitlin when we slept together. It was long over by then. She's with someone else, it's great, everyone's happy.'

'It's fine.' Elle shook her head, wanting to say, *Well, I know that now.* 'I wasn't asking.'

'I know you weren't, but I want you to know,' he said. 'Because obviously, I don't wish things had been different, with Caitlin, because of Dora. But in one way I wish they had.'

She could hear Gray talking in his low, charming voice to the girl at the counter, hear the rustle of his plastic bag as he took the book. Elle gazed at Tom, almost desperately. 'What way?'

'Well . . . I fell in love with you that summer all those years ago, Elle. And I never really told you, because of everything that happened. But I suppose I've been in love with you ever since.' The hard lines of his face were rigid, his jaw tight, as he looked over at Gray. 'Everything's been wrong with us, timing-wise. Hasn't it?'

451

'Tom –' she began.

'I just wanted you to know. To know I wasn't an idiot, some stupid bastard who wanted to hurt you. I could never do that to you. There were reasons.'

She shook her head. 'Don't say anything,' she said, her voice thick. 'Please, don't.'

He lowered his voice. 'I have to just say this one thing. I did love you and I'm glad we had that night together. It was – well, it was wonderful. I know what happened afterwards with your mum changes everything, but to me it was something special.'

His hand was on hers, crossed in front of her. Elle swallowed. She knew him so well, the amused, detached tone of his voice, the scroll of his ear, his eyes, his bony frame. Someone whom she always wanted to be in the room, someone who saw the world in the same way, and it had always been like that.

'I think,' Tom said, 'I think sometimes the bits of your life happen in the wrong order, or all at the same time and you waste time feeling angry about it, but that's the way it is, it's real life. You meet the person who you think could make you happy for the rest of your life, but at the same time your ex-girlfriend who's told you umpteen times she never wants to see you again tells you you're going to be a dad.'

Elle took up the story. 'And then you move to another country and then the next time you see that person, even though it's like no time's passed, you sleep together and then – your mum dies.' She gave a short, sad laugh. 'Yep. That's rubbish timing. But Tom, perhaps –'

Gray appeared between them. 'Hello!' he said. 'So, I think we should go, honey. Tom, it was great to meet you, and your beautiful daughter, and see the shop. They're both a credit to you. Good luck.' He shook Tom's hand graciously. 'Elle?'

'Sure,' Elle said woodenly.

'Right,' Tom said mechanically.

She slung her bag over her shoulder, not knowing what else to do. 'So – bye.'

'Bye,' Tom said. 'I'm glad I saw you.' He turned away.

Gray put his arm around her again as they exited the shop together, and she didn't look back once. On the pavement, he kissed her. 'This has been a great trip, hasn't it? I feel as if you've come through something. Laid ghosts to rest. Is that a terrible thing to say?'

'No, it's not.' Elle gripped his arm as they walked away, pulling him as fast as she could. She couldn't look back. She squared her shoulders, and glanced at him. 'Thank you, darling, thank you for coming. I'm glad you came.'

'Sometimes it's the only way with you,' Gray said. He stuck his hand out and cried, 'Taxi!' A cab pulled over and Gray turned to her. 'Honey, I'm going to miss you. I'll call you when I'm in the hotel. I love you. I'm glad you've come back to me. It was worth it in the end.'

Elle kissed him. 'What do you mean?'

'I don't know . . .' Gray smiled. 'Sometimes I wondered if we'd make it. Or if it was just going to be too hard.' He nodded, and gripped her wrists. 'But it was! It was, honey. I love you. See you back at home. At home!'

He climbed in, wound down the window and leaned out. She walked towards him.

'Where you going?' the cabbie asked, annoyed.

'One second, please,' Gray said, frowning. 'Goodbye, my darling girl. Keep yourself safe. Remember.'

Elle put her hand on his cheek. 'Thank you,' she said.

The cab moved off, and she wondered why she'd said it. *Thank you.*

She stood alone on the pavement, watching the black cab disappear up the High Street, and then she looked at the books in the shop window. Rows of beautiful books, different

453

colours, sizes, promising different things, a new world inside each one. She didn't know how long she stayed there, watching the movement inside, looking for someone she didn't see.

The rain was falling lightly, a fine mist like a soft blanket. She could feel droplets of water soak into her hair, on the back of her neck, on her skin. She turned around, and there was the shop again, glowing warm in the grey light of a late London afternoon. She stared longingly at it. Someone was moving around by the shelf next to the window, a dark head. It disappeared from view.

Elle turned her back on it. She bit her lip, and started walking down towards Mayfair. She should call Courtney. She should pack and check her email. She had to—

'Elle?'

It was so faint, it could have been anything, not her name.

'Elle?'

She turned around. Tom was running up the street, towards her.

'Thank God, I thought I'd missed you.' He held out his hand. 'Elle –'

'Yes?' she said.

'Here. You forgot your umbrella.' He put the small black object into her hand, and kept it there.

'Oh.' She gripped his hand for a moment, then took it. 'Thank you,' she said. 'How stupid of me.'

Tom said, 'Well, I just thought . . . You'll need it if you ever move back to London. Very important.'

'I'm not moving back to London,' she said.

'I thought you might.' He ran his fingers through his short black hair, brushing the rain away.

'Well, Gray doesn't want to.'

'And you?'

She shook her head. 'Don't ask me that.'

'Why not?' His voice was insistent. 'Why not, Elle?'

'Oh –' She put the umbrella up and moved towards him, so they were both standing beneath it. 'A week ago I'd have said you were mad. But you don't know what's round the corner, do you?' She laughed, slightly hysterically – some inexorable emotion was creeping over her, what the hell was she doing? 'I feel like . . . I just have this feeling. I can't explain it. Like, it wouldn't necessarily be better here. It'd just be *right*. Does that make sense?'

'Yes,' he said. 'Yes, it does make sense.' His grey eyes were the colour of the sky. 'I don't want you to go back, Elle,' he said. 'I want you to stay.'

'Do you?' She brushed rain out of her eyes, and looked around.

'Come with me,' Tom said suddenly. He took her hand and she went with him, mutely. They walked up the road in silence, his fingers clutching hers, and he propelled her into a coffee shop, where she sat down at a table by the window, and he ordered.

'Shouldn't you be at the shop? Don't they need you?'

'They'll know to look for me in here if they do, this is where we come for coffee,' he said, sliding a paper cup firmly over towards her. 'Drink up.'

The coffee was strong, hot and delicious. Elle closed her eyes, breathing in the smell. 'I'm so tired,' she said.

Tom put his elbows on the table and rested his chin in his hands. 'What have you been up to? Burning the midnight oil?'

She didn't mean to pour it all out, but she did. She told him everything. About how her mum had died, about what it was like back in New York, how she couldn't talk to anyone, about the image, the nights alone in front of the TV. Her mum and her mum's father, the day he died, supper on Monday night and what had come out. And he just listened. He didn't say anything or jump in and tell her what to do, just sat there watching her intently and listening.

At the end, when Elle had finished, she added, 'I don't know why I'm telling you all this.'

'I'm glad you did.' He took her hand, and held it. She let him.

'I have to go back tonight,' she said. 'And I can't. I can't face it. I want to stay here, and I don't know why. I'm having some kind of a moment of madness, and I can't explain it. Because it makes no sense. It's just that I don't want to leave and I don't know why. And I don't know what to do.'

Tom turned her hand over, and ran his fingers over the creases in her palm. He pinched each of the tips of her fingers. Elle watched him. All of a sudden, she didn't feel stressed, or hurried, or confused, or angry. Peaceful, as if it was just the two of them, and everything else was imaginary.

'Look, I have to say it again . . . I'm in love with you,' Tom said, after a moment. 'I always have been. And I think you should come back here and be with me. And Dora, I'm afraid, but me mainly.'

He bit his lip, not looking at her. The coffee shop was quiet; they were alone in the world.

She squeezed his fingers and looked down. His hands, her hands, clutched together.

'The trouble is, I'm not very good at trusting my own instincts,' she said. 'I've been wrong before. A lot.'

'About what?' Tom leaned forward and wiped a tear from her cheek. 'You worry too much, Elle, about everything. You're too hard on yourself.'

'I was wrong about Rory –'

'You were twenty-five, twenty-six! Everyone's allowed to be in love with the wrong person at some point. In fact, it's a mistake not to be. Come on.'

Elle cleared her throat, to try and quell the rising tide of emotion inside her. 'Um – I was wrong about Rhodes and Melissa. I thought they were horrible, and they're not.'

456

Tom cleared his throat. 'None of my business, but seems to me they got you wrong too. And your mum.'

'Well, but that's it. I was wrong about my mum, totally wrong. And that's –'

She made a sobbing sound in her throat, and bent her head forward, her hair hanging over her face.

'That's what?' Tom said softly. He tucked a lock of her hair behind her ear.

'That's my fault most of all. I had my head in the sand, for years and years, and I didn't notice, I should have, I could have saved her.'

Elle's throat was aching with the effort of not crying. Tom reached over and rubbed her back and tears started falling onto the ground, more and more. 'It's OK,' he said. 'You should just cry. A lot. It's awful, what happened to her.' Elle shook her head, sobbing softly, not caring if anyone was watching, unable to stop. 'But Elle, you've got something wrong, just one thing. You think you could have saved her. You couldn't. No one could. She was ill, Elle. She drank in secret for years, and she knew it would kill her. Honestly, you may think you had your head in the sand, but that's a totally separate thing. There's nothing you could have done.'

Elle's shoulders heaved. 'If I'd got home earlier that night—'

'No,' Tom said firmly. He bent forward so his breath was in her ear. 'I persuaded you to stay with me. She'd have done it again, the next night, the night after you left. Elle, there isn't anything you could have done. And I met her, I saw how much she loved you, she did, she loved you so much. She was so proud of you, it was obvious, she lied so you wouldn't be ashamed of her, so you could be a success and not worry about her. She'd be horrified to think you blamed yourself.'

'Gray says I need to go and see the therapist again,' Elle said, in between hiccuping sobs, the wall of her hair still shielding her from everything. 'He says I –'

'Well, maybe you should, or a grief counsellor or something,' said Tom. 'Because your dad, your brother, they're not in such a state, are they? Do you think they're still like this about her death, four years after it happened?' He stroked her hair again and she sat up and blew her nose.

'No, they're not,' she said, calmly. She took a deep breath. 'Her father was an alcoholic. He hit her. He died the summer she started drinking properly again. I only really found out on Monday.'

Tom nodded. 'Blimey,' he said.

'I still think we should have—'

'Listen, Elle,' Tom said firmly. He caught her hands in his once more, and held them tightly, his thin, kind face only inches away from hers. 'My mum died of a disease, and I blamed my dad for it, I still do in some ways, but I know I'm being stupid when I do. That's the point. Your mum had an illness. Her dad had it. You might have had it too but in a way you could say that summer you backed away from it. And then you tried to help her, but she didn't want you to. She knew it wouldn't work. I think you think it's in your nature to be a failure, but it's the opposite. You're a star, you're wonderful, and you don't realise it.'

'Bleurgh,' Elle said, embarrassed, but he leaned forward and kissed her. Her cheeks were flushed and hot from crying, her lips swollen. He put his hands around her head, pulling her gently towards him, so that their lips touched, lightly at first and then hard against each other. His skin was cool on hers. She closed her eyes briefly, remembering the feel of him again; it was so strange how years and oceans had separated them, but she could still remember how he tasted, what it felt like to kiss him. She put her hands on his shoulder, on the back of his neck, and something winked at her. She pulled away, hastily.

'I can't,' she said. 'I'm – I can't, I'm engaged, Tom, I can't do this.' She stood up. 'Jesus, what am I thinking.' She wiped her eyes again, light-headed from the crying, and turned to the window, expecting to see the clouds parting, but the grey sky hung steadily over them, without a break. He pulled softly at the cuff of her coat.

'You can,' he said. 'Do you love him?'

'Yes,' she said. 'Only – oh, I can't explain it. I shouldn't be here. I should go,' she said, talking a gulp of her coffee.

'What happens if you stay, one more day?' Tom said. 'Come to dinner with me.'

'I just can't do things like that,' Elle said. She smiled. 'I have to fly back tonight. I've got a board meeting tomorrow, and a presentation to an author, and we have to budget for next year, and negotiate the pay rise. I can't just bunk off.'

She thought of Felicity's email again, of the cool green of a London spring, of the dinners with Gray's friends, of the way he wanted to fix her.

'What do you want?' Tom asked, insistent.

'To be happy. To make someone else happy. To do my job well, be a good person. And that means –' Elle shrugged, took a deep breath, shook her head. 'It means – I don't know. You tell me. I seem to spend my life telling people what to do, these days. What do you think I should do?'

'I can't tell you that.' His hand closed on hers. 'You have to decide what you want.'

'What do you want?' Elle asked him. 'Do you even know?'

'I want you,' he said. 'I want to be with you. I want Dora to be happy, I want to open another bookshop, and I want to be with you.' He shrugged his shoulders. He'd been so lanky when she'd first met him, awkward and cross in his suits. Now he was still lanky, but it suited him. He was himself. 'I know what I want, you see.'

They were standing, facing each other across the small round cafe table, and then suddenly the door was opened and someone was calling his name. 'Tom – Tom –'

They turned around. The bookseller who'd sold Gray his

book burst into the shop. 'I knew you'd be here. Dora's going mental, Tom, I don't know what she wants but she keeps shouting "Cobweb",' she panted. 'The shop's full and –'

'OK, OK,' Tom said. He turned back to Elle, and rubbed his face. 'Can I meet you when I've finished work? Are you staying at the conference hotel?'

'Yes,' she said. 'It's horrible. And Tom – I have to go back tonight, I do.'

'*Tom* – look, she's going mad, it's not fair –'

'I'd better get back. You go for a walk. You need some fresh air, cooped up all day. Think it all over. Think about it. I'll call you.'

He touched her arm, and then he was gone. She didn't want him to leave. Outside was fresh air, and it was cool. Elle rubbed her eyes, rolled her head around her neck, and realised she felt a little lighter, somehow. She could feel the warmth of his skin on her hands, on her lips. She turned to walk back to the hotel, south, and then abruptly crossed the road and set off through Marylebone, going east, without much thinking about where she was going. She took out her phone and rang Courtney.

'Hi, Elle.' Courtney sounded a little nervous. 'How's it going? Celine's assistant told me there was a problem with your schedule. Was everything OK?'

'Yes, it was fine,' Elle said. 'Just me, being an idiot. I'm sorry if you worried about it. I got something wrong.'

'Oh, OK.' Courtney breathed out. 'Wow. Phew.'

'How's everything there? Any messages?'

'Sure.' Courtney rustled through some papers. 'Caryn asked me to remind you again about the figures for tomorrow's meeting. But I told her you'd done them already and they were printed and ready to be handed out. I hope that was OK.'

There was something so soothing about Courtney's ultra-professional, neutral tone. 'Yes, that's perfect.' Elle sometimes

460

wondered if Courtney could just do her job for her, operating the switches like the man behind the Wizard of Oz. 'Anything else?'

'I have a car booked to pick you up at eleven tonight, but I wanted to remind you it's Newark and not JFK.'

Elle hesitated. 'Yep, got that,' she said. 'I was wondering. How easy would it be to change my ticket? By a few hours? Or even a day or two?'

'Oh.' Courtney sounded confused. 'You mean catch an earlier flight?'

'No,' Elle said. 'A later one.'

'Do you want me to check flight times, find one that'd get you in for the board meeting?'

'I was thinking I might miss the board meeting. Maybe come back later instead.'

Courtney cleared her throat. 'OK – um – I'll, should I –' She tried again. 'It's just Caryn has asked me twice today, when does she get back, what time does she land, does she have the presentation ready. I think they're expecting you here for the meeting, and –'

'Courtney, don't worry,' Elle said, scratching her cheek. She didn't want to alarm her. 'I'll let you know. It probably won't happen. Just – there's a few things to sort out.'

'Got it. Just let me know if there's anything I can do.'

She sounded younger on the phone; Elle had to remind herself she was, in fact, still only twenty-four. She was so efficient, like a robot, sometimes she forgot. 'Thanks, Courtney. I'll let you know, love,' she said, not sure why she'd called her love – you didn't do that at Jane Street, drop terms of endearment into conversation. She rang off, and carried on walking. *Go for a walk.*

Pounding the grey pavements, her black boots slick with the rain, Elle thought again about the previous month when Courtney had had a bad case of the flu. She'd sounded so miserable that Elle had left work a little early and taken her some chicken soup. Visiting her assistant's bare but cute apartment had made her nostalgic; vintage lampshades and throws, a battered old bookcase full of Penguin classics and modern girl's classics: *The Girl's Guide to Hunting and Fishing*, Marian Keyes, Jonathan Lethem and Converse in the hallway, half-eaten bags of Goldfish crackers and a copy of *People* magazine on the old oak trunk that was the coffee table.

'I just got it last weekend, in Brooklyn,' Courtney had told her with pride, running her hands along the warm wood of the trunk and sneezing. 'Saw it a couple of months ago and I've been saving for it ever since. Isn't it beautiful.' She'd tucked her feet underneath her and sunk even further into her comforter. Elle had looked at her, suddenly longing to kick off her shoes and stay here with Courtney and Sarah, her roommate, who'd just arrived home. They were about to embark on a *Golden Girls* marathon; there were chips and dips, ice cream, and Gatorade for Courtney, as well as the beautifully packaged, small tub of chicken soup from her boss.

But just then she'd glanced at the two of them and realised they were waiting for her to leave. It was strange for her to be here. She was the boss lady in heels, not their friend who lounged on the couch with them. She had walked down the stairs, feeling chastened, not a little embarrassed, and gone back to Gray's apartment, reminding herself as she put her keys down on the smooth marble countertop that this was much better, this was what she worked for.

The afternoon light was already fading. The white stucco buildings broke apart in places, the gaps revealing mews streets, pubs with golden light streaming from them. Elle carried on walking east, knowing this was the wrong direction, but somehow unable to change her path. It struck her then that she was worse off than Courtney, in fact. She had nothing to show for her hard work, except an engagement ring and a flashy apartment that someone else had bought. Courtney had the wooden trunk, she'd saved for it and lugged it up four flights of stairs. Elle had a car to meet her at the airport, an assistant, a fiancé, a career, and yet she didn't have anything that was really hers.

She realised then she wasn't quite sure where she was. She'd lost her way in London, in the streets she used to know so well. She walked down Cleveland Street, past the ancient chemists, the George and Dragon and the irate sign on the front door of a house that said firmly THIS IS NOT A BROTHEL!! next to a house that was, unmistakably, a brothel: broken windows boarded up with cardboard, weeds growing out of cracks on the bricks, naked light bulbs in each room visible from the street, a skinny, chapped-lipped woman sitting in the bare front room, a cigarette in one long hand. She glared at Elle, and Elle stared back at her, then shook herself out of her reverie and hurried along.

The traffic along Tottenham Court Road was heavy, the road was wide, engines and drills from roadworks thundering in her ears. Elle scurried along the pavements, suddenly realising why she'd come here, and crossed the road, almost running down the street. She turned off and she was there. She walked across Bedford Square, looking up at the houses, till she found the one she wanted.

Panting slightly, Elle stood at the bottom of the steps, just as she'd done on her first day over eleven years ago, and stared up at the front door. Her phone started ringing. It was Caryn. Elle shut it off, still looking up at the old Bluebird building. There was no trace of Bluebird there, though; the sign had gone with Felicity on that freezing cold day before Christmas, and the windows on the top two floors had thick white blinds. There was a new brass plaque where the old buzzer had been, with three different buttons. She climbed up the front steps to peer at it.

463

Ground Floor: BRIGHTSTAR MEDIA PROPERTY LTD
First Floor: ADEX DIGITAL RESOURCES
Second Floor: PAUL HURRIDGE

Elle stepped back, smiling. What had she been expecting? A bookbinder's and archivist's with a workshop full of elves making glass slippers in the basement? She remembered throwing coffee over Felicity, running down the steps in the evenings with Sam or Libby, hanging around the corner waiting for Rory, sitting in the square on a bench reading a book, any book, with her prized Pret sandwich and her Pied a Terre shoes, bought in the sale, worn till they fell apart.

But it wasn't here any more, it was in the past, and she wasn't a girl any more, she was a woman, standing on her own in the rain, looking for something she wouldn't find.

It was time for her to go home.

EPILOGUE

Four Months Later

'HERE IS WHERE we keep the tea and coffee. We contribute to the kitty, four pounds a month, but I provide the biscuits. And ah – your desk is here.'

'This is my desk?'

'Yes.'

'I thought I was getting an office.'

'Find a million-copy best-seller and you'll get an office.'

Elle put her hands on her hips. She smiled and said firmly, 'I need an office.'

'I was joking,' Felicity said. 'Here is your office.'

She opened another door onto a tiny room with a view over Curzon Street. On the desk was a bunch of flowers, a computer, and a slim black package.

'That's your e-reader,' Felicity said. 'This is a new computer, and your assistant has your BlackBerry.' She smiled at Elle's obvious surprise. 'This isn't the age of Caxton, you know. Move with the times, Elle.' She paused. 'So, you've been back for over two months, what have you been up to?'

'Nothing really,' said Elle. 'Seeing my family. Spending time with . . . people. Old friends.' She smiled quickly, looking down, because she wanted to keep it private, but then she remembered: Felicity wouldn't pry. She wouldn't be interested. To Elle, it was wonderful, the most wonderful thing that had ever happened to her. To Felicity, she saw now, love was something that only really happened within the pages of a book. For long periods of Elle's life, she'd thought that was true, too. But it wasn't. It was you and him, the two of you, a team to face the world together, and that was what she'd been looking for all those years; not an idol, or someone to lust after, or someone to fix her. 'I rented a flat near the river, and I put my mother's sideboard in it, and bought a sofa, and lay on it and did nothing. I read, mainly.'

'How lovely,' said Felicity. She glanced quickly at Elle. 'I'm very glad to hear it.'

She looked at her watch. 'Now, shall I let you settle in? Our editorial meeting's at eleven on Mondays. If we meet first thing after the weekend it gives us a jump-start on the opposition. I remember when –'

It was good to know some things didn't change, and that Felicity still loved a long pointless story. Elle listening politely to an anecdote about the time Felicity had told Carmen Callil how she should be running Virago, and then smiled politely, turning on her computer, and opening the post in her in tray. There was a large manilla envelope, already opened. She tipped the contents out. A postcard was on top, a Veronese print, and written in looping, large handwriting:

You haven't given me your new address, so I'm forwarding on your post to Aphra Books. Good luck, my dear. Be well. Gray

She smiled. She hadn't quite forgiven Gray yet, for wearing his injured pride like a cloak around New York that caused people to look at Elle, in the couple of months she spent back there, through narrowed eyes. 'She went crazy,' she heard someone at a book launch say, a few days before she flew back. 'He had a hard time with her, you know. She's still very young. Poor Gray,' whereas poor Gray had, in fact, hooked up with Jessica, a fellow lecturer and widow, less than two weeks after his split with Elle. It had taken her under an hour to pack her things up in the loft, and move into a hotel, after she'd broken up with him.

'This wasn't ever your home,' he'd said, matter-of-factly.

'It was,' she'd told him. 'It was. It's just it's not any more.'

Leaving Gray and leaving Jane Street sent her New York ranking plummeting so drastically that, by the time she flew back to London, just before Christmas, she was free of almost any guilt. They'd told Elizabeth Forsyte she'd had a breakdown. When Elle heard, she was furious, then she shrugged and smiled. Perhaps she had. Was it insane, to hand your notice in on a job like that, leave behind that life, to come back to London in the depths of winter, to do a job she employed other people to do?

Maybe, maybe not. Caryn got Courtney to courier her things over to the Midtown hotel where she was staying, on her final day, and sign a release form.

'I'm only moving to a tiny start-up,' Elle had told her boss, exasperated. 'I just want to read something good, edit some books for once, do it all over again. I'm not defecting to our rivals, you know.'

'I know, but you can't be too careful,' Caryn replied. She was almost uninterested. She patted Elle on the back. 'It's business. We're gonna miss you. Come back when you've got whatever it is outta your system.'

The package of post from the States was mundane stuff: renewal reminders on her subscriptions, invitations to come shop at Dean & Deluca or extend her credit on her Bloomingdale's card. She pushed it to one side and turned to the rest of the in tray. There were several cards from agents and other publishers welcoming her to Aphra Books.

The last one was a picture of Sherlock Holmes smoking a pipe. It said:

> By the time you get this, paper will probably be obsolete. So treasure this and good luck. We can't wait to see you for supper tonight. Lots of love Tom and Dora xx

Elle smiled, took out the old paperback copy of *Venetia* from her handbag, and propped it up on the windowsill next to the card. She opened the window, smelling the fresh air, and spun joyfully round on her chair, her hands clutching the armrests. Spring was on its way.

ACKNOWLEDGEMENTS

I'd like to say a special thank-you to Jane Morpeth for hiring me all those years ago and believing in me. She is my real-life heroine, a brilliant boss and a lovely person, and I miss working with her every single day.

Massive thanks to Nikki Barrow, Auriol Bishop, Lindsey Evans, Abigail Hanna and Tora Orde-Powlett for the wine-soaked memories of the good old days, and for the good old days themselves. Also to Lance Fitzgerald, Georgina Moore, Rebecca Folland, Sophie Linton and Roland Philipps for their help. Especially thanks to Chris for the plot rehearsals and for everything, basically.

Big *muchas gracias* to everyone at Curtis Brown, especially Melissa Pimentel, Alice Lutyens, Lucia Rae and OF COURSE Jonathan Lloyd.

And thanks to everyone at HarperCollins, especially Kate Elton, Thalia Suzuma, Kate Stephenson and the one and only Elinor Fewster. Special thanks to Liz Dawson, I am very lucky to have you on my side. Lastly to my editor Lynne Drew who has put up with me for many years, taught me so much and is very great, and that is why this book is for you, with my love.